NANUET PUBLIC LIBRARY

3 2824 00988 6180

D1046149

JUN 13 2006

NANUET PUBLIC LIBRARY
149 CHURCH STREET
NANUET, NEW YORK 10954
845-623-4281

Also by Judith Henry Wall

A Good Man

The Girlfriends Club

My Mother's Daughter

If Love Were All

Death Eligible

Mother Love

Blood Sisters

Handsome Women

Love and Duty

A Chain of Gold

NANUET PUBLIC LIBRARY
149 CHURCH STREET
NANUET, NEW YORK 10954
845-623-4281

The Surrogate

JUDITH HENRY WALL

SIMON & SCHUSTER PAPERBACKS

New York London Toronto Sydney

SIMON & SCHUSTER PAPERBACKS
Rockefeller Center
1230 Avenue of the Americas
New York, NY 10020

This book is a work of fiction. Names, characters, places, and incidents either are products of the author's imagination or are used fictitiously. Any resemblance to actual events or locales or persons, living or dead, is entirely coincidental.

Copyright © 2006 by Judith Henry Wall, Inc.

All rights reserved, including the right of
reproduction in whole or in part in any form.

First Simon & Schuster paperback edition 2006

SIMON & SCHUSTER PAPERBACKS and colophon are
registered trademarks of Simon & Schuster, Inc.

For information about special discounts for bulk purchases,
please contact Simon & Schuster Special Sales at
1-800-456-6798 or business@simonandschuster.com

Designed by Kyoko Watanabe

Manufactured in the United States of America

1   3   5   7   9   10   8   6   4   2

Library of Congress Cataloging-in-Publication Data

Wall, Judith Henry.
The surrogate / Judith Henry Wall.—1st Simon & Schuster pbk. ed.
p.   cm.
1. Surrogate motherhood—Fiction. 2. Houston (Tex.)—Fiction.
3. Celebrities—Fiction. 4. Secrecy—Fiction. I. Title.
PS3573.A42556S87 2006
813'.54—dc22
2005054090

ISBN-13: 978-0-7432-5851-7
ISBN-10:   0-7432-5851-7

Acknowledgments

No book is created in isolation. Special thanks go to my brilliant editor, Amanda Murray, who did a terrific job helping me turn a rambling, overly long manuscript into a publishable book, and to my fantastic agent, Philippa Brophy, for hanging in there with me for all these many years.

I also am grateful for the assistance, expertise, and encouragement I received from JoAnna Wall, Joan Atterbury, Dr. Jim Wall, Lanella Gray, and certified midwife Michelle Robidoux.

And I want to express my gratitude to all those unheralded, knowledgeable, and diligent copy editors who, over the years, have cleaned up my manuscripts.

Oklahoma City

THE BABY WAS GONE.

Only a blanket and a pacifier remained in the crib. Jamie stood there, clutching her own baby to her chest, trying to make sense of what she was seeing, thoughts racing frantically through her mind. She was aware that she had only seconds to convince herself that what she was seeing was true and to act on that knowledge.

She reached down and pushed the blanket aside—just to make sure.

It was like the morning that she found her grandmother dead. Jamie had felt as though there must be some other explanation for her grandmother's lifeless body. Anything but death. Jamie had even tried to lift Granny's head and place a pill between her lips. Then to shake her awake. To make it not be so.

That was how she felt now. She wanted to do something that could reverse the reality of what she was seeing.

Sounds came through the open window—a distant siren, a train whistle, the slam of a door. Normal sounds that belied that reality.

If her neighbor's baby was truly gone, it would mean that once again her life had been irreversibly changed.

But was there some other explanation? Had Lynette come in the night to take her baby home? Jamie looked at the door—her apartment's *only* door. The security chain was still engaged.

Even though her neighbor's baby was only two months old and could not climb, could not walk, could not even crawl, Jamie—still holding Billy in her arms—dropped to her knees and, with a fervent, whispered prayer, looked under the baby bed.

She scrambled back to her feet and, laying her cheek against the top of Billy's head, took a deep breath and willed her pounding heart to slow

1

down. Perhaps there was a logical explanation. She was overlooking something. Sometimes her keys weren't in her purse, and she would look everywhere for them only to realize they had been in the purse all along.

She ran her hands over the baby bed and shook the blanket.

The bed was definitely empty.

She forced herself to look out the open window, half expecting to see a small broken body on the ground three floors below.

Nothing was lying there.

She looked up and down the alley. Everything seemed so normal. It was just an ordinary-but-somewhat-seedy neighborhood near downtown Oklahoma City where she had come to put hundreds of miles between her and a ranch in the Texas Panhandle. To start over.

Jamie thought of all the other nights when her Billy had been the baby sleeping in the bed near the open window. How could it have been done? She doubted if an ordinary ladder could reach the third-floor window. Had someone lowered himself from the roof? Or crawled along the ledge? But still disbelief clouded her senses. Perhaps she had only dreamed that Lynette dropped her baby by last night. Just as she sometimes dreamed that her grandmother was still alive.

But Lynette's polka-dotted diaper bag was still on the coffee table.

A sob escaped from Jamie's throat. She closed her eyes and begged God to protect Lynette's baby.

Billy was whimpering. She needed to change him. Needed to nurse him.

She pressed her lips to Billy's forehead. They were one creature, she and her baby. There was no line between where she ended and he began. Love for him coursed through her veins. She would do anything to keep him. She would rather die than lose him.

Whoever had taken Lynette's baby had made a terrible mistake. The baby that person meant to take was Billy.

"Oh, God, Lynette, I am so sorry," Jamie whispered, imagining the anguish that Lynette would go through. "So sorry," she said again.

She looked around the two-room apartment she had called home for more than a month now. If her neighbor's baby was truly gone, she and Billy were no longer safe here.

Maybe they had never been safe here. Maybe it had only been a matter of time until they were found.

She would have to leave. *Now.* Everything had changed. *Everything!*

Chapter One

JAMIE'S EARLIEST MEMORY was of flying, of looking out the window of her daddy's airplane and seeing the whole of Galveston Island, which from the ground seemed a world unto itself.

Her father was a flight instructor and sometimes took her and her mother on Sunday afternoon flights.

Jamie preferred flying through clear blue skies with only occasional puffs of pretty white clouds floating by. She didn't like being surrounded by clouds. She was afraid they would get lost in them and never find their way home.

Sometimes her daddy flew so low over the ocean Jamie thought they were going to crash into the waves, and her mother would squeal for him to stop. Jamie realized it was a game that her parents were playing.

Perhaps they had died playing that game.

It was her parents' tenth anniversary. They planned to fly to Cozumel, an island off the coast of Mexico, and spend a week in a big hotel. But first they flew north to leave Jamie with her grandmother. Granny met them at the Mesquite airpark. Jamie held Granny's hand while they watched the plane take off. Jamie waved until it was only a tiny speck in a blue, cloudless sky.

The plane never arrived in Cozumel. There was an investigation, and eventually her parents were declared dead.

Sometimes Jamie imagined that the airplane had had engine trouble and her daddy had been forced to land on some uncharted island like the castaways on *Gilligan's Island,* and someday they would be rescued and come back to her. Every time a small plane flew overhead on its way to the Mesquite airpark, Jamie wondered if it was her parents coming back to get her. Long after she could not imagine living anyplace other than her grandmother's small white house, she would dream of her mother

3

and father opening the front gate, coming up the walk, and knocking on the door.

In her parents' will, Jamie's half-sister Ginger had been named her guardian. Their mother's child from an earlier, unhappy marriage, Ginger was sixteen years older than Jamie, married, and not at all interested in raising her.

Ginger had never had warm, cozy feelings for her half-sister. She had wanted to be royally pissed when her mother married and they moved to Galveston. But thanks to her stepfather's generosity, Ginger was able to attend Southern Methodist University and pledge a sorority instead of living at home and attending a community college. Ginger was totally mortified when she learned that her mother was expecting a baby at age forty-three, but when the baby was born, she did a pretty good job pretending to be enchanted by her little sister. When Ginger met Mr. Right, her stepfather coughed up enough money for her to have a storybook wedding, but Ginger found it very difficult to live on her husband's salary as a stockbroker at Merrill Lynch. She had thought stockbrokers made a lot of money and felt cheated when she realized that was not so.

Except for a ten-thousand-dollar bequest to Ginger, six-year-old Jamie was the sole recipient of her father's estate, and it didn't take Ginger long to realize that being named her sister's guardian was an answer to her prayers. She sold her stepfather's interest in the flight school and his family home on Galveston Island, and—so that little Jamie could have a room of her own—bought a brand-new house with a swimming pool in north Dallas and promised herself that she would do right by the kid.

Ginger tried to love the little girl. Or at least like her. But she became pregnant with twins and, what with feeling so damned tired all the time and decorating her new home, she just didn't have the energy. Sometimes she forgot to pick Jamie up at school, and the school secretary would call to remind her, her voice icy with disapproval. One day Ginger got a note from the school nurse saying that Jamie's shoes were too small and as a result she was suffering from severely ingrown toenails and needed to be taken to a podiatrist.

Ginger decided the kid was bound to feel more at home with their grandmother Gladys and started leaving Jamie in Mesquite for longer and longer periods of time until Gladys finally hired an attorney. By the time Gladys had been granted permanent custody of Jamie, the money that was supposed to pay for raising her was almost gone. The lawyer suggested that Gladys sue Ginger on Jamie's behalf. The court could force Ginger to sell her house and whatever else she had bought with the money.

"I can't do that," Gladys told the lawyer. "Ginger is my granddaughter, too."

Gladys was then well into her seventies. She didn't much believe in asking the Lord for favors but did suggest in her nightly prayer that it would sure be nice if she could live long enough to get the child raised.

Jamie understood that her sister had not wanted her and that her grandmother had decided to do what was best for her. It took her a while to realize that her grandmother also loved her. Granny didn't grab her in her arms and swing her around the way her father had done. And Granny didn't hug and kiss her all the time like her mother. Her Granny was simply there. Always calm. And firm. Granny didn't take any sass. And she had her rules. Muddy shoes came off at the door. The bathroom basin and tub were to be wiped clean after every use. Beds were to be made as soon as a body got out of them. The Lord was to be praised before every meal. And before the kitchen light was turned off at night, the counters and tabletop were to be washed with soapy water and the floor swept clean. At her sister's house in Dallas, Ginger had constantly been making up rules and then changing them. Granny's rules never changed. Jamie always knew what was expected of her, and there was comfort in that. And if she sat on the footstool in front of her grandmother's chair and laid her head against her grandmother's knee, Granny would stroke her hair.

Being raised by an elderly grandmother made Jamie different from the other kids. A few of her classmates also lived with their grandmothers, but those grandmothers weren't elderly. They didn't wear cotton dresses that had been washed so many times the printed flowers had almost faded away. They didn't wear their granddaughter's outgrown athletic shoes. They didn't clean houses to supplement their Social Security checks.

And there was the matter of Jamie's height. She was the tallest kid in her grade until some of the boys caught up with her in high school, and it didn't help a bit that her last name was Long. By the time she finished growing, she was five feet ten.

Jamie had always loved to run. Granny said she was as swift and graceful as a gazelle, but it was the grandson of their back-fence neighbors who encouraged Jamie to try out for the high school track team.

Joe Brammer lived in Houston but every summer came to spend a month with his grandparents. Joe was almost six years older than Jamie, and his grandparents would send him over to help with the heavy stuff, like pruning trees, digging out a stump, changing a tire, or hauling off a broken-down washing machine. Granny would always feed him for his trouble. He would tell her in a conspiratorial tone that *her* apple pie was better than his grandmother's. Sometimes Joe would play dominoes with Jamie and Granny on a Sunday afternoon. Other times Jamie would help him work on his Jeep, or sometimes it was her grandmother's car getting the oil changed or the spark plugs cleaned. And when it cooled down in the evening they would shoot baskets at the hoop mounted over his grandparents' garage door, or one of them might challenge the other to a foot race. He was better at shooting baskets than she was, but from age ten she could outrun him, and Joe would groan and moan and swear he would cut out her tongue if she ever mentioned it to anyone. Then after one particularly humbling defeat, he announced that she was going to try out for the high school track team, and if she didn't, he would personally drive up here from Houston and drag her down to the track. "You're a natural, Jamie," he said, punching her arm and mussing her hair.

Joe was right. Jamie had excellent times for both long and middle distances. And was competitive at the long jump.

High school was better than grade school. She felt at home with the other girls on the track team, some of whom were as tall as or taller than she was. They called one another on the telephone and went to the movies together. One girl, Charlene, even became her best friend, and they often slept over at each other's houses and both worked Saturdays at the VIP Car Wash.

Jamie never had a boyfriend, though. Never had a real date. Sometimes this or that boy would hang out around her locker between classes and act like maybe he wanted to say more than "Hi" or "See you in class," but she always pretended she didn't notice. The only boy she ever had romantic thoughts about was Joe Brammer, which was silly of her. She knew Joe's feelings for her were of the big-brother variety, but maybe when she was older . . .

By this time, however, Joe was in college and working summers as an oil-field roustabout. The only time he came to Mesquite was with his parents for Thanksgiving, Easter, and an occasional weekend. There were no

more foot races or shooting hoops in the driveway. But instead of thinking about him less, thoughts of Joe were always there at some level of
Jamie's consciousness. In her mind she would playact entire conversations with him. When she closed her eyes at night, she imagined more
than conversations.

Whenever he was in town Joe would come over to pay his respects to
Jamie and her grandmother and admire Jamie's growing collection of
track medals. He said he didn't feel quite so bad now that she had beat him
whenever they raced to the highway and back.

Easter weekend during Jamie's junior year, Joe stopped by like always.
He asked Jamie about school and track and inquired about Granny's
health. And he told them about his college classes and how he couldn't
decide whether he wanted to be a high school history teacher or go to law
school. When Granny announced it was past her bedtime, Joe and Jamie
went for a walk. It was a clear night, the air filled with the sounds of crick-
ets and the air brakes on the big rigs over on Highway 352 as they slowed
to make the Scyene Road exit.

"If you went to law school, would you stay in Austin or go out of
state?" she asked Joe, thinking that if she got a track scholarship to UT and
he was a law student there, they might see each other from time to time.
Maybe he would stop thinking of her as a kid sister of sorts if she were a
college student.

"I'm not sure," Joe answered. "The girl I'm going with is majoring in
broadcast journalism. If she gets a job out of state, I might apply someplace else."

"Oh," was all Jamie could say. She felt as though all the air had gone
out of her lungs. As though her bones had gone soft. When she stumbled,
Joe grabbed her arm, but as soon as she got her balance he let go.

"Come on," he said. "I'd better take you home before your grandmother comes looking for you."

That night, Jamie sobbed into her pillow. What a silly girl she had been
to hope that Joe Brammer might someday realize that deep down he had
always loved her but had denied those feelings because she was too young.
He was the only boy she had ever imagined kissing. The only boy she had
imagined making love to.

Stupid. That's what she was. A stupid, silly girl.

Jamie was recruited by the track coaches at several state colleges, but at the last meet of her senior season, she injured her knee going for a conference record in the long jump. At first, the operation to repair her torn ligaments seemed like a success, but her knee was never the same. She would be able to walk without a limp and even run—but not competitively.

Charlene's family moved to California after graduation. The two girls promised to stay in touch, but Jamie wondered if they would ever see each other again, if she would ever have another best friend.

Thanks to her good grades and her scores on college entrance exams, Jamie was granted a tuition-waiver scholarship at the University of Texas in Austin. Her grandmother sent a hundred dollars every month to help with her dorm bill, and Jamie worked twenty hours a week at a dry-cleaning establishment. She had little time for a social life but did have several friends—girls like herself who had to work and were not in a sorority.

During the second semester of her freshman year Joe Brammer started to stop by the dry cleaner's, and they would visit in between customers. He was thinking about applying for a fellowship that would allow him to study international law at Oxford during his last semester of law school. And he sometimes mentioned his girlfriend, but mostly they talked about their classes, music, current events, and what they wanted to do with their lives. Sometimes he came by just before her shift was over and walked her back to the campus.

That summer he didn't come to Mesquite at all.

Her grandmother was well past eighty by then and no longer strong enough to clean other people's houses. When Jamie left for her sophomore year at UT, her grandmother cried because she could no longer afford to send her any money. Jamie assured her that she could manage just fine, which she did by working longer hours and counting every penny.

She was thrilled when Joe dropped by the dry cleaner's her first week back, and she dared to hope that maybe he wasn't serious about the girl he was dating. But a couple of weeks later he came by to tell her that he was going to get married. When he left, Jamie went into the tiny bathroom and cried, running the water to muffle the sound of her sobs. She stayed in the bathroom so long that the manager knocked on the door and asked if she was all right.

Jamie tried to stop thinking about Joe, especially at night while she was waiting for sleep. She knew now that he was never going to fall in love with her. That she was still just a kid to him. But she didn't have anyone else to take his role in her nighttime imaginings and wondered if she ever would.

Mid-November it became apparent that her grandmother was not well. Jamie finished out the semester then packed up and came home. When Granny protested, Jamie told her the decision was not negotiable.

It was strange to see her grandmother's house unkempt. The only food in the refrigerator was on dishes Jamie recognized as belonging to Joe's grandmother. When she returned the dishes, Mrs. Washburn hugged her and insisted on pouring her a cup of coffee. "I'm glad you're home," she said, patting Jamie's arm affectionately. "Your grandmother needs you."

Jamie spent several days cleaning the little house. In the process, she found a drawer full of unpaid bills and threats to discontinue service from the utility companies. She also discovered that her grandmother's property taxes had not been paid in years, the mortgage company had begun foreclosure proceedings, and Granny's bank account was overdrawn.

When she asked her grandmother about the bills, Granny said not to worry. "I'm expecting a check for thirty-eight thousand dollars any day now," she explained.

"Who's sending the check?" Jamie asked.

"I won it," Granny said with a proud smile. "I kept getting these letters promising me a prize if I made a contribution to the war on cancer, so I finally sent a donation. And a nice man called and said I had won all this money. All I had to do to secure my winnings was send a check for eight hundred and seventy-two dollars. My winnings should come any day now."

"I'm sure they will," Jamie said with a sinking heart.

"And in the meantime, there's some money in an oatmeal box on the top shelf of the pantry," Granny said.

When Jamie looked, there was no oatmeal box in the pantry or any-place else in the kitchen. Jamie applied for a credit card and used cash advances to cover Granny's overdraft and pay the overdue bills. She used a cash advance on a second credit card to appease the mortgage company, which agreed to wait six months before foreclosing on the loan. She also got a job at a hardware store but had to quit when Granny could no longer get herself to the bathroom. Jamie told her grandmother that the prize money had finally arrived and began charging groceries, gas, and medical expenses not covered by Medicare. She made monthly payments on the first two credit cards with cash advances from a third.

With her grandmother all but bedridden, Jamie encouraged her to fill her waking hours with reminiscing and listened while her grandmother dug up old memories—good and bad. Jamie realized how difficult her grandmother's life had been—being widowed as a young woman and raising her daughter on her own.

"The best of my life has been the last," Granny told Jamie. "You have been my greatest joy and my crowning achievement."

She died the next day.

After the men from the funeral home had taken Granny's body away, Jamie called Ginger, whom she hadn't seen in years. "I thought you'd want to know," she told her sister.

After several seconds of silence, Ginger said, "I know you're going to miss her."

That night Jamie dreamed that their parents arrived just in time to be with her and Ginger at the cemetery when they buried their grandmother next to her husband, who died so long ago that no one except Granny remembered him.

Ginger arrived the next morning and walked through the house. "Did she have a will?" she asked.

Jamie shook her head.

That afternoon, Ginger returned with a rented truck and two burly men. "Some of this old stuff might be worth something," she said. "I talked to a Realtor about selling the place."

When Jamie explained that the house belonged to the mortgage company, Ginger accused Jamie of stealing her share of the inheritance.

Jamie walked through the house gathering up the things she wanted to keep and carried them out to the old Chevy, which Granny had already put in her name. That night she slept on a mattress apparently deemed too old and lumpy to be of value.

Ginger didn't even stay for the funeral.

A surprising number of people did come, however, including Joe Brammer's grandparents. "Your grandmother was a fine woman and our dear friend," Mr. Washburn said with a bear hug. Mrs. Washburn embraced Jamie and kissed her cheek. "We're going to miss her," she said, "and you, too." Jamie knew that the Washburns had purchased a retirement home in Georgia and would soon be leaving Mesquite.

She stayed in town long enough to scrub the house from top to bottom and settle her grandmother's affairs. Then she carried the last of her things and Granny's houseplants out to the car and, taking one last look at the little white house that had been her home for more than a dozen years, drove away with tears streaming down her face.

She stopped at the cemetery on her way out of town.

As she stood there staring down at the patch of raw earth, a favorite memory of her grandmother came into her mind. They were doing the spring cleaning and had propped open the back screen door so that they could carry the mattresses and rugs out to the backyard for an airing. A young sparrow flew through the open door and went completely crazy when it couldn't find a way out. Fluffy little feathers fluttered about like snow as it beat its wings first against the window over the sink and then the window by the table. Back and forth it went. Granny stood perfectly still in the middle of the kitchen talking in a low, soothing voice, telling the frantic little creature that it was a very beautiful bird and that she had always wished that she could be a bird for a day so she could fly high in the sky and better see what God hath wrought. Finally the exhausted creature lighted on top of the refrigerator, and Granny reached out to it. The bird perched on her finger and, still talking softly, she carried it to the door and watched it fly away.

What Jamie would miss the most was her grandmother's calmness. It had soothed like a balm.

"I love you, Granny, and I thank you from the bottom of my heart," she said.

She was alone in the world, deeply in debt, and two and a half years away from a college degree.

But she did have a plan.

Chapter Two

BENTLEY ABERNATHY WAS awake when the phone rang.

He had been staring into the darkness hoping for some indication from his wife's side of the bed that she might also be awake and possibly receptive to a little middle-of-the-night sex after which he was always able to fall asleep immediately. Brenda had made it clear to him years ago that she did not want to be awakened in the middle of the night for sex and that he should go jack off in the bathroom or take a sleeping pill when he was suffering from a bout of sleeplessness. But occasionally she, too, would be wakeful and roll willingly into his arms without expectation of foreplay, her own fantasies apparently having been at work, and they would come together for an immediate, intense coupling followed by a bit of affectionate snuggling as they both fell soundly asleep.

Even though Bentley was an attorney and not unaccustomed to late-night phone calls from desperate clients, the demanding ring of a telephone in the still of the night was always startling. Always made his heart lurch. And in the span of a millisecond, that first harsh ring precipitated an avalanche of possibilities that had nothing to do with clients. As disappointed as he was in his four spoiled and seemingly worthless children, he realized how much he still loved them when the middle-of-the-night phone calls came and his greatest fear was that something terrible might happen to one of them—something an attorney father could not make go away. The possibilities were many. Automobile accidents topped the list, followed closely by overdoses. Or the fear would resurface that his daughter's jerk of a husband was capable of abuse. Or one of his sons might have been severely injured in a barroom brawl. Or had driven into Mexico and been murdered by *banditos*. Or been mugged. Carjacked. Kidnapped. One of his children could be bleeding to death on a hospital gurney or cold and dead on a slab at the county morgue.

Without his glasses, Bentley did not even try to read the number on the caller ID. He grabbed the phone before it rang a second time. An instant later Brenda turned on her bedside lamp.

"What's taking you so goddamned long?" a rasping male voice immediately demanded.

Bentley fell back on the bed and took in a deep, calming, grateful breath. His spoiled, worthless children lived on.

"You said to take all the time I needed to find the perfect young woman," Bentley said into the receiver, reminding himself of the almost impossible list of criteria he had been given.

"It's been four damned months, and I pay you a great deal of money to look after our affairs down there. I told you that this particular affair was to have top priority."

"It *is* my top priority," Bentley assured his caller, carefully keeping any sign of irritation from his voice.

"My sister says you haven't found a single girl for her to interview."

"That's because we didn't want to waste her time with unsuitable applicants. Amanda was very specific about the sort of young woman that she and her husband were looking for. But I can assure you that we have narrowed down the search. In fact, I have a promising candidate coming into the office in the morning."

"E-mail me something on her."

"Now?"

"*Now.*"

Before Bentley could respond, the caller hung up, and he allowed himself a single "Shit!"

"God almighty, I presume," Brenda said.

"Yeah. I've got to take care of something downstairs."

Brenda was sitting up. One strap of her nightgown had slipped from her shoulder, revealing a portion of her right breast. For an old broad, his wife was still a looker. Still had a great body. Great tits.

Bentley took a chance and reached over to pull her nightgown even lower and rub a fingertip around the exposed nipple. He was rewarded with just the tiniest suggestion of a smile.

"How long will 'something' take?" she asked.

"Five minutes," he said.

"Well, I *might* still be awake," she said.

Bentley leaped from the bed. He beat on his chest and let out a Tarzan yell as he went racing across the room. Brenda's laughter followed him.

In his downstairs office, Bentley looked in his Rolodex for his secretary's home phone number and dialed it.

"Hi, boss," she said sleepily. Obviously Lenora didn't need glasses to read her caller ID.

"I'm sorry to bother you, but I had a late-night call from Gus Hartmann. He thinks we're neglecting his sister's search. Didn't you say the young woman you have scheduled in the morning looked like the best of the lot?"

"Yeah. At least on paper and over the phone she seems promising."

"I need you to e-mail her file to Gus Hartmann ASAP. He's at home."

"I'm heading for my computer now."

"Do I pay you enough?" he asked.

"For the time being."

Bentley thanked her then hurried back upstairs.

At the top of the stairs, he could see the flicker of candlelight from the open bedroom door. His heart surged.

Brenda was naked. "I want you to kiss me for a long time," she said. Her voice was low and sultry.

"God, you're beautiful," he said, taking her in his arms. God yes, he would kiss her. Every inch of her. He was doing just that when the phone rang. "Don't answer it," Brenda said. "He'll just upset you."

Bentley shook his head and reluctantly reached for the receiver.

"There's no picture. I need to know what this girl looks like."

"We'll take one tomorrow," Bentley said and hung up the receiver. He wanted to disconnect the phone before returning to his wife's lovely, warm, delicious body but didn't dare.

Gus Hartmann printed out the e-mail and read the report again before putting it in his desk drawer. Then he pushed back his chair and headed for the open French doors. A fountain gurgled pleasantly in the meditation garden, and the soft hooting of an owl could be heard from the grove of pine trees just beyond the brick wall.

The garden was just as it had been when his mother would come here. A willow draped its branches elegantly over the fountain, and a sculpture of Jesus, his arms outspread, beckoned from the shadows of a stone grotto. The gaslights still came on every evening at dusk. The plantings were kept the same. Not a weed, fallen leaf, or cobweb was allowed to mar the garden's pristine beauty.

Gus seated himself on a stone bench where his mother used to sit for long periods of time without moving, seemingly without breathing. He would watch her from the French doors until she realized that he was there. She would smile and open her arms. "Come here, my darling boy," she would say.

It was an image he clung to.

Gus and his sister Amanda had kept the house and grounds of the northern Virginia estate much as it had been when they were children and lived here with their famous parents. And the Texas ranch, too. Both were monuments to another time.

Gus looked through the open doors at the portrait of his parents that hung above the mantel. What a striking couple they had been. And tragic. An irresistible mix—beauty and tragedy. Even after all these years, people still made their way to the gate of the estate to leave tacky little bouquets of flowers and silly little messages, especially in remembrance of his and Amanda's mother. Amanda read the messages and had a secretary respond if there was an address. Each address was added to the mailing list for the Alliance of Christian Voters, and the writer was extended an invitation to join the organization and help bring the God of our fathers back to American life and government. If an individual made a large enough donation to the Alliance or a clergyman brought his congregation into the fold, he or she would be invited to a retreat or seminar at Alliance headquarters in Washington, D.C. And depending on the size of the gift, that person might even be invited to a reception or a dinner here at Victory Hill and meet Amanda Hartmann in person. Gus never attended these affairs, but he did sometimes stand in the shadows of the upstairs hallway and watch Amanda receive guests, all of whom seemed to have a pathological need to shake her hand and gush about how important her books had been to them and how much they had enjoyed her appearances on *Oprah* or *Regis* and how they remembered her mother with such awe and admiration. Even corporate moguls and those elected to high political office fawned over Amanda, and those who were old enough to remember her father told her what a fine man he had been, what a great president he would have made. And, of course, there would be a photographer waiting to take each guest's picture with Amanda. Such photographs were autographed and mailed to the visitor with a personalized letter.

The only gatherings Gus attended were board meetings and private dinners for a small group of powerful men who had a vested interest in making sure the correct side of the political spectrum maintained a firm control of the nation's destiny. For, like his father before him, Gus was a political animal. Unlike his father, however, he was not a politician.

Jason Hartmann had been the youngest governor in Texas history. He was midway through his first term when he married Mary Millicent Tutt, who was already known to millions for her inspirational books and her nationally syndicated newspaper column and her television and radio shows. Their wedding had been a media event. Pictures of the bride and groom appeared in countless newspapers and on the covers of magazines. The accompanying stories usually pointed out that Jason's gubernatorial election had been financed by his whiskey-drinking, cigar-smoking billionaire father, Jonathan "Buck" Hartmann, who had struck it rich wildcatting for oil and claim-jumping in western Texas, and that Mary Millicent was the daughter of Preacher Marvin Tutt, an old-time tent evangelist who died after being bitten by one of the poisonous serpents that he sometimes wrapped around his neck during his hellfire-and-brimstone sermons. In spite of their notorious fathers, the bride and groom were heralded as Texas "royalty."

Gus had no memory of the governor's mansion or his father's election to the U.S. Senate. His first memories were of the Texas ranch and this house, where his family had lived during his father's Senate years. Jason Hartmann had been on track to be nominated as his party's presidential candidate when he was stricken with a malignant brain tumor. Gus had been eight years old at the time and his sister Amanda ten. They went with their parents to the Texas ranch and watched from the sidelines while their father languished and finally died. Their mother became even more beloved as she traveled around the nation bringing millions of lost souls to the Lord and launching the Alliance of Christian Voters as a memorial to her late husband. The Alliance was dedicated to returning the United States of America to its staunch Christian roots. Many of Mary

Millicent's supporters wanted her to run for political office, but she preferred to endorse candidates rather than become one. She'd often told her son that it was the kingmakers who ruled the world and not the kings themselves. But, of course, she realized that political office was out of the question for Gus.

Americans have a penchant for electing tall candidates, and Gus was a very short man. He stood barely five feet tall and, having been diagnosed as an infant with a rare form of dwarfism, achieved that height only because he had been treated with growth hormones throughout his childhood. He was not only exceptionally short, his head was overly large for his frame, his arms and legs too short.

Gus and Amanda had grown up knowing that he would someday administer both the Alliance and the oil company founded by their grandfather Buck Hartmann and that she would eventually take over their mother's ministry and become the spiritual leader of the Alliance.

Gus left the limelight to his sister. If people had heard of him at all, it was as the brother of Amanda Tutt Hartmann. Only the most astute observers of the political scene realized that he had played a pivotal role in the current president's rise to the White House and was perhaps one of the most powerful men in the country. Gus refused to be interviewed when contacted by the occasional perceptive reporter who realized that the reclusive chairman of both the vast Alliance of Christian Voters and Palo Duro Oil and Gas was more than what he seemed. Nevertheless, every few years an article about Gus would appear in one of the nation's more astute publications. A photograph almost never accompanied such articles, for almost no photographs of him existed in the public domain. He never appeared at public events. Never appeared in public at all. Palo Duro and Alliance board meetings were generally held at Victory Hill or the ranch or via teleconferencing. Whenever he went to the White House, he entered through a back entrance used mainly by delivery people and servants. If he wanted to speak with the president from his home, all he had to do was punch a button on his phone. Gus spoke to the president almost daily to remind him of his priorities and that he had run for office as a devout Christian and damned well better do nothing to destroy that image.

His sister, however, was quite well-known and continuously sought after by reporters and photographers, and her face was often on the covers of magazines. Amanda was as elegant and well-spoken as their mother had been and had inherited their mother's skill with the written word but carried a softer message to her flock. Amanda's God was more loving and forgiving than her mother's had been. Amanda's book, *Peace from Within*, had been an international best seller. And, like her mother before her, she was a frequent guest on talk shows, and there would be standing room only at the rallies and revivals she held all over the country, during which she urged attendees not only to give their heart to Jesus but to register to vote and to use their vote to bring the United States of America back to God.

Gus realized that his sister had always assumed he shared her religious faith, and he never bothered to tell her otherwise. For him, religion was now and had been throughout history a way to control the masses. He placed his faith in power—in *political* power—and religion had become the defining force in American politics. Gus had masterminded the president's election by bringing together the power and wealth of giant corporations and the religious right. Under Gus's direction and Amanda's ministry, the Alliance of Christian Voters had become a powerful political action group.

In spite of his disdain for all things religious, Gus loved and admired Amanda immensely. He had been relieved when her brief marriage to a professional football player ended, and she and her infant son came home to Victory Hill. The football player, who had a history of bar fights and an addiction to gambling, refused to give up parental rights and allow his son's last name to be changed to Hartmann, but less than a year after the divorce, the man had been the victim of a drive-by shooting.

Amanda's son had no memory of his father. Gus had been the father figure in Sonny's life, a role he had cherished. Still, he had never completely realized how profoundly he loved his nephew until the accident. It was almost six months ago now since Sonny had been found pinned under an all-terrain vehicle at the bottom of a shallow canyon in the far northwest corner of the ranch. He had been taken by helicopter to Amarillo, but after more than a month in intensive care, Amanda had him moved back to the ranch, away from prying eyes, and taken up the mantle of a grieving mother. Her millions of followers assumed that Sonny was dead and grieved along with her, but the press had not given up so easily. With their telephoto lenses and audacity, they drove up the isolated road that led to Hartmann Ranch. They stayed until the frigid reality of a Panhandle winter drove them away.

Technically, Sonny Hartmann was still alive. He still moved and even mumbled at times. But the essence of the boy who had been Gus's beloved Sonny lived no longer.

Gus now conducted his life under a staggering burden of grief.

His sister had prayed a thousand prayers to her God, asking that Sonny be restored to her. Gus even reconsidered altering his own religious beliefs for a time. Even though he had not prayed since childhood, when his grief became unbearable Gus had given it a try. On bended knee he made his bargains and promises, but they had been to no avail.

He looked into the face of the stone Christ and pondered trying once again.

Chapter Three

"YOUR TEN O'CLOCK appointment is here," Lenora's voice announced when Bentley picked up the phone.

"What do you think?" Bentley asked. "Does the young woman live up to your expectations?"

"My expectations aren't what matters. Her file is on your desk."

"Offer her coffee and give me a few minutes."

Bentley headed for his private bathroom to take a leak, run a comb through his hair, and remove a speck from his right contact lens. With the lens back in place, he grinned at his face in the mirror, remembering last night. He thought he'd lost Brenda after Gus's second phone call, but she'd hung in there. And turned into a tigress. A fuckin' tigress. And he had risen to the occasion. *God, had he ever.* And he hadn't even taken Viagra.

Bentley gave his crotch an affectionate pat.

Still wearing a self-satisfied smile, Bentley emerged from the bathroom and took a quick glance around his office—at the book-lined walls, the Persian rugs on dark wood floors, the carefully selected works of Native American art on the walls. He picked up a remote from his desk and adjusted the blinds on the wall of windows overlooking the river.

The room was designed to impress, of course. Lately though, Bentley had begun to wonder if the decor was a bit too contrived.

He used to take more satisfaction in the trappings of his success. After all, his first law office had been over a garage, and he and Brenda set up housekeeping in a one-bedroom apartment. Of course, that had all changed after Gus Hartmann anointed him. Now he drove a late-model Mercedes sedan and lived in a mansion in a fine old Austin neighborhood, but sometimes he found himself foolishly longing for those days of yore when he and Brenda were young and struggling. Sometimes he wondered how she would react if he closed his practice and went to work for legal aid, helping the down-and-out instead of the filthy rich. Or if he gave up law altogether, and they took up fishing and gardening and enjoying their grandchildren—if their kids ever got around to providing them with any. But with a million-dollar mortgage, three sons still in college, and a daughter married to a worthless bum, he was pretty much locked into the present arrangement.

Bentley put on his suit jacket, adjusted his cuffs, and sat on a corner of the desk while he looked over the fact sheet Lenora had prepared on Jamie Amelia Long.

- Twenty years old.
- Dropped out of college midway through second year to care for dying grandmother.
- Outstanding ACT scores.
- Ran track in high school.
- Parents killed in a plane crash when she was six.
- Raised by aforementioned grandmother.
- One sibling—a half-sister sixteen years her senior from whom she is estranged.
- Blond hair.
- Blue eyes.
- Five feet ten inches tall.
- Weight 135 pounds.
- Right-handed.
- No serious illnesses.
- No known genetic disorders in her family.
- Doesn't wear glasses.
- Never been married or pregnant.
- No current romantic involvement.

Sounds good, Bentley thought. He hoped she looked okay. One of Amanda Hartmann's specifications was that the young woman be "winsome of face and body." In addition, she was to be "extremely intelligent, in perfect health, athletically gifted, willowy, graceful, soft-spoken but articulate, virtuous, industrious, and loyal." She also must belong to a church and believe in God, and must never have been married. And Amanda "strongly preferred" a young woman *without* family ties.

On paper, at least, Jamie Long seemed like a match.

He really would like to get this business settled. Of course, he would bill the Hartmanns for every hour he'd spent educating himself on the legal aspects of surrogate motherhood and the time he and Lenora spent looking for and screening the candidates, but he needed to move on. He had two important trials coming up—both concerning environment infractions by Palo Duro Oil and Gas.

Bentley put down Jamie Long's file, straightened his tie, and opened the door that separated his office from Lenora's domain. Lenora and the young woman were seated on the sofa, coffee cups on the table in front of them.

Bentley extended his hand. "Bentley Abernathy. Nice to meet you, Miss Long."

She had a firm handshake and met his gaze. "Thank you for seeing me," she said.

Bentley escorted Jamie Long into his office and seated her on the leather sofa. After establishing that she did not want another cup of coffee, he retrieved the file folder from his desk and sat across from her.

Jamie Long was pretty in an unassuming way. Good cheekbones. A full mouth that would be sexy on another face but somehow only made her look sweet and vulnerable. Her eyes were a deep shade that must have some more exotic name than simply "blue," and her hair was a glistening pale blond that surely could not have come from a bottle. With a little makeup and a better haircut, the girl could be a knockout.

"I assume that you saw our ad in a student newspaper," Bentley began.

"Yes, in *The Daily Texan*. But that was a couple of months ago. I was a bit surprised that you were still looking for someone."

"What would you have done if we weren't?"

"I've found similar ads on other college newspaper Web sites and met several interested parties in chat rooms. I knew from the phone number that you were in-state, so I decided to start with you."

"And just what made you interested in becoming a surrogate mother?" he asked.

Her hands were folded in her lap. She was very young to be alone in the world, Bentley thought.

"Well, I thought it would be a satisfying way to help a couple who really wanted a baby and at the same time earn the money I need to finish my college education and pay my debts," the girl said.

"I see," Bentley said. "I want to make sure you completely understand what would be expected of you. Before being artificially inseminated, you would be required to sign a contract in which you agree to terminate all parental rights to the child and to abide by my clients' terms. You would be paid handsomely for your services, which would end with the child's birth. My clients have specified that you would not be allowed to see the baby, know its sex, or have any sort of relationship with it whatsoever. Have you really thought this through, Miss Long? Are you sure you will be able to give up a baby that you have carried for nine months?"

Jamie nodded, her expression solemn. "I hope to have babies of my own someday, but at this point in my life I don't want the responsibility that comes with being a mother. Right now I just want to finish my education and not have to worry all the time about money." She paused as though considering just how much more of an explanation was needed. "I grew up poor and have always had to make do," she continued. "And while I realize that my upbringing prepared me better for life than kids who have everything given to them on a silver platter, once in a while I would like to be able to walk into a nice store and buy something just because it's pretty." Then she buried her hands in her lap and blushed. "I know that makes me sound frivolous, but really I am a very serious person. I have always studied hard and made good grades. I never skipped school and never got into trouble. My grandmother never had to remind me to do my chores. She raised me well."

"I am sure she did," Bentley said. He liked Jamie Long. So much so that he wasn't sure he wanted to introduce her to Amanda Hartmann. Not that he disliked Amanda. His dealings with her had always been pleasant and civil, and she was revered by millions of followers. But Amanda was, after all, Gus Hartmann's sister.

If he passed on Jamie Long, however, he would have to keep on interviewing candidates, and the process had gone on long enough. Amanda and her brother were growing impatient. And maybe Amanda's new husband was, too. Anyway, Bentley needed to move on to other things.

"Should my clients select you as their surrogate, they will expect you to agree to some terms that are a bit unusual," Bentley explained. "For starters, you would be required to live on their ranch and be under strict supervision throughout the entire process—from the moment you sign the contract until you deliver the baby."

Jamie Long's eyes widened. "But I want to go back to college," she protested.

Bentley shrugged. "I'm afraid that would be impossible. My clients are intent on protecting their investment and doing everything possible to ensure a good outcome. They believe that close supervision is the only way they can be sure that the young woman carrying their child remains drug- and alcohol-free and that she doesn't smoke or engage in any other risky behaviors. My clients own a ranch in the Texas Panhandle. The woman they engage as their surrogate will have her own apartment in the ranch house. All meals will be prepared for her. A nurse will look after her. She will not be allowed to swim unattended nor will she be allowed to ride a horse or drive a car. And she will not be allowed to leave the property unattended."

"So basically, I would be incarcerated for nine months," Jamie said, her tone incredulous, her eyebrows raised.

"I think that 'a guest with limited privileges' might be more accurate," Bentley said. "And it might be for more than nine months. The insemination process can involve several menstrual cycles. But such restrictions are not unreasonable when you think about it. My clients want to do everything within their power to protect the surrogate and their unborn child. Should you and my clients come to an agreement, throughout the entire process you must think of the baby as *their* baby. The husband will donate his sperm and therefore be the child's natural father, and the wife will become the baby's adoptive mother. The contract you sign will stipulate that after the baby is born you are never to contact my clients or make any future demands on them. You will be provided transportation to the destination of your choice. If you experience any medical complication as a result of your pregnancy or the delivery, they will continue to provide for your medical care until the situation is resolved. As for financial compensation, if my clients select you as their surrogate, they will pay you ten thousand dollars up front. If you don't become pregnant after three menstrual cycles, you will be paid an additional five thousand dollars and dismissed. If you are successfully inseminated but miscarry, you also will be given an additional five thousand dollars and dismissed. The contract also stipulates amounts of compensation for other circumstances, such as a stillborn child or a child that is aborted because prenatal testing reveals a defect in the fetus that is unacceptable to my clients. But if you are successfully inseminated and deliver a live baby, you will be paid an additional ninety thousand dollars, making your total compensation one hundred thousand dollars."

"Oh, my God!" Jamie said. "That's a lot more than I expected."

"Yes, it is a great deal of money," Bentley allowed. "But there is yet another incentive for you to consider. Privacy is a *major* issue with my clients. If you deliver a viable infant, they will create a trust fund in your name. According to the terms of this trust, if you do not contact the child and never reveal your relationship to the child to another living soul, for the rest of your life you will receive an annual payment of twenty thousand dollars from the proceeds of the trust."

A small gasp escaped from Jamie Long's lovely mouth.

"I must warn you, Miss Long, that you should not enter into a contract with my clients unless you are absolutely certain that you will abide by its terms. Even though it is not unheard of for surrogate mothers to change their minds and decide to keep the baby, those who do find themselves in a very compromised legal situation. While the courts might very well recognize her as the child's legal mother, the father also has legal rights to his child. And the woman could face lawsuits for breech of contract, be held responsible for her and the baby's medical expenses, and might very well be expected to reimburse the couple for their legal fees and any other expenses they incurred.

"So, Miss Long," Bentley continued, "you need to decide what putting your life on hold for up to a year is worth. If you agree to my clients' terms, you will undergo a comprehensive medical workup. If you receive a clean bill of health, we will arrange an interview with my clients. Now, do you have a place to stay here in Austin?"

Jamie shook her head.

Bentley rose and went to the door. "Lenora, would you please join us."

Lenora smiled at Jamie, then seated herself in the other armchair and crossed her legs.

"I want you to book a room for Miss Long at the Driskill and see that she has everything she needs," Bentley said. Then he scribbled a few additional instructions on a notepad, tore off the page, and handed it to Lenora.

NANUET PUBLIC LIBRARY
149 CHURCH STREET
NANUET, NEW YORK 10954
845-623-4281

"Lenora will go over the contract with you and answer any questions you may have," he told Jamie. Then he stood, and the two women followed suit.

"If I do agree to all the terms in the contract, do you think I'm the sort of person your clients are looking for?" Jamie asked.

"I think you just may be," Bentley said. "Just be sure in your own mind that this really is what you want to do."

But of course she would agree to their terms, he thought. No penniless young woman in her right mind would turn down such an offer.

Chapter Four

JAMIE'S HEAD WAS spinning as she followed Lenora from Mr. Abernathy's office and sat on the sofa across from her desk. She took a deep breath in an effort to calm herself and mentally replayed the conversation with Mr. Abernathy while Lenora made phone calls and gave instructions to her assistant.

One hundred thousand dollars! That was far more than had been suggested on any of the surrogate mother Web sites she'd visited. And, in addition to that, she would have an annual income for the rest of her life—not enough to live on but certainly enough to give her wonderful options as to how she would manage her life.

Taxes would take part of the money, of course, but she could pay off her credit cards and have more than enough money to finish her undergraduate degree. And it made going to medical school not seem like a pipe dream.

It was overwhelming. So much so, she began to tremble. She took several deep breaths and put her shaking hands between her knees to still them.

But to earn this bonanza and get on with the rest of her life, she would have to take the better part of a year off to have a baby, she reminded herself.

A baby.

Even though she had done all that research online, perhaps she had not completely thought through what being a surrogate mother entailed. She touched her stomach. *A baby growing inside of her that didn't belong to her.* By knowing from the very beginning that it was not hers to love and raise, she could deal with it, though. She was certain of that. After all, she didn't want a baby of her own. Not yet. Not until she could have a baby that was conceived because she and a man loved each other and wanted to have a family together. And she was a long way from that.

She wondered what Mr. Abernathy thought of her—of a woman willing to have a baby for strangers. Was he appalled that a seemingly decent young woman would even consider such a thing? Jamie found the idea of surrogate motherhood rather appealing, however. It seemed like a beautiful thing to do for a childless couple. She'd read on one of the Web sites that some women even volunteer to be surrogate mothers for free. They like being pregnant and having babies. Some of them even have lifelong relationships with the parents and the child.

Of course that wasn't going to be the case if she carried a baby for Mr. Abernathy's clients. They would never want to see their child's surrogate mother again after the baby was born, which might be better for all concerned. How confusing it would be for a child to have two mothers.

But what about all those other stipulations to which she would have to agree? Was not having to mortgage her future in order to complete her education worth becoming a virtual prisoner for up to a year of her life?

Then she thought how glorious it would be to attend the university without having to hold down a job and worry about money all the time.

She watched Lenora put a sheaf of papers in her briefcase and take her purse from the bottom drawer of her desk. Jamie followed her out of the office. On the elevator ride to the underground garage, Jamie dug around in her purse for a tissue.

"Are you all right?" Lenora asked.

Jamie blew her nose. "Just a bit overwhelmed," she admitted.

"What you need is a nice lunch at the Driskill Grill," Lenora said. "Then we are going to have manicures and pedicures on the boss's dollar before we settle down for the afternoon in your hotel room to go over this contract."

Her grandmother's Chevrolet, packed with all of Jamie's possessions, was parked across from Lenora's late-model BMW. Jamie followed Lenora as she navigated her way through the midday downtown traffic.

She parked behind Lenora in front of the entrance to the historic hotel, which made Jamie think of a huge, overdecorated wedding cake. A young man in livery came hurrying over to open her door.

"You know, it wasn't so many years ago that a black person would have had to enter from the rear—and then only if he or she was employed by the hotel," Lenora mused as they walked through the lavishly decorated lobby with marble floors and soaring columns. "My grandmother worked here as a chambermaid back in the fifties. I bring her here every year on her birthday. She wears her best church hat and white gloves and carries herself like a queen." Lenora paused, and then added, "Your grandmother raised you, didn't she?"

Jamie nodded, thinking how wonderful it would have been to bring Granny to a place like this.

The restaurant, with its paneled walls and ceiling, was more sedate than the lobby. The other diners were dressed like Lenora—in smart outfits and expensive shoes. Jamie self-consciously crossed her feet, which were shod in twelve-dollar sandals from Wal-Mart, and shoved them under the table.

She envied Lenora, who exuded self-confidence. And for good reason. With her hair pulled sleekly back in a tight chignon, perfectly fitting suit, velvety brown skin, flawless makeup, bare silky legs, and obviously expensive sling-back pumps, she looked like a professional model. Or a successful executive. Jamie wondered if Lenora had ever driven around on bald tires or wondered where her next meal was coming from.

Jamie had no expectations of ever being rich. It would be nice, however, not to be poor.

A waiter brought them goblets of water and placed a breadbasket between them.

"Are there lots of other candidates for this . . . this *position*?" Jamie asked.

"I am not at liberty to say."

"Have you taken any other candidates to lunch at the Driskill?"

Lenora smiled. "No, I haven't."

Jamie nodded knowingly. "Mr. Abernathy seemed to think that his clients would like me."

"Well, then, you must think this through and decide if being a surrogate mother is something you would always regret or something you could look back on with satisfaction."

"Do you know the clients?"

Lenora shook her head. "Not really. In the three years I've been with Bentley Abernathy, the woman has come to the office only once. Bentley has known her and her brother for years, however. They are quite wealthy, as I am sure you already realize. The woman lost her only child in an acci-dent and apparently can no longer have children, and she recently married a younger man who has never had children."

"And this woman and her husband really want this baby more than any-thing?" Jamie asked.

"I think you can assume that a baby is a high priority for them," Lenora said. "Why else would they go to all this trouble?"

Jamie thought how only people who were well off financially could afford to hire a surrogate mother, which was unfair, of course. But she had figured out a long time ago that life was not about fairness. It was about making the best of what came one's way. While her grandmother was dying, she decided that she was not going to wait for life to come to her; she was going to go use what few assets she had and meet it on her own terms. Which was why the surrogate-mother idea appealed to her in the first place.

"What you need to do is read the contract and do the arithmetic," Lenora said. "Determine just how meaningful the money would be in your life. Then have the medical workup and meet with the couple. You can walk away at any point up until you sign the agreement. And—as I am sure Bentley explained—even though some surrogate mothers do change their minds and decide to keep their baby, that could turn out to be one *very* bad decision. In fact, you must not even entertain such a notion. You must think of the terms of this contract as being cast in stone."

Jamie sighed. "I keep wondering what my grandmother would think."

Lenora placed her hand on top of Jamie's. "Our grandmothers grew up in a different time. This is a decision for a young woman of *this* time."

Jamie stared down at Lenora's hand resting on top of hers—a beauti-ful hand with long, tapered fingers. It felt nice to be touched by another human being.

She had slept in her car last night because she had no cash and didn't dare try to use one of her maxed-out credit cards for a motel room. Every time she thought about her credit-card debt, she felt as though she were sinking in a sea of quicksand. She couldn't remember the last time she'd had her car serviced, and she desperately wanted to put a head-stone on her grandmother's grave. Such thoughts made the decision seem like a no-brainer.

Lenora picked up a menu. "I recommend the poached salmon and steamed vegetables if you're counting calories and the fried catfish and hush puppies if you aren't. And save some room for dessert."

After a visit to a nail salon, they followed a bellhop carrying Jamie's one small suitcase to her fourth-floor room.

"Oh, my," Jamie gasped as she took in the huge bed and elegant decor. "What a beautiful room."

Lenora tipped the bellman, ordered coffee from room service, then took the contract from her briefcase and placed it on the round table in front of the window. "Might as well get this over with," she said.

At times the legalese seemed incomprehensible, but Lenora was patient and explained every clause thoroughly. The document attempted to cover every possible contingency, but at its core things were pretty much as Mr. Abernathy had explained in his office.

"I want to emphasize that if you violate any terms of this contract, you will be liable for every cent of the money you have been paid for your services," Lenora said as she put the contract back in her briefcase. "And I can't stress strongly enough how serious these clients are about the privacy issue. If you sign this contract, you must never reveal any information about it or the couple's identity to anyone. You must not even hint to anyone where you are going and what you are doing. You cannot have visitors or contact anyone in the outside world while you are living at the ranch, which means you will not be allowed to make phone calls or have access to a computer. If there's anyone who will be alarmed by your disappearance, you need to think of a cover story and inform them you will be studying abroad or volunteering in a Third World country or something of the sort. You must make sure that no one will be reporting you to the police as a missing person or hiring a private detective to track you down."

"I'm pretty much alone in the world at this point in my life, so I can't imagine anything like that happening," Jamie said. "But isn't all that a little excessive?"

"It may seem so to you or me, but I am sure the clients have their reasons. You have to understand that privacy is often a major issue with the very rich. I'm sure these particular rich people worry about someone learning the identity of the child's biological mother and somehow exploiting that information," Lenora said as she leaned back in her chair.

"But if I do enter into a contract with 'the clients,' I'll need some sort of address in order to open a bank account, and I'd like to enroll in a correspondence course," Jamie pointed out.

"With your banking needs in mind, the clients plan to rent a post-office box for you here in Austin and have your mail forwarded to the ranch by a third party."

"That sounds like something out of a spy movie," Jamie said in disbelief.

"Perhaps," Lenora allowed. "But I think these people just want to be very, very careful. They are investing a lot of money and a world of emotion into this project. They want to do everything within their power to assure its success. I can't imagine them objecting to your enrolling in a correspondence course, but just to be sure I'll have Bentley mention it to them. Now, do you have any other questions?"

Jamie shook her head. "No, you've made everything quite clear. You should go to law school."

"I already do. Three nights a week, thanks to Bentley Abernathy's encouragement and financial backing. In two more years, provided I pass the bar, I will become his partner." Lenora leaned back in her chair. "So, tell me, Jamie Long, should I arrange for you to have a physical examination tomorrow?"

"Can you do that on such short notice?"

Lenora nodded. "You might as well go ahead and have the exam. The office will pay for it—and bill it to the clients, of course. Then, if you're certified healthy, you'll be examined by the fertility specialist who will be doing the insemination procedure. If you get the nod from her, I'll arrange for you to meet the clients. There won't be any contract signing until everyone is in agreement. In the meantime, you can stay here in the hotel and charge food and sundries to the room until all parties have made up their minds. If I were you, I'd enjoy a bit of luxury and not stew over things until all the cards are on the table. So what do you think? Should I schedule the exam?"

Jamie nodded.

Lenora reached for the phone and made arrangements for Jamie's physical examination, reading a long list of medical tests that she was to undergo. At the conclusion of the call, she closed her briefcase and stood. "I'll pick you up in the morning at nine," she told Jamie.

Jamie was sorry to see her leave, sorry to be alone again.

After eating a solitary meal in her room, she undressed and took a long hot bath in the luxurious bathroom. And tried to do what Lenora had suggested—not think about *it* until all considerations were known.

When she got out of the tub, Jamie looked at her body in the mirror and tried to imagine herself pregnant. Then she tried to look at her body through the eyes of another person. A man. Would he find her pleasing? Would he want to make love to her?

Maybe after she had the hundred-thousand-dollar baby she would be flabby and have stretch marks. Maybe her breasts would droop.

But just the thought of a man looking at her naked body made her feel flushed and light-headed. She touched her breasts and felt warm, mysterious stirrings deep inside her belly. It felt as though her body were waiting for something. Not a baby. Something else altogether.

In this day and age, it was almost weird to be a virgin at age twenty. But that was what she was. A virgin who was willing to rent out her womb to the highest bidder. Who was about to sell a year of her life because she was poor and tired—so tired, with a weariness that seemed to flow through her veins and sap her very soul.

Chapter Five

LENORA ENTERED BENTLEY'S office carrying two cups of coffee. She handed him one and seated herself on the sofa.

"How did it go this morning?" he asked.

"We don't have the results of the lab tests yet, but the doctor found no problems during Jamie's physical examination. In fact, he said she seems exceptionally healthy. I've scheduled an appointment with the fertility specialist for tomorrow afternoon."

Lenora paused and took a sip of coffee before adding, "She's a virgin."

Bentley digested this last fact. Somehow he would have preferred otherwise, although he would be hard-pressed to explain why. Amanda Hartmann originally had insisted the surrogate be "chaste." Bentley had pointed out that such a requirement would severely limit the pool of possible candidates since most young women were sexually active by the time they were old enough to enter into a surrogate-mother arrangement, but it was her husband Toby who had convinced Amanda to keep an open mind. "Every baby is born pure in the eyes of our Lord," he assured his wife. "And we have entered into a special covenant with Him. It is Him we serve."

Amanda touched her husband's face. "Sometimes the disciple teaches the master," she had said with an adoring smile.

But now, it would seem that Amanda was going to get her wish. A virgin would bear a child to carry out their "special covenant."

Which was nonsense, of course. Bentley told himself. It wasn't as though he were a high priest sacrificing a virgin to appease the gods.

Or was it?

Bentley cleared his throat. "So, after spending all this time with Miss Long, what do you think of her?" he asked Lenora.

"I think she is sincere, honest, intelligent, lonely, and desperate," Lenora said without hesitation.

Bentley took a sip of coffee before asking, "Do you think she is emotionally capable of coming through this arrangement unscathed?"

Lenora shrugged. "I suspect that no woman goes through a pregnancy without being changed in some profound way—whether she keeps the kid or gives it away. But I think Jamie is resilient enough to resume her life afterward." Lenora paused before adding, "I do find myself wishing, however, that there was some other way for her to solve her financial problems."

Bentley absently stared out the window thinking of his own spoiled daughter who had never earned a dime in her life yet had such a sense of entitlement about money and the things it could buy. His sons, too. He sometimes wondered if he had done the lot of them any favors by never insisting they get a job and at least buy their own vehicles.

"Jamie asked me what sort of people 'the clients' were," Lenora said.

"What did you tell her?"

"That I've only met the woman once, which is the truth. Of course, I have handled countless phone calls from Amanda Hartmann and have found her to be unfailingly cordial and charming. She always remembers my name and seems to sincerely care about me as a human being, which I find quite flattering. She is, after all, a very famous person. Of course, I resent the hell out of people who want to do away with the separation of church and state—and that includes Amanda Tutt Hartmann. But it is hard to be angry with a woman who has been through what she has. So if she and her new husband want a kid and this is the way they want to go about it, I hope it works out for them."

Lenora rose and headed for the door. With her hand on the doorknob, she said, "Hey, boss, promise me you won't get involved in any more cases like this one."

Bentley answered with a noncommittal laugh, then asked, "How's law school?"

"Drudgery punctuated by moments of sheer enlightenment."

Jamie took special care with her appearance, washing her hair and applying a touch of eye shadow and blush. She was wearing black slacks and a white cotton blouse, which she hoped would make her appear mature and businesslike. She added a narrow black belt and a pair of small pearl earrings, then checked her appearance in the mirror—and decided that she looked like a waitress.

She took off the white blouse and put on a blue one.

Today was the day she would meet Mr. Abernathy's clients. She hoped that by this evening she would know one way or the other how she would be spending the next segment of her life.

After deciding that there was nothing more she could do to improve her appearance, Jamie sat down at the desk and placed a call to Dallas. To her sister.

Her heart pounded while she listened to the phone ring. When her sister answered, she said, "Ginger, it's Jamie."

"What do you want?"

"I want you to know that I truly wasn't hiding anything from you. There was no hidden bank account. No hidden assets. Granny mortgaged the house just so we could get by. We pretty much lived hand-to-mouth."

"So?"

"You left angry. I hated to leave things like that. I wish we could be closer. I'd love to see you sometime and get to know your daughters."

"I suppose you think I should feel guilty because I didn't raise you, but I don't. I had my own life to live. I wish you well, but that is the best I can do."

"I wish you well, too," Jamie said.

"It wasn't fair the way Mother fawned over you," Ginger continued. "I was a latchkey kid, and then you came along and she treated you like a princess."

"Good-bye, Ginger," Jamie said, and carefully replaced the receiver as though it were made of glass.

"I am not going to cry," she told her reflection in the dresser mirror. But she did.

Then she tidied up the room so the maid wouldn't think she was a messy person and headed for the elevator.

Ten minutes before the appointed hour, she was waiting in front of the hotel for Lenora. She was nervous. So much so, her stomach hurt.

* * *

The woman and her husband stood when Lenora showed Jamie into Mr. Abernathy's office. They were two of the most dazzlingly attractive people Jamie had ever seen in person. They looked like movie stars. Like the sort of people who kept a yacht docked at some posh resort on the French Riviera.

Mr. Abernathy introduced them as Amanda and Toby. Amanda's age was difficult to discern, but Jamie decided that she must be at least a decade older than her husband. Maybe more. She was obviously one of those women who took impeccable care of herself. She had perfect skin, perfect cheekbones, perfect posture, perfect figure, perfect makeup. Her pale lavender pant suit fit her slim body to perfection. Her gold jewelry was understated but impressive. Her watch was a Rolex. Her shoes and handbag were of the finest leather.

And she had a radiant smile. "You are every bit as pretty as Bentley said you were," she said as she shook Jamie's hand.

Toby stepped forward. He was perfect, too. Like a model in *Gentleman's Quarterly,* down to the perfectly folded silk handkerchief in the breast pocket of his perfectly fitting tan blazer and his perfectly manicured nails. His smile revealed the whitest teeth Jamie had ever seen. "I am so pleased to meet you, Miss Jamie," he said, taking her right hand in both of his.

Amanda seated herself on the sofa and patted the cushion next to her. "Come sit by me, Jamie. We need to get acquainted. Lenora will get you something to drink. What would you like, dear?"

"Just a glass of water, please," Jamie told Lenora.

"I am so sorry about your grandmother," Amanda said, once again clutching Jamie's hand. "How dreadful for you to be left all alone in the world at such a young age."

The look on Amanda's face was so sincere that Jamie's eyes filled with tears. And she felt herself relaxing. She liked this woman. Amanda seemed as kind and caring as Jamie had hoped she would be.

Amanda immediately fished a handkerchief from her handbag and handed it to Jamie. "You poor dear," she said. "What you need is some time to heal, and our ranch is just the place for that. We have two swimming pools and a library full of books. Our excellent cook will prepare your meals, and our very competent nurse will look after you. And I think you'll find your accommodations attractive and homey. Bentley told us that you're thinking about continuing your studies while you're at the ranch. I think that's a wonderful idea, and I'll see that a desk is put in your room. You won't have a care in the world, my dear."

Toby knelt in front of her. He had the most beautiful skin Jamie had ever seen on a man. His eyes were a pale golden brown. Arresting eyes that captured her gaze like a magnet.

"You've never seen anything until you see one of our West Texas sunsets," he told her in a voice so gentle, he sounded as though he were trying to lull her to sleep. "Amanda and I travel a great deal, but we always look forward to our time back home at the ranch. And for as long as you are there, our home will be your home."

Jamie had expected to be interviewed. To be asked dozens of difficult and personal questions. Instead she was being courted. They had already made up their minds. *They wanted her.*

Jamie felt the tension flow from her body and smiled.

Amanda explained their plans. According to Jamie's menstrual cycle, the first attempt at insemination could be made the following week and would be done by the fertility specialist here in Austin. Should any further attempts at insemination be necessary, a fertility specialist in Amarillo would perform them. Jamie would receive a ten-thousand-dollar advance payment today and have the week prior to the insemination procedure to get her affairs in order. After the procedure, she would be flown to the ranch in their private plane.

"I'd rather drive," Jamie said. "I have my grandmother's car."

The room got very quiet. Mr. Abernathy, Lenora, and Toby all looked nervously at Amanda. "But I thought Lenora had explained the terms of the contract to you," Amanda said in her same soothing voice, but the look on her face was one of displeasure—a look that made her seem less lovely. "Once the contract has been signed, you will not be allowed to drive a vehicle."

"But I have several things I need to take care of over the next week. And I'll need my car after the baby is born."

"It can be stored here in Austin. We'll see that you have transportation back to Austin after the birth of the baby."

"Everything I own is in that car," Jamie explained. "I would just feel more comfortable if I had it with me at the ranch."

"Very well," Amanda said with just a touch of irritation in her voice. But the smile had returned to her face. "If the car is that important to you,

Lenora can arrange for it to be transported to the ranch. And you can go ahead and run your errands. Just remember that you will be drug-tested before the insemination procedure, and from the minute you are inseminated, you will be closely supervised, Jamie. I want you to understand that. We want this baby so very much and will make sure that everything possible is done to assure a successful pregnancy."

"Does that mean I will have no privacy?" Jamie asked.

Amanda shook her head. "Not at all, dear. But we do expect you to adhere to our wishes, and I hope you can see things from our viewpoint. Everything we know about you says that you are an exemplary young woman who has every intention of fulfilling her end of the bargain, but we have to make sure of that for our own peace of mind. Once we have ascertained a level of trust, you will have a reasonable amount of privacy, but you must realize that you are never to leave the premises unaccompanied or communicate with anyone outside the boundaries of the ranch."

Jamie nodded and swallowed a dose of reality. These people seemed nice enough, but they were not going to be her new best friends. This was a business deal. She was a brood mare. They were paying to use her womb.

She had no best friends. She had only herself.

"I'd like to get a dog," she said, surprising herself. Where had *that* come from?

"I beg your pardon," Amanda said, a frown marring her smooth forehead.

"I want to bring a dog with me."

"I didn't realize that you had a dog."

"I don't. Not yet, at least. But I will by the time I leave for the ranch."

"I see," Amanda said, her lovely smile back in place. "Well, I think that's a fine idea. Now, before we sign the contracts, I would like for us all to join hands and pray for the success of our endeavor."

Amanda stood and waited while everyone else followed suit. She reached for Jamie's hand and that of her husband, who in turn reached for Mr. Abernathy's hand. That left only Lenora, who seemed unsure as to what she was going to do. Mr. Abernathy held his hand out to her, and with a shrug, she joined the circle, and Amanda began her prayer. "Our heavenly Father, we thank you for bringing us this innocent young woman. Bless the journey we are beginning with Jamie Long this day and continue to guide our footsteps as we carry out your bidding . . ."

The complete adoration in Amanda's voice struck a cord in Jamie's mind. She had heard that voice before. She opened her eyes and regarded the woman's uplifted face. Her expression was one of pure rapture. Jamie had seen her before. On television. Praying, just as she was now.

Jamie joined the others in echoing Amanda's "Amen." Amanda opened her eyes and greeted Jamie's gaze with a beatific smile.

Amanda's prayer had touched Jamie's heart. These were godly people. She would be safe with them.

Chapter Six

THEIR LAST NAMES were different. She was Amanda Tutt Hartmann, spiritual leader of the Alliance of Christian Voters. He was Toby Travis and apparently also involved in the Alliance. They were constantly exchanging looks and touches, which led Jamie to believe that they were very much in love. The ring on Amanda's finger was a simple gold band. For some reason that impressed Jamie. It seemed more sincere than an ostentatious show of diamonds.

With the contracts signed, arrangements discussed, and an envelope in her purse containing a ten-thousand-dollar cashier's check and a post-office-box number, Jamie shook hands with Amanda and Toby. In a daze, she walked to the nearest bank.

It was really happening.

The plan she had hatched out of desperation had come to fruition. She was both relieved and . . .

And what?

Afraid, perhaps.

But what did she have to be afraid of?

Well, for one thing, pregnancy itself. And her own emotions. She was setting sail on an uncharted sea.

She opened a checking account and with a new checkbook, an ATM card, and more cash than she had ever carried in her life tucked in her purse, she walked back to the office, her mind racing ahead as she thought of all the things she needed to take care of during the upcoming week.

When she entered the law office, Lenora looked up from her computer. "You okay?" she asked.

Jamie nodded.

"The procedure—an inner-uterine insemination—is scheduled for

Monday morning, and you will be required to give a urine specimen for a drug test before it takes place. Afterward I will be spending every minute with you until I deliver you to the airpark on Tuesday morning, at which time you will be flown to the ranch."

"I want to check out of the hotel this afternoon," Jamie said, "and move to someplace that will let me keep a dog."

"I guess that's okay. Just let me know where you are as soon as you've made the change, and I'll arrange to have the room billed to the office. So, what kind of dog are you going to get?"

"A lonely dog."

"Good idea," Lenora said.

Jamie sat at the table in her hotel room and wrote checks to pay off her credit cards, a task that left her feeling giddy with relief.

It took her less than thirty minutes to pack and check out. She threw her suitcase on top of the pile of assorted possessions stored in the backseat of her car and drove first to a post office and then to a motel just across the river that claimed to be pet-friendly in its Yellow Pages ad.

Once she had checked in, she grabbed a sandwich and headed north on I-35.

The monument company was located near the cemetery. The late-afternoon sun beat down unmercifully as the stonecutter showed her through the display yard. Jamie chose a simple monument that looked much like the one Granny had placed on her husband's grave all those years ago.

In the air-conditioned office, Jamie wrote out an inscription—just her grandmother's name and dates. There was no way to say in a few words what an incredible woman she had been and how much she had been loved by the granddaughter she had raised. "But I would like for you to carve a bird over the inscription," she told the stonecutter. "My grandmother loved birds."

Her business concluded, Jamie drove into the cemetery and placed a rose on her grandmother's bare grave. "I won't be visiting you again for a long time, Granny," Jamie said, "but I'll think of you every day."

It was dark when she returned to the motel. She walked to a nearby Mexican restaurant, where she had a platter of sizzling chicken fajitas and a plate of sopaipillas. She didn't even wince when she looked at the check.

The next morning, she had her car serviced and bought four brand-new tires. Then she drove to an animal-rescue establishment on the far west side of the city.

"I can't bear to look at the animals," Jamie told the woman behind the desk. "I'm afraid I'll want them all. Just bring me a nice, friendly dog that nobody else is going to want."

The animal the woman brought was about as homely as a dog could be. One ear stood straight up and the other flopped over. He was a non-descript shade of grayish brown, and his coat appeared to have the texture of a Brillo pad. His legs seemed too long for his slender body, and the last three inches of his tail veered off at an angle. But the crooked tail was wagging, and his big brown eyes were looking up at Jamie with such hope. When she knelt in front of him, however, he cowered a bit and backed away. She held out her hand for him to sniff, and he took a tentative step forward, then she gently scratched his neck. And with great solemnity, the dog licked her chin.

"I love him," Jamie declared.

The woman smiled. "He's been with us for several months. Apparently he'd been fending for himself for some time when he was brought in. He was little more than skin and bones and had a serious case of mange. He's about eight months old now, and I wouldn't hazard a guess about his breeding. We've been calling him Ralph for no particular reason, but you can change that, of course."

"No, Ralph is fine," Jamie said.

She paid for his immunizations and neutering and was told that she could pick him up in the morning. "We'll have him bathed and ready to go," the woman said. "You'll need to bring a collar and a leash."

Jamie knelt in front of Ralph and explained that she would return for him tomorrow. "We're going to be a family, you and me," she promised. "And I hope you like to walk. I plan for us to walk miles and miles every single day."

Jamie felt almost happy as she drove back to the motel. She would have a dog to keep her company during the strange journey on which she was embarking.

Perhaps it was just as well that Amanda Tutt Hartmann and Toby Travis did not plan to fawn over her and make her feel like a member of the family, Jamie decided. That would be dishonest of them, and she really didn't want to have any sort of lasting relationship with them. It was better that way. Tidier.

She spent the following day getting to know her dog and taking him for his first walk at the end of a leash. He was smart and eager to please. "We're going to get along just fine," she told him. That evening she folded a blanket on the floor by the bed, and he dutifully curled up on it.

The next three days went by quickly.

She went shopping and bought socks, underwear, jeans, knit tops, hiking boots, a windbreaker, and a warm coat.

Twice she drove to a nearby greenbelt and took Ralph for an extra-long walk.

She visited the UT distance-learning office. The clerk told her that yes, the university still offered old-fashioned correspondence courses, although most of their students enrolled in online courses. Jamie left the office with a catalog of course offerings.

She spent one afternoon writing letters. The first was to her sister, Ginger. "I just wanted you to know that I'm okay but will not have a permanent address for a number of months. Please remember me to my nieces. I know you are so proud of them."

Then she wrote to Charlene in California, two other high school friends, and her closest college friends, saying only that she had a "domestic" position with a wealthy family and would be living on their ranch and that she hoped to return to college next summer and would let them know when she had a permanent address.

And she wrote to Joe Brammer's grandparents, thanking them for years of friendship and their help during her grandmother's illness. "Tell Joe I said hello," she added at the end.

She wondered what Joe would think of what she was doing. Would he be appalled? Or would he think she had made a sensible decision?

And she wondered if Joe was married yet. If he ever thought about her at all.

She recalled the day he stopped by the dry cleaner's to tell her that he was going to get married. He had tried to make it seem like a by-the-way sort of announcement on his part and not something that he felt the need to tell her because there had been any sort of understanding between them. Which there hadn't been. Not ever. But that was the last time she saw him, and if he thought of her as just a friend, wouldn't he have continued to drop by to say hello when he was in the neighborhood?

Of course, only a few weeks later, she had taken her semester finals and gone home to take care of her dying grandmother, so she never had a chance to discern the nature of his exact feelings for her. But even if Joe had fostered some level of romantic feelings for her, apparently they weren't deep enough or strong enough to keep him from wanting to marry someone else.

The afternoon before the insemination procedure, Jamie watched her car being loaded on to a flatbed truck for its journey to the Hartmann Ranch. That evening she purchased a carry-out meal at a nearby restaurant and tried to watch television but couldn't concentrate. She paced for a while, which made Ralph nervous. Finally, she took a bath and crawled into bed. Ralph took his usual position on the blanket beside the bed, but she patted the place beside her. Once he had resituated himself, she put an arm around him and curled her body against his.

She wondered about tomorrow. Would Amanda and her husband be there? Or would Toby have been there earlier to . . .

She struggled for a term that was not indelicate to describe the act that Toby would be required to perform but could not come up with one. God, it was so weird. Toby would masturbate to provide the semen that would be used to impregnate her. She hoped that Toby had already left the clinic by the time she arrived. She would blush if she saw him. Which would be mortifying. Maybe he had already done his part. He'd said that he and Amanda traveled a lot. And mentioned a trip to Florida and then a ten-city "crusade." Maybe she wouldn't see him and Amanda again for weeks and weeks.

The next day, Dr. Betty Winslow showed Jamie the instruments she would be using and explained that Jamie might experience some discomfort but it would be over very quickly.

Jamie closed her eyes and tried to keep her mind blank while Dr. Winslow carried out the procedure.

Once it was completed, the examining table was tilted so that her feet were higher than her head, and she was told that she would need to remain in that position for a half hour. As Jamie lay there staring up at her feet, she wondered what the baby's last name would be. Would he be given his father's last name or his mother's far more famous one?

Then she put such thoughts out of her head. The baby's name was none of her business. She didn't *want* to know its name. Didn't want to know anything about it at all. Except that it was healthy. She would like to know that.

She wondered if a woman who had been penetrated by an instrument could still be considered a virgin. Would she someday have to explain to a man that she had never had sex but had given birth?

Or did one just keep such things a secret?

"How'd it go?" Lenora asked when Jamie entered the waiting room.

"Okay," Jamie said. "I'm sorry you got stuck with making sure I don't go on some sort of a binge."

"No problem," Lenora said, linking arms with her. "Let's go treat ourselves to a wonderful dinner, then curl up in bed and watch a movie."

They had dinner at T.G.I. Fridays, then watched a Harry Potter movie on pay-per-view and called it a night. Jamie knew that sleep was once again going to be difficult for her. She tried to put aside the events of the day so that she could mentally and emotionally prepare herself for tomorrow's flight.

Jamie hadn't flown in an airplane since those childhood trips that ended when her parents died in a plane crash. Her stomach was knotted with apprehension, and she was afraid to close her eyes lest she dream of planes plunging from the sky.

Finally she gave up on sleep. If it weren't for Lenora in the other bed, she would have watched television or turned on the lamp and read. Ralph sensed her wakefulness and came to comfort her. She curled her body around his, and the next thing she knew, the alarm was going off. An hour later, she and Ralph were in Lenora's car on their way to the airport.

The Hartmann airplane was a great deal larger than her father's had been and had jet engines instead of propellers. The words *The Messenger* were painted in script on the side. Beneath the words was a golden cross.

The uniformed pilot and copilot introduced themselves. They were father and son—Russ was the father and Rusty the son. They were based in Virginia and flew regularly for Miss Hartmann and her brother, Russ explained.

Suddenly the moment of departure was at hand.

"You'll be fine," Lenora said. "Amanda and Toby are not your run-of-the-mill folks, but you will be well cared for."

Jamie hugged Lenora and thanked her for everything. They promised to stay in touch, and yes, Jamie would let her know if she needed anything.

Ralph was hesitant about climbing up the steep steps, so the young copilot carried him. Jamie turned and waved at Lenora before entering the spacious cabin. No, this wasn't like her father's little airplane at all, she thought as she took in the easy chairs and individual television monitors. In the back were a conference table and chairs.

As soon as Jamie took her seat, Ralph jumped onto her lap. Jamie let him stay there, putting her arms around him and burying her face against his neck while the plane raced down the runway and lifted heavenward.

She avoided looking out the window during the short flight, but when she felt the plane bank and begin its descent, she moved to a window seat and looked down on the emptiest landscape she had ever seen. Not a house, not a road, not a hill, only an occasional clump of stunted mesquite along a creek bed. But already there were the beginnings of one of those spectacular sunsets Toby Travis had promised.

Then miraculously there was a landing field, and beyond it were a water tower, a silo, and rooftops emerging from an oasis of trees and cultivated fields. As they descended farther she spotted a large greenhouse and a trailer park.

The plane made a looping turn over the large L-shaped stone ranch house with a turreted tower. Behind the house were two swimming pools, one a large free-form pool with a small island in the center and the other a rectangular pool with swimming lanes. Beyond the pools were tennis courts. The place looked more like a resort than a home.

Obviously, the people to whom she was now contractually bound were wealthy beyond anything she could even begin to imagine, which represented enormous good luck for the baby she would carry for them. The child would have every advantage that money could buy. He or she would never be made fun of for wearing secondhand clothes.

Which hadn't been the worst thing in the world, she decided.

The plane descended very quickly and soon the wheels were touching the ground. When it had rolled to a stop, Rusty emerged from the cockpit. "Welcome to Hartmann Ranch, home to the only bowling alley in Marshall County," he said with a grin. "If the ranch were a town, it would be the second largest in the county, which may not be saying too much since there are only two so-called towns in the whole damned county, and one of them is just a wide spot in the road."

Chapter Seven

WAKEFULNESS INTRUDED on the woman's sleeping brain like water slowly seeping into a hard, dry sponge. She struggled against it for a time, then opened her eyes and took in her surroundings. Always the same place. The room that wasn't square and wasn't round and had lots of skinny windows with diamond-shaped panes.

Her neck hurt. It always did when she nodded off in her wheelchair.

And she was hungry. Surely it was time for the witch to bring up her tray. She didn't like her anymore, but at least *she* spoke English. The witch used to work for her, but now somehow she was the boss. Which was irritating. *Very* irritating.

The woman was trying to decide what time of day it was and whether her next meal would be breakfast, lunch, or dinner when she heard the roar of a plane.

Frantically she spun her wheelchair around. Maybe someone was coming to see her. Her daughter, maybe. Or even her son.

She saw the plane roaring by and knew it would make a big curve before coming in for a landing. She waited until it completed the curve and rolled her wheelchair to the correct window in plenty of time to watch it touch down and roll to a stop.

She used to fly in airplanes all the time. Handsome men in limousines would be waiting for her. Sometimes she sat up front with them. Sometimes she invited them inside.

She watched while a figure climbed down the airplane's steep stairs. The person was too far away for her to see who it was. And it was getting dark.

She continued watching as headlights approached the house, then she leaned forward hoping to see who was in the vehicle, but it disappeared under the portico.

"Shit!" she called out angrily.

A young Mexican man in a golf cart met the plane.

Jamie held Ralph on the short ride to the ranch house. The setting sun reflected in its many windows, making it look as though there were a raging fire within the stone structure and its octagon-shaped tower.

Two women were waiting for her by the imposing front door of rough-hewn wood with heavy iron hinges. One woman was tall and somewhat formidable-looking with very erect posture and her coal-black hair pulled back into a bun. She was wearing a tailored navy suit with sturdy navy pumps on her feet. The other woman was younger with a stocky build, very short hair, and dressed in khaki pants and shirt, with a holster and flashlight hanging from her wide leather belt.

"Good evening, Miss Long," the older woman said, extending her hand. "I am Ann Montgomery, head housekeeper, and this is Chief Katy Kelly, who is in charge of ranch security."

Jamie shook hands with both women. "Everyone calls me Kelly," the younger woman said.

"And this is Ralph," Jamie said, looking down at her dog, who was looking up at the two women expectantly, with his crooked tail wagging. After living most of his life in a cage, Ralph was turning out to be a very friendly dog.

Kelly dropped down on one knee and scratched Ralph's head. "Hey, buddy, why don't you take a walk with me while Montgomery shows your mommy around?" Ralph dutifully wagged his tail again, and Jamie handed the leash to Kelly. Then she followed Miss Montgomery through the front door into the delightfully cool interior of what she realized was a solid stone structure. Like a castle.

An arched entryway opened onto a pillared hall with a beamed ceiling. Twin curving staircases led to a landing with three enormous windows comprised of small round panes of brilliant gemlike colors. From the landing the staircase branched again and continued to a second-floor gallery.

"I feel like I'm on a movie set," Jamie said.

"Yes, it is rather impressive, isn't it?" Miss Montgomery said. "The original ranch house was built by Amanda Hartmann's grandfather, who was a cattle rancher and founder of Palo Duro Oil and Gas Company," she explained, speaking with authority and a touch of reverence in her voice. She was older than Jamie had at first thought. Well into her sixties. Or older. Her erect bearing belied her age. Her blue-black hair was obviously dyed. Her dark red lipstick had bled into the creases that radiated outward from her mouth.

"Every stone used to construct both the original structure and the south wing was quarried in the state of Texas," Miss Montgomery continued, "and all the lumber was milled from Texas trees with the exception of the hand-hewn doors, which were made in Mexico. The south wing was added by Amanda's parents—Senator Jason Hartmann and Mary Millicent Tutt Hartmann—to provide additional accommodations for guests and to increase the size of the kitchen and service areas. They loved to entertain at the ranch. When Amanda and Mister Toby had their wedding here, it was like old times," the housekeeper said with a wistful sigh. "Some of the stockmen even put on a rodeo for the guests."

"How long have you worked here?" Jamie asked.

"I have lived here almost all of my life," the housekeeper said as she started up the stairs.

Jamie listened as Miss Montgomery explained that the ranch had long served as a retreat for family members and friends, Palo Duro board members, and board members of the Alliance of Christian Voters, which was founded by Mary Millicent. In addition to family quarters, there were six guest suites. The ranch-house compound was enclosed by a security fence and included a large garage, a shed used by the gardeners, four bungalows for in-house staff and their families, and two bungalows for overflow guests. Other ranch employees lived in an area north of the ranch known as Hartmann City.

From the second-floor gallery, Jamie paused to look across the great hall at the soaring stained-glass windows as they captured the last rays of the setting sun.

"Amanda's grandfather saw similar windows while touring in Italy with his wife back in the early 1900s," Miss Montgomery said. "He had Italian artisans duplicate the windows and hired an architect to design a house that would properly showcase them."

"Was the tower his idea?" Jamie asked.

"No, actually the tower was Mary Millicent's idea. It was added when the south wing was built."

"What's it used for?" Jamie asked.

"The first floor is a storeroom, and there's a chapel on the second floor," the housekeeper said. "The upper part is just an empty shell."

Jamie followed the housekeeper through a doorway that led to the south wing. On the left was an arched entryway to a tiny chapel with a softly illuminated altar. As they walked down the hall, Jamie noticed that each door had a brass plate with the name of a biblical landmark. The housekeeper stopped in front of "Cana."

"Do you know why I am here?" Jamie asked.

Miss Montgomery nodded.

"Do other people here at the ranch know?"

"Only myself, the nurse who will care for you, and Chief Kelly. As far as everyone else is concerned, you are Miss Amanda's guest. It isn't unusual for her to allow individuals to live here for a time—to heal, to meditate, or to write. When it becomes apparent that you are pregnant, those who live and work here will assume that you are an unmarried young woman that Amanda has taken under her wing. And you will tell *no one* otherwise. I understand that you have signed a confidentiality agreement with Amanda and her husband. That agreement began the minute that you signed it."

Jamie nodded. "Yes, I understand that."

"All of us here at the ranch think *very* highly of Amanda," Miss Montgomery went on. "She is not only our employer, she is our spiritual leader."

Unsure if a response was required of her, Jamie fiddled with the handle on her small traveling bag.

"And you, too, will feel the same as time goes by," Miss Montgomery continued, moving closer to Jamie and placing a hand on her arm. With her face so close that Jamie could see the pores in her nose, the housekeeper said, "You will come to understand that God put you on this earth to bear a child for Amanda Hartmann."

Jamie took a step backward. She started to tell the woman that she had not come here to carry out a godly mission. She had a business arrangement with Amanda Hartmann and Toby Travis that had nothing to do with God.

But she decided to change the subject instead. "Is there another stair-way that I should use to the take the dog in and out?" she asked.

Miss Montgomery pointed to a door at the end of the hall and, return-ing to her businesslike demeanor, said, "The stairs lead to a back entrance by the kitchen. The security alarm is activated between ten P.M. and six A.M. You will be served your meals in your rooms, except for Sunday morning, when the kitchen is closed. Laundry should be bundled and left outside your door. Other than the immediate grounds, Amanda has spec-ified that you are not to leave the house unless I or a member of the secu-rity staff accompanies you. The cook will visit with you in the morning about your food preferences. Now, if you'll tell me what you would like for dinner, I will see that it is prepared. In the meantime, make yourself at home."

"What about my car?"

"It is parked in the garage behind the house. After you remove what-ever of your possessions you'll need during your stay here, the car will be stored in the motor pool in Hartmann City." The housekeeper said good-night and promised to take her on a tour of the ranch in the morning.

Jamie thanked the woman and entered the rooms that were to be her home for some months to come. French doors opened onto a small bal-cony. A large cabinet housed a big-screen television and several pieces of colorful Native American pottery. Indian blankets hung on the walls, and the furnishings were handsome handmade Mexican pieces. A kitchenette hidden behind folding doors was already stocked with dog food, bottled water, and snacks. A small desk sat under a window; beside it was an elec-tric typewriter on a metal stand. Jamie remembered her father typing on a machine like that but hadn't seen one in years.

The spacious bedroom was furnished with a king-size bed, an easy chair and ottoman, a lamp table, and a cabinet with a second smaller tele-vision set. The bathroom had a large oval tub, a glass-enclosed shower stall, a large mirrored vanity, and a skylight. A cabinet by the tub held stacks of thick white towels and washcloths and a basket of bath soaps and toiletries.

Jamie put away the things from her traveling bag, then sat on the sofa waiting for Kelly to return with her dog. For now, this apartment was her home, but it would feel homier when she had some of her own possessions in place.

Jamie took another look around and did some push-ups and crunches. Then she opened the door and looked up and down the empty hallway.

She went back to the sofa and reached for the remote control. Soon the familiar voice of a CNN anchor filled the small room. She watched the news and then tried to plan how she would make the two rooms seem more her own. She would move the Indian blanket over the sofa to another wall and hang her great-grandmother's mirror there. Or she might leave the blanket there and move the sofa.

She looked at her watch, trying to decide how long it had been since she and Ralph arrived at the house. More than an hour. Maybe an hour and a half.

What was taking Kelly so damned long? She needed her dog so she wouldn't feel so alone.

What if he had slipped out of his collar and gotten lost? Maybe the reason Kelly was taking so long was because she was out looking for him.

By the time the security chief finally arrived, Jamie was frantic. "Sorry to have taken so long," Kelly said. "A deputy from the county sheriff's office dropped by for a chitchat."

Jamie dropped to her knees, put her arms around Ralph's neck, and accepted his doggy kisses on her chin. She planted a few kisses of her own on the top of his head.

"I guess Montgomery explained the rules," Kelly said. "Miss Hartmann wants you looked after, and I plan to carry out her wishes."

"Fine," Jamie said, without looking up at her.

She waited until Kelly left before bursting into tears.

She was homesick for a home that no longer was hers. For a grandmother who was dead and buried. For parents she barely remembered. The only family she had left was a sister who didn't want her and two nieces she didn't know. And without being able to tell anyone where she was or what she was doing, she was cut off from her friends. This dear, homely dog was all that stood between her and loneliness as vast as the treeless plain that surrounded this isolated place.

Chapter Eight

THE NEXT MORNING, Jamie awoke to a sunlit bedroom and her dog standing on the bed using all the body language at his disposal to tell her that it was time for his walk. She stretched and accepted Ralph's urgent kisses. "Yes, I know," she told him. "Give me just a minute to wake up."

She closed her eyes, trying to recall a dream. A nice dream.

About her grandmother.

Yes, she had dreamed that Granny was sitting in the easy chair in the corner of the room holding Ralph on her lap. Jamie had started to call out to her but realized that Granny and the dog were both sound asleep, so she went back to sleep herself feeling safe and peaceful and no longer alone.

Jamie smiled. In a very real sense, her grandmother would always be with her.

"You are a happy dog," Jamie said, scratching behind Ralph's ears. "My grandmother would have liked you."

With the dog waiting impatiently, his tail thumping on the floor, Jamie pulled on her jeans and sneakers and, with Ralph following, headed down the back stairs. She could hear voices in the kitchen—animated female voices speaking in Spanish as the women went about their work.

She watched while Ralph carefully inspected the large backyard, which was completely enclosed by a six-foot-high wall and a precisely clipped boxwood hedge. The yard was beautifully landscaped and included a graceful gazebo, a rose garden, and an enormous live oak tree that shaded stone benches and a beautiful life-size statue of a kneeling Christ. At the rear of the yard, a padlocked wrought-iron gate led to the swimming pools and tennis courts she had seen from the airplane.

Shortly after she had eaten her breakfast, the cook arrived. A slight, unsmiling woman, Anita listened without expression as Jamie explained her food preferences. Midmorning, Miss Montgomery arrived to take her on the promised tour of the house and ranch. At first Jamie thought the woman was wearing the same outfit as yesterday but realized this was a different navy blue suit—less tailored and with looser sleeves.

Briefly, Miss Montgomery showed Jamie the kitchen and formally introduced her to the "in-house" staff. In addition to Anita, there were two younger women named Rosa and Dolores and an older woman named Teresa. The women each acknowledged the introduction with a glance and a nod in Jamie's direction, then continued what they were doing. Miss Montgomery explained that the three women assisted Anita in the kitchen and did general housecleaning and the laundry. When the Hartmanns were in residence, other employees filled in as needed.

Once they were back in the hallway, Jamie asked, "Why are they so unsociable?"

"They have been told to be courteous but to respect your privacy," Miss Montgomery said. "Now, shall we continue? This door leads to the basement, where the laundry and storerooms are located—and where we maintain a significant food larder, which allows us to manage when the roads are impassable."

"Does that happen often?" Jamie asked.

"We usually have two or three major snowstorms every winter, and every so often a road will wash out," the housekeeper said as they entered the great hall.

In the light of day, the soaring room seemed more welcoming. The morning sun streaming through the magnificent stained-glass windows bathed the room in glorious light. Graceful palm and weeping fig trees in enormous pottery urns filled the corners of the room, and large Native American rugs were scattered about the stone floors. "Mary Millicent used a mixture of southwestern, Mexican, and European furnishings, art, and rugs to decorate the house, and Amanda has kept this part of the house much as it was when she and her brother were children," Miss Montgomery explained.

Arched doorways opened into a dining hall and a library, each with a stone fireplace large enough to stand in and soaring windows with leaded panes. The dining room held a massive table large enough to seat a dozen or more. Two walls of the library were lined with books, and numerous handsomely framed portraits and photographs were displayed on the other walls. Standing in front of an imposing painting of Amanda and Gus Hartmann's grandfather, the housekeeper explained that her father had served as Buck Hartmann's ranch foreman. "That was back in the days before feedlots, and thousands of cattle roamed free on the ranch. Buck Hartmann spent much of his time wildcatting for oil all over the Southwest. My father pretty much ran the ranch, and my mother was in charge of the house. Buck's wife didn't like it here, and as the years went by she spent most of her time in Houston. They had only the one child, Jason, who was born here at the ranch. My father told me that when Jason was born, Buck called all the help together, including the cowboys and field hands. They gathered out there in the great hall, and Buck stood on the second-floor gallery and, holding up his newborn son for all to see, declared that the boy would one day be president of the United States. Jason would have been, too, if he had lived long enough," Miss Montgomery said with a sigh, looking up at a picture of a handsome young man in western attire sitting on a horse and cradling a rifle in his arms.

"Jason loved the ranch but came less and less often after he began his political career," Miss Montgomery continued. "He served first in the Texas Legislature and was governor when he married Mary Millicent Tutt, who was already famous in her own right," the housekeeper said, pointing to a picture of the handsome couple on their wedding day.

The next picture they viewed was a framed *Life* magazine cover from the early 1960s. The black-and-white photograph on the cover had been taken from offstage, capturing not only the woman occupying the center of the stage but a sizable portion of the audience, all of whom were standing, their hands in the air, their uplifted faces filled with rapture. The woman was wearing a white robe, her arms wide, her fingers outstretched, and her face—bathed in a circle of light—tilted heavenward. She fairly radiated energy and power, and every single person in that audience appeared to be under her spell. The words below the picture read: *Televangelist Mary Millicent Tutt shepherding in a new breed of Christianity.*

Jamie found the picture disturbing. It made her think of other pictures—ones with a uniformed dictator standing on a balcony and masses of people in the square below with their arms uplifted in salute.

"Oh, my," Jamie said. "That's quite a picture."

"Yes," Miss Montgomery agreed. "Mary Millicent Tutt was the first woman to have a nationwide radio ministry and the first woman to preach God's word to a nationwide television audience.

"After their children were born," Miss Montgomery continued, "Mary Millicent traveled less and devoted more of her time to writing. She and the children loved the ranch and came here often. After Jason's death, she founded the Alliance of Christian Voters and began traveling again, but the children spent their summers and school vacations here with me," she said with a wistful smile as she pointed to a photograph of two children in a pony cart with the ranch house in the background. "Those were good times," she said, her gaze lingering on the photograph.

"Where does Amanda's brother live now?" Jamie asked.

"Gus Hartmann lives in northern Virginia and is a very busy man, what with the oil company and the Alliance to oversee. We don't see him here at the ranch as often as we would like. Amanda, too, although she comes more often than her brother."

Jamie pointed to a picture of a gloriously handsome youth with unruly golden hair and a beautiful smile sitting on the top rail of a fence. "Is that Amanda's son?"

The housekeeper closed her eyes momentarily as though dealing with a sudden sharp pain. "Yes, that is a picture of Sonny," she said.

Jamie wanted to see other pictures of Sonny, to ask more questions about Amanda Hartmann's only child, but Miss Montgomery turned abruptly and walked briskly from the room. Jamie hastened after her. "Does Gus Hartmann know that his sister has engaged a surrogate mother to have a child for her?"

"I am sure that he does," Miss Montgomery said. "Gus and Amanda are very close."

After they finished touring the ranch house, Miss Montgomery drove Jamie in a pickup truck over the mile or so of gravel road that separated the ranch-house compound from Hartmann City. In her suit and pumps, the housekeeper looked out of place behind the wheel of a truck, but she seemed no stranger to the vehicle and drove with a heavy foot, leaving a cloud of dust in its wake.

"Do you live in Hartmann City?" Jamie asked as they sped along.

"No, I have an apartment in the ranch house," Miss Montgomery explained. "I was raised in a two-story house that stood where the garage is now. When the south wing was built, Mary Millicent included a spacious apartment for me on the first floor."

Miss Montgomery parked alongside the ranch store, which had gas pumps in front and offered a snack bar and a surprisingly wide range of merchandise, including groceries, household items, gardening tools, clothing, cosmetics and pharmaceuticals, and even toys. As they walked by a mail drop and a bank of post-office boxes, Miss Montgomery said, "According to the contract you signed, any mail you send must go through me."

"Yes, I realize that," Jamie responded.

As they drove away from the store, Miss Montgomery pointed out a large building that housed the motor pool where Jamie's car would be kept. Then they drove by the schoolhouse, power plant, and a trailer park with several dozen trailers, each with a small garden plot. Across the road from the trailer park, Miss Montgomery pointed out two bunkhouses where the single workers lived. Behind the bunkhouses was a long, narrow building that housed a two-lane bowling alley.

Miss Montgomery paused in front of a charming church with arched windows and a small bell tower. "Our people are very devout," she noted with pride. "Amanda looks after their souls, and Gus takes care of their legal status. After they have been with us three years, they are allowed to bring their families here."

"So, most of the employees are Mexican?" Jamie asked.

Miss Montgomery nodded. "At least two-thirds. The rest are home-grown. But we are one people in our love for the Lord and for Amanda Hartmann."

Unable to think of an appropriate response, Jamie viewed the church in silence. The glare of the sunlight on its white exterior and polished windows was blinding.

Miss Montgomery slowed as she pointed out the medical clinic. "Our nurse, Freda Kohl, looks after folks who live here at the ranch and in the surrounding area."

Miss Montgomery explained that Nurse Freda would be taking care of Jamie unless there were complications, in which case she would be taken to a hospital in Amarillo.

"What if I have to be inseminated a second or third time?" Jamie asked.

"If that becomes necessary, I will accompany you to Amarillo," Miss Montgomery said.

Just beyond the cluster of buildings were a baseball diamond and basketball court, a huge silo, and a stable and corral. Amanda and her husband liked to ride, Miss Montgomery explained. And even though most of the cattle were now kept in feedlots located well away from Hartmann City and horses were no longer needed to work the herds, the ranch still kept quarter horses, mostly for recreational purposes, although they did come in handy during winter weather.

Before heading back to the ranch house, Miss Montgomery stopped at the greenhouse, where an elderly gardener helped Jamie select three small holly bushes for her balcony that he would transplant into terra-cotta pots and deliver later in the day.

"Thank you for showing me around," Jamie told Miss Montgomery as the truck stopped in front of the ranch house.

"You're welcome," she said, her usual stern expression softening somewhat. "I know this must be quite an adjustment for you, and I do want to make things as comfortable as possible. But part of my job is to make sure that you uphold your end of the bargain you made with Amanda Hartmann and her husband."

"I understand," Jamie said.

After lunch, one of the gardeners helped Jamie unload the things she wanted from her car and carry them upstairs. He also helped her move the sofa and hang her great-grandmother's mirror before he went back to his usual chores. Jamie placed her houseplants around the sitting room and put her address book, tablets, pencils, pens, and the like in the small desk, which was already stocked with two packages of typing paper. She unpacked a box of books—mostly textbooks and well-read favorites from her childhood—and arranged them on the shelves and put her grandmother's sewing stand by the chair in the bedroom. She put pictures of her grandmother and her parents on the bedside table. Then she put away her clothing and looked around for a safe place to keep her grandmother's garnet and pearl ring along with a spare set of car keys, her ATM card, and cash. After ruling out several locations, she removed a couple of the tacks from the sewing stand's floral lining and slipped the items under it.

She considered other decorative touches she might add—throw pillows, a wall clock, another plant or two—but decided there was no point in spending money on a place that, no matter how homey she made it, would never really feel like home.

During her first week, Jamie quickly fell into a routine of walking her dog, swimming laps, and eating solitary meals either in front of the television or seated at the small round table with a book propped in front of her. When she walked, one of Kelly's security guards walked with her. When she swam, one of them sat by the pool. By the end of the first week, Lester Thompson, the youngest member of the force, was usually the one sent to watch over her.

With little else to occupy her time, the daily walks grew longer. At first glance, the countryside was boring, but gradually Jamie began to see beauty in fields of wheat and native grasses waving gracefully in the wind and in the splashes of yellow, orange, red, and purple provided by wildflowers. Often she spotted the various creatures that inhabited the high prairie—jackrabbits, prairie dogs, snakes, lizards, armadillos, deer, and antelopelike animals known as pronghorns. Using her grandmother's well-worn guide to Texas birds, she began keeping a log of all the birds she saw during her walks. Already she had spotted prairie chickens, wild turkeys, Western kingbirds, a scissor-tailed flycatcher, red-tailed hawks, and a pair of horned larks.

And there were landmarks along the way. A wooden bridge over the creek. A large pond that a pair of heron called home. And atop a rise about a half mile from the ranch house was a tiny cemetery surrounded by a tall ironwork fence. She would have liked to take a closer look at the cemetery, but Lester had informed her that it was off limits.

Since the library off the great hall offered almost no current titles, Jamie selected books by the Brontë sisters, Edna Ferber, and Mark Twain to begin her reading program.

And she wrote a letter to the UT distance-learning office requesting enrollment in the correspondence course American History, 1870 to Present, and enclosed a check for the tuition.

She asked Miss Montgomery what return address she should use and reminded the housekeeper that Amanda knew about her plan to enroll in a correspondence course.

"Just give your mail to me, and I'll take care of it," Miss Montgomery said.

Two weeks after she had been inseminated, Jamie was awakened quite early by a knock on her door. Before her feet were even on the floor, Miss Montgomery had already unlocked the door and was standing in her bedroom. "I have a pregnancy-test kit," she said. "The first urine in the morning is more reliable."

Miss Montgomery had already read the instructions and went over them with Jamie. Jamie was allowed to urinate in private, but Miss Montgomery performed the actual test herself.

It was positive.

"The Lord be praised!" Miss Montgomery called out, clasping her hands and looking heavenward. "I must notify Amanda immediately," she muttered as she went rushing out of the bathroom.

Jamie sat on the side of the tub, staring at the purple line across the tiny round opening in the tester. Purple for pregnancy.

She should be experiencing some sort of emotion—relief or joy or even apprehension. But all she felt was a need to be out-of-doors. She made her bed and called the security office.

"But I haven't had breakfast yet," Lester said with a groan.

"Neither have I," Jamie said. "I'll meet you out front in ten minutes."

It was a glorious morning for a walk. Ralph fairly danced along. And she saw what she thought might be a brown-headed cowbird, but it was too far away for her to be certain.

The week following her pregnancy test, Jamie took one look at her breakfast tray and rushed to the bathroom to throw up.

Not ten minutes after Rosa had come for her tray, Miss Montgomery was at her door. "Anita said you didn't eat any breakfast. Are you sick?" she demanded.

That afternoon, Lester drove Jamie to the Hartmann City medical clinic, where Freda Kohl, a sturdy woman with salt-and-pepper hair, greeted her.

Freda explained that as a nurse practitioner she had advanced training that allowed her to diagnose and care for patients. In addition, she was trained and certified as a midwife. Nurse Freda also was a nonstop talker.

When Jamie emerged from the changing room, Freda weighed and measured her. "You're a tall one," she said as she adjusted the weights on the scale. "A bit on the skinny side, but not too bad. Now, have a seat on the end of the examining table.

"Just look straight ahead, sugar," Freda said, ophthalmoscope in hand. "That's good. You're the second OB case this month. At least the pregnant girls come into the clinic. I look after a number of shut-ins, and sometimes folks are just too sick to get themselves out of bed. You ought to see inside that camper shell on the back of my truck," she said as she checked Jamie's ears. "I travel around like the large-animal vets with a whole clinic worth of stuff in the back of my truck. Sometimes when folks have a bad heart attack or get themselves messed up real bad in an accident—mostly with farm equipment—I have to send them to Amarillo. Just last month old Judd Choate had himself a massive heart attack, and I called out the medevac folks in their helicopter, but Judd passed before they got him to the hospital. Most things, though, I can take care of on my own or sometimes by talkin' things through with an MD over at the medical college in Amarillo."

Freda paused in her dialogue while she checked Jamie's blood pressure and pulse. "Some folks don't have any money to pay me," she continued as she put the stethoscope to Jamie's chest. "Now, breathe in and out, sugar, nice and deep. That's good. Now let's do it from the back, nice big breaths. Good girl. Your lungs sound nice and clear," she said, stuffing the stethoscope back in the pocket of her white jacket. "And I end up with more chickens and eggs and homemade bread than you can shake a stick at, but let me tell you, Amanda Hartmann is my guardian angel, and there's not a thing I wouldn't do for that woman. Not a single thing. Amanda is a saint. A *real* saint. The pope in Rome, he should just make it official. *Saint* Amanda. She set up this clinic here at the ranch and pays me well to come here to look after her people. And let me tell you, these Mexican folks love their Amanda like they love the Madonna. Maybe more. Amanda has offered to build my husband and me a house if we'd move over here. I'd like to sell out and do just that, but my husband won't leave the old home place. His people are all buried over there, and when the time comes, that's where he wants to be planted. But if he goes before I do, I'm taking Amanda up on her offer.

"Now, as for the morning sickness, I want you to keep soda crackers on your bedside table and eat two or three before you even lift your head off the pillow. Then wait a while before you get up and put anything liquid in your stomach."

Jamie nodded.

"I understand you are going to have the baby here at the ranch."

Jamie nodded again.

"Amanda and Mister Toby certainly are looking forward to having a baby," Freda said as she helped Jamie lie back on the examining table and put her feet in the stirrups. "You'll never know how she suffered after her son's accident, but then the Lord sent her Mister Toby, and now all her followers are so happy for her and praying that she'll have a baby with her pretty young husband," Freda continued as she poked around on Jamie's abdomen. "When they find out she's in a family way, they will be so thrilled."

Confused by the nurse's words, Jamie asked, "Is Amanda expecting a baby, too?"

The nurse said nothing for several seconds. "We should not be talking about Amanda's private business," she said in a chastising tone and continued her examination in silence. Then she helped Jamie return to a sitting position. "You can leave as soon as you pee in a cup. Don't forget about those soda crackers. I'll give you a call tomorrow and see how you're getting along."

Chapter Nine

OVER THE NEXT few weeks, Jamie was able to control her nausea by never allowing her stomach to be completely empty. If she awoke during the night, she ate crackers. And she ate crackers while still lying in bed in the morning. Which helped but didn't cure her.

She no longer had the energy for swimming laps, but she still went on walks with Ralph, always with a packet of saltines in her pocket. Lester usually accompanied her, but he no longer did so on foot. With country music blaring out the open windows, Lester would follow along behind her in a white pickup with the words "Hartmann Ranch" painted on the side. Jamie could have done without the music, but she liked the privacy that the arrangement provided. And sometimes he would drop far enough behind her that the radio wasn't an issue. Then the only sounds were the wind rustling through the prairie grasses and the calls and chirps of the many grassland birds. When she saw a bird she didn't recognize, she would pull Granny's field guide from her pocket.

After her morning walk, Jamie would eat a light lunch and read or watch television. But more often than not, she would succumb to the drowsiness that was also a symptom of early pregnancy. She wished her correspondence course would arrive so she could make better use of all this free time, but probably she wouldn't be any more wakeful if she was trying to study.

Actually Jamie felt rather proud of how well she was managing the nausea. It just took a little planning and sticking to a routine. She was losing weight, but Freda said that wasn't unusual during the first trimester and was not a worry.

Gradually, however, the nausea began to increase, each day worse than the one before. Jamie's two main concerns were looking after her dog and not throwing up, and it was becoming difficult to do either. Being on her feet not only made her more nauseated, it made her dizzy. When she fell and hit her head on the corner of the coffee table, Freda stitched up her scalp and ordered her to bed. When Ralph was sent to stay in the security office, Jamie didn't even protest.

In spite of the bed rest, the nausea increased. Just the act of lifting her head from the pillow made Jamie feel sick. She wished she had never heard of surrogate motherhood. She'd rather be homeless on the streets of Austin than enduring a continuous state of nausea. Her tortured stomach rejected even the tiniest sip of water and had her reaching for the basin on her bedside table.

Freda came twice a day to give her IV fluids. "This will pass, sugar," the nurse assured Jamie. "I promise that it will. And don't worry about your baby. Nature looks after babies first and mothers second."

Jamie wanted to correct Freda. The baby in her womb was not *her* baby. It belonged to Amanda Hartmann. But talking took too much effort. And to think that she had *willingly* subjected herself to this torture! If she ever decided to have a child of her own, she would adopt one.

Once a day, Miss Montgomery and Freda would help Jamie to the shower, where she would sit on a metal stool and allow the hot water to stream over her body. Which was heaven. For a time she could almost forget about the nausea. Then her two keepers would decide she had been in heaven long enough and dry her off, then help her into a nightshirt and back into bed. She hated being so helpless, but she was grateful to them. "You're very kind," she would say. Of course, a little voice inside her head would remind her that it was not just kindness that motivated the two women. Caring for her was one more way they could serve Amanda Hartmann. When Miss Montgomery was alone with Jamie, she was less gentle as she helped her back and forth to the bathroom or lifted her head so she could take a sip of water. "One of the reasons Amanda selected you was because you seemed so strong and healthy," the housekeeper mumbled on one occasion. "And just look at you. You have no idea what you are putting that dear woman through."

Jamie now slept most of the time. Wakefulness meant the return of nausea. When she felt herself waking, she would concentrate on going back in the other direction. Often she would find herself stalled just on the edge. Not asleep. Not awake. Balancing there like a trapeze artist on a high wire.

She was seldom alone. If the nurse or Miss Montgomery wasn't with her, one of the housemaids would watch over her. And even at night, she was aware of Miss Montgomery coming into her bedroom to check on her. Sometimes she would sit in the corner chair for a time. Or kneel beside the bed and pray that God would watch over the blessed baby in this young woman's womb.

But sometimes it was Jamie's grandmother sitting in the corner chair. At times, she could even feel her grandmother's gentle hands placing a damp washcloth on her forehead.

When Jamie woke during the night, she would look to see if anyone was sitting in the chair, hoping that her grandmother would be there. Of course, she knew perfectly well that Granny was dead and that she was hallucinating because she was so weak. But she didn't care about the reason why. She liked having her grandmother look after her.

One night Jamie felt well enough to speak to her. "Is it hard for you to come here, Granny? Do you have to ask permission?"

Granny cackled like an old hen laying an egg. Which seemed strange. Jamie couldn't ever remember her grandmother laughing like that.

Jamie struggled to rise onto an elbow and gave the shadowy figure in the corner a better look. The woman had long white hair rather than her grandmother's frizzy halo.

"You're not my grandmother," Jamie said accusingly.

"Never said I was," the shadowy figure said.

"Who are you, then?" Jamie asked, allowing her head to sink back on the pillow. She felt light-headed. Maybe she was still asleep and having a strange dream. Then she realized the most incredible thing.

She wasn't nauseated.

The figure in the corner rose from the chair and came closer to the bed. It was an old, disheveled woman who smelled bad. "I am Mary Millicent," the woman said. "I can save your soul if you want me to."

"Mary Millicent *Tutt*?" Jamie asked.

The old woman sat on the side of the bed. "*Tutt?* Yes, that's my name. And there was another name, too." She frowned and looked around the room as though searching for her other name. "Oh, dear, what was it?"

"Hartmann?" Jamie suggested.

"Yes. The man I married was named Hartmann. *Jason* Hartmann. He had a penis as long as a hammer handle."

I must be dreaming, Jamie decided. She closed her eyes and eased her body back into a sleeping position. But the woman *smelled,* she reminded herself. She couldn't remember ever smelling someone in a dream.

Maybe she should take a second look.

But when she opened her eyes, the malodorous old woman was gone.

First light was coming through the window when next she woke. Jamie lay very still and put her hands on her stomach, which was tender from all that retching. With great effort, she stretched her legs and lifted her arms over her head. Her muscles felt as though they were made of Jell-O. But the nausea had retreated.

She glanced at the corner of the room recalling her strange dream, which was already growing fuzzy. A dream about Amanda Hartmann's mother? That was just too weird. If she was going to keep on having dreams about old dead women, she would much prefer limiting them to just her grandmother.

Jamie rolled onto her side and tentatively put one foot and then the other on the floor and pushed herself to a sitting position. She felt hollow and weak but not queasy. "Hot damn!" she said.

Very carefully, she made her way into the bathroom, where she used the toilet and brushed her teeth. Then, feeling stronger with each step, she went into the sitting room, where she got a bottle of water from the refrigerator. She opened the French doors and stepped out onto the balcony. She inhaled several breaths of the clean morning air then sipped the deliciously cold water and watched as daylight crept across the sky, erasing the stars as it went.

"A new day," she whispered, then turned to go inside and get on with her day—a day that would not be spent in bed.

As she closed the doors, she realized the holly bushes were dead. The inside plants were still alive but no one had thought to water the ones on the balcony. She wouldn't bother to replace them, she decided.

She walked over to her desk and looked at the calendar. She wasn't sure what day it was, but it must already be well into September. She had been sick for almost a month.

The first thing she was going to do was take a nice hot bath, she decided—*all by herself!*

That was where Miss Montgomery found her—in the bathtub. "What do you think you're doing!" the housekeeper shrieked.

"I'm feeling better," Jamie said, covering her breasts with her arms. "Thank you so much for all you have done to help me get through this, but I need to have my privacy back."

The woman stood there for a time, glowering. "You don't even have a bath mat on the floor. You could slip and fall."

Jamie took the bath mat hanging on the side of the tub and dropped it to the floor. "Thank you," she repeated. "I know this has been difficult for you, but I'm fine now. Really I am. I would appreciate it if you closed the bathroom door when you leave. It's rather drafty with it open."

With a huff, the housekeeper turned heel and left. She did not close the bathroom door.

Jamie leaned back in the tub, planning to luxuriate a while longer in the hot water, but the draft from the open door chilled her shoulders. With a sigh, she carefully got herself out of the tub. She was going to start locking the door to her apartment, she decided. Of course, Miss Montgomery had a key, but locking the door would send a message.

After she had dried off, she looked at herself in the mirror on the back of the door and hardly recognized herself. "You look like hell," she told her emaciated self.

She put on a robe and made two phone calls. The first was to the security office. "This is Jamie Long," she said. "I need for you to bring my dog back. As soon as possible, please."

Then she called the kitchen. "I'd like some hot tea and toast," she said when Anita answered.

Ralph arrived just as she was finishing her second cup of tea. His joy was boundless. Jamie wept as she buried her face against his neck.

She took him out into the backyard. While he raced around, she sat on the steps of the gazebo and lifted her face to the sun. Fall was in the air, she realized, with leaves just beginning to turn on the trees. It would be spring before she could leave here. Before she could have her life back.

Ralph came to sit beside her, and she put her arm around his shoulders. "I wish I could get us back to the starting line and withdraw from the race, but that's not going to happen."

Ralph thumped his tail on the step and licked her chin. Jamie hugged her dog and sighed. There was no going back.

"We'll get through this," she promised, planting a kiss on the top of Ralph's scruffy head. "Less than seven months from now, we'll be on our way back to Austin. I'll find us a little house with a backyard near the campus where we'll be safe and happy and never have to think of Hartmann Ranch ever again."

But no matter how much she wanted to forget this time in her life, she knew she never would. And sometimes she would pause to think of this other time and place and the child she had borne here.

Not wanting to push her luck, Jamie had only a bowl of soup for lunch, after which Lester came to drive her to Freda's clinic.

"Montgomery says that you've made a miraculous recovery," Freda said. "Climb up on the table, and let me give you and the baby a once-over. I told you the nausea would pass, didn't I? I told Montgomery that a big, strong, healthy girl like you would bounce back just fine. Matter of fact, I was more worried about Montgomery worrying herself into a nervous breakdown or a stroke than I was about you."

When she was finished with her examination, Freda pronounced Jamie "fit as a fiddle."

"I'll call Montgomery and let her know," she said. "And Amanda. She's been worried sick about you."

"Where is Amanda?" Jamie asked.

"In Virginia right now. She travels a lot, you know, speaking at revivals and political rallies. She's a very important woman," Freda said with pride in her voice. "Some folks say the only reason our dear president got himself elected was because Amanda Hartmann raised all that money and let righteous people know that it was their Christian duty to vote for him. You should hear the woman speak. You can just feel her love for the Lord. It fills up the room and fills up people's hearts. It gives me goose bumps just thinking about it," Freda said, rubbing her arms. "Course she'll start tapering off now that . . ." Freda's voice trailed off and she turned her attention to making an entry on Jamie's chart. "Leave a specimen on the way out," she said, nodding in the direction of the bathroom.

When Jamie came out of the clinic, Lester was dozing behind the wheel. He awoke and stretched when she got in the truck.

Back at the ranch house, instead of climbing the stairs to her apartment, Jamie walked to the end of the first-floor hallway and stopped in front of the door to Ann Montgomery's apartment. She paused a minute, getting up her courage, then tapped on the door.

"Can I help you?" the housekeeper's voice asked from behind her.

Startled, Jamie turned around. Miss Montgomery was wearing her usual navy blue—today's attire was a double-breasted dress with white buttons. "I want to ask you a question," Jamie explained.

"Well, what is it?"

"If Amanda Hartmann is expecting a baby, do she and her husband still plan to raise the one I am carrying?"

"Who told you that she was expecting a baby?" Miss Montgomery asked, a frown deepening the creases in her forehead.

"Freda sort of indicated that she was."

Miss Montgomery digested this information, then forced a smile and patted Jamie's arm. "You need not concern yourself with what is going on in Amanda's life," she said, her tone firm but pleasant. "All you need to know is that the child you are carrying is destined to be *her* child. And Mister Toby's, too, of course. They want this child very much, more than you could ever know."

Ann Montgomery watched as Jamie headed down the hall and started up the stairs. Under other circumstances she might actually have allowed herself to like the girl. As it was, all she felt was wariness.

Ann unlocked the door and went inside her spacious apartment with its handsome rugs, custom-made drapes, and elegant furnishings. It was a beautiful room that usually gave her great pleasure every time she opened the door and stepped inside. Her pleasure was muted, however, by what Jamie Long had just told her.

Amanda claiming to be pregnant?

She went into her bedroom, which was austere compared with the living room. Her father had made the sturdy bedroom furniture for his only daughter.

She sat on the bed that she had first slept in as a girl, the same bed that she had shared with Buck Hartmann for more than twenty years. She and Buck had made love under this same quilt.

She looked at her ugly old face in the speckled old mirror that hung above the dresser. She had been beautiful back then. Buck would call her his "raven-haired beauty." But the years had not been kind to her. Her once willowy body was now thick and buxom, her once smooth skin criss-crossed with a maze of wrinkles.

After Buck's son, Jason, married, Mary Millicent came into Ann's life and immediately began transforming the ranch house and making it her own. That was when the guests started coming. So many guests—mostly wealthy men and powerful politicians who came to hunt and play poker into the night.

Mary Millicent was often dismissive of Ann and never sought her advice, allowing both her personal maid and her secretary to usurp Ann's authority at the ranch. But Ann was a faithful listener of Mary Millicent's Sunday morning radio show. On her knees, she would pray along with Mary Millicent and ask the Lord to forgive her for welcoming a married man into her bed. She wondered if serving a woman of God would help balance out the transgressions in her life. And as the years went by, Mary Millicent came to rely on Ann more and more to look after things at the ranch and care for her children.

After Jason died, Mary Millicent once again took up her ministry, and Amanda and Gus were sent away to school but spent their summers and school vacations at the ranch.

Jason's death had been more than Buck could bear. Not only had he lost his only child, he lost the dream that his son would one day be pres-ident of the United States. A month or so after Jason's death, Buck went out to the paddock and managed to get his weak, old body on top of an unbroken colt. They found him the next morning miles from the ranch house, his neck broken, the colt grazing nearby.

Buck had promised to leave her enough money that she would never want for anything, but his last will and testament made no provision for the housekeeper whose legs he had crawled between night after night for decades. She chose not to hate him. He had just forgotten.

It was Buck's grandchildren, her beloved Amanda and Gus, who made things right for her. Ann Montgomery wasn't wealthy but she had all the money she would ever need and a home for life.

Ann allowed her vision to become soft-focus as she stared into the mir-ror. Instead of the formidable old woman she had become, she saw instead the raven-haired beauty who had loved Buck Hartmann. And continued to love his grandchildren.

Then she took a deep breath and reached for the telephone on her bedside table. First she called Freda. Then she called Gus. He answered on the second ring.

"My darling boy, there's something I think you need to know," Ann said.

Jamie was watching CNN—which she had come to think of as her best friend, after Ralph, of course—when she heard a knock at the door. When she opened the door, one of the housemaids handed her a cardboard box.

Jamie thanked the girl and shut the door. Inside the box was her correspondence course. *Finally,* she thought. She didn't even mind that Miss Montgomery had opened the box and probably riffled through the lessons and textbooks. After all, she had to make sure that the University of Texas wasn't sending her a stash of drugs or cartons of cigarettes.

Jamie wondered if the university had inadvertently omitted a cover letter from the professor or if Miss Montgomery had confiscated it.

That evening Jamie began reading the assignment for the first lesson. When she started nodding off, she picked up the remote control and scrolled through the channels until suddenly she was startled to see Amanda Hartmann's face on the screen. "Oh, my God!" she said, causing Ralph to jump to his feet.

Jamie sank onto the sofa and stared at the screen. Amanda's eyes were closed. She was telling God that more than seven thousand souls had gathered here this night to ask his forgiveness for their sins and offer him their souls. The prayer was accompanied by a harpist playing "Swing Low, Sweet Chariot."

The camera was tight on Amanda's face, which was even lovelier than Jamie remembered. She seemed to glow with an inner radiance. Or maybe it was just clever lighting. Whatever, the woman looked like an angel. Her voice was as beautiful as her face and filled with such hope and exultation as she promised the Lord's forgiveness. All they had to do was ask, and their souls would be washed clean. They would live the rest of their days on this earth with joyful hearts, and when they died they would rise through the clouds and be welcomed by all of those who had gone before them and would see the face of the one true God.

Then the scene was shown through another camera's eye, with Amanda a small kneeling figure in the middle of a huge stage at the front of a vast auditorium. Huge television screens, one on each side of the stage, showed close-ups of Amanda's face.

A trailer running across the bottom of the screen announced that this was the Amanda Tutt Hartmann Crusade being broadcast live from Cincinnati.

Ralph slipped into Jamie's arms, and she hugged him close, her eyes glued to the screen. The baby inside of her belonged to this woman. A holy woman. A woman pure of heart and soul.

I should be happy, Jamie told herself.

Chapter Ten

SINCE THERE WERE only four guests, dinner was being served in the smaller of Victory Hill's two dining rooms. The paneled walls and stone fireplace of the more intimate "petite salle" offered a relaxed atmosphere and did not call for formal attire, although Amanda was wearing a red silk gown with a plunging neckline that drew admiring if surreptitious glances from their male guests.

Gus always enjoyed watching the disconcerting effect his sister had on men, who were never quite sure how they should respond to a female spiritual leader with sex appeal, which she still had in abundance even though she was approaching her fiftieth birthday.

Of course, none of the men seated around this table were devout. At least Gus didn't think so. Although he had known them for decades, such a topic had never been discussed. And even if they went regularly to places of worship with their families and celebrated holy days in their homes, he knew that these men practiced politics first, with religion a distant second if they practiced it at all.

Not that any of tonight's guests were *politicians*. In the United States of America, politicians—whether they were believers or not—were now required to make a big show of their piety. They interspersed their public rhetoric with biblical references, expounded their faith at every opportunity, and equated belief in God with patriotism.

But Gus and the other men seated around this table had no need for public shows of faith. Few people even knew they existed. They called themselves the Committee of Five. Gus was their chairman.

No matter how diversified their holdings or how many disparate corporate boards they sat on, his fellow committee members were, in their hearts and souls, oilmen like Gus himself. Oil was their Holy Grail. They understood that oil was the world's most important commodity and knew that governments, economies, and their own private fortunes could not endure without it. At its core, their interest in politics came from a need to make sure no law was passed and no regulation enforced that impeded the flow of oil into the pipelines and money into the coffers of oil companies. To accomplish these goals, it was necessary for those who controlled the oil industry also to control the White House and other key positions in the U.S. government.

Like Gus, the four guests seated around the table had been born to great wealth. Even though few in this country and abroad even knew who they were, they were among the nation's most powerful individuals. They were the kingmakers who bought and sold politicians, who put them into office and cast them out. It was Gus who had brought them together. And it was Gus—through the Alliance of Christian Voters—who had provided the swing votes that had put their candidate in the White House.

Amanda understood all this at some level but did not concern herself with the details. Her motives were purer. She unequivocally believed that a nation in which everyone was a devout Christian—preferably of the evangelical variety—would be a better place for all. And to achieve that end, the United States of America needed a devout Christian electorate and a devout Christian in the White House. Her passion and sincere beliefs were what moved her flock, what brought people to their knees before a God who wanted them to regard voting as a holy sacrament.

Amanda had just completed a triumphant tour of ten cities, speaking in churches, auditoriums, and even sports arenas, mixing political ideology with religion as only she could do. After all, she wasn't running for office, nor was her husband. Her motives were sincere. She envisioned a country where abortion clinics closed their doors because no one wanted or needed an abortion, where the rich fed the poor and the strong helped the weak and homosexuals repented. To achieve such a nation, voters must elect individuals to public office—from city hall to the White House—who believed as they did. Gus was always quite moved when he heard his sister preach, not because she made him want to praise the Lord but because he found her quite amazing and so very lovely. Her ability to reach people never ceased to astonish him. When she held out her arms inviting people to come forward and give their lives to Jesus, endless lines of them came, many on their knees, all with tears streaming down their faces, their arms lifted in praise, *hallelujahs* on their lips. Amanda, angelic in white, would descend from the stage and put a hand on their forehead or shoulder, telling them how much God loved them, how joyous God was that they were allowing Him into their hearts. Some would call out to her that her mother had saved their soul many years ago and they wanted to rededicate themselves to the Lord. And some came to be healed, and while Amanda had never presented herself as a healer, there were always those who swore that a touch of her hand had cured their arthritis, stuttering, seizures, infertility, or whatever. People would wait for hours to receive Amanda's blessing. Afterward, she would be so drained that she needed help to walk to the waiting limousine. Now that she had Toby the muscle man as her consort, he probably lifted her in his arms and carried her.

The revival in Cincinnati had been nationally televised, and before dinner their little group had watched a video of the event over cocktails in Gus's study. During the viewing, their guests would steal sidelong glances in Amanda's direction, amazed that this slender, calm woman had turned an audience of thousands into a swaying, arm-waving, weeping, praying mass of humanity.

Of course, Amanda had learned her craft at the knee of a master. She was, after all, the daughter of Mary Millicent Tutt. And the granddaughter of Preacher Marvin Tutt. Evangelism flowed in her veins.

According to the stories Gus had heard about his and Amanda's grandfather, Preacher Tutt had been a disgusting old man who loved drinking and whoring as much as he loved the Lord. But put a revival tent over his head and a Bible in his hand, and Preacher Tutt could quote entire chapters of Scripture. And he could speak in tongues, heal the sick, save souls, and even tame poisonous serpents—except for that last one, which had bitten him on the nose then disappeared under the side of the tent, never to be seen again. Gus regretted never having known the infamous old reprobate, but that serpent had ended his life long before Mary Millicent had married Jason Hartmann and brought their two children into the world.

With her father dead, Mary Millicent sold the tent and enrolled at a small Bible college in southeastern Oklahoma for a year or so—long enough to be ordained as a minister of the Pentecostal Church of the Brethren. During this period, she also wrote a book about her life as the daughter of a colorful, itinerate preacher who loved the Lord but sometimes strayed from the path of righteousness, with his loving daughter always helping him find his way back. In *Hell Bent for Glory* she chronicled their life on the road, going from one small town to the next throughout Oklahoma, Texas, Arkansas, and Louisiana. She wrote about her mother, who had slipped away one night when Mary Millicent was only eight years old. Her father had not only raised her, he was her only teacher, with her only textbook the Bible.

Their arrival in a community generated a great deal of excitement since they went places where not even a shabby, one-ring circus with scrawny, mistreated elephants and tigers would go. People began to gather before the tent was even up. If her father was "indisposed," Mary Millicent did the preaching, delivering her first sermon at the age of twelve.

Mary Millicent had included some of her father's sermons in the book. Gus found them to be a wonderful hodgepodge of bullshit, Bible stories, visions, dreams, and vivid portrayals of the fate that awaited those who did not repent and accept the Lord Jesus Christ as their personal savior. After his sermon, Preacher Tutt would invite those assembled to come forward to confess their sins and get their souls saved. And he asked the town folk to "dig deep into their pockets and help this old country preacher keep on savin' sinners from eternal damnation."

Mary Millicent wrote that before her father died in her arms, he told her, "Sister, you've got the call. You're the reason I was born."

When no publisher would buy her book, Mary Millicent took it to Hollywood, where it was made into a movie starring Loretta Young, with Burl Ives memorable in the role of Preacher Tutt. When the movie became a box-office success, publishing companies came begging. With the money Mary Millicent received for the film and publishing rights, she bought a decaying old movie palace in downtown Dallas, and she enticed a local television station to broadcast her weekly services. Soon an Oklahoma City station also began to carry the services. Then other stations. By this time, she had written her second book, *The Road to Heaven*.

Mary Millicent had been a statuesque, handsome woman with an orator's voice. Her daughter was willowy and soft-spoken. Even so, Mary Millicent had realized early on that her daughter had the call and trained Amanda to follow in her footsteps.

In the beginning, Amanda tried to imitate her mother, but over the years, she developed her own style and tempered her mother's message. Like Preacher Tutt before her and in spite of her own transgressions, Mary Millicent had evoked a sense of fear in people, convincing them that if they didn't change their lives, they would suffer eternal hellfire and damnation. Amanda took quite another tack. She urged her followers to live better lives and help make the world a better place, a world that God could look down upon and smile. On the rare occasions when Gus challenged any of his sister's beliefs, Amanda would smile benignly at him and assure him that God had told her it was so.

Gus had asked her what God thought of her decision to imprison their mother at the ranch rather than commit her to some posh sanitarium for lunatic elders who had developed a penchant for calling out obscenities and disrobing in public. Amanda said that God would expect them to hide his longtime faithful servant away from prying eyes and protect her reputation. And perhaps Amanda and God were right. Still, it did seem like a mean thing to do to one's own mother.

Amanda had always known that she would bear a child to carry on the Tutt family's high calling into the fourth generation. She claimed to have known from the minute Sonny was born that he was blessed of God and that he, too, carried "the call." Gus had been more interested in the Hartmann side of Sonny's heritage. Someday the boy would inherit the oil company founded by his great-grandfather and the vast Hartmann Ranch.

Now the Tutt-Hartmann bloodline would die. This child that his sister planned to bring into the world would be the child of a gigolo and a hired surrogate.

Or would it?

Toby had joined the group for cocktails and to watch the video, then excused himself, saying he had "pressing business" to take care off, which meant Amanda had suggested beforehand that he might be bored by the dinner conversation. Gus had to give the man credit; he did understand his place in Amanda's life. He was her masseur, personal trainer, gofer, prayer partner, and lover, which left him plenty of time to pump iron, swim laps, and be fitted for the custom-made clothing and shoes of which he had grown so fond. Gus had never seen him overstep his carefully assigned boundaries, and he did seem to genuinely care for and respect Amanda. In fact, he seemed genuinely in awe of her, as well he should be.

At first Gus tried to tell himself that Toby was gay, but there was too much touching and sexual innuendo that passed between him and Amanda for that to be the case. Gus didn't like the thought of his sister having sex with anyone, but it was something he had to live with. And having Toby take care of her sexually meant she was less likely to engage in unseemly liaisons with lowlife men.

Sex was one thing, however. Raising Toby's child was quite another.

Gus realized that his sister was a pro at delusional thinking, but surely she didn't believe that the child of Toby Travis and a girl who answered Bentley Abernathy's newspaper ad could take Sonny's place as the family's heir apparent.

Amanda had eaten little of her meal, mentioning that she had been bothered by a queasy stomach of late. And while she never drank wine in public, in private she enjoyed it with her meals, yet she had drunk no wine this evening. And she was either a bit pale or had used a lighter shade of makeup than usual.

Gus knew that if she was planning what he thought she was planning, Amanda did not begin to understand the ramifications. But he would not stop her. If this was how she had come to terms with what happened to Sonny, if this was what it was going to take for her to let that dear boy finally die, then so be it. It was Gus's job in life to look after his sister and remove pitfalls from her path.

He felt Amanda's gaze from the other end of the table and met it. She smiled and mouthed the words "I love you," and his heart swelled so painfully in his chest that he had to close his eyes and grasp the arms of his chair.

He did not believe in God, but he did believe in love.

Chapter Eleven

AFTER THE DINNER dishes had been cleared away, Amanda announced that she was a bit weary from her travels and would not be staying for coffee and dessert. "I'll leave you men to your business," she added.

As she stood, the men scrambled to their feet. "Please join me in prayer," Amanda said, reaching for the hands of the men on either side of her. Somewhat clumsily, the others around the table followed suit.

She lifted her face and carefully composed it as she always did when she prayed, knowing that people could not resist a peek or two in her direction. She barely closed her lids in order to avoid unsightly creases at the corners of her eyes.

"Dearest Lord," she began, "please bless the efforts of these good men as they endeavor to make our beloved country the most Christian nation on earth. Like me, they dream of a day when every American is a believer; when no unborn child is murdered; when every child is raised in a Christian home; when lawmakers, educators, businessmen, judges, and all others who influence people's lives ask for your guidance in all that they do. We praise thy holy name and ask these things in the name of your beloved son, Jesus."

The men joined her in saying "Amen" before hastily letting go of one another's hands.

Amanda walked around the table to kiss her brother good night. In her bare feet, she was considerably taller than he was; in heels, she towered over him. He would always be her little brother in age and in stature. Her feelings for him were both sisterly and motherly. She loved and trusted him completely. He had always attended to the things she cared nothing about, which had allowed her to concentrate on her ministry and her son.

"Are you all right?" he asked softly.

"Yes, my darling," she said, softly stroking his face with her fingertips. "I'm just a little tired."

"Are you okay with the changes we talked about tonight?" he asked.

"Probably. Let's have breakfast together in the morning, just the two of us."

Gus nodded.

Amanda bent down to kiss his cheek. "I love you," she whispered.

"And I you," he whispered back.

She felt everyone's eyes on her as she left the room. Admiring eyes. She smiled to herself. The evening had gone well. Of course, there had been some talk of having the president not run for reelection, using a manufactured health problem as an excuse, and having the younger and more articulate vice president take his place on the ticket. The president had overstepped himself at times. No question about that. But while the vice president made a great show of his Christian faith, his eyes did not glow when he spoke of the Lord. And on two occasions she had heard him blaspheme.

She stopped by the kitchen to thank the staff for another lovely dinner party, calling each person by name and wishing God's blessing on them all. Then she put her arm around a young sari-clad woman known as Randi who had been working at Victory Hill for only three or four months and guided her out into the hall. "Are you with child?" she asked the girl.

With downcast eyes and a shy smile, the girl nodded.

"You're married to one of the groundskeepers, aren't you?" Amanda asked.

Again the girl nodded.

"Are you both happy about the baby?"

"Oh, yes, madam. We are very happy. My mother will take care of the child so I can keep working."

"You shall have six weeks off with pay when the baby is born," Amanda said.

The girl grabbed Amanda's hand and kissed it. "You are the kindest lady I have ever known. My mother says you are a saint."

"No, no," Amanda said with a smile, stroking the girl's smooth brown cheek. "Not a saint, dear. Just a woman who loves the Lord. Is this your first child?"

"Yes, madam. Our first."

"Tell me, Randi, can you keep a secret?"

"Oh, yes!" Randi said, her beautiful dark eyes wide.

Amanda stepped closer and whispered, "I, too, am expecting a child."

Randi's eyes immediately filled with tears. *She knows about my Sonny,* Amanda realized. But of course she would. Everyone knew. Sometimes Amanda wondered if God had planned Sonny's accident to make her a more sympathetic spiritual leader. Or to test her. She had to believe that Sonny's accident was part of God's plan; otherwise she would not have been able to continue. She would have had to curse God and dissolve her ministry. But that would mean she would have had to stop being herself. To stop being the person she was born to be. It had taken her countless hours of prayer and meditation to cleanse her heart of doubt.

Amanda understood that all those people who claimed that she had healed them had in truth been healed by opening their hearts and minds to the power of prayer. Sonny could no longer do that. It had taken her a while to understand why God had left him so, but with knowledge came peace. And with peace came God's reward—her beautiful Toby and a plan for the future.

"Oh, madam, I am so happy for you," Randi was saying, once again kissing Amanda's hand. "I will pray for you and your baby every day."

"And I will pray for you and yours," Amanda promised, embracing the slender young woman.

Amanda slowly climbed the stairs to her spacious suite on the second floor, her fingers trailing along the curving banister. Her mind shifting gears from the dinner gathering and the pregnant kitchen worker to her husband. To Toby, who was waiting for her.

She had primed him earlier in the evening, telling him just what she was in the mood for. She chuckled to herself. Toby was such an obliging boy. And he loved their sex games as much as she did.

How wonderfully smooth the wood felt under her fingertips. Like satin. Like the skin on Toby's back. Toby was her Adonis. When they were in Madrid, she had taken him to the Prado for the express purpose of showing him Titian's painting of *Venus and Adonis.* "There you are," she had said, pointing to the gorgeous youth, with Venus's arms wrapped around him, drawing him downward toward her nude body.

"I think she's trying to seduce him," Toby said.

"I think she probably succeeded," Amanda said.

Toby leaned close. "Your body is much better than hers," he had whispered.

Amanda smiled, remembering how they had playacted the scene that night in their hotel room. She was the pagan goddess; he was the undefiled young boy. And when she was satiated, she had curled her body next to Toby's and silently thanked God for bringing her this beautiful young husband.

Once, Toby had asked her what God thought of such games. She had assured him that God had given them vivid imaginations to make their physical life fulfilling and keep them from sin.

With her free hand Amanda reached inside her dress to caress her breasts. Climbing each step became an erotic act. A step higher, a step closer. She could feel her body opening. Feel the moistness gathering between her legs.

The bedroom was aglow in candlelight. Toby was waiting for her, lying facedown on the bed, his wrists handcuffed to the headboard, the leather whip waiting on the bedside table. As soon as she entered the room, he lifted his head and began to whimper. "Please don't whip me," he begged.

Amanda unzipped her red dress and stepped out of it, revealing her nude body underneath. She stepped into a pair of stiletto-heeled boots and tied a black velvet cape around her neck. "But you've been a bad boy, haven't you, Toby?"

"Oh, yes, I've been a very bad boy. A very, very bad boy," Toby said.

Amanda picked up the whip. "And tell me, what happens to bad boys?" she cooed.

It was well past midnight when Gus placed his call to Ann Montgomery. But her voice was alert. "Gus," she said immediately. "How are you, my darling boy?"

Gus felt a smile tug at his lips. Good old Montgomery, he thought. His mother might have gone loony in her old age, but Montgomery never changed. He counted on that. "Not so good," he admitted.

"Tell me," she said.

"You were right. It looks like Amanda plans to pass off the baby that

Jamie Long is carrying as her own—as the rightful heir to the family ministry and the family fortune. We had guests for dinner tonight, and Amanda made a great show of only nibbling at her food and not drinking anything alcoholic."

"I believe that the baby Jamie Long carries truly *is* the rightful heir to all things Hartmann," Montgomery said.

Gus sat up straighter in his chair. "What are you talking about?" he demanded.

"I believe that she is carrying Sonny's child."

"But that's impossible."

"Is it?" Montgomery asked.

Gus drew in his breath. "What makes you think such a thing? Did Amanda tell you?"

"No, but I know my Amanda. She was at the ranch the night before the insemination procedure was done on Jamie. She flew in, then turned right around and left first thing the next morning. She said she needed to pray at Sonny's bedside."

"Did she bring someone with her—a doctor or technician?"

"Nurse Freda was with her," Montgomery said.

"Are you saying that she . . ."

"Yes, that is exactly what I'm saying."

Gus rubbed his forehead, trying to think, trying to decide what the implications would be if what Montgomery believed could actually be true.

"I'm not sure about the legality of harvesting sperm from an unconscious man," he said, "but I don't suppose anyone is going to arrest Amanda for somehow managing to have that done. After all, Sonny is her only child."

"Probably not," Montgomery agreed. "But I assume that the contract Jamie Long signed with Amanda and Toby specified that he would be the natural father of the child. If the true circumstances of this child's conception were ever to become known, the contract could be declared null and void, and Jamie could be awarded full custody of the child."

Gus picked up a letter opener and stabbed at the blotter on his desk. He already had some idea where Montgomery was going with this and didn't want to hear it.

"I've been thinking about this a lot, Gus," she continued. "If Jamie ever realizes that the baby she is carrying is Amanda Hartmann's grandchild, she is certainly not going to give up her parental rights to the sole heir to the Hartmann family fortune."

"But there is no way for her to know that," Gus insisted.

"At this point, Jamie thinks that Amanda *may* be pregnant. But she does watch a lot of television and is bound to hear that Amanda has put the word out that she herself is expecting a baby. Then, when Amanda and Toby end up with just one baby to raise—one that Amanda claims is her natural-born child—Jamie will wonder what happened to the baby that she had carried and delivered. What if she hires a private detective or starts snooping around herself? What if she finds out that Amanda doesn't have a uterus, and Sonny was still alive when he was taken from the hospital in Amarillo? What if the girl demands that she and Toby and the baby undergo DNA testing? What if she sues to get her baby back?"

"Then I would make sure the judge awarded custody to the baby's grandmother," Gus said, rubbing his forehead, wanting desperately to reject Montgomery's line of reasoning.

"Perhaps," Montgomery allowed, "but in the process, Amanda would be exposed as a fraud."

Gus drew in his breath. "Jesus Christ," he muttered.

"Don't be blasphemous," Montgomery said, her voice stern. "Your mother and I raised you better than that. I want this baby, Gus. It's *Sonny's* baby. And you will want it, too, when you think about it. This baby is a gift from God."

Gus stared at the lighted statue of Christ in the meditation garden. For years he had been telling himself that he was going to have the damned thing carted away. But his mother had put it there. And moving it would upset Amanda.

Gus had always found it strange how easily devout people were able to convince themselves that the evil things they wanted to undertake were somehow the will of their one true God. If there were a God, Gus knew that he or she would have to spend all his or her time weeping.

Being an atheist meant that he was unable to rationalize or pray away evil. He had to look it square in the face and acknowledge it for what it was.

He wished that he had never insisted that Bentley Abernathy send him a photograph of the girl. Wished that he had never seen Jamie Long's lovely young face.

Gus shook his head in an attempt to refocus his thoughts.

"And what about Toby? Does he know what's going on?"

"I really don't know," Montgomery admitted, "but he's nothing more than a lap dog. He'll believe whatever Amanda tells him to believe."

"I don't know how we're going to manage this," Gus said.

"The Lord will provide," Montgomery said.

Chapter Twelve

BENTLEY SELDOM SAW Gus Hartmann in person. Mostly the man existed for him as a disembodied voice on the other end of a telephone. He had to remind himself at times that the authoritative utterances of this extraordinarily wealthy and powerful individual came from a man who stood no higher than Bentley's chest.

When Gus called, everything else was put on hold. The conversation was transferred to speakerphone, and Lenora hurried into his office to take notes.

This time Gus had called to discuss issues dealing with real estate. He wanted to purchase the mineral rights for several tracts of land in the Texas Panhandle. But his main concern was the county road that crossed the Hartmann Ranch. The road's official designation was Rural Road 12 but locally was known as Hartmann Road. It continued north of the ranch for thirty-two empty miles until it eventually intersected a state highway. Buck Hartmann's original landholdings were all to the east of RR 12, but with additional acquisitions to the ranch over the years, the road now divided the Hartmann property almost in half.

Bentley doubted if more than a few dozen vehicles a day traversed the gravel road, which was used mainly by other county residents and an occasional hunter. Gus complained that Hartmann City had become a stopping place along the road, with people expecting to buy gas and soft drinks at the ranch store.

"Why is this an issue?" Bentley dared to ask.

"Privacy," Gus's voice had boomed over the speaker. Bentley reached over and turned down the volume.

"I'll cede the county land along the western boundary of the ranch and reimburse whatever it costs to build a new segment of the road there," Gus continued. "I want this taken care of, Abernathy. I told the county commissioners two years ago that I wanted this done. You remind those yokels that I pay more goddamned property taxes than anyone else in the county and that Hartmann Ranch is by far its largest employer. You remind them that Hartmann money built their high school gymnasium and put a new roof on the schoolhouse. And let them know in no uncertain terms that I want this project implemented immediately. You let them know that the only reason my sister and I have hung on to the ranch is for the privacy it provides. I want to maintain tighter security around the ranch house, and I can't do that if there is a public thoroughfare passing right in front of it. And you remind them that Hartmann City is not a 'city' at all. It is *private property*. We've had people driving onto *our* property looking for Amanda and expecting her to heal their lumbago or pray with them. And reporters come snooping around. I had to install a security fence to keep people from driving right up to the ranch house and knocking on the door."

"I understand," Bentley said in his most conciliatory voice. Then he made eye contact with Lenora and added, "I'll tell you what, Gus, Lenora and I will fly up there. I'll talk to the county commissioners at their next meeting, and Lenora would like to see Jamie Long."

Lenora nodded her approval.

"Why does she want to see the girl?" Gus demanded.

"Well, Lenora became quite attached to Jamie and is concerned about her. She has tried to call the girl numerous times but has never gotten through to her. And Jamie has never responded to her letters."

"I'm not even sure she's still there," Gus said flatly. "If she is, I'm sure she's fine."

Lenora frowned and leaned forward, ready to add something to the conversation. Fearful she might say something that would annoy Gus, Bentley shook his head at her.

And to think that only a couple of months back, he had actually been thinking about ending his association with the Hartmanns and cutting back his practice, Bentley thought with a sigh. That had changed when his wife found a rundown Victorian mansion out near Round Top and decided that she had been put on this earth to restore it, a project that would cost a king's ransom.

Of course, he could protest all he wanted to, but in the end, Brenda would get her derelict mansion, which would take away any hope he had of ever ending his association with the Hartmanns.

At least the old house would keep Brenda busy for years.

The correspondence course was a godsend. The textbook was well written, the supplemental readings fascinating. Jamie immersed herself in American history. When she finally had the first two lessons ready to mail, she felt elated. She addressed a manila envelope and put the lessons inside. She left the envelope unsealed, certain that Miss Montgomery would feel it her duty to make sure she hadn't violated any rules, and slid it under the housekeeper's door. To celebrate, she called Lester. "I want an extra-long walk this afternoon," she told him.

"Don't you get bored with all that walking?" he asked.

"Not really. I experience something new every time we go out." Which was true, Jamie thought. Only yesterday, she had watched an armadillo ambling down the middle of the road as though it didn't have a care in the world and not minding at all that Jamie, her hand firmly on Ralph's collar, was following along behind it.

She had learned to listen to the ever-changing music of the prairie—the sounds made by animals and insects, the whisper of the prairie grasses waving in the wind. And she admired the ever-changing palette of color as the sun traversed the sky and slid behind an occasional cloud.

The daily walks also had led to a deeper awareness of her own body— a different sort of awareness than when she was on the track team. Running was all about pacing and required intense concentration. With walking she was able to relax and enjoy the feel of her muscles working in concert as she strode along. Sometimes she would take a deep breath just to feel her lungs fill and expand and to relish the health and youth and strength of her own body. The muscles in her legs were almost as firm as they had been when she was running track and working out almost daily. She sometimes wondered if walking had become an obsession with her. Or was it simply a coping mechanism that helped her deal with isolation and loneliness? And with fear? She was sailing in uncharted waters. The changes in her body went further than the muscles in her legs and the capacity of her lungs. She could no longer button her jeans, and there was a firmness to her belly that had nothing to do with the underlying muscle structure.

"Actually I have a specific destination today," she told Lester. "I asked Freda about any points of interest I might visit on my walks, and she told me about an abandoned farmhouse a few miles north of here. Do you know where it is?" she asked.

Lester said that he did and would be out front in fifteen minutes.

Ralph's tail started wagging when Jamie got her hiking boots out of the closet. "So you think you're going to go with me?" she teased.

She and Ralph made their way down the main staircase and headed for the front door. Lester hadn't arrived yet, so she and Ralph sat on the front steps. Freda's pickup truck with its camper-shell clinic was parked under the portico, a seemingly daily occurrence. Jamie assumed that the nurse came to visit Ann Montgomery. In spite of the difference in their ages, the two women seemed to be close friends. Probably it was their devotion to Amanda Hartmann that brought them together.

A visit with a friend would be nice, Jamie thought. Or a letter from one. Without knowing her current address, Jamie realized that her friends and sister would not be writing to her, but she wondered why she hadn't heard from Lenora. Other than her correspondence course, the only mail she had received were her monthly bank statements, which were being mailed to the ranch by the anonymous "third party" and opened by Miss Montgomery before passing them along to Jamie. Such measures seemed ridiculously extreme to Jamie, but then, as Lenora had pointed out more than once, privacy was a major issue with the Hartmanns.

When Jamie saw Lester's truck approaching, she stood. He pulled up beside her and rolled down the window. Jamie could hear Vince Gill singing "A Little More Love" on the truck radio.

Lester turned down the radio. "I have to be back by noon, so you're going to have to ride at least part of the way."

"I'll walk first—for an hour," Jamie said, glancing at her watch then heading down the drive. Lester turned up the radio. When Vince finished his song, Reba began pondering "Is There Life Out There?"

Jamie jogged a bit to get ahead of the radio. She liked Reba but didn't want the distraction.

She slowed as she approached the main gate, waiting for Lester to activate the opener. As soon as the gate swung open, she and Ralph headed north.

She walked down the middle of the empty roadway. Ralph ran excitedly from side to side, sniffing clumps of prairie grass and frantically digging up gopher runs. She wondered what he would do if he actually caught a gopher.

At the end of an hour, Lester honked at her, and she and Ralph rode the rest of the way. "There it is," he said, pointing toward a mailbox hanging crookedly on a fence post. The name on the box was "McGraf." At the end of an overgrown lane she could see a listing barn, a windmill with a missing blade, and a stone chimney jutting out of a rooftop.

"I want to take a look," she told Lester as she reached for the door handle.

"No way. I'd lose my job if you fell down an old well or through a rotten floor."

Jamie started to protest but decided she didn't want to get Lester in trouble. Disappointed, she stared at the desolate scene. "Why did the McGrafs leave?" she asked.

"Actually there are several deserted farmhouses on the ranch," Lester explained. "Word has it that Mr. Hartmann paid the back taxes on the farms and had the occupants evicted. The McGrafs didn't get very far, though. They loaded up their truck and drove off right before a blizzard hit. No one knew they were missing, so no one went looking for them. It was a week or so later when some hunters spotted the truck out in the middle of a field. Mr. McGraf and the missus and three kids were all packed into the cab of the truck. Apparently they lost their way in all that snow and ice and froze to death."

"How horrible!" Jamie said. A family had tried to make a living here and failed. But they shouldn't have had to pay with their lives.

"Yeah," Lester agreed. "Every few years something like that happens. Sometimes a farmer gets lost on his way back from his own barn. Weather gets that bad sometimes."

She imagined the family members taking what they could fit in the back of an aging truck and leaving the rest to be scavenged by drifters over the years. Had Gus Hartmann given them a deadline, threatening to send the sheriff to evict them, or had they simply not realized a blizzard was on the way?

"So this property is part of Hartmann Ranch now?" Jamie asked.

Lester nodded. "I guess it's all right for me to tell you since it's public record. All the Hartmann land used to be on the east side of the road, but now they own several thousand acres along the west side."

"Why do they need so much land?" Jamie asked, taking in fields that had once been cleared but were now covered with prairie grass and scrubby mesquite trees. Obviously, Gus Hartmann had no pressing use for the land when he made the McGraf family leave.

Lester shrugged. "My dad says that owning a lot of land makes rich folks feel safe or something like that. Kind of like owning an island, I guess. Instead of being surrounded by water, or by walls like the movie stars in Hollywood, some rich people surround themselves with a sea of land. Except what's the point if they never visit their safe place. Gus Hartmann hasn't been to the ranch since I started working here. And Miss Amanda has only been here once since she married the greenhorn."

Jamie took a last look at the deserted homestead as Lester turned the truck around and sighed.

"You feeling okay?" he asked.

"Just a little melancholy. Those poor people. By now Mr. and Mrs. McGraf should have had grandkids running around the yard."

"Yeah. Or maybe the Lord was ready to call them home," Lester said. "Maybe they're living in a whole lot better place than they had back there and not having to work so damned hard to put food on the table and shirts on their backs."

"So we shouldn't grieve when people die?" Jamie asked. "Or question the circumstances when their deaths seem so unnecessary?"

"I wouldn't know," Lester said. "I leave stuff like that to Miss Amanda."

They rode in silence for a time. Then Jamie asked, "Would you really lose your job if I got hurt?"

"Yep. And this is a damned good job. Better than any job I'd have working in Alma, that's for sure. I've got health insurance, a retirement plan, and two weeks' paid leave a year. And I live in one of the bunkhouses for nothing. Miss Amanda takes good care of her people."

"I saw Amanda the other night on television," Jamie said. "She was amazing."

"Yeah, whenever one of her revivals is televised, all the Hartmann City folks gather at the church to watch on the big screen. Everyone who works on the ranch thinks the world of Miss Amanda."

"What about Gus Hartmann?" Jamie asked as she stroked her dog. "What do people think of him?"

"Everyone respects him, but he doesn't know everyone's name like Miss Amanda. When I was a little kid, he used to come to the football games in Alma with Amanda's son. Mr. Hartmann is a short little guy. *Real* short. Sonny Hartmann went to a private school back East, but when he was at the ranch, he'd drive into town and hang out some. You'd think a rich kid like that would be a snob, but he wasn't. Sometimes he even played pickup basketball at the school yard. Shame about what happened to him. Everyone in town was real tore up over it. But you know what? I'm not supposed to talk about the Hartmanns. It's a habit, I guess. Folks who live here on the ranch are more interested in the Hartmanns than they are in movie stars or football heroes or the president in Washington, D.C., but we all signed a paper promising not to talk about the Hartmann family to outsiders."

"A confidentiality agreement?"

"Yeah, that's it," Lester said. "But since you're living here now, I guess that kind of makes you one of us."

"Not really," Jamie said. "I'm just passing through. I won't ask you any more questions about the Hartmanns. I wouldn't want to get you in trouble."

"You know, we've all been mighty curious about you," Lester admitted. "At first we thought you were going to work for Montgomery—a secretary or bookkeeper, maybe—but it seems like you don't do much of anything except walk."

"So, why do people think I'm here?" Jamie asked.

"Well," Lester said, staring at the road, "Freda says that Miss Amanda invited you to come to the ranch to get away from a mean boyfriend and then you turned up pregnant so she's letting you stay here till the baby is born. But Miss Amanda is still afraid that the boyfriend might come looking for you, so she doesn't want you wandering off by yourself."

"That's pretty close," Jamie said.

"You're just lucky to have someone like Amanda Hartmann to help you get your life back on track," Lester said.

"That's true," Jamie said.

*   *   *

Back in her sitting room, Jamie removed the decorative items from the two rooms, leaving only her books and photographs and the potted plants from her grandmother's house. She even took down her great-grandmother's mirror and put it in the closet alongside her grandmother's sewing stand. She could no longer think of these two rooms as home. Not even a temporary one.

Chapter Thirteen

JAMIE AWOKE IN the night to the sound of singing.

A thin, quavery female voice was singing a strange song about a woman longing for her "sweet little Alice blue gown."

Jamie rolled over and looked toward the chair in the corner.

It was empty.

The singing was coming from the sitting room. Light was pouring through the open door. Jamie rose and padded across the bedroom.

The old woman was sitting next to Ralph on the sofa, her hand stroking his back. His tail thumped when he saw Jamie.

Their visitor was wearing a lacy black nightgown that hung loosely over her bony shoulders and chest. Her feet were bare. Red lipstick covered her mouth and much of her chin. A well-worn red leather pocketbook rested on her lap. When she finished her song, she applauded, the loose skin on her underarms waving back and forth.

Jamie applauded, too.

The woman looked at Jamie, apparently noticing her for the first time. She acknowledged Jamie's applause with a shy smile then let forth a delighted cackle. Jamie remembered that laugh. The first time she'd heard it, she thought she was dreaming. Now she was wide awake, and the woman was obviously quite real.

"I'm Jamie," she said as she sat across from the woman. "What is your name?"

"I told you last time I was here," the old woman said. "I'm Mary Millicent, and this is my house."

"Do you live here all the time?" Jamie asked.

The woman nodded. "Up in the tower. My children are going to burn in hell for keeping me a prisoner in that room with the witch as my jailer."

"You're not in that room now," Jamie pointed out.

"The witch thinks she is so smart, but she's forgotten that this is my house, and I have a magic key that opens all the doors." No sooner had she said these words than she gasped and put her hands over her mouth.

Jamie jumped up and rushed to the old woman's side. "What's the matter?" she asked, kneeling in front of her.

Mary Millicent took her hands from her mouth. "You won't tell them, will you?" she asked in a whisper, her gaze darting from side to side.

"About your key? No, I won't tell," Jamie whispered back.

"And promise you won't tell the witch that I was here."

Jamie nodded.

"Cross your heart and hope to die."

Jamie solemnly crossed her heart. Then Mary Millicent looked around as though to make sure no one else was in the room. "The witch doesn't know I can walk," she whispered. "The nurse, too."

"You're kidding!"

Mary Millicent shook her head. "If the witch knew I could walk, she would lock me up or chain me to the bed."

Jamie sat on the sofa. Ralph gave her a quizzical look, as though asking if he should abandon his position on the other side of Mary Millicent and come sit beside her. With a gesture of her hand, Jamie told him he was fine where he was.

"I added on the wing because we needed more room for all our important visitors," Mary Millicent said, sitting up straighter and lifting her chin. "We had presidents and senators and ambassadors and even a sultan come here. Sometimes they brought their wives, and sometimes they didn't. They liked to dress up like cowboys and ride horses and hunt deer and quail, then sit around smoking Cuban cigars and drinking Tennessee whiskey."

"Tell me about the tower," Jamie said. "Did you build it to make the house look like a castle?"

"Nope. I built it so I could have a private place. Sometimes I would invite one of the gentlemen visitors to meet me up there. Now the only excitement I have is watching people out the windows. That and making the witch mad," she added with a chuckle. "I watch you from up there. You and the pooch walk all the time with that boy following you in the truck."

"Why do they keep you up there?" Jamie asked, not sure if she believed the woman.

"Because I'm a secret," Mary Millicent said. "They don't want a crazy old woman going around saying things she shouldn't say and embarrassing Amanda. She's on television now just like I used to be. Everyone would notice me when I walked into a restaurant or through an airport. People would come up to me and tell me they'd seen me preach on television, and they wanted me to bless them and to touch my hand. You want to touch my hand?"

"Sure," Jamie said, taking one of Mary Millicent's clawlike hands in her own. Her nails were carefully trimmed, as were her toenails. Her hair was combed. She had smelled before, but not now. Obviously someone was trying to look after her needs.

"Do you like me?" Mary Millicent asked, tilting her head to one side.

Jamie started to say that she didn't know her very well, but the look on the old woman's face was so beseeching, like a small child in search of a friend. "Of course, I like you," she said.

Mary Millicent put her head on Jamie's shoulder, and Jamie put her arms around her. Her skin felt like parchment. Jamie could see down the front of the lacy nightgown. Mary Millicent's bony chest was flat with no flesh at all. Just baggy skin and two shriveled-up nipples.

Mary Millicent became so still that Jamie wondered if she was falling asleep. "Maybe you should go back to your room now?" she asked. "You don't want the witch to find you here."

"Will you sing with me first?"

"What would you like to sing?"

Mary Millicent began rocking back in forth in Jamie's arms singing a familiar hymn. Jamie closed her eyes. She remembered standing next to her grandmother in church singing the very same hymn. In their simple little frame church.

"What a friend we have in Jesus," Jamie sang along with her elderly visitor, "all our sins and grief to bear/ What a privilege to carry everything to God in prayer."

At the end of the hymn, Mary Millicent kissed Jamie on the mouth, then, clutching her red purse and with Jamie's help, she shakily rose to a standing position.

Jamie watched the barefoot, frail figure in a lacy black nightgown slowly make her away across the room.

"Good night," Jamie called after her.

Without turning around, the woman waved a hand, then opened the door just an inch or two and peeked out into the hallway. Apparently assured that the hall was empty, she left, closing the door behind her.

"Seems we have a friend," she told her dog. "How about you and me going back to bed?"

Before turning off the light, she opened the door and looked up and down the hall. There was no one in sight.

She locked the door, an act she distinctly remembered performing when she and Ralph came in from their evening foray into the backyard. It was a defiant act she performed nightly with Miss Montgomery in mind. Even though she realized the housekeeper had a passkey, Jamie wanted her to know that uninvited visitors were not welcome.

Mary Millicent also had a passkey, it seemed.

She assumed that Mary Millicent's "witch" was Ann Montgomery. The designation made Jamie smile.

The next morning when she set out on her walk, Jamie wanted to turn and wave to Mary Millicent. She didn't, of course. Someone might see her. When she reached the road, however, she looked toward the house—at the tower with its many narrow windows. Was Mary Millicent watching her?

After her walk, Jamie took Ralph to the apartment then headed back downstairs to the library. After her conversation with Mary Millicent, she wanted to study the pictures on the wall.

Yes, the pictures were definitely of a much younger Mary Millicent. Such a striking woman she had been—more stately and commanding than her daughter. She and her husband had been a handsome couple—like a duke and duchess.

She stopped in front of the picture of Mary Millicent in a pony cart with her two young children. Amanda was sitting on her mother's lap with Gus beside them.

Not your usual family, Jamie thought as she studied picture after picture. Not with an oil baron, a politician who almost became president, and three generations of evangelists.

After viewing the pictures for several minutes, she realized she was not alone. She turned around, and there was Amanda Hartmann herself watching her from across the large room. She was sitting on a cushioned window seat, a stack of file folders in her lap. "Good morning, Jamie," she said. "You're looking well."

"I didn't realize you were here at the ranch," Jamie said as she tentatively crossed the room.

"I have some things to take care of here, including a baptism and a wedding," Amanda said with a welcoming smile. "And three of the Alliance board members are coming in tomorrow for a couple of days of hunting. Freda tells me that you're progressing nicely with the pregnancy."

Jamie nodded. "Apparently all is well."

Amanda was simply dressed in jeans and a white cotton shirt. Her shining blond hair was pulled back into a smooth ponytail. She wondered if Amanda would see her mother while she was here. And if she and her brother really had banished Mary Millicent to the tower.

Amanda put aside the stack of files and reached for Jamie's hand. "Come sit by me, Jamie dear."

Once she was settled beside Amanda, Jamie asked, "Is your husband here with you?"

"Oh, yes," Amanda said with a brilliant smile. "Toby and I are seldom apart. He's out swimming laps now. He wanted me to join him—he's not only my husband, he's my personal trainer—but the sun is bad for my skin, and I prefer to swim after the sun goes down. It's more romantic then, anyway," she said and actually blushed. "Oh, my," she said, putting her hands on her red cheeks. "You'd think I was a schoolgirl. Tell me, Jamie, have you ever been in love?"

"Not really," Jamie said, but then to her surprise she began telling Amanda about Joe Brammer, who came to Mesquite to visit his grandparents and had never been her boyfriend but had been very nice to her. She paused, thinking she would explain that she was a lot younger than he was and that he had fallen in love with someone else. But she changed her mind and said instead, "I probably need to let you get back to your work."

"Oh, I am always behind with my correspondence, it seems," Amanda said with a wave of her hand. "Each of our donors deserves some sort of personalized response, but a few more minutes won't matter," she said.

"I guess it's too early for you to show," Amanda continued, patting Jamie's tummy. "You look very trim. You're not dieting or anything like that, are you?"

Jamie shook her head. "I lost weight while I was so nauseated, but I've gained all that back and more. I can't button my jeans. I guess I'll need to get some stretchy clothes."

"I'll see to that," Amanda said. "I was very worried about you while you were so sick and so very grateful that you had Montgomery and Freda to look after you."

"Yes, they were diligent."

"You walk a lot, I understand," Amanda said. "And swim laps."

"I was swimming daily before I got sick, but now I mostly take my dog on long walks twice a day. We both enjoy it. And I've taken up bird watching."

"That's nice," Amanda said, stroking Jamie's cheek. "I had forgotten what a pretty girl you are. You remind me of a young Julie Andrews in *The Sound of Music*."

Jamie liked the way Amanda smiled, liked the way she leaned forward as she listened, as though the words coming out of Jamie's mouth were very important to her. And she liked the warmth of Amanda's touch. She found herself wanting the woman to approve of her, to *like* her.

"I understand that you're pregnant, too," Jamie said.

Amanda's smile faded. "Freda never should have told you that."

"You mean, it's not true?"

"I'm . . ." Amanda began then paused. "I am much too old for child-bearing and having some problems, so I prefer that no one know anything about my condition just now. You know, just in case . . ." Her voice trailed off and her eyes were downcast.

"I hope everything works out all right," Jamie said.

"Montgomery tells me that you were worried that I wouldn't want the baby you're carrying if I had one of my own. You must put such a silly notion out of your head, Jamie. My husband and I are thrilled about both pregnancies—the one we planned so carefully and the one that caught us totally by surprise. Now, tell me, my dear, other than maternity clothes, is there anything you need?"

"I'd like to borrow binoculars for my bird watching if there's a pair available."

"I'll see that you get a pair," Amanda said. "Are your accommodations satisfactory?"

"Yes, I am quite comfortable."

"Now, you would tell me if there was anything bothering you, wouldn't you?"

Jamie nodded again, this time feeling a bit dishonest. Lots of things were bothering her. She was none too fond of Miss Montgomery, and she was lonely as all get out. A part of her wished she had never signed on for this gig, but she would see it through to the end because that was the sort of person she was and because she was tired of being poor. But she deliberately did not think about the life growing inside of her because she was afraid that if she thought about it and got the least bit sentimental, she might find herself wondering if she wanted the baby to be raised by a televangelist and a man who seemed to have no job or purpose in life other than to keep himself beautiful and to adore and serve his wife. Of course, there was a community of several hundred people on this ranch who also lived to adore and serve Amanda, which had seemed odd to Jamie, but here in the woman's presence, she understood why people felt that way. At this moment, she would have liked to linger a while longer, basking in Amanda Hartmann's glow.

Probably weird old Mary Millicent was confined in the tower to keep her from wandering off or getting into mischief, Jamie decided. If she hadn't promised Mary Millicent that she would keep her visit a secret, she would have asked Amanda about her mother.

"You seemed quite engrossed in the family pictures," Amanda observed, nodding toward the wall of framed photographs.

"Miss Montgomery told me some of your family history. I find it very interesting."

"Yes. And sad. My father died in his prime. And I suppose that Bentley Abernathy told you about my son's accident," Amanda said, her gaze growing distant, her eyes filling with tears. "I have never felt such despair. I wanted to curse the Lord, but He lifted me up and told me how to survive. I wish you could have known my Sonny. He was so beautiful. So dear. No child ever filled a mother's heart more."

Jamie reached into her pocket for a tissue and handed it to Amanda. "I'm sure that Sonny loved you very much and was very proud of you."

Jamie paused while Amanda dabbed at her eyes then asked, "What about your mother? Is she still alive?"

Amanda hesitated before saying, "My remarkable mother is no longer the guiding light in my life. But I have my dear brother, and the Lord sent me my darling Toby. And soon we will be parents. You can't imagine how that knowledge fills my heart."

Feeling a wave of discomfort at Amanda's deceit, Jamie moved an inch or two away from her.

"I watched you on television last week," Jamie said.

"I am so pleased," Amanda said, smiling through her tears. "Did you pray with me? Did you accept our Lord Jesus Christ as your personal savior?"

"Not really," Jamie admitted. "I just watched."

Amanda took both of Jamie's hands in hers. "You must look after your soul, child. I want you to pray with me now."

Jamie dutifully bowed her head and listened while Amanda thanked God for the beautiful day, for the birds that gave Jamie such enjoyment. "And I ask your blessing on this young woman and the precious infant she carries. She is a good person and accepts that you are the one true God."

Jamie joined her in saying "Amen."

Chapter Fourteen

LENORA HAD NEVER been to the Texas Panhandle before. Most of what she knew about the region came from weather reports on the evening news. The Panhandle had more winter storms and tornadoes than the rest of the state.

As their flight banked for a landing at the Amarillo airport, she was surprised to see the sprawl of a large city spread below them after flying over hundreds of miles of emptiness. "Why do so many people live down there?" she asked Bentley.

Bentley chuckled. "Amarillo is a major distribution center for oil and cattle," he said, closing his briefcase. During the flight they had been going over his notes in preparation for the Marshall County commissioner's meeting that he would be attending this afternoon.

"And there's a huge facility for slaughtering cattle and a number of petrochemical plants," he added.

Lenora made a face. "Sounds lovely," she said.

Once they were on the ground, Lenora headed for the car-rental counter while Bentley made a few phone calls. Less than twenty minutes after landing, they were on their way. Lenora followed the signs that led her from the airport and soon was heading west on Interstate 40.

"Think you can light a fire under the county commissioners?" she asked.

"Actually, they really aren't dragging their feet," he admitted. "They're having the motor rebuilt on their forty-year-old bulldozer. Your concern for Jamie Long has begun to rub off on me, though, and I took a certain perverse pleasure in prolonging Gus Hartmann's irritation."

"You know, either Gus Hartmann is getting more cantankerous or you're suffering from burnout," Lenora observed.

Bentley sighed. "Maybe it's some of both. But the truth of the matter is I need Gus more than he needs me."

"You signed the papers on the haunted house yet?" Lenora asked.

"Day after tomorrow. I've never seen Brenda more excited. She drives out there every single day, and yesterday I heard her *whistling*. I've been married to her for almost thirty-five years and never once heard my wife whistle."

"So?"

"So I'm jealous of a goddamned house that would fall over if I leaned on it."

"I'm sorry," Lenora said.

"Me, too."

Once they had left the outskirts of Amarillo, the landscape was unvaried but majestic in its vastness and loneliness. The drive to Alma took about an hour.

The most noticeable thing about Alma was the overpass that allowed motorists to sail over the town without even slowing down. Lenora parked in front of the Main Street Café, where they both ordered the blue-plate special—chicken-fried steak with mashed potatoes and gravy.

After lunch, Bentley headed for the courthouse, and Lenora drove north. Within minutes she had left the town far behind her, with only an occasional lonely farmhouse and its cluster of outbuildings to break the monotony of the landscape. Lenora realized as she drove along that she hadn't seen another vehicle for miles, which she found disconcerting. She was a city girl. What if she had a blowout? Did AAA send tow trucks to such remote places? And where did one go to the bathroom?

Her first indication that the ranch was near was a high fence posted with signs warning DANGER! HIGH VOLTAGE. Then she saw a stone tower rising above treetops. As she drove a bit farther, she could see that the tower was part of a very large stone house set about a half mile or so back from the road in a grove of trees. And some distance north of the ranch house, she could see other structures, including a water tower and a large silo.

She expected some sort of impressive sign to tell her she had arrived at Hartmann Ranch, but all that greeted her was a closed gate and a large sign that said PRIVATE PROPERTY. NO HUNTING ALLOWED. TRESPASSERS WILL BE PROSECUTED.

She pulled up to an intercom speaker mounted beside the gate and pressed the button. Shortly a female voice said, "Can I help you?"

"Yes, I'm here to visit Jamie Long."

"Just a minute," the voice said.

The minute proved to be a very long one. The house was not visible from this vantage point, just a curving drive lined with cedars. After five minutes, Lenora turned off the motor. After another fifteen minutes, she pressed the button again. This time a male voice responded.

"I am here to visit Jamie Long," Lenora repeated. "I have come all the way from Austin for this purpose and have been waiting twenty minutes for the gate to open."

"One minute, please."

After several more minutes, Lenora once again pressed the button.

"Yes," the same male voice said.

"I am here to see Jamie Long, and if you don't open this gate, I plan to climb over it."

"You would get quite a shock," the man said. "And if you got inside, we would have to detain you."

"Are you a policeman?"

"The ranch has a security force that has law-enforcement jurisdiction over ranch property."

"Okay. Let's start over. My name is Lenora Richardson. I work for Bentley Abernathy, who is the Hartmann family attorney in Austin. I have been trying to reach Jamie Long for months. She has not responded to my letters or phone calls. I am concerned about her and would really appreciate it if you told her that I am here to see her. If she does not want to see me, I want her to call me on my cell phone and tell me so in person. Now, pick up a pencil and write down this phone number."

"Folks don't have much luck with cell phones out here," the man said.

"Then I want to speak to the person in charge."

"I'll see what I can do," he said.

Lenora looked around for a tree or a bush. She really needed to go to the bathroom but was afraid to get too far from the intercom. Finally, she looked up and down the empty road to make sure no one was coming, then opened the door, pulled down her slacks, and squatted beside the car.

She had no sooner finished buckling her belt than she heard a woman's voice saying, "Miss Richardson?"

"Yes," she responded.

"This is Ann Montgomery," a woman's voice said pleasantly. "I am the head housekeeper here at the ranch and am so sorry you drove all the way out here to see Jamie Long. She no longer lives here."

"Why is that?"

"I am not sure. She was with us for a time and then left."

"Where did she go?"

"I have no idea. She had her car here at the ranch and simply packed up and left. Such a quiet young woman. I will let Miss Hartmann know that you came by. Perhaps she knows something about Miss Long's plans."

"I would appreciate that," Lenora said. "Miss Hartmann can get in touch with me at the office of Mr. Bentley Abernathy in Austin."

"Yes, I understand that. Again, I am sorry for your inconvenience."

"You know, I have been trying to reach Jamie by telephone and by mail for some time now."

"Perhaps she did not wish to respond," the woman suggested.

"Yeah. Maybe."

Lenora uttered an obscenity and got into the car. She backed onto the road and drove north toward the water tower and silo. As she drew closer, she realized that an entire community was spread out below the two soaring structures.

She turned onto the gravel road and stopped at a building with gas pumps in front and went inside what proved to be an old-fashioned general store with a serve-yourself concession area. A young Hispanic woman stopped stocking a shelf with breakfast cereal and stepped behind the cash register.

Lenora poured coffee into a Styrofoam cup. "I think I'm lost," Lenora told the woman as she paid for the coffee.

"Where do you want to go?" the woman asked in accented English.

"Alma," Lenora said.

"That way," the woman said, pointing south. "Turn left at first road. Soon there is a road sign for Alma."

Lenora tried to look suitably relieved. "It seemed like I had been driving forever. I was afraid I'd gotten lost. So, what is this place called?"

"Hartmann City. Is part of big ranch."

"I met a young woman in Austin who said she was going to live at the Hartmann Ranch. Her name is Jamie. Would you happen to know her?"

The woman shook her head.

"Well, thank you for the directions," Lenora said, taking a sip from her Styrofoam cup.

Back in the car, she drove through the community, drawing stares from children in the school yard and from a man in a pickup truck. Obviously they did not have many visitors here.

She made a U-turn and headed back toward Hartmann Road.

Lenora pulled into a drive-in on the way out of town. Bentley ordered a milkshake, and she requested a Coke.

"What I really want is a martini," Lenora said.

"No luck, I take it," Bentley said as she backed out of the parking space.

"You first," Lenora said.

"The commissioners will rent a bulldozer from Oldham County. They hope to start the project in a couple of weeks. Now, what happened at the ranch? Did you see Jamie?"

Lenora explained what had transpired and concluded her story by saying, "Boss, I'm really worried about Jamie."

"Well," Bentley said, "the contract specified that she would be paid for her time and dismissed if she didn't become pregnant after three insemination procedures. Maybe she drove off in her grandmother's car and is back in college or gone back to wherever she came from."

"Mesquite," Lenora said.

"Yeah, maybe she's back in Mesquite."

"Maybe so," Lenora acknowledged. "The whole experience was spooky, though. The Hartmanns have a regular fiefdom out there, with a feudal village for the serfs. The ranch house looks like a castle complete with a turreted tower, and in lieu of a drawbridge and moat, there are miles of electric fences."

"You know what a big issue privacy is with them."

"More like an obsession, I'd say," Lenora said.

"But if the whole insemination deal is off," Bentley pondered, "it does seem strange that Amanda didn't let us know and request that we find another girl. Maybe she and her husband have changed their minds."

Bentley thought of Gus and Amanda's impatience during the search for a surrogate. Which had made him nervous. The Hartmanns' annual retainer accounted for more than half of Bentley's income. Pleasing them was a condition of his life.

"I saw Amanda the other night on television," Lenora said. "She really is remarkable. There were moments when I got tears in my eyes and other times when I wanted to jump up and down and yell 'Hallelujah.' Amanda Tutt Hartmann is either the genuine article or the world's greatest con artist."

"I think she is sincere," Bentley said. "Gus Hartmann is more pragmatic."

And more ruthless, he thought. Back in the days when Bentley was dealing with angry landowners who claimed Gus or his grandfather before him had swindled them out of their mineral rights, lawsuits would quietly be dropped for no apparent reason. Bentley had always wondered what sort of intimidation had been used.

He also had wondered if Gus had something to do with the death of Amanda's ex-husband. Bentley had tried to persuade the man that it was in his best interest to accept the Hartmanns' generous offer and get the hell out of Amanda and Sonny's life, but Lenny Bradford joined AA, swore off gambling, hired a lawyer of his own, and sued for shared custody. Both sides were gearing up for a huge court battle when Bradford was shot while coming out of a restaurant by a still unidentified assailant.

And more recently, Bentley had been bothered by Gus's determination to find someone to blame for Sonny's tragic accident. The company that manufactured the all-terrain vehicle Sonny had been driving claimed that the rollover had caused a wheel to come off. Gus hired one of the best trial lawyers in the country to prove that just the opposite was true—that the wheel coming off was the cause of the accident. When the manufacturer offered a huge settlement, Gus turned it down. The next day the CEO was found hanging from the rafters of his horse barn. His death was ruled a suicide. At first his family had refuted that finding but soon withdrew their protest.

Not that Gus would harm Jamie Long, even if she tried to back out of her contract. The Hartmanns were powerful people and not to be trifled with, but they could always hire another surrogate mother.

Probably Jamie had miscarried or the insemination procedure had never worked in the first place and she had been dismissed.

Yes, something like that must have happened, Bentley assured himself. They had given her some money and sent her on her way. Any day now Gus probably would be calling to demand that he find another young woman to replace her.

Chapter Fifteen

IT HAD BEEN CHILLY when Jamie and Ralph began their walk, but now it was downright cold with a biting wind that cut right through her. And grayness had settled over the land, robbing it of beauty and making it seem inhospitable and cruel.

When she opened the door to her apartment, there were two boxes waiting for her—one of them quite large. True to her word, Amanda had sent her maternity clothes—jeans, knit shirts, sweaters, underwear, and two flannel nightgowns. In the smaller box was a pair of binoculars.

She went to a window and focused the binoculars on a lone red-tailed hawk circling near the road and watched with fascination as it suddenly dove with breathtaking speed. Just when it seemed as though it would crash into the ground, the bird swooped upward with a small creature—a field mouse, probably—firmly held in a grasping foot. The powerful do prey on the weak, she thought philosophically. She wondered if the field mouse struggled or simply accepted its inevitable fate.

She put away the clothing and wrote a thank-you note to Amanda and slipped it under Miss Montgomery's door. Then, more out of boredom than fatigue, she decided to take a nap. "Just an hour or so," she told Ralph, who curled up beside her on the sofa.

She dozed until her dinner tray arrived—at straight-up six o'clock, like always. She fed Ralph then turned on the television and decided which anchorperson she would have for a dinner companion. Other than Lester and Ralph, television people were her only friends. And Mary Millicent. Except that Amanda's mother hadn't made a middle-of-the-night visit since their songfest more than a month ago.

Jamie selected an Amarillo station, more to hear a weather report than from any desire to know what was going on in the Panhandle's largest city, and removed the domed cover from her dinner plate. Tonight's entrée was a baked chicken breast served with green beans and scalloped potatoes. Tonight's weather, according to a perky brunette weatherperson, was scattered showers and intermittent sleet. Jamie didn't mind her solitary breakfasts and lunches, but dinner was a meal she associated with companionship. At her grandmother's house, dinnertime meant a cloth on the table, a blank screen on the television set, and a reporting of one's day. In Austin, she usually had dinner in the residential-center cafeteria with one or more of her dorm mates.

After she'd put the dinner tray in the hall for pickup, Jamie curled up in bed to watch *Breakfast at Tiffany's*. She'd seen the 1960s movie before but was charmed all over again as she watched Audrey Hepburn and George Peppard fall in love. How lovely that would be, she thought, to fall in love with someone and have that someone love her in return. She didn't even have anyone to daydream about. Except Joe Brammer. And he was probably married by now. He would have finished law school and most likely was ready to settle down and have a family.

When the film ended, Jamie turned out the light. But her mind refused to settle down.

Finally, she got up and paced up and down the living room, much to Ralph's bewilderment. When the dog finally got so upset over her strange behavior that he began to whine, she stopped pacing and heated a cup of milk in the microwave. She had just taken the first sip when she heard a key in the lock. Ralph heard it, too. His crooked tail began to wag in expectation.

Mary Millicent had on the same black lace nightgown as before with a tattered quilt around her shoulders and men's argyle socks on her feet. "You're not in bed," she noted.

"No, I'm having trouble sleeping," Jamie explained.

"You're pregnant, aren't you?"

"What makes you ask?"

"I hear and see things," Mary Millicent said with a girlish giggle. "The witch and the nurse talk in front of me sometimes. They think I'm just a crazy old woman and don't pay me any mind. I always had trouble sleeping when I was pregnant. It gets your whole body out of whack."

Mary Millicent placed a hand on Jamie's abdomen. "Yep. Between four and five months, I'd say. Felt any quickening yet?"

"No," Jamie said, moving away from the woman's touch. *Quickening.* The nurse had asked her the same thing and then explained that the term meant a woman had reached the stage in pregnancy when she could feel the fetus move. Jamie had no choice but to talk to Nurse Freda about such things, but she didn't have to discuss it with other people.

Or even to think about it.

"It's time you met Sonny," Mary Millicent declared, wrapping the quilt more tightly around her emaciated body.

"Sonny? I thought he was dead."

"Might as well be," Mary Millicent said.

"Where is he?" Jamie asked.

Mary Millicent shook her head and put a finger to her lips. Then she grabbed Jamie's hand and pulled her along as she tiptoed across the room and carefully opened the door. Jamie closed the door behind them.

Hand in hand they walked down the long, silent corridor. When they reached the entrance to the tiny chapel, Mary Millicent pulled Jamie inside. For an instant, Jamie thought Mary Millicent was going to kneel in front of the softly lit altar. Instead the old woman pushed on one side of it.

Jamie watched in amazement as the altar and the wall behind it swung inward. Mary Millicent stepped inside and switched on a light, revealing a bare wooden staircase. She waved Jamie through the opening, pushed the hidden door back in place, and started up the stairs.

Jamie followed as Mary Millicent slowly climbed, pausing on each step. At the top of the staircase she found herself in an octagon-shaped room that smelled of disinfectant. Half of the room was cordoned off with heavy curtains, like those used in hospital rooms. This side of the room held a large reclining chair, a small table with a lamp, and a second flight of stairs that disappeared into an opening above.

Jamie held back, not sure she wanted to see what was behind the curtain, but Mary Millicent pulled it back, revealing a metal bed with railings. On the bed, lying on his back, was the slight form of a person with longish blond hair.

"Come meet Sonny," Mary Millicent said.

Slowly Jamie approached the bed.

She stared down at the wasted body on the bed. His eyes were closed, his cheeks sunken, his chin covered with stubble, but his hair looked as though it had just been brushed. "Is he conscious?" she whispered.

"Sometimes he mumbles and moves his arms and legs," Mary Millicent said, "and every once in a while he opens his eyes and looks at me, but I'm not sure he sees me."

The man was little more than a skeleton. Like Mary Millicent. Fluids were dripping into a vein in his arm, and his urine was being drained into a large plastic bag that hung from the side of the bed.

Jamie thought of the pictures of the glorious young man with the unruly blond hair and wonderful smile that she'd seen on the wall of the library and felt overwhelming sadness that he was now reduced to such a state.

"Who takes care of him?"

"The nurse and the witch—and one of the Mexican men helps out some. They feed him through a tube, but he's nothing but skin and bones. Once he was the most beautiful boy I'd ever seen. When he smiled at me, I felt like I had been given a wonderful gift. I loved this boy more than I've ever loved anyone in my entire life. More than I loved God. My heart loved him and my eyes and my ears and my fingertips and my soul."

Jamie realized the old woman's cheeks were awash with tears and put a comforting arm around her bony shoulders. "It must be wonderful to love someone like that," she said.

"No, it's not. It makes you weak when you love. It gives God a way to punish you," Mary Millicent said, pulling away from Jamie's embrace. "After the accident, Amanda brought Sonny here and spent weeks and weeks doing nothing but praying to God to save her son. Even Gus came and prayed, and I tried to. I really did. But all I could do was curse. Do you think that's why God won't let Sonny wake up—because I cursed at Him for not doing a better job watching over my darling boy?"

Mary Millicent picked up Sonny's hand and kissed it. "He was a holy being from the moment he was born," she continued, laying her cheek against her grandson's hand. "We all knew it. And felt it. You could see it in his eyes. In his smile. He was a holy being, and I knew that he was going to save more souls than my daddy or me or Amanda ever even thought about. But he never got the chance. God isn't ever going to let him wake up," she wailed, "and it's time to let the poor boy go. I thought since you were going to have his baby that Amanda would have let him go by now. The last time she was here, I thought that was why she came. She spent hours and hours sitting here by the bed and holding Sonny's hand and kissing him and washing his body and talking to him."

"What does my pregnancy have to do with Sonny?" Jamie asked, backing away from the bed, not sure if she really wanted to hear Mary Millicent's answer.

The anguish vanished from Mary Millicent's face and she emitted a lewd-sounding cackle. "He's your lover," she said and used her hands to mimic intercourse.

"I don't have a lover," Jamie said.

"Honey, you don't have to pretend with me. I live right up there," Mary Millicent said, pointing toward the ceiling. They think I don't know what goes on down here, but I do. I heard Amanda tell Sonny that he was going to be a father. She said the mother of the baby was a pretty girl with blond hair and blue eyes, just like him. And she was tall and smart, just like him. And a good Christian, just like him."

Jamie took another step back. She shouldn't have come here. She didn't want to know about this poor shell of a man who was more dead than alive. And she didn't want to hear nonsense coming from the mouth of an addle-brained old woman.

"You want to go upstairs and see where I live?" Mary Millicent asked.

Jamie shook her head as she turned and walked shakily toward the stairs.

"Don't you want to kiss him good night?" Mary Millicent asked.

"No," Jamie said, grabbing hold of the banister and hurrying down the stairs. She could hear Mary Millicent singing in her quavering old-lady voice,

> *Sleep, my child, and peace attend thee,*
> *All through the night;*
> *Guardian angels God will lend thee,*
> *All through the night . . .*

Frantically Jamie pulled open the door and crept into the chapel then pulled the altar back in place and, with a pounding heart, looked up and down the corridor, half expecting to see Miss Montgomery or Amanda Hartmann waiting to accost her.

But she had done nothing wrong. All she had done was befriend a lonely old woman. It wasn't as though she had set out to discover what was apparently a carefully guarded secret, a secret being kept by an incredibly wealthy family that practiced power and subterfuge along with religion.

But maybe they kept Sonny hidden away because they didn't want reporters to hover around like vultures. Maybe that was why Amanda and her brother were so security-conscious.

Back in her apartment, Jamie sank onto the sofa and buried her face against Ralph's neck, who was pathetically glad to see her. Not that she had been gone long, but he was unaccustomed to being left alone in the middle of the night.

Jamie willed her heart to stop racing and took several deep breaths in an attempt to slow it and to control the troubling avalanche of thoughts tumbling through her mind. She placed a hand on her stomach in a rare acknowledgment of the pregnancy that was changing the contours of her body. Had Mary Millicent really overheard Amanda saying that Sonny was the father of this baby?

Jamie shook her head in denial. She wasn't going to believe the raving of a crazy old woman. Toby Travis was the father of the baby. She had signed a contract agreeing to have a baby for him and Amanda. The nice fertility doctor in Austin had used Toby Travis's semen to inseminate her.

Could someone have taken semen from poor Sonny Hartmann and had the doctor use it instead?

Jamie remembered reading about an Aberdeen-Angus bull in Canada that was thought to have fathered more offspring than any other bull ever. His semen was packed in dry ice and shipped all over the world. Which meant that human semen could surely be transported from Marshall County to Austin.

Did a man have to give his consent before his semen was used to conceive a child, she wondered. Of course, men became unwilling fathers all the time, but at least they had realized that was a possibility when they had unprotected sex with a woman.

Jamie recalled an old movie that she had watched late one night after her grandmother had gone to bed. *The World According to Garp*. An army nurse had crawled into a bed with an unconscious soldier and gotten herself pregnant.

If that was possible, then it might be possible for someone to masturbate an unconscious man to an orgasm.

Jamie shook her head to clear her mind of such an image. *No way,* she told herself.

Or Nurse Freda might have done some sort of surgical procedure.

Jamie touched her stomach. If she *had* been impregnated with Sonny's semen, the baby inside her would be Amanda's grandchild. But the birth certificate would say that Toby was the father and that Amanda was the baby's *adopted* mother.

What about Amanda's own pregnancy? Was she just pretending to be pregnant?

Maybe she was planning to raise Jamie's child as her own flesh and blood, which it truly would be if Sonny was its father. But what could possibly be the reason for such deception? Whether Amanda was the baby's grandmother or adopted mother, she would end up raising it.

Jamie groaned and put her hands to her head. It was too confusing. Too insane. She had gotten herself locked up in a loony bin. She needed to talk to someone on the outside, someone who could help her make sense of things.

She got up and went to the desk. She opened first one drawer and then another, searching for her address book.

It wasn't there.

She looked in the bedside table. Between the sofa cushions. Under the bed. In every drawer. The top of the closet. Behind every book.

Then she looked again.

Maybe it had fallen in the trash can and been thrown away by accident.

Convinced that the address book was nowhere to be found, she picked up the phone, hoping Lenora's number was not unlisted. Lenora already knew why she was at the ranch. Surely talking to her would not be a violation of the privacy clause.

When she punched zero, a recording informed her that the ranch switchboard was closed and that outside lines were available between the hours of eight A.M. and eight P.M. After-hour emergency calls should be made through the security office.

Probably she didn't want to use the ranch phone system anyway, Jamie thought as she hung up. Someone might be listening in.

God, she was getting so paranoid.

But just to make sure, she would call Lenora from the pay phone at the ranch store. *Tomorrow.*

Still restless, she opened the door onto the balcony. Immediately a bone-chilling cold ripped through her flannel gown. But she stood there for a minute hoping the cold would clear her brain. Ralph was whimpering behind her.

When she closed the door, he continued to whimper and stand by the door to the hall, his way of informing her that he needed to go outside.

"Oh, Ralph, are you sure?"

His whimpering became more insistent. Jamie pulled on her coat and shoes then picked up the phone and punched in Miss Montgomery's number.

"What's wrong?" the housekeeper's voice demanded.

"I need to take the dog out," Jamie said.

"At this hour?"

"I'm sorry, but he's pretty insistent."

"Very well. I'll meet you at the back door."

Miss Montgomery was wearing a plaid bathrobe, her hair in two long braids, a put-upon look on her face. Placing herself carefully in front of the alarm so that Jamie could not watch, she punched in the security code and opened the door. "I'll wait here for you," she said. "Please hurry."

Jamie wrapped her coat closely around her body as she waited for Ralph to race around and find just the right spot to relieve himself. Then he ate grass. For a long time he ate grass. Jamie could almost feel Miss Montgomery's displeasure radiating through the back door.

Finally Ralph raced up the steps. Jamie followed and tapped on the door.

"He has an upset stomach," Jamie said before the housekeeper could complain about the length of time. Miss Montgomery said something that sounded like "hurrumph" and turned around to activate the alarm. Jamie stood on her tiptoes and watched over the woman's shoulder.

It was a simple code. Three fours and a five.

Chapter Sixteen

AFTER RETURNING TO her bed and spending the next hour trying to fall asleep, Jamie had given up and crept down the hall, past the chapel, down the stairs. The night was moonless, and the library's soaring windows admitted only a lesser degree of darkness. She could just make out the silhouette of the dictionary stand. Jamie felt around on the shelf below the dictionary for the leather-bound atlas she knew resided there and carried it back to her room.

Sitting at the desk, she carefully drew a replica of the Texas and Oklahoma panhandles and their environs, showing each town and road. She put a dot where she thought Hartmann Ranch would be and a line that represented Hartmann Road, which eventually connected with U.S. Highway 54, then angled its way across the northwest corner of the vast Texas Panhandle before crossing into the narrow strip of land that made up the Oklahoma Panhandle.

Once her task was done, she carefully folded the paper and put it in an envelope, which she taped to the bottom of a dresser drawer. Then she carried the atlas back downstairs.

Back in bed with her thoughts, she asked herself just what that little excursion had been all about. Of course, it was always nice to have a better geographical perspective on one's location. And she was going to drive away from this place at some point in the future and would need a map to guide her.

But she was months away from leaving the Hartmann Ranch—unless she changed her mind about staying.

She tried to put her situation in perspective. How much would it matter if Sonny Hartmann was indeed the father of the child she carried?

* * *

The following morning, the aroma of freshly cut evergreen greeted Jamie before she reached the top of the staircase. An impressively large Christmas tree was awaiting decorations in the middle of the great hall. She was aware that the month of December had begun, of course. More than a week ago. When she had turned the page on her calendar, she decided that the only significance she would attach to the month was that midway through it she would reach the halfway mark of her pregnancy. But there was no escaping the season, she realized.

She and Ralph were waiting on the front steps when Lester arrived. "It looks like rain," he announced.

"I know, but I just have to get out for a little while," Jamie said.

She jogged down the lane toward the road then waited while Lester pointed the remote opener at the large metal gate. She wondered just how much electrical current ran through the fence. Ralph sometimes scooted under with no ill effect. Maybe only the top part was electrified.

As soon as the gate had swung open a few feet, she and Ralph went through and headed north on Hartmann Road.

Ralph ran ahead of her like a beast possessed, flushing out a jackrabbit then racing back and forth across the road in search of other prey. Jamie trotted along after him. Her body was no longer sleek, but it felt good to push herself a bit. When her life was back to normal, she would enjoy getting back into shape.

Back to normal. That was all she wanted. To be away from this place. To put this time of her life behind her.

As she jogged after her exuberant dog, her breath condensing into white clouds, she willed herself to stop thinking about Sonny in the tower and her missing address book and her growing disquiet with her entire situation and tried instead to imagine what her life would be like after she left Hartmann Ranch.

She would run a couple of miles every day and work out three or four times a week at the student fitness center. After nine months of solitude, it would be wonderful to be in such a busy, bustling place, filled with other young, athletically inclined people like herself. Maybe a guy would invite her to play handball. Or maybe she would invite him. Afterward they would walk over to the union together for coffee.

Thoughts of this imaginary guy occupied her mind for a time—until he started to turn into Joe Brammer and tiny bits of ice began to strike her face. The sleet promised during last night's weather report had arrived. She continued on, struggling against the biting wind until the sleet began to come in sheets. As she turned to wave at Lester, she lost her footing on the frozen ground and slipped into the drainage ditch that ran along the side of the road. Almost immediately Ralph was beside her licking her face, and the truck was sliding to a stop on the road above her.

"Are you all right?" Lester yelled as he jumped out of the truck.

"I'm fine," Jamie said.

Lester grabbed her arm and pulled her to her feet. "You need to watch where you're goin', girl," he said, brushing dirt off her coat. "Kelly will have my hide if anything happens to you."

"I am fine," Jamie repeated, pushing his hand away. "Your concern for my well-being is touching."

She climbed out of the ditch and headed for the truck, her head ducked down to protect her face from the sleet.

Lester maneuvered a tight U-turn and headed back toward the ranch.

"I still want to go to Hartmann City," Jamie said.

"I don't have clearance to take you there," Lester said.

"*Clearance!*" she said angrily. "You take me to the store right this minute or I am going to get out and walk over there. I don't want to go back to the ranch house. I am sick and tired of the damned ranch house! I want to go to the store and walk up and down the aisles and drink a cup of hot chocolate. Is that too much to ask, for God's sake!"

"All right. All right," he said.

Silence filled the cab of the truck as Lester drove to Hartmann City.

At the store, Jamie wandered around a time then sat on a bench and drank her cup of tepid vending-machine hot chocolate while Lester visited with the cashier. After Jamie put the cup in the trash, she walked over to the pay phone. Lester and the cashier were both watching her.

There was no slot for her coins. A sign on the front of the phone said PHONE CARDS ONLY. She walked over to the cashier. "I need to buy a phone card," she said.

"We have to go," Lester said, taking Jamie's arm.

"But I need to make a phone call," Jamie said, jerking her arm away.

"I can't let you do that," he said.

On the short drive to the ranch house, she didn't bother with conversation. She watched glumly while Lester put the truck in gear and headed for the stretch of gravel road that separated Hartmann City from the ranch-house compound. As they approached the security gate, he fished around in the compartment in the door, patted the pockets of his jacket, and felt in the crevice between the seat and the seat back. Then he leaned forward and felt under the seat. "Damn!" he said. "What have I done with the remote? Do you see it anyplace?"

Jamie scrunched down in her seat and folded her arms across her chest. It was his problem, not hers. She had wanted to think that Lester was a friend of sorts, but she had no friends at Hartmann Ranch.

He pulled to a stop in front of the gate, got out, and looked behind the seat. Then he slammed the door, walked over to the intercom, and pressed a button. Jamie watched while he conversed with someone at the security office and the gate began its slow opening arch. Lester continued talking. Probably he was telling on her. The bad girl who tried to make a phone call. Or maybe he was reporting the lost gate opener.

"I probably dropped the damn thing when I had to pull you out of the ditch," he said as he got back in the truck. "I'll have to drive back there and look for it."

"You didn't pull me out of the ditch," Jamie reminded him. "I got myself out."

Once through the gate, Lester drove a little faster than usual, using speed to sooth his frustration. Just before reaching the circular drive to the ranch house, he braked abruptly, and the missing opener came sliding out from under the seat. Jamie glanced at him to see if he had noticed, then surreptitiously dropped one of her gloves on top of it.

When the truck came to a stop, Jamie made a show of looking for the missing glove, then bent over and scooped up the glove and opener together.

Even as she performed this act, she wondered what exactly was motivating her. Perhaps it was just that the opportunity had presented itself. Most likely she would never have any use for the device, but if at some future moment in time she found herself needing to open a gate and drive a vehicle through to the other side, it would be good if she had the means to do so.

"Come on, Ralph," she said and jumped out of the truck without a thank-you or a good-bye. Before opening the front door, she thrust the opener in her pocket.

When she entered the great hall, she found it abuzz with activity. Boxes of decorations were scattered about the room, and the house staff and gardeners were busy decorating the tree and hanging garlands. Someone had set a boom box on a table, and Elvis Presley was singing "White Christmas."

Miss Montgomery, wearing a heavy white sweater over a navy dress, was overseeing the decorating. She offered a small nod in Jamie's direction but did not invite her to join in. Everyone else avoided eye contact with her as she self-consciously wound her way among the boxes on her way to the stairs. She was not a member of the ranch family. She would not be included in their Christmas celebration.

Jamie wondered if Amanda and her husband would celebrate Christmas at the ranch. And Gus Hartmann.

Jamie would be curious to see Amanda. Would she be wearing maternity clothes, or had the problem she'd alluded to during her last visit brought an end to her pregnancy?

If she really had been pregnant in the first place.

As she climbed the stairs, the sound of Elvis singing about glistening treetops and sleigh bells in the snow filled the vaulted space of the great hall. She'd never experienced a white Christmas, which probably wasn't an unusual occurrence in the Texas Panhandle, but Jamie couldn't bring herself to care one way or the other if she woke up to snow on Christmas Day. She wished there were some way to banish the day from her calendar. She thought of melancholy prisoners in their jail cells on Christmas Day longing for their families and better times. That's how it would be for her. Except that she didn't have a family to long for. "Oh, just stop it!" she told herself as she and Ralph walked past the chapel. Ralph looked up at her. "Not you, sweetie," she said, bending to stroke his head. "*I* need to stop it. If there's one thing I can't stand, it's self-pity. I have my health and my darling dog," she said. Then, thinking of Sonny Hartmann, she added, "And a future."

Back in her apartment, she put the remote gate opener under the lining of her grandmother's sewing stand alongside the other items hidden there. Then she picked up the phone.

Listening ears or no, she had an almost pathological need to speak to someone from the outside world. And Lenora had encouraged her to call if she had any concerns. Well, she had some now. Of course, maybe all she needed was to hear how stupid her misgivings sounded when she said them out loud. "I need to make a call to the office of attorney Bentley Abernathy in Austin," she said.

"I have no authorization for you to make a long-distance call," the man's voice said.

"How do I get authorization?" Jamie asked.

"You need to speak with either Chief Kelly or Miss Montgomery."

Jamie put down the phone then fumed for a while, walking back and forth and working up a head of steam. Then she headed back downstairs, anger coursing through her veins, ready for a confrontation.

Square-shouldered, she made her way through the boxes and bustle. People with startled faces were stepping to one side, allowing her to pass. When she reached Miss Montgomery, she said, "I need to speak with you."

Jamie had expected a reprimand. Instead the housekeeper nodded. "Let's go into the library," she said.

Jamie followed her. Every eye in the room was on them as they crossed the hall.

In the library, Miss Montgomery closed the heavy double doors. She turned and, wearing an uncharacteristically benevolent look, said, "I understand that you tried to make a phone call."

"My, word certainly travels fast around here," Jamie observed.

"I know you are upset, Jamie, and you have every right to be. I am so sorry. I should have explained things more carefully."

Taken aback by the woman's unexpected apology, Jamie studied Miss Montgomery's face, trying to judge her sincerity. "I was told that I had to have permission to make a phone call," Jamie said. "Okay, I request permission to make a phone call. I want to call the secretary in the legal office where the contract with that all-important *privacy clause* was created. She already knows who I am and why I'm here."

"The contract states that you are not to have any outside contacts while you are here at the ranch," Miss Montgomery said. "Surely you can understand that. Nowadays so many telephones are equipped with caller ID."

"But Lenora already knows that I'm here," Jamie insisted.

"But someone else might be listening on the line. I'm sorry, dear, but I just can't allow it. I should have reminded you that communication of any sort violated the contract, but I didn't want to upset you—not in your condition. Pregnancy is such an emotional time under usual circumstances, and your circumstances are unusual."

For a minute Jamie thought the housekeeper was going to put a hand on her arm and took a step backward.

"The Hartmann name is so well-known, Jamie," Miss Montgomery continued. "Surely you can see how careful we must be. But instead of making friends with you, as I should have done, I have isolated you. That was cruel of me. I can see that now. Could we just start all over again? I will be completely up front with you from this time forward."

Miss Montgomery was doing her best to sound sincere. The expression on her face was hopeful.

"Okay," Jamie agreed. "For starters, what about my address book? You took it, didn't you, to make it more difficult for me to contact someone? And I've completed six lessons from the correspondence course and have yet to receive any sort of grade or comment from the professor. You never mailed them, did you?"

"Perhaps the professor is waiting until you have completed all the lessons," the housekeeper suggested, her tone less conciliatory than before.

"Am I even enrolled in the course?" Jamie demanded. "Or did you somehow manage to get a copy of the lessons just so you could keep me busy and I'd have less time to ponder the fact that I am being treated like a criminal in a prison? Come to think of it, the check I wrote to pay for the course has yet to show up on my bank statement."

Without waiting for a response, Jamie turned heel and, with a pounding heart, marched from the room.

Back in her room, she opened a desk drawer and pulled out her copy of the contract she had signed. Yes, if she read the legalese carefully, she could see that she was indeed prohibited from having any contact with individuals or entities not directly involved with her day-to-day life on the Hartmann Ranch. No contact at all. Lenora had said as much when they went over the contract, but Jamie had not understood how absolute her isolation was going to be.

Probably calling the secretary of the attorney who had drawn up such a document had been a stupid idea anyway. Bentley Abernathy was the Hartmann family's attorney. His job—and that of his secretary—was to look after the Hartmanns' interests. Jamie realized that she should have hired her own attorney and had him or her look over the contract before she signed it. As it was, she didn't have anyone looking after her interests. Not anyone at all.

Even if she wanted to contact a lawyer after the fact and ask about her legal options, she would not be allowed to do so. Moreover, if she told someone that she was carrying a child for Amanda Hartmann, she forfeited her right to all that money, which was the whole point of her entering into the arrangement in the first place.

But if Amanda planned to pass the baby off as one to which she herself had given birth, security became an even greater issue, Jamie realized. Probably Amanda wanted to make sure the surrogate mother of her child didn't call some tabloid and offer to sell her story for more money than Amanda planned to pay her.

Jamie put the contract back in the drawer, wishing she had never heard of the Hartmann family.

The week before Christmas, Jamie woke to the sound of howling wind. She took Ralph into the backyard but decided that she would forgo her morning walk. She looked over the assigned readings for her next correspondence-course lesson, trying to decide if she would bother with them. She didn't even have copies of the lessons she had completed. She had her notes, however. If she did decide to retype them and complete the additional lessons, she could deliver the completed course in person to the professor in Austin—after she had served out her sentence on this godforsaken ranch.

For now, though, she gave herself over to watching a morning's worth of mindless television programs.

At noon her lunch arrived. As Jamie placed the tray on the coffee table, she felt a strange sensation in her abdomen. Like a bird fluttering around inside of her.

She put a hand on her stomach. But the sensation had ceased.

She waited a minute to see if it was going to happen again. For several seconds she waited. Maybe it was just her stomach protesting its emptiness. Or a muscle spasm.

She sat down, switched on the television, and took a bite of the turkey sandwich.

Then it happened again.

"Oh, my gosh!" she said, placing both hands over her protruding belly.

The fluttering lasted longer this time, for several seconds. And Jamie knew what she was feeling. It was *life*.

Of course, the baby had been alive all along, but she hadn't felt it before. She recalled the word that Mary Millicent and Nurse Freda had used. *Quickening*.

She couldn't bring herself to pick up the sandwich for a second bite. She just sat there, staring at nothing.

For a long time she sat there. Not thinking. Not eating. Finally, though, she picked up the sandwich and took another bite. And another. Then she pushed the tray away and headed for the bedroom, where she wrapped herself up in a blanket and lay across the bed.

She slept for a time, waking to the sound of the wind, which seemed even more ferocious than before. An afternoon walk was out of the question. She stretched and was trying to decide what to do with the rest of the day, when it happened again. Movement. More pronounced than before. She imagined a tiny arm or leg moving about. A tiny human being flexing its muscles. She wanted to yell at it to stop. If it was going to start moving around like this, there was no way she could continue ignoring what was going on inside of her.

She buried her face in a pillow and began to cry. She wanted the baby to go away. She didn't want it moving around in there. But she didn't want it to die either, and if it went away it would die.

Dear God in heaven, what have I done?

Ralph jumped up on the bed and began licking her face. She put her arms around him and buried her face in his coarse hair. "What are we going to do, Ralphie? What *are* we going to do?"

Finally, she calmed herself, feeling a bit ashamed that she had overreacted in such a way. It was time for her to face up and grow up. Of course the baby moved. It was supposed to move, supposed to grow, and eventually get itself born. She had put off dealing emotionally with her situation long enough. She was now five months' *pregnant*. A small living creature was swimming around in her uterus. A baby. A human baby.

She was not to think of it as *her* baby. She had signed a contract saying that in exchange for a handsome amount of money, she agreed to forfeit her legal rights to the child. In the eyes of the law, he or she would belong to Amanda Hartmann and Toby Travis. Biologically, she was the mother, however. And Toby was the biological father.

Unless what Mary Millicent had said about Sonny was true.

Which was too far-fetched to be believed.

Jamie wondered what life would be like for the child she was carrying, other than being raised amid extreme wealth and never wanting for anything. She did not doubt that Amanda and Toby would love the child. She did worry, however, that much of the child's upbringing would be left to Miss Montgomery or a nursemaid while Amanda, with Toby at her side, traveled about saving souls and raising money for political candidates handpicked by her Alliance. And Jamie wondered how she would feel if the child that she was now carrying followed in Amanda's footsteps and someday told a national television audience how God wanted them to live and think and vote. Would she feel proud? Or would it make her squirm?

That night, it was Jamie who initiated the middle-of-the-night visit with Mary Millicent. She crept down the hall to the chapel, then she pushed open the hidden door, felt around for the light switch, and climbed the bare wooden stairs to the first of the two tower rooms. A dim light glowed from behind the curtain that divided the room. She slipped behind the curtain and stared down at the emaciated face of the unfortunate young man lying there. All the family riches had not protected him from grave misfortune.

She pulled back the covers, lifted one of his hands, and placed it on her belly. "Is that your baby in there?" she whispered.

Then she leaned forward and softly kissed his lips.

He had been greatly loved, she thought as she backed away from the bed. Perhaps she would have loved him, too, had she had a chance to know him. She wondered if, in spite of being the heir to a vast fortune or maybe because of it, Sonny Hartmann had also known what it was like to be an outsider.

She climbed the stairs to Mary Millicent's room. Once she had reached the top, she stood for a time, allowing her eyes to become accustomed to the darkness. The sound of soft snoring reached her ears. She waited until her eyes adjusted and she could make out the outline of the bed, then tiptoed across the room. "Mary Millicent," she said, leaning over the sleeping form.

When the old woman did not respond, Jamie felt around for her hand. "Hey, Mary Millicent, it's Jamie, the girl from downstairs."

"I know who you are," Mary Millicent said in a hoarse whisper. "Did the witch see you?"

"No," Jamie said, turning on a bedside lamp. "I wanted to tell you that the baby moved today."

"You came all the way up here to tell me that?"

"Well, yes," Jamie said, helping the woman to a sitting position. "You asked me if I had felt any quickening, and I thought you might be interested to know that it had, indeed, occurred."

"Well, it was bound to happen unless the baby was dead," Mary Millicent said, struggling to swing her legs over the side of the bed. Jamie helped get her situated and extracted her bunched-up nightgown from underneath her hips.

"So, this is where you live," said Jamie, taking a look around the room. Like the room below, a pair of narrow windows was set in each of the room's eight sides. The floor was bare wood, and the walls were painted white. A rack of clothing and a chest of drawers stood by the stairwell railing. A shelf held a large television set. In the middle of the room was a round mahogany table with claw feet and two matching chairs. On the other side of the bed were a sink, a portable toilet, a trash can, and a rectangular table that held a box of adult diapers, a large plastic container of wipes, a stack of towels, and another of washcloths. Jamie was surprised to see an old-fashioned wood-and-wicker wheelchair parked by the head of the bed. Then she remembered Mary Millicent's claim that Miss Montgomery thought she could not walk. The nurse, too.

"Do you really use the wheelchair?" she asked.

Mary Millicent nodded. "All the time."

"Well, aren't you the sly one!" Jamie said.

"You got it, sister," Mary Millicent said with pride, and offered Jamie a high five.

Jamie sat on the bed beside the old woman. "How long have you lived up here?" she asked.

"I don't know. Could be one year or a hundred for all I know. They started putting me up here just when there were guests in the house—after Amanda got all upset when I showed up at a dinner party wearing just a hula skirt. I think someone really important was there—like a king or a movie star. Then I was sick for a long time and couldn't move or talk, and for a long time after that I was too weak to walk. But when I got stronger again, I jus' kept on pretending to be weak. Sometimes when Amanda and Gus are here, they have one of the Mexican gardeners carry me downstairs so I can have dinner with them in the dining room. I like having men carry me. I like the feel of their muscles and the smell of their sweat," she said with a sigh. "Sometimes I reach down and pat their pee-pee. You should see the look on their faces when I do that. They don't know if they should scream or laugh. I miss doing it with a man. I miss it a lot."

Jamie listened to Mary Millicent's outpouring in open-mouthed wonder. She didn't know if she should put her fingers in her ears or laugh out loud. When Mary Millicent finally stopped, Jamie said, "You are one outrageous old woman."

Mary Millicent put her hands on her hips. "Well, what of it?"

Jamie had to laugh. *What of it, indeed?* She put a hand over her mouth, fearful of making too much noise, but continued to laugh, her shoulders shaking with mirth. And then she stopped abruptly, putting a hand to her belly. She grabbed Mary Millicent's hand and placed it under hers. "Can you feel it?"

"Yep. Feels like the kid has the hiccups."

"Isn't that just wonderful?" Jamie said in awe.

"Not particularly."

Jamie put her arms around Mary Millicent Tutt Hartmann, retired evangelist and outrageous old lady, and said, "Oh, but you're wrong. Baby hiccups are wonderful, and so are you."

Chapter Seventeen

THE NEXT DAY, there was a midafternoon knock on her door.

Amanda and Toby were standing in the hallway, their arms full of gift-wrapped packages. "Merry Christmas," they said in unison.

Jamie returned their greeting and invited them in. Ralph backed away from the door, unsure of what his reaction should be to the two strangers invading his domain.

Amanda paused and looked around the room. "You've changed things quite a bit," she observed, her tone a bit less warm.

"Yes," Jamie agreed, somewhat surprised that Amanda even recalled how the rooms had been decorated. She started to say that she hoped Amanda didn't mind her changes but stopped herself. What happened in these two rooms was the only part of her life over which she had any control, and she wasn't going to apologize.

There were a few seconds of awkward silence before Toby said, "You're looking well, Jamie."

"Thank you," she said.

"We brought you a few gifts," Amanda said as she and Toby placed the packages on the table.

"That's very kind of you," Jamie responded. "Won't you sit down?"

Amanda and Toby both seated themselves on the sofa. "Mostly the gifts are things you might need when you start your new life," Amanda said with an airy wave toward the packages. "We wanted you to have something to open Christmas morning. I know how lonesome it must be for you here—especially during the holidays—and I feel terrible that I haven't been able to spend more time with you. I so enjoyed our little visit when I was here last month."

What a handsome couple they were, Jamie thought with genuine admiration. Toby was muscular and fit, his hair a bit lighter than it had been last summer, his skin tan in spite of the season. Both were wearing jeans, turtleneck sweaters, and expensive-looking western boots. They sat close to each other, their thighs touching, and holding hands. Amanda's fleecy white sweater was long and loose-fitting, making it impossible for Jamie to judge whether she was expecting a child or not. She considered inquiring about her condition but decided against it. The woman was either pregnant or she was not. It was none of Jamie's concern.

Ralph crept toward the two guests warily, his tail wagging. Toby reached out and scratched his head. "What an unusual dog," he said. "What kind is it?"

"Just a mutt, but a very sweet one," Jamie said.

"Freda says that you and the baby are both doing splendidly," Amanda said, clasping her hands together and smiling broadly. "Freda now has five obstetrical patients, and we decided that it was time that we buy sonogram equipment for the clinic. The sonograms will be sent by computer to the university medical center in Amarillo to be read by an expert, like the X-rays she takes. So many more things are possible now with computers."

Jamie nodded.

"Actually, I want you to go to the clinic tomorrow so Freda can do a sonogram on you. I can't wait to actually *see* the baby. Knowing that I will be a mother once again has helped heal my broken heart and filled it once again with joy. You can't imagine the heartbreak of losing a child, Jamie. It is the worst thing that can happen to a woman."

Jamie thought that was a strange thing for Amanda to be saying to the woman she was paying to give up a child.

"Toby and I pray for you every day," Amanda said. Beside her Toby was smiling his agreement.

Jamie was surprised when Amanda rose from the sofa and came to kneel in front of her and take her hands. "We pray for you, dearest Jamie, not just because you are carrying our child," Amanda said, "but because we care about you and want you to feel good about what you are doing."

Jamie felt herself falling under Amanda's spell, as she had when the two of them were sitting on the window seat in the library. Amanda's voice was so soothing. Her eyes as clear and blue as sapphires. Her hair smooth and shining. Her lips moist and full. Amanda was lovely and seemed so very sincere.

Jamie wanted to put her head on Amanda's shoulder and feel the comfort of her embrace. And, as though the woman could read her mind, she felt Amanda drawing her close and placing a cheek against hers. Jamie closed her eyes and relished this unexpected moment of human contact.

"You're very lonely, aren't you?" Amanda said softly into her ear. "But you must remember, my darling Jamie, that you are never alone. You can always confide in our Lord. He is with you always and wants to hear your prayers. He will lead you to the other side of these lonely times and enrich your life for having so dutifully fulfilled your mission here. It is His wish that this very special baby be born. You must remember that always. You can put your trust in Him. Always, my darling girl. *Always*."

Jamie watched with regret as Amanda rose to her feet. She rose with her, feeling a bit light-headed. Not wanting the moment to end, she asked, "Will I ever see you again afterward?"

"After the baby is born? No, dear child, but I will think of you and pray for you ever single day of my life," Amanda said, taking Jamie's face in her hands and looking deeply into her eyes. "And there will be times when you actually *feel* my thoughts and prayers and well wishes. We are irrevocably connected in this life, you and I, and in the next we will also be. Don't ever forget that, Jamie. Not ever." Amanda kissed Jamie's cheek and then her lips and offered her a last smile before holding her hand out to her husband.

Jamie watched the door close behind them and felt as though all the life and air had gone out of the room with them. With Amanda.

Jamie stood there for the longest time, like a statue. Or a person who had forgotten how to move and think.

Nurse Freda was like a child with a brand-new toy as she showed off the new equipment to Jamie. "It's as good as anything you'd find in any obstetrician's office in Amarillo," she said proudly.

Lying flat on her back on the examining table, Jamie was a bit startled at how round her belly was. Freda listened to the baby's heartbeat then poked around for a bit. Then she covered Jamie's abdomen with a gel that felt as though it had just come out of a refrigerator and began moving a paddle slowly back and forth over it. Jamie was able to watch the images on the screen. It took a while for her to make out the baby. It was moving languidly in its dark little aquatic world, oblivious to spying eyes. Bentley Abernathy had said she would not be allowed to see the baby or even to know its sex, but she was seeing it now after a fashion. And just in case Freda didn't know all the rules, she asked, "Can you tell what sex it is?"

"Looks like a boy to me," the nurse said, pointing to the screen. "There's his scrotum right there. Yep, a healthy, normal baby boy, all body parts present and accounted for. Amanda and her husband are going to get themselves a fine little fellow."

She picked up a towel and wiped the gel from Jamie's abdomen. "I'm finished. You can get dressed now. And don't forget to pee in a cup. I'll see you next week."

Midafternoon, Freda called the radiologist in Amarillo. "Have you had a chance to look at that prenatal ultrasound yet?"

"It's on my screen now. Looks like a good baby. Male. No discernible anomalies."

Freda called Amanda at the ranch house. "Congratulations," she said joyously. "The baby is a normal, healthy boy."

The day before Christmas, while Jamie was walking Ralph, she watched while the Hartmann plane banked overhead and landed on the ranch landing strip.

That evening she crept down the hall toward the second-floor gallery. Taking great care to remain in the shadows, she moved around the gallery until she could see into the dining hall. Symphonic music wafted softly from hidden speakers. The table was resplendent with crystal and candles. Seated around the table were Amanda and her husband, Miss Montgomery, Mary Millicent in her wheelchair, Nurse Freda, Chief Kelly, and a man Jamie recognized from the pictures in the library. Gus Hartmann had come to the ranch for Christmas.

The next morning, when she took Ralph out into the backyard, Jamie heard singing floating across the frigid morning air—many voices singing "Away in a manger, no crib for a bed . . ." Harmonious, joyous, well-rehearsed voices singing so beautifully that she had to stop and close her eyes. A shiver that had nothing to do with the cold brought chill bumps to the skin on her arms.

It was Christmas. Always before she had been with someone she loved on this day. Memories poured over her. The large tree in the high-ceilinged living room on Galveston Island. Her mother playing carols on the upright piano. Her sister Ginger home from college. The four of them singing together. The Christmas tree at Granny's house had never been large, but they lovingly decorated it with mostly homemade ornaments. And they sang along with the carols on the radio—including the same carols now being sung by the hidden choir.

Jamie sang along. "It came upon a midnight clear,/ That glorious song of old . . ." And at just that instant, the baby moved as though to remind Jamie that she was not alone. She carried life within her. Beside her was Ralph with a stick in his mouth, his tail wagging in anticipation. And there was Mary Millicent in her tower. Jamie would creep up there tonight so the two of them could sing Christmas carols together. Jamie glanced upward. The narrow tower windows were golden in the morning sun.

She threw the stick for Ralph, then walked over to the far side of the yard, climbed into the low branches of an oak tree, and peeked over the high brick wall. Dressed in crimson robes, the carolers were standing under the portico. She recognized many of them—the young woman from the ranch store, Anita the cook, the man from the greenhouse, one of the security officers.

Jamie could not see the front door, but the carolers were all looking in that direction. Amanda and Gus Hartmann would be standing there, and Toby, smiles on all their faces as they graciously acknowledged the devotion of their faithful vassals. And probably Miss Montgomery would be hovering nearby, the steadfast family retainer, like a figure from a Dickens novel.

Back in her room, Jamie made herself a cup of hot chocolate and, with the radio tuned to a station playing Christmas music, tried to make a ceremony out of opening the presents that Amanda and Toby had brought—gifts selected to help her start a new life. The first package was a bottle of French perfume cradled in a satin-lined box. Then she opened a box with a sterling silver compact in a leather pouch. The next box held a pink silk peignoir set. A sterling silver bud vase occupied the next box. The last one contained a handsome leather billfold.

The billfold would come in handy, but Jamie found the other gifts puzzling. They had nothing to do with the sort of life she would be leading. Perhaps Amanda wanted her to have some pretty things to relieve the otherwise utilitarian life that most college students led. Or perhaps she had asked a secretary or servant to buy some gifts for a twenty-year-old female.

She put the gifts back in their boxes and stored them under the bed.

She waited until after dinner to visit Mary Millicent.

As soon as she opened the secret door, she heard voices. Her curiosity getting the best of her, she crept halfway up the stairs. The voices were coming from Mary Millicent's room.

She peered through the railing into Sonny's room, which was illuminated by the light from dozens of flickering candles. Candles were everywhere—on the windowsills, on the tabletops and bureau, set in trays on the floor—illuminating the still form on the bed.

Jamie wondered if Sonny was dead and the candles were part of a wake. But the catheter tube was still connected to its bag.

She knew that Amanda had done this and that she had sat with her son in the candlelight, holding his hand, kissing his lips, remembering Christmases past when he was a beautiful young man and had his whole life ahead of him.

Jamie wondered how long a person in his condition could be kept alive.

She climbed the last few stairs, tiptoed over to the bed, and touched Sonny's hand. She agreed with Mary Millicent. It was time for Amanda to let Sonny die, but she also understood why a mother might put off such a decision and instead pray for a miracle.

She had no doubt that Amanda had genuinely loved her son, who had apparently been a very nice young man. Jamie wondered if Sonny had really wanted to follow in his mother's footsteps. Not that there was anything wrong with that. Except she wondered how you know that other people's religion is wrong for them and that your own would be better. What if all God cared about was that people be good to one another?

Amazed at her own daring, Jamie carefully climbed the second staircase far enough to peek under the railing that guarded the stairwell. A small Christmas tree with twinkling lights stood in the middle of the table. Mary Millicent in her wheelchair was wearing a new sweater with the tags still on it. Sitting with her at the table were Amanda and Gus—her children. Gus was telling a story about their father, recalling the Christmas when he drove their brand-new pony cart right into the great hall. He had been wearing a Santa Claus hat and jingle bells were attached to the pony's harness.

Feeling very much the intruder, Jamie crept back down the stairs.

Chapter Eighteen

AFTER TUCKING THEIR mother into bed, Gus followed his sister down the stairs to Sonny's room. The room was incredibly beautiful with all the candles reflecting in the hundreds of diamond-shaped windowpanes.

Gus stood beside his sister at her son's bedside and watched while she stroked Sonny's forehead and spoke to him in a soothing voice, like a mother would talk to an infant in a crib. Suddenly Gus couldn't stand it anymore and grabbed Amanda's arm. "Let him go," he begged. "Please let him go. You promised that you would."

"It's already begun," she said. "Freda removed the feeding tube last week. She says that starvation is actually a very gentle way to die."

"How much longer will it take?" Gus asked, staring at his nephew.

"Not long," Amanda said, kissing Gus's cheek and stroking his back. "Aren't we lucky that the Lord allowed us to have this wonderful boy to know and love for twenty wonderful years? Just think of all those lovely memories. We have been blessed."

One of those memories came to Gus's mind. Sonny was racing ahead of him across the great hall and up the stairs on sturdy little legs, anxious to show off his new hamster that went round and round in its own little Ferris wheel. Beautiful Sonny, the sunlight streaming through the stained-glass windows highlighting his golden curls, looked over his shoulder and called out, "You're going to love him, Uncle Gus. His name is Brownie." Sonny waited at the top of the stairs for him and slipped his hand into his.

Gus had to pause and close his eyes for a moment to deal with the ache that filled his chest. And for an instant, he could feel that small, sweet, warm hand in his own. He had loved the boy Sonny without reservation—and the young man he had become, a young man who had shared his uncle's love for the ranch and wanted to live here always. Sonny had asked Gus to help him make his mother understand that he was not cut out to be an evangelist or to run an oil company or a political movement. He did not want to follow in anyone's footsteps. He wanted to be himself. And Gus had said yes, that he would side with him against Amanda, and remembered feeling amazement at how correct that decision seemed. Sonny wanted to be his own man. And that made Gus proud.

But Amanda refused even to discuss the matter, and less than a week after that conversation, Sonny had been reduced to a vegetable.

If Gus thought there was even the tiniest chance that there was a heaven and he would see Sonny again, he would become the devoutest of believers and give away all his worldly goods and wear rags like Saint Francis of Assisi. As it was, every single day he cursed the God that he didn't believe in for taking away that precious boy. And he had insisted on finding someone mortal to blame when maybe the accident had been just that. *Accidental.* No one's fault—except perhaps Amanda's goddamned God if he did happen to exist.

Amanda smoothed Sonny's hair from his forehead and planted a kiss there. "I love you, my darling," she told him. His face was gaunt, but she could still see the beautiful boy he had been—physically and spiritually. Everyone who saw him responded to his beauty. They wanted to be near him and bask in his smile, shake his hand. Her son had the power to save the world. After the accident, she hadn't been able to understand why God had let such a thing happen to him. Finally, she had given up trying and simply bowed before God, submitting herself completely to his will. It was the only way she could find peace. That was when God had pointed the way. He was calling Sonny home, but he had shown her the way to have Sonny's child. She would have another child to raise and adore. Yet, if an angel were to appear before her and tell her that she could have her son back if she would tear the baby from Jamie Long's belly and kill it with her bare hands, she would do it.

Amanda sighed. What must God think of her for having such thoughts? And she banished them from her mind.

Gus was standing beside her, his face buried in his hands. The poor darling. He had vowed never to return to the ranch as long as she kept Sonny like this but had relented when she told him it was time to say good-bye—

time for their boy to float up to heaven. But oh, how hard it was going to be not to have Sonny's warm, living skin to caress. His lips to kiss. His body to wash. His physical self would be lost to her.

She embraced her brother. Gus buried his face against her shoulder, his entire body shaking with sobs. She stroked his back and kissed the top of his head as she would a child's and told him that she loved him dearly and that they would always have each other. Then the two of them went around the room putting out the candles before making their way down the wooden staircase. They would have a nightcap before Amanda returned to watch over Sonny through the night.

The lights on the Christmas tree had been turned off, but its towering ghostly presence still dominated the great hall. Their footsteps echoed on the stone floor as they crossed to the library, where embers still glowed in the massive fireplace.

Gus turned on a lamp, threw a couple of logs on the fire, and stoked it a bit. Amanda seated herself on a leather sofa facing the fireplace and poured two glasses of sherry from a crystal decanter.

Gus sat beside her. Seated, he and his sister were almost the same height. He leaned back, making himself as comfortable as he could with his short legs jutting out in front of him. How he loved this room. For him, it was the heart of the house—the place where they had come after dinner when his father was still alive. In the winter, there was always a fire in the fireplace. He and his father would play chess, or he would play cards or checkers with Amanda while their parents read and enjoyed an after-dinner drink. Gus had always adored his sister, but after her marriage ended and she and Sonny came to live with him in Virginia, they had become even closer. Sometimes he found himself wishing that she wasn't his sister so that he could love her in other ways. As it was, however, their love was purer and deeper and would last a lifetime.

"To us," he said, lifting his glass.

"Yes, to us," Amanda said, taking a sip. "My darling Gus. How I love and count on you. We have survived so much together, and now, with Sonny soon to be lost to me, you are the only constant in my life. Of course, we'll still have Mother," she added somewhat dismissively, "but the mother I once loved and respected no longer resides in that woman's body. And there is Toby, my adorable playmate, and our diligent and faithful Montgomery, and all the other employees here on the ranch and in Virginia, and our staff at the Alliance for whom I feel lovingly responsible. But you are my rock. Only you."

His eyes misting over, Gus reached over and stroked her hair. "Thank you, my darling," he said. "You are far and away the most important person in my life."

Amanda leaned close and kissed him. Just a soft brush of her lips, but it left him light-headed. He took a sip of sherry then cleared his throat and said, "Mother seemed glad to see us."

"Perhaps. Poor Montgomery. Can you imagine putting up with Mother day in and day out? But with her unpredictable behavior and not knowing what trash is going to come out of her mouth, it's best this way. She has her television to watch, and I think she takes a perverse pleasure in giving poor Montgomery a hard time."

Gus put his glass on the side table and turned to face his sister. "There's something we need to talk about, Amanda," he said.

"Oh, dear," she said, affecting a pout. "You're using your stern voice."

"I have seen stories in several publications from supermarket tabloids to *Newsweek* that claim you and Toby are expecting a baby in April," Gus said.

"So?" Amanda said with a girlish smile. Then she actually giggled. "I've bought this little padded thing that looks quite authentic. I plan to start wearing it after Christmas. And I'm having some perfectly lovely maternity clothes made for me. In the meantime, I have opted for a loose, more ambiguous look."

"So you plan to pass this girl's baby off as your own?"

"It *is* my own baby," Amanda said. "I have a contract that says it is."

"Do you plan to pass this baby off as one to which you yourself gave birth?" he amended.

Amanda nodded. "You sound displeased. Would that bother you?" she asked.

"Is Toby the biological father of Jamie Long's baby?" Gus asked.

Amanda squared her shoulders. "Damn it, Gus. It is *not* Jamie Long's baby. It is *my* baby."

"Answer my question, Amanda," Gus said, his voice quite firm. "Is Toby the biological father of this baby?"

"What difference does it make?" she demanded.

"It could make a great deal of difference. When I first started hearing these rumors about your being pregnant, it occurred to me what your motivation might have been for keeping poor Sonny alive all this time when there is no hope of him ever recovering. After his accident, you were absolutely incapacitated by grief, refusing to leave his bedside, hardly eating anything, and putting your own health in jeopardy. And then all of a sudden you announce that God is great and you are going to get married. Don't play games with me, Amanda. If I am going to protect you, I need to know if Sonny is the father of the baby that now resides in the womb of Jamie Long."

"Of course, he is," she said, anger in her voice. She took a deep breath, downed the last of her sherry, and carefully put her glass on the table. Gus could see her mentally shifting gears. Anger was not her style.

She took his hand and leaned very close, her lovely scent filling his nostrils. For an instant, he thought she was going to kiss him again. She looked so beautiful in the firelight. Her skin glowing, her eyes glistening, her lips moist. "Just think, Gus, this baby is of *our* blood. A baby that will continue our mother's ministry and the Hartmann legacy. A baby for you and me to love and raise. He will be blessed by God, just like our Sonny was. And he will have the call. God has promised me. It will be like having Sonny back with us," she said. "Freda did a sonogram on Jamie. She is carrying a healthy baby boy. That's why I can let Sonny go. I will have his son to raise."

The son of his beloved Sonny. Gus closed his eyes, imagining the love he would feel for such a child, who would be beautiful and perfect and incredibly dear, just like Sonny. A child who would love him in that same sweet, uncomplicated way that Sonny had loved him.

"And what does Toby say about this plan?" he asked.

She shook her head. "He doesn't know. Of course, he realizes that I plan to assume the role of the baby's natural mother and agrees that it's better that way. Our people will more readily accept the baby if they think he is my flesh-and-blood son. Just think of the television ratings when we introduce him to the world," she said, clasping her hands together.

Gus realized that there was some rationale to this logic. Many of Amanda's flock had been followers of their mother before her. It would indeed mean a great deal to them if the baby was of the Tutt lineage and had entered the world with a birthright and would carry the Tutt ministry into the fourth generation. And the child would inherit the ranch and the family's vast oil and gas business. Gus could groom him to take over. Like he had once planned to do with Sonny. Perhaps the child would be more interested in the family business than Sonny had been. There was so much he could teach the boy, things that only he could impart.

But the warming of his heart to Amanda's scheme did not erase his anger at her. She should have told him from the beginning what she had in mind. He could have managed things better.

"How could Toby *not* know?" Gus asked.

"All it took was a little dry ice," she said with a shrug. "When the day came for the insemination procedure, Toby and I made a little game of it. I 'helped' him, so to speak. When we were finished, I carried the semen out of that little room while he got himself back together. But the contents of the vial I gave to the nurse came from Sonny. We left before Jamie arrived. It was quite simple, really."

"And how did you get Sonny's semen?"

Amanda folded her hands in her lap and looked down, avoiding her brother's gaze and his question.

"Freda helped me," she said, staring into the fire. "I did what I needed to do. Sonny would have wanted me to."

"I'm not so sure of that," Gus observed.

"Of course it is," Amanda insisted. "He will have a son to carry on for him. And we will have the next best thing to Sonny."

"Amanda, I don't think you've thought through the implications of what you have done."

She lifted her chin. "Such as?"

"Such as Jamie Long realizing that the baby you are publicly claiming to be your own natural-born child is no such thing."

"Jamie believes that I also am carrying a child," Amanda pointed out.

"A child that just happens to be born the same time as the one she is carrying? You are a very famous woman. The girl is going to see photographs of you and your miracle child everywhere. And read heartwarming stories about how God miraculously healed you with another child after your son's tragic accident even though you were postmenopausal or whatever. Those stories will say nothing about a second adopted child. There will only be *one* baby, Amanda, unless you and Toby plan to go out and find yourself a kid to adopt and raise alongside the miracle child."

"I'll tell Jamie that my baby was stillborn," Amanda said.

"And maybe she will believe you and be ever so happy that you have the baby she carried to raise. But she will still know that the baby you are claiming to be your own child is no such thing. She would know that you, Amanda Tutt Hartmann, who is supposed to be above reproach and has millions of followers who think that you have a direct line to God Almighty and can save their souls and heal their bodies and make their pitiful little lives seem worthwhile, you are living a lie. The girl could blackmail you, Amanda. Or sell her story to the media. And if all those millions of followers lose faith in you, they are not going to donate the money we need to elect our candidates to high office. The Alliance of Christian Voters would wither up and die. We wouldn't have friends anymore in Washington, and without the right people in Washington, the oil industry would suffer. We'd have to live at the ranch and feed out more cattle in those cruel, smelly feedlots you hate so much. Maybe we could turn the ranch house into a hunting lodge for rich, old cigar-chewing men—as long as the deer and quail population holds out, of course."

"Stop it," Amanda demanded, her beautiful face made hard and almost ugly with anger. "You are making too big of a thing out of this. Jamie Long signed a contract promising never to tell anyone about anything. She would have to give the money back if she ever told."

"Amanda, that girl could get twice as much from some tabloid for telling them that she is the biological mother of your baby."

"Then we would have to sue her and the tabloid for libel."

"And then there would be a trial with the whole world watching. The judge would order DNA tests on you and the baby and Jamie Long and Toby. Those tests would not only prove that Jamie Long is the biological mother of the child, but they would also show that the child is related to you, which offers only two possibilities as to its father—me or Sonny—which would certainly give rise to all sorts of unseemly speculation. That girl signed a contract with a legally married husband and wife, Amanda. She did not sign a contract with a woman and her dying son. Your actions have made that contract null and void. She could sue you not only for breech of contract but for the money she needs to raise the child."

"You don't know that any of that is going to happen," Amanda insisted. "Jamie is a dear girl, and she loves me. We have prayed together. It would never occur to her to cause trouble."

"You may be exactly right," Gus said in his most reasonable tone. "But how will she feel if she learns that you have lied to her? That the high and holy Amanda Hartmann has knowingly entered into a fraudulent contract?"

"Well, then, let's make a new contract and give her some more money to sign it."

"And what will you do if she says no?"

"The girl *loves* me," Amanda said emphatically, her chin set, her eyes wide. "She is not going to say no."

"You don't know that, Amanda. When she signed on for this gig, the idea of a baby was just an abstraction to her. It was just a way to make a lot of money. Now there's a living child moving around inside of her and all these maternal hormones racing around her body. If it had just been Toby's kid, it wouldn't have been such a big deal if the girl decided to renege on the deal. But now the equation is different. It is not Toby's child. It's Sonny's."

"So, what are you saying, Gus?" Amanda asked, her eyes narrowing.

Gus paused a few seconds before answering. "That you don't need to worry about anything," he said, patting her hand. "I'll see that nothing goes wrong. You will have your baby."

"Thank you," she said and kissed him once again, then held out her empty glass for a refill.

When Jamie crept back up to the tower, the candles had been extinguished in Sonny's room, the light over his bed dimmed.

Mary Millicent's room was dark. Jamie waited for her eyes to adjust then tiptoed over to the bed. "Are you asleep?" she asked.

"Not unless I'm dreaming."

"I thought you might like to sing some Christmas carols," Jamie said, switching on the bedside lamp. "I came earlier but your children were here. Did you have a nice evening with them?"

"Of course not. My children have ruined my life."

"That's a terrible thing to say about your own son and daughter," Jamie said.

"I say terrible things about them because they are terrible people, and don't you forget it, girl."

Mary Millicent grabbed hold of Jamie's arm. "Help me sit up," she demanded, and Jamie obliged, propping up pillows behind the old woman's frail body.

"Terrible people," Mary Millicent repeated. "And if you don't do exactly what they say, they'll lock you up in a tower, too. Or they will have you killed, like they did with Sonny's father. Amanda went crying to Gus that Sonny's father wouldn't let her have Sonny all the time and wouldn't let her change his name to Hartmann, and then someone shot the man in the head," Mary Millicent said, making an imaginary pistol with her hand and pointing it to her temple. "I wonder how long it will be until Amanda gets tired of her new husband and asks her brother to get rid of him. And don't you look at me like that, young lady," she said, shaking a finger at Jamie. "I may be as old as dirt and have a few screws loose, but I know what I know. Maybe it's my fault Amanda and Gus turned out the way they did. I raised them like they were God's anointed, like they could do no wrong. And now God is punishing me. But you know what? I wish that God would just strike us all dead. Me, Amanda, Gus, and Sonny, too, and put an end to all things Hartmann. God should just open up the earth and let this whole damned ranch and everyone who lives here drop right down into hell. Except for Sonny, of course. Sonny should go to heaven. *Just Sonny.* Yes, I'm going to pray for God to do that—to drop all of us except Sonny into hell, so if I were you I would be hightailing it out of here. And when that baby of yours is born, don't you ever tell him how he came to be. Don't tell him that his father was a dead boy being kept alive past his time. You just tell him his daddy was killed in a car wreck or in some war."

Jamie took a step backward.

"Hey, where are you going, girl?" Mary Millicent demanded. "I'm not through talking yet. And I want to sing Christmas carols."

She grabbed a plastic water pitcher and threw it at Jamie. "You come back here, girl. You come back here right this minute or I'll tell the witch and Amanda that you've been coming up here to see me. I'll tell them to kill your dog."

Jamie latched the door to her apartment behind her and pulled the sofa in front of the door. And put the coffee table on top of the sofa.

Angrily she wiped her cheeks. No tears, she told herself. She had gotten herself into this mess. She had to see it through to the end or . . .

Or what?

She knelt and petted her dog, who was confused by her late-night activity. He became more confused as she began to pace. He sat there watching her go back and forth, like a spectator at a tennis match, occasionally offering a whimper to express his disapproval.

She needed to think.

Or maybe not so much to think as to organize all the disparate thoughts that were tumbling around in her brain. To sort things out. To work through her confusion.

Not that she believed everything that Mary Millicent said. After all, the woman was afflicted with senile dementia. Or Alzheimer's. Paranoia. Or maybe she was just plain nuts.

But not all the time. Sometimes Mary Millicent seemed perfectly lucid. Which didn't necessarily mean that she was telling the truth.

Was Sonny Hartmann really the father of the baby inside of her, she agonized. And was Gus Hartmann some sort of underworld figure who could arrange for people to be murdered?

Long after Amanda had excused herself and gone upstairs to bed, Gus sat staring at the glowing embers, sipping sherry and making plans. Just to be on the safe side, he'd have Montgomery destroy the girl's copy of the contract. He didn't want her showing it to anyone or it falling into the wrong hands.

After the baby was born, the girl would be followed when she drove away from the ranch in her grandmother's car.

No one would ever know what happened to her. She would simply vanish from the earth. Probably no one would even file a missing person's report.

When Freda said it was time, Gus followed his sister up the wooden stairs, this time for the deathwatch. It was dark outside, and the candles had been lit once again. Montgomery was already there with Freda. Kelly joined them for a while then walked over to Sonny's bed and offered a military salute. When she turned to leave, her face was covered with tears.

One of the gardeners—a burly man named Enrique—brought Mary Millicent's wheelchair down the stairs to Sonny's room and then carried Mary Millicent herself, which made Gus feel acutely inadequate. With his stubby legs, it was all he could do to get himself up and down the steep stairs.

They seated themselves in front of the bed and waited while Sonny's respirations grew farther and farther apart and progressively shallower. Gus found himself holding his own breath while waiting for Sonny's next one.

On and on it went. For hours, it seemed. Each time Gus was sure that he was gone, Sonny would take another breath.

He tried to convince himself that what was about to happen was, in a sense, after the fact. The living force that had been a wonderfully kind and gentle boy was already gone from Sonny's body and had been since the day of the accident. Nevertheless, as long as his nephew's flesh was warm and his heart was beating, the still form lying there on the bed represented Sonny to him.

Gus had surprised himself by agreeing to be here. But if his sister wanted him with her, how could he say no? He needed Amanda's love more than he needed life itself. More so now than ever before.

Amanda asked Freda to lead them in singing "Amazing Grace." Mary Millicent's quavery, old voice rose above the rest. At the end of that hymn, Mary Millicent said they must sing Sonny's favorite hymn and began singing,

> A mighty fortress is our God,
> A bulwark never failing;
> Our helper, He amid the flood
> Of mortal ills prevailing . . .

Gus remembered the words to every verse. He was, after all, the son, grandson, and brother of evangelists, and actually it felt good to sing the familiar words from his childhood. He moved his chair close to his mother's wheelchair so they could harmonize, as they had done so often all those years ago.

Suddenly they realized that Sonny's breathing had stopped. Freda put her fingers to his neck. Then she kissed his forehead, put her hands to her face, and began to sob.

Gus and Amanda helped their mother to her feet. She kissed her grandson's lips and stroked his hair and face. "Good-bye, my poor little Sonny boy," she whispered in his ear. "You can go be an angel now."

Then Gus kissed Sonny's lips and chin and forehead. And his eyes. His hands. His silent heart. He felt as though his own heart were bursting inside his chest.

Amanda lingered, caressing her son's face. "Take good care of my baby, Lord," she implored. "Take him to your breast and love him for eternity."

"Amen," Gus said.

He envied his sister her faith. How nice it would be to think of Sonny in a bright warm place with love all around.

Jamie awoke to the sound of the wind—a howling wind that sounded like a horde of enormous creatures enraged because they could not force the stone fortress from its foundation. She glanced at her clock and realized it was morning—a very dark morning.

She dressed in layers and pulled on her coat. "Let's get this over with," she told Ralph.

She was surprised to see Miss Montgomery, Nurse Freda, and Kelly coming out of the housekeeper's apartment and heading in the direction of the great hall. Jamie waited on the bottom step as they walked past her, the expressions on their faces solemn. Miss Montgomery and Kelly acknowledged Jamie's presence with perfunctory nods. The nurse seemed not to notice her.

Outside the cold took Jamie's breath away. As soon as Ralph had found just the right spot to relieve himself, he came racing back up the steps, obviously eager to go back inside.

Her breakfast tray was waiting outside her door. She carried it inside and, telling Ralph she would be right back, headed down the corridor toward the chapel. She pushed open the hidden door and climbed the wooden stairs. The room where Sonny had been was empty, the bed stripped.

She thought of the little windswept cemetery with its iron fence. Soon Sonny Hartmann would be laid to rest in that sad, lonely place.

Chapter Nineteen

"MY GOODNESS—seven months," Freda said as she palpated Jamie's abdomen. "Time flies, doesn't it?"

Jamie didn't bother to respond. If she had, she would have disagreed. For her time dragged by like a brick harnessed to a snail.

She lay quietly while Freda continued her examination. "You're doing fine, sugar," the nurse said as she helped Jamie to a sitting position. "Do you have any questions?"

"Not really," Jamie said.

"Well, you should. Your due date is still two months away, but sometimes babies come early. I want you to call me at the first sign of labor or if your water breaks or even if it just begins to dribble some. Or sometimes the first sign of impending labor is when the mucus plug is expelled, which always has some blood mixed in. No cause for alarm. But whether it's labor pains or your water breaking or passing the mucus plug, I want you to have Montgomery get in touch with me. Day or night."

"Then what happens?" Jamie asked.

"Hard to predict. Even lean girls like you with great muscle tone usually take a while with their first baby. I'll keep you as comfortable as possible throughout, but it won't be a walk in the park. You know that, don't you?"

Jamie nodded.

"Afterward, you'll be drowsy from the pain medication and bleeding quite a bit," Freda explained. "You'll need to stay here at the clinic for several hours so I can keep an eye on you and then you can recuperate over at the ranch house for a couple of days."

When she was finished at the clinic, Jamie walked over to the security office. Lester must have been watching for her. The door opened, and he walked over to his truck. "You walking or riding?" he asked.

"Walking," she said and headed toward the stretch of road that led to the ranch house. She settled into a brisk pace then took a deep breath of the cold air, willing it to clear her head of all but pertinent thoughts. As her grandmother would have said, it was time for her to fish or cut bait. She needed to figure out how she was going to navigate herself through the next two months of her life.

It was *not* going to be easy.

Jamie still had no qualms about the practice of surrogate motherhood per se. Her disillusionment began when she realized that trust was not to be a part of her relationship with Amanda and her husband. And Jamie had always found it odd that the baby was going to be born on an isolated ranch in the middle of the Texas Panhandle. Amanda had gone to such lengths and expense to have this baby. Why would she allow it to be born in such a remote location without an anesthesiologist, obstetrician, and pediatrician in attendance? To some extent, Jamie had been able to put aside such concerns when she met Freda and saw the clinic. Freda was a certified midwife and no stranger to delivering babies. Deliveries sometimes turned into true medical emergencies, however. Why take the risk? Why not have the baby delivered in a hospital in Amarillo?

There was only one rationale that Jamie could see for having the baby at the ranch. If the baby were delivered in a hospital, she could screw up the whole deal by refusing to sign the adoption papers and simply walk out the door with the baby in her arms. Legally no one could stop her. At the ranch, she knew that the baby would be whisked away the minute it was born. Even if she refused to sign the papers, she knew that she would never be allowed to see the baby, much less leave with it.

Of course, if Amanda really was having a baby herself, it shouldn't matter all that much if Jamie backed out of the deal—unless the baby she carried was Amanda's grandchild.

God, it was all so confusing. At times her brain felt as though it had turned into mush.

Just have the baby and leave, she told herself. The words had become her mantra as she walked up and down dirt trails and gravel roads, as she paced up and down her living room, as she ate her solitary meals and lay sleepless in her bed.

There was nothing she could do to change the terms to which she had agreed. And she didn't really want to do anything to jeopardize the life she had planned for herself. The child she carried was Amanda's child and *not* her own, she told herself for the umpteenth time. She didn't want a child at this point in her life. She wanted a chance to live for herself.

Except that Mary Millicent possessed a passkey left over from the days when she was the chatelaine of Hartmann Ranch and had come tiptoeing into Jamie's corner of the castle. And the things Mary Millicent had told her made her afraid.

But Mary Millicent was a crazy old woman who disliked her own children, Jamie reminded herself. How could she possibly put any credence in her tales?

She remembered Lenora's warning that powerful people have methods of getting their own way and that if Jamie signed the contract, she must be absolutely committed to upholding her end of the bargain and never looking back.

Just have the baby and leave. That was the only safe and sensible thing to do.

She tried to imagine what would happen following the baby's birth. After she had signed away her legal rights to the child, Miss Montgomery or Freda probably would take him to Amanda.

How would she receive the money owed to her, Jamie wondered. And how soon after the delivery would she feel well enough and strong enough to leave? Not days. No way was she waiting around here for days. Jamie wanted to have her car packed, gassed up, and waiting for her in front of the clinic. With Ralph waiting in Freda's office.

She imagined herself telling Miss Montgomery that she had decided to leave. *Now.* This very afternoon. After all, the housekeeper had no legal jurisdiction over her. She couldn't lock her up in the tower and chain her to a bed until she delivered the child.

Except that was exactly what Jamie was afraid of.

Just have the baby and leave, she told herself once again as she arrived at the security gate. Ralph darted under it and stood waiting on the opposite side. Lester slowed as he approached and pointed the opener at the gate.

As soon as the gate had swung open a few feet, Jamie strode through.

When she reached the portico, she climbed the steps and went inside without bothering to wave at Lester.

It was well past lunchtime. Her tray would be waiting for her. But instead of returning to her apartment, she marched down the corridor to Miss Montgomery's apartment, where the housekeeper usually spent the early part of the afternoon.

Jamie knocked on the door and waited.

The housekeeper opened the door. Jamie could hear the voices of soap-opera characters dealing with their daily allotment of crises.

"What is it, Jamie?" Miss Montgomery asked in a reasonably pleasant tone.

"How will I be paid after the baby is born?"

Miss Montgomery frowned. "I'm not sure."

"Well, I need to know," Jamie demanded. "I want it taken care of as soon as the baby is born. I don't plan to stay very long afterward."

"I will inquire and let you know," Miss Montgomery said, already pushing the door closed.

Jamie put her hand on the door. "And I want my car brought back over here. I want to start packing things and loading them into the car."

"Isn't it a little early for that?" the housekeeper asked.

"I want to be ready to leave when the time comes."

"I will see if that is possible," Miss Montgomery said.

Jamie shook her head. "I want the car brought over here *this afternoon*," she said, making her point by carefully enunciating each word.

Miss Montgomery's eyes narrowed.

"I would like to know about the money by tomorrow," Jamie continued. "I want it wired to my bank in Austin as soon as I give birth, and I need official documentation that arrangements have been made for the payment and also for the annual stipend I am to receive."

"I will see what I can do," the housekeeper said curtly.

Jamie turned and headed back down the hallway, Ralph hurrying along behind her. She waited until she was halfway up the back stairs before allowing herself to breathe.

As she ate her lunch, she went over her conversation with the housekeeper. Maybe Miss Montgomery didn't know how or when Jamie would be paid because no arrangements had yet been made. Maybe arrangements were never going to be made.

And what if Amanda wasn't pregnant at all?

"Stop it!" Jamie yelled at herself.

Ralph jerked awake and began whimpering. Jamie opened her arms, and he jumped up beside her on the sofa then crawled onto what was left of her lap. She put her arms around him and buried her face against his neck. "Everything's okay," she lied. "We'll always be together, you and me. I'll always take care of you."

Once she had terminated the conversation with Jamie, Ann Montgomery went back to her soap opera. But even though her favorite character was trapped in an abandoned mine shaft, she found herself wondering if she should call Gus and tell him about Jamie's demands.

Gus depended on her to manage things, though. She decided that she would call Amanda instead, and tell her to call the girl and reassure her about the money. As for the business about the car, she would stall Jamie along for a time. After all, it was a very old car and could plausibly have all sorts of mechanical ills. That decided, she gave herself over to the life-or-death situation being played out on the television screen. The mine shaft was filling with water. And Pamela was losing consciousness.

Chapter Twenty

LATER THAT AFTERNOON, Miss Montgomery called Jamie to report that the mechanics at the motor pool had not been able to get her car started. The fuel pump needed to be replaced. A replacement had been ordered from Amarillo, but it would be several days before it would arrive—perhaps longer what with a winter storm on the way.

It began snowing that evening. The weather reporter on the evening news warned that both the Texas and Oklahoma panhandles could expect blizzard conditions. Jamie groaned. "Looks like there will be no walks for us tomorrow," she told Ralph.

By the following evening, the drifts on the north side of the house had buried the back door. Miss Montgomery escorted Jamie and Ralph on brief forays in front of the house. The housekeeper would wait on the top step while Jamie—fighting the wind with every step—walked the dog down the driveway and back. "Like she thinks I'm going to run off in a snowstorm," Jamie would mutter under her breath.

After one of the outings, Jamie asked the housekeeper if she'd found out about the money.

"Amanda said that she would call you and explain about the arrangements," Miss Montgomery said.

"I want something in writing," Jamie said. "And I want it signed and notarized."

The snow continued off and on for three days, and even when it was not actually snowing, daylight was reduced to a flat gunmetal gray. The snowdrifts on the north side of the ranch house were so high that the first-floor windows were completely covered. Even though the furnace continued to function, Jamie wore her coat all day long and wore long johns day and night. There would be no mail deliveries, she realized. No fuel pump for her car.

She waited until a thaw had set in before asking Miss Montgomery if the repairs had been made.

"It's such an old car," Miss Montgomery said. "The head mechanic said he hasn't been able to locate the right part."

Jamie thought of all those afternoons helping Joe work on his Jeep and Granny's Chevy. She wasn't an ignoramus when it came to cars. The small-block V-8 engine used in Chevys of that era was probably the most popular engine in automotive history. A fuel pump for such an engine would be quite easy to locate in a city the size of Amarillo.

But she said nothing.

That night she made sure her set of car keys was still under the lining in her grandmother's sewing stand. They were—along with her stash of cash, ATM card, grandmother's ring, and the remote-control gate opener she had taken from Lester's truck.

She put the ring on her finger for a minute and admired it. Someday maybe she would wear it on a special date with a nice normal boy. But would she ever be a nice normal girl? The "nice" part she could handle, but would she ever feel normal again?

She put the ring back in its hiding place and returned to the bed, which had grown icy-cold in her absence. It was stupid to worry about what some imaginary boy would think of her, she told herself as she tried to find a position of maximum warmth and ease for her pregnant body.

First she had to assure herself that she had a future to worry about.

Miss Montgomery had lied to her. Obviously the housekeeper didn't want her anyplace near the car. But why? Did she think that in spite of all the surveillance and the security gates Jamie was going to run away?

Not that the thought hadn't crossed her mind. She had, after all, intentionally hidden a spare set of keys to her car and the remote gate opener that she had taken from Lester's truck. And she had memorized the access code for the ranch-house alarm system.

But she had done those things just in case . . .

In case what?

In case she decided it was not in her best interest or that of the baby to honor the contract she had signed.

If indeed, as doddering old Mary Millicent had insisted, Amanda's dead son was the father of the child Jamie carried, and if Amanda planned to raise this child as her own natural-born offspring, then she might very well worry that the biological mother of the child could present a threat. Amanda's life would certainly be tidier and more comfortable if the baby's birth mother ceased to exist.

And even if Amanda herself did not harbor such thoughts, her brother might. And if Jamie were to believe Mary Millicent, Gus Hartmann had the power to do anything he wanted and never pay the piper. If that were true, would he really allow her to drive away in her old Chevy?

And there was the other consideration. The most important one of all. What was her responsibility to this baby?

Jamie put her hands on her stomach and thought of how her grandmother, as a woman well past seventy, had taken in a seven-year-old child. Granny had done that because it was the right thing to do.

The next morning, Jamie called the security office for an escort, explaining that she wanted to take a walk and stop at Hartmann City on the way back.

A burly, middle-aged man named Hugh picked her up, explaining that Lester had the day off.

Jamie headed down the driveway. Ralph was ecstatic and took off at a dead run. Even though the temperature was above freezing, the biting wind cut right through her. Still she struggled on for fifteen more minutes before waving at Hugh.

She opened the door, and Ralph jumped inside. "Dogs 'posed to ride in the back," Hugh said.

"Not my dog," Jamie said as she got in. "I'm ready to go to Hartmann City now."

When Hugh stopped the truck in front of the ranch store, Jamie told him that she would be at least an hour. Maybe he should return for her later.

Amazingly Hugh didn't object. Apparently no one had briefed him as to the limited extent of Jamie's privileges.

"What about the dog?" he asked.

She reached in her pocket and pulled out a leash. "He'll be fine."

With Ralph at her side, she walked into the store and bought a small coffee. At noon, men began drifting into the store, buying sandwiches and soft drinks and congregating on the wooden benches grouped around a pot-bellied stove. Jamie meandered around the store for a few minutes before leaving through the side door.

The front office of the motor pool was empty. Ralph followed her as she walked the length of the building, past vehicles in various states of repair, smiling and nodding at two mechanics working on the motor of a John Deere tractor, making her way to the back corner where her Chevy resided. On blocks.

The car was covered with a thick layer of West Texas dust.

Jamie turned on the lamp and knelt beside the old woman's bed. "Mary Millicent, it's Jamie," she said.

"I don't know anyone named Jamie," Mary Millicent said without opening her eyes.

"Jamie, the girl from downstairs."

Mary Millicent's eyes fluttered open. "You had the baby yet?"

"Not for six more weeks. Has Amanda said anything to you about the baby?"

"She told me it's Sonny's baby. A baby boy. She's going to let me hold it if I behave myself. I want to hold a baby again. I love babies."

"Tell me what else Amanda said."

"She said that it was all God's plan. The baby is God's chosen. She said that maybe the baby will pray for me and get me into heaven after all. I wonder if my husband still loves me. He never knew that I fooled around on him. God wouldn't tell, would he?"

"No, I'm sure that God will keep your secret," Jamie said. "Did Amanda say what would happen to me after the baby is born?"

"I asked her that very thing, and she said that you were Gus's problem and none of her concern."

"And how would Gus handle this 'problem'?" Jamie persisted.

Mary Millicent tilted her chin back, took her index finger, and swiped it across her throat.

Jamie scrambled to her feet. "But Amanda is a good person. She wouldn't let something like that happen."

"It's easy to be 'good' when you have someone do your dirty work for you," Mary Millicent said with a giggle. "When her new puppy chewed up her favorite doll, Gus hung it by its neck from the second-floor gallery. Amanda had a wonderful time putting on a funeral out in the backyard. She made a floral wreath and wore her favorite dress and sang her favorite hymns and even shed a few tears."

Jamie backed away from the bed.

"Hey, where are you going, girl?" Mary Millicent demanded. "I'm not through talking yet."

Jamie turned and hurried across the room, with Mary Millicent yelling for her to stop. With her heart pounding, she hurried down the stairs—for the last time, she promised herself.

Back in her apartment, she calmed herself by hugging Ralph. She still didn't know anything for sure. Except for one thing. She was going to leave this place and have the baby someplace else. Someplace where she felt safe. And then she would find an attorney to help her untangle the mess she had gotten herself into. But not just any attorney. She would go to a public library and use a computer to track down Joe Brammer. If he didn't want to represent her, he would help her find someone else. Someone she could trust.

Her decision made, Jamie felt as though a world had been lifted from her shoulders.

Except that she had to get herself off this ranch. And that would take planning. Careful planning.

Chapter Twenty-one

GUS WAS JUST heartbeats short of ejaculating when he realized that Felipe was knocking on the door.

The door opened just the tiniest crack, and Felipe announced that Gus had a phone call.

"Shit!" Gus muttered. Something must be terribly wrong for Felipe to interrupt. But he would have his pleasure before dealing with whatever it was.

"Quickly," he told the woman, rolling onto his back.

Suzette was her name. She crouched beside him and within half a minute Gus's body shuddered its way to a climax. Then he pushed her away and told her to leave.

She regarded him for a heartbeat or two with her huge dark eyes before grabbing her clothes and racing toward the door.

Gus clutched a pillow to his chest, allowing himself a moment for the aftermath of the orgasm to subside. He took a deep breath and willed his racing heart to slow down. "Damn," he muttered. "Damn! Damn! Damn!"

Beautiful Suzette. She was like something out of a Toulouse-Lautrec painting, with those eyes and her masses of dark curls, pouty mouth, lily-white flesh, black garter belt, and even an authentic French accent. The last time he had asked her to stay with him for a time. And they had talked about French cinema. She was quite knowledgeable.

This time he had planned to have her stay the night. She had sung French cabaret songs for him and made a production of taking off her clothes. He had pulled her to the bed and kissed her all over.

But the mood had been destroyed. And probably it was just as well. He liked her too much.

And suddenly tears sprung to his eyes. It was one of those moments when he would have gladly given all his worldly goods just to be normal.

When he was twelve years old, he had asked the endocrinologist in Zurich to promise him that if he ever had children, they would not be dwarfs. The doctor had refused to make such a promise.

Gus had undergone a vasectomy when he was seventeen. By then he knew that he was as tall as he was ever going to be and that his ugly, disproportioned body would be his for life. With his family's vast wealth, he realized there would be women willing to marry him, but no woman was ever going to love him. He had kept a succession of mistresses, each for a shorter period of time than her predecessor, until he decided to end the practice. For several years now, Felipe—who had served as Gus's bodyguard/valet since his prep-school days—arranged his sex life for him, booking both the hotel suite and the woman, always in the middle of the night, when it was easier for Gus to slip in and out back entrances unobserved. Because of his short stature, Gus preferred to be in bed when the woman arrived. Nothing pleasured Gus more than watching a beautiful, long-legged woman pleasure him, especially if she was skillful at prolonging the process. He preferred never to have the same woman twice but on occasion broke his own rule. This was Suzette's fourth time.

Felipe brought his cell phone. "The ranch," he said.

Gus called Montgomery's private line.

"Jamie Long is gone," she said in a near-hysterical voice as soon as she answered the phone.

"*Gone?*"

"Oh, Gus, I am so dreadfully sorry," she moaned. "The security office called to say that the front gate had been opened. I went immediately to Jamie's apartment. She's gone, Gus," she said, her voice breaking. "Packed up and gone."

"On *foot*?" Gus asked.

"No, in her car," Montgomery admitted, her words interspersed with gasping sobs.

"Okay, Montgomery, take a deep breath and calm down," Gus said.

He could hear her sniffling a bit and drawing in her breath. "That's good," he said. "Now, how did the girl get access to her car?"

"She demanded that it be brought over here so she could start putting her possessions in it. She said she wanted to be ready to leave here as soon as possible after the baby was born. At first I told her that the car wasn't in running condition and a part had to be ordered for it. Then I stalled for more time, telling her it was hard to find parts for a car that old. But she went to the motor pool and saw the car up on blocks and covered with dust and realized that no one had touched it in months. She told me that she was going on a hunger strike and wouldn't eat a morsel of food until the car was up and running and parked out back. I didn't know she had an extra key to the car," she moaned, the sobs beginning again. "I'd gone over her apartment with a fine-tooth comb. Not just when you told me to take her copy of the contract. I went through it several times. Every inch of it. And there were no keys. Not a one. I swear there weren't. I would have taken them if there were."

"Well, obviously, the girl got the car started some way," he said, his tone hard and flat.

There were several seconds of silence before Montgomery said, "Yes. Of course, she did." Her voice was calmer now. Almost too calm. "I am so sorry, Gus. I have failed you and our darling Amanda. And Sonny. I have failed you all, and I want to die. I just want to die."

Gus took a deep breath in an effort to control his anger. "Now, Montgomery," he said in what he hoped was a soothing voice. "What we need to do is work our way through this. How long ago did the girl leave?"

"Less than thirty minutes."

"Do you have any idea what caused her to bolt?"

"I think she was getting suspicious. Jamie knew that Amanda was claiming to be pregnant with a baby due about the same time as the one she was carrying. And she got upset when I wouldn't allow her to call the secretary in Bentley Abernathy's office and when she realized that she wasn't really enrolled in the correspondence course. Then she quizzed me about when and how she would receive the money that would be owed to her after the baby was born. She wanted some sort of documentation showing that arrangements had been made and the money would be put in her bank account as soon as the baby was born. I told Amanda to call and reassure her, but I don't think she ever did. And . . ." Montgomery paused.

"What?" Gus demanded.

"I probably should have told you sooner, but I didn't think it was all that important . . ."

"Told me what?" Gus demanded.

"I think that Jamie may have been up in the tower. That maybe she talked to your mother and saw Sonny."

"What makes you think such a thing?" Gus asked, trying to keep his voice calm.

"Mary Millicent asked me about the blond pregnant girl," Montgomery admitted. "She was upset because the girl stopped coming to see her. She said that Jamie was Sonny's girlfriend and that she was going to have Sonny's baby."

"Jesus Christ!" Gus yelled, no longer trying to hold back his anger. "How could my mother have known that? And how did that girl get access to her?"

"I don't know, Gus," Montgomery moaned. "Somehow Jamie found the hidden door. I didn't tell her about it. I swear that I didn't."

"You should have put a lock on the door and installed an alarm. Your two most important responsibilities were to keep Mother away from other people and to keep tabs on Jamie Long. Now you call me in the middle of the night to tell me that you have screwed up on both. I counted on you to take care of things down there."

"I am so sorry, Gus," she wailed. "I don't understand how it could have happened. Should I call the county sheriff and tell him Jamie stole the items in the car?" Montgomery asked, her voice frantic. "Or I could send some of our people out to look for her. The weather has turned bad, and she couldn't have gone very far. I couldn't let her stop eating, Gus. I was afraid it would hurt the baby."

"Just shut up, damn it, and let me think!" Gus yelled.

Ann Montgomery dropped the receiver on the floor and put a hand to her throat. She found it difficult to breathe.

Gus had yelled at her. Her darling boy had yelled at her. The boy she had raised and mothered.

He didn't love her anymore.

She had failed them. Failed Amanda and Gus. And Sonny, too.

She stared down at the telephone receiver. Gus was still yelling, using the Lord's name in vain, demanding that she pick up the phone and talk to him.

"I am so sorry," she whispered. "I wanted that baby more than anything."

Now even if Gus let her stay on at the ranch, she would no longer be in charge. And even if Jamie Long was found and brought back here to have the baby, Ann knew that she might be allowed to spend the rest of her life wiping Mary Millicent's bottom but she would never be permitted to care for Sonny's baby.

She stretched out on the bed she had shared with Buck, the bed in which she had birthed his baby. Her poor little dead baby boy. She had bathed his lifeless little body and kissed him all over and smoothed talcum powder on his skin and wrapped him in the blanket she had crocheted for him. When Buck came, she placed the baby in his arms. He told her it was for the best. She hated Buck for saying that, but he had gone with her to the cemetery and dug a grave. And weeks later, a wooden marker with the inscription "Stillborn Baby" appeared on the grave.

For the longest time afterward, Ann would sprinkle talcum powder on her pillow and pretend it was her baby while she rocked it in her arms. And she begged God to please let her baby into heaven, a baby who had been born of sin but had not sinned himself.

After Mary Millicent arrived at Hartmann Ranch, she had asked about the nameless infant buried in the family cemetery. Ann never told her whose baby it was but said that no preacher had ever said words over it. Immediately Mary Millicent grabbed her coat and the two of them marched up the path and knelt beside the little marker, and Mary Millicent Tutt herself, the famous evangelist who had written books on salvation and preached on radio and television and had saved millions of souls, raised her arms heavenward and asked the Lord to hold this baby close and give him everlasting life.

After Mary Millicent gave birth to Gus and Amanda, Ann's arms didn't feel so empty anymore. She had Buck's grandchildren to love. Those were the happiest years of her life. Now every time Ann became exasperated with Mary Millicent, she reminded herself that Mary Millicent had saved her baby's soul and allowed her to love and mother Gus and Amanda. The call had long since left Mary Millicent, but back then she had the ear of God. Ann had no doubt of that.

The phone was silent now. Gus wasn't yelling anymore.

She rose from her bed and regarded her reflection once again. So old and ugly. She didn't want to see that old ugly face ever again.

She walked through the living room of the spacious, beautiful apartment that had never meant as much to her as the creaky old house that used to be out back—where she had lived with her father until he died and Buck had starting coming to her in the night.

She didn't bother to close the door behind her when she left the apartment for the last time. At the back door, she punched in the security code. She opened the back door, walked down the steps, and crossed the backyard to the side gate by the driveway.

It was starting to snow. The weatherman on television had said it might snow south of here, but not in huge, empty Marshall County, where she had spent her entire life in service of the Hartmann family. And she had allowed her heart to be filled with love for them and had told herself that they loved her in return. But probably they were just using her. Dumb old Ann Montgomery. She had spread her legs for old Buck and raised Mary Millicent's children and taken care of her when she was old and useless and her children couldn't deal with her anymore. Ann had run their ranch and kept their secrets. Now she had failed them, and Gus had yelled at her. It felt as though he had stabbed her with a knife. Stabbed her dead.

She knew it must be very cold, but she didn't feel it. Maybe she was already dead. Maybe she had been dead for years.

She took the winding path up to the windswept little cemetery and opened the iron gate, its rusty hinges squealing in protest. The wind whipped her nightgown around her legs as she walked past Buck's headstone to the back corner where their baby was buried. She wished she could dig down into the frozen earth to where her baby lay and hold him in her arms while she died. But at least she was close to him. She curled her body around the small headstone and began crooning to her baby. Her pretty little baby boy. His little chest had shuddered. She had tried to breathe for him, tried to put air in his little lungs. But he had never taken a breath. Buck had refused to give him a name, but in her heart she had named him David.

She recited the Lord's Prayer and the Twenty-third Psalm. Then her mind roamed through the Bible and she recited favorite passages until she realized that light was filling up the sky. The light was warm, and it was coming closer and closer until she was in the middle of a soft warm cloud that smelled of talcum powder.

Almost immediately Gus knew that he had gone too far. It was *Montgomery* he was yelling at. The woman had practically raised him and Amanda. The woman who loved them completely and would have laid down her life for either one of them.

But he kept yelling, demanding that she answer him, saying that he was sorry, that he loved her. He and Amanda loved her. More than they had loved their own mother. Then he hushed, sensing that she was no longer listening.

He yelled for Felipe to get Kelly on the phone.

"Oh, God," Gus moaned, rubbing his eyes with the heels of his hands.

When Felipe handed him the phone, Gus said, "Kelly, you need to go over and check on Montgomery ASAP!"

"What's going on?"

"Jamie Long flew the coop, and Montgomery is freaking out."

Kelly let out a low whistle. "So, that's who went through the front gate."

"Apparently so. You have any idea how she managed that?"

"One of the remotes is missing," she admitted.

Gus resisted the urge to let forth a stream of obscenities. No more yelling. He needed to stay calm. Needed Kelly's help.

"Go see about Montgomery," he told her, "and get me the license-plate number on the Long girl's car. Don't make a big deal of this, Kelly. If anyone at the ranch asks, just say the girl decided to have her baby elsewhere."

"Will do."

"I'm worried about Montgomery," he admitted. "She was pretty upset when I talked to her. Call me back right away."

Chapter Twenty-two

WHEN JAMIE POINTED the remote control at the front gate, she half expected an alarm to sound and the car to be bathed in bright spotlights and men to appear suddenly and drag her from the vehicle.

Until that moment she had told herself that she could always change her mind. That this was just a trial run and not the real thing.

But in bed early this morning, she had felt a tightening of her abdominal muscles. Not exactly painful, but uncomfortable. She experienced the same feeling again in the bathroom, along with the beginnings of hysteria. Freda had warned her about the possibility of a false alarm. About Braxton Hicks contractions. Sometimes they could be pretty strong, but they came intermittently and then went away. Real labor didn't go away. Jamie prayed that was what she was experiencing. *Braxton Hicks.*

She experienced another episode midmorning but nothing else for the rest of the day. She had been thoroughly shaken by the experience, however.

What if the pains she had felt were a lead-up to true labor?

What if her labor started during daytime? She'd never be able to leave in broad daylight, and if she waited until dark, she risked having the baby alone and unattended.

Jamie had known all along that leaving would not be simple. That fact in itself is what finally convinced her. Miss Montgomery and Kelly were not about to allow her just to get in her car and drive away. They would find some grounds to stop her—accuse her of stealing something most likely. And it would be almost impossible for Jamie to prove otherwise. It would be her word against theirs, and they worked for the Hartmanns. In Marshall County, the Hartmanns were above the law.

She knew her departure would have to be clandestine. She needed to get as far away from Hartmann Ranch as she possibly could before anyone realized that she had left.

Getting access to her car had been a major problem. She hadn't planned to threaten a hunger strike. The words just came out of her mouth. She wouldn't have done it, of course, at least not to the extent that it would hurt the baby. But Montgomery didn't know that. Montgomery had called her a "wicked girl."

Once the car was in running order and parked in the ranch-house garage, Jamie went about the business of packing up her possessions and carrying them out to the car, always accompanied by a gardener or sometimes by Miss Montgomery herself. Jamie made a deliberate effort to be cheerful around Miss Montgomery and Nurse Freda, telling them how excited she was about returning to Austin and continuing her college education and getting in touch with her friends. "I know you think I'm rushing things," Jamie told Miss Montgomery, "but I'm bored and don't have anything better to do."

The garage was locked at night, but Jamie had been able to unlock a window on the back of the building while her current escort was out front smoking and chatting with his *compadres*.

With the only possessions left in her apartment the articles of clothing and toilet articles she would need for the remainder of her stay, the two rooms looked bare and impersonal. She considered putting back the decorative items that had been in the room when she arrived but decided against it. The bare look signified that the end of her incarceration was near.

With the packing done, she was anxious to leave. Her plan was to wait until the danger of winter storms had passed but not so long that she would be in danger of going into labor. She hoped to have enough time to get herself settled and make arrangements for the delivery of her baby.

Her baby. That was how she now thought of the baby boy she carried. *Her baby. Her child. Her son.* And with acknowledgment came love. She continuously caressed her swollen belly. Her love for her unborn child made her strong and determined. She must plan her escape thoroughly and well so she would be the one who raised her son.

Since the area north of the ranch was so vast and empty, Jamie was fairly certain Miss Montgomery and Kelly would assume that she would head south to Interstate 40, which would take her either east to Amarillo or west into New Mexico. Jamie planned, however, to drive north into the Oklahoma Panhandle. If all went well, she would have breakfast in the town of Guymon. According to the atlas in the library, Guymon was a town of more than five thousand people, or at least it had been twenty years ago when the atlas was published. It was large enough to have restaurants and motels, and a stranger in town could go unnoticed. Not that she would be staying long.

She tried to imagine what was going to happen at the ranch when it was discovered that she had left. Would Kelly contact the county sheriff and the Texas highway patrol and claim she'd run off with the silverware or the family jewels? Jamie knew that she would feel safer once she crossed the state line and was in a different legal jurisdiction.

Jamie imagined Amanda's fury when Miss Montgomery called with the news. She would expect her brother to track her down. Jamie hoped to make that impossible.

Just last night she had crept down the stairs in the middle of the night to make sure the security code had not been changed. At the back door, she punched in three fours and a five, then opened the door a few inches. No alarm sounded. The code was still in effect. She went down the steps and tried the code on the back gate. It worked.

This afternoon she and Ralph took their usual walk with Lester following behind. She was too nervous to eat much dinner and flushed most of the food down the toilet so that nothing would seem amiss. Then she took Ralph downstairs for his last outing before Miss Montgomery locked up for the night. Back in her apartment, she put on her granny gown—just in case Miss Montgomery decided to stop by—and pulled back the covers on her bed. She even stretched out on the bed for a while, watching the weather. The weather reporter said that what should be the Panhandle's last winter storm of the season was now located over central New Mexico. The storm would affect the Texas Panhandle as far north as I-40, with only isolated flurries predicted farther north.

A good thing she was heading north, Jamie told herself. She should have clear sailing.

She forced herself to stay in bed until midnight. Then she got up, dressed warmly, and packed the remainder of her possessions in a plastic bag.

Ralph followed her down the stairs. She paused briefly at the back door, took a deep breath, and punched in the security code. The minute she opened the door, Ralph raced past her, headed down the steps, and lifted his leg at the closest tree.

As always, the backyard was lit by floodlights mounted on the roof of the house, but the gate was close to the house and deep in shadows. She couldn't read the numbers on the touch pad but counted to the fourth button, punched it three times, and the button next to it once.

Ralph followed her as she hurried across the paved area in front of the garage, then went around back. She put Ralph through the window, then crawled through herself.

The garage door made a frightening amount of noise, but no lights came on in the ranch house. She peeked around the corner of the garage. No lights were on in the employee cottages.

She drove at a crawl past the house and down the front drive. Then, after weeks of agonizing and planning, she arrived at the point of no return.

In her gut, or wherever it was within the human psyche that one puts logic aside and blunders forward if for no other reason than inaction feels wrong, Jamie had found the courage to point the remote at the metal gate and press the button. Ghostly and silent in the darkness, the gate swung open.

She held her breath.

There were no spotlights. No alarm. No men racing toward the car.

"Maybe this is going to work," she whispered to Ralph, who seemed as apprehensive as she was by this strange late-night outing.

With her heart pounding furiously, she drove through the open gate.

"Oh, my God," she whispered. She was on the other side. She looked over her shoulder and watched the gate close. The front drive was empty.

So far so good.

Except it was starting to snow. Just a little, though. Just those isolated flurries the weatherman had mentioned. Not a cause for concern.

The tires crunched on the gravel as she turned north on Hartmann Road and drove ever so slowly, squinting into the darkness of the moonless night. She strained to make out the edge of the roadway, which she used as a guide. She wanted to be well past Hartmann City before she turned on the headlights.

The snow was coming down harder now. She replayed the forecast in her head. The snowstorm would be *south* of the interstate. She was certain of it. The ranch was more than twenty miles *north* of the interstate.

She would drive out of it soon. At least she hoped so. She'd never driven in snow before.

After she passed the Hartmann City turnoff, she turned on the headlights, which did little to help visibility. All she could see in front of her was swirling snow. She slowed to a crawl, continuing to use the edge of the road as her guide.

The swirling snow was hypnotic. She kept blinking her eyes and shaking her head to clear her vision. Surely the snow would let up soon. She just needed to keep going.

After what seemed like an eternity of tedious driving, she forced herself to relax a bit. All she had to do was inch along and stay on the road.

Then suddenly she saw something other than snow reflected in the headlights. What looked like a pair of glowing coals was floating a few feet above the road. It took her several seconds to understand what she was seeing. The eyes of a deer. She put her foot to the brake.

Only then did she realize how slippery the road had become. The car began to swerve out of control.

As she let up on the brake, she had a fleeting image of the deer leaping into the underbrush along the side of the road.

Somehow she managed to keep the car on the road. Then ever so carefully she slowed to a stop and buried her face in her hands. Why tonight of all nights did the TV meteorologist get the forecast wrong? This didn't look like isolated flurries to her. She was in the middle of a damned blizzard!

Which made her think of the family that had frozen to death in their truck after being evicted by Gus Hartmann. The McGraf family. Had she already gone past what once had been their property?

She was looking around for some sort of landmark when she felt the beginning of a contraction.

It lasted only a short time and ended as quickly as it came. Another Braxton Hicks contraction. *Not* the beginning of labor.

She took several deep breaths and put her foot on the accelerator, and slowly—ever so slowly—the car began to move again. The snow was getting worse. No doubt about it. At the rate she was going, it would be a long time before she reached any sort of civilization. Maybe she should turn around and go back. Maybe no one had realized that she was gone. She could get back in bed and try again another night.

The road was narrow. If she turned around here, she would have to be careful not to slide off the road.

Already the snow was drifting against vegetation and blurring the edge of the roadway.

What if Montgomery had already discovered that she was gone? If she went back, Montgomery would have her locked up. In the tower with Mary Millicent. Or maybe in the cellar. She would never have another chance to escape.

She continued driving forward. Her speed barely registered on the speedometer. She leaned forward, peering over the steering wheel. She blinked her straining eyes and almost missed a curve in the road.

As she inched around the curve, another pain grabbed hold of her body. She lifted her foot from the accelerator, clutched the steering wheel, and waited for it to pass.

Not too bad, she told herself. *Not* the real thing. There was no reason for her to go into labor three weeks early. She was healthy and had had a normal pregnancy. Freda had said so. In fact, Freda had said she was amazingly healthy. Not a single sign of anything amiss. Her blood pressure was perfect. No sign of toxemia. The baby had a strong heartbeat.

She began to inch forward again. At this rate she would reach the Oklahoma Panhandle sometime next week.

But surely she would run out of the snow soon. *Just keep going,* she told herself.

She checked to make sure the windshield wipers were on the highest setting.

Her neck and shoulders hurt more than the pains in her belly. Jamie rolled her head around in an attempt to relieve the tension in her neck.

The road curved again, and she spotted something just ahead. A mailbox mounted on a fence post. A place where she could turn around—if that was what she decided to do. She slowed to a stop.

Then the muscles in her abdomen began to contract and another pain grabbed hold of her body. She clutched the steering wheel and willed the pain to pass. This one was harder than the other two and took longer to recede.

She turned off the motor and headlights, then waited in the darkness to see if there was another pain. Without the heater, the temperature in the car immediately began to drop. She reached in the backseat for a blanket and covered herself with it. Then she reached for Ralph and tucked him under it, too.

She stroked his head and prayed. *No more pain. Please.*

What the hell was she going to do if she was in labor? She would have to go back to the ranch. She had no choice. She would be risking the baby's life if she didn't.

What if God was on Amanda's side?

With that discouraging thought, she began to moan. "I'm sorry, God, if I wasn't supposed to do this, but I was afraid of what was going to happen to me afterward. And I don't want Amanda to raise my baby. She might not do bad things herself, but I think she looks the other way and lets bad things happen. Please, if you're mad at me, don't take it out on the baby. He hasn't done anything wrong. I want him to live. Please let him live," she sobbed. But her sob turned into a gasp as another pain took hold of her body.

When it ended, she stared at her watch with its glowing dial, hoping to determine how much time passed in between pains. But when the next pain started, she forgot to check the time. She grabbed hold of the steering wheel and waited for it to end.

Then she forced herself to stare at the watch as she waited. Almost ten minutes passed before the now familiar pain began once again. And ten more minutes before the next pain. When that pain subsided, she actually felt calmer. She knew what the situation was and knew what she had to do. What she was experiencing was not false labor. Not Braxton Hicks. Snow was drifting against the windshield. The roads were becoming impassable. Pretty soon the car was going to be buried. Unless she found some sort of shelter, she and her baby and her dog were going to freeze to death.

Jamie turned on her headlights and squinted to make out the faded name on the mailbox. It was McGraf. There would be no help for her at the end of this lane, but at least she would be out of the weather.

The lane was completely buried under snow, but she was guided by the fence posts that marched along both sides. Just as she pulled up in front of a small frame house with a sagging roof and boards nailed over the windows, she had another pain—a hard pain that took her breath away.

She took a flashlight from the glove compartment, found her boots among the pile of things in the backseat, and exchanged her sneakers for them. At one time the front door of the house had probably been padlocked, but now it stood open. She shined the light around the small front room. The floor was littered with beer cans and trash. A broken chair lay in one corner. She walked over to a stone fireplace. There was cold air coming down the chimney. A good sign. The chimney would draw.

Working in between the pains, she began gathering wood and piling it beside the fireplace—any sort of wood she could find—twigs, sticks, fallen fence posts, the broken chair, loose boards from the front porch. Ralph was always at her side. Poor little dog. How confusing this must be for him. She would have to remember to feed him and put out water for him when they settled down inside.

She slipped and fell several times, at one point striking her forehead so hard against the edge of the porch that she saw stars. Another time she slipped and slammed her hip against a tree.

Once she had a sizable pile of wood, she dug around in the trunk and backseat, locating blankets, quilts, towels, a box with the few dishes and utensils she had kept from her grandmother's kitchen, and another box with snacks, dog food, and water bottles she'd packed with her journey in mind.

The pains seemed somewhat closer together. Not unbearable but getting harder. She kept fear at bay with busyness. Doing what had to be done.

There were two old mattresses in one of the bedrooms. She dragged them both into the living room, putting the least filthy one in front of the fireplace.

She piled wood in the fireplace then tore open the spare mattress and pulled cotton batting from it to use for kindling. She had no matches but found a tin can among the trash scattered about the house and poked some of the cotton batting inside it. Then she took the can out to the car and used the cigarette lighter to ignite the cotton.

She knew that one was supposed to boil water before a delivery, although she wasn't quite sure why. Since she had only three water bottles, she filled her grandmother's soup pot with snow, and set it close to the fire.

What else might be useful? she asked herself.

She would need string and scissors for the umbilical cord. She waited for the next pain to end, then went back out to the car and located her grandmother's scissors in the sewing stand. In lieu of string, she cut a narrow strip from a towel. And she placed the scissors and strip by the mattress.

She closed the living room off from the rest of the house to prevent heat from escaping and continued making forays outside in search of more firewood and to collect snow to melt in the pan by the fire. She discovered that it took a lot of snow to make only a little water.

The snow was getting ever deeper, but she had no way of knowing how much wood she would need and decided she would keep gathering wood as long as she was physically able. She tore rotting boards from the front gate and a collapsed shed.

She would fall to her knees when the pains began. And moan with Ralph whimpering beside her.

Finally, too exhausted to do anything more, she put out food and water for Ralph and spread a blanket over the mattress by the fireplace. It crossed her mind that she might be preparing her deathbed. And that of her son.

If she thought she was about to die, she would try to open the door so that Ralph would at least have a chance of surviving. But probably he would be eaten by wolves or coyotes if he didn't freeze to death first.

Before she gave herself over to the mattress, she tried to think. Was there anything else she could do?

She remembered a movie she had seen about a woman having a baby alone on an island in the far north country of Canada. The woman had tied a rope to a bedpost to give her something to pull on while she was in labor. But Jamie had no rope and no bedpost. What she wanted was someone's hand to hold. Someone's soothing presence and voice to get her through this.

The only sounds she heard came from the howling wind.

At the end of each pain, Ralph would lick her face and put his head on her shoulder. And she would fall asleep thinking what a good little dog he was. A perfect dog for a little boy.

Then she would awaken to another pain. Terrible, agonizing pain. Pain that took over her body and her mind. Pain that took away her self-control and brought forth frantic thrashing and scream after scream. Pain that made her not care if she lived or died.

She would look at her watch and immediately forget what she had seen. Time lost all dimension. She never knew if the time between pains was seconds or hours. She forced herself to check the fire after each one. And she would reach between her legs, hoping to feel the top of the baby's head. Then she would sleep until the pain began again.

She knew that it would end only if she could push the baby out of her. Out of desperation, she grabbed hold of her knees and pushed with all her might. Which only increased the pain.

She let go of her legs but felt such an urge to push that she pulled them back again. Toward her chest. It felt as though her insides were being pushed out of her body. She was being turned inside out. But the pushing was no longer a choice. It was something she had to do. Along with screaming. She pushed and screamed. Then dozed. And then she repeated the cycle. Again and again.

After each pain, she reached down between her legs.

He was stuck in there. In the birth canal. They were both going to die. Sooner rather than later, she hoped.

If they didn't survive, she wondered how long it would be before they were found. Would their deaths even be reported, or would they be secretly buried and forgotten? It really didn't matter, she supposed. Dead was dead. And with every pain, she felt closer to death. With every pain, she wondered if it was time to open the door so that Ralph could escape.

She grabbed her legs once again. And this time she felt something happening. Something moving. When the pain ended, she reached down once again and felt the top of the baby's head.

She pulled her legs back and pushed with all her might.

This time when she checked, she felt his neck and a tiny shoulder.

Again she pushed, with all the strength left within her body. *"I will not die,"* she screamed. *"I will not die."*

She felt the rest of the baby slide from her body. He was born.

She rolled onto her side and scooted her body around him. The baby wasn't moving. His arms and legs were blue. His lips were blue.

She pulled his wet, slippery body toward her and shook him. Then she put her mouth over his and blew air into him.

And again. But to no avail.

"Breathe, baby," she implored. *"Please* breathe."

She stuck a finger in his mouth, which was full of mucus. She suctioned it out with her own mouth, spit out the mucus, and breathed into him again.

Then his little chest moved up and down.

And he cried. A thin, weak cry.

She clutched his slippery, bloody body to her chest. Only then did she realize how cold it was. She was shivering. The fire was almost out.

But there was more stuff happening down there. She pulled a corner of the blanket over the baby's wet body and waited until she felt the afterbirth come sliding out.

The baby's crying grew stronger as she tied off his umbilical cord. Then she cut the cord and wiped the blood and mucus from him with a towel, wrapped him in another towel, and laid him on a corner of the mattress. Then she wrapped the afterbirth in the blanket she had been lying on, carried it outside, and shook it into the snow.

A new day was dawning, and the storm was over.

She covered the mattress with a fresh blanket, wrapped a quilt around her shoulders, and turned her attention to the fire, leaving a trail of blood with every step she took. She stuffed the towel she had used to clean the baby between her legs, knelt in front of the fireplace, and blew on the coals. The blowing took such effort. And she felt so weak. But somehow she found the strength to blow again and was able to ignite a fresh wad of cotton batting. Then she continued blowing until it was safe to add more wood.

She closed her eyes, relishing the blessed heat that the fire emitted and worrying that the smoke from the chimney could be seen from the road.

She couldn't stay here long. Just a few hours to get her strength back.

With the fire going, she turned her attention back to the baby. His eyes were open. "Hello, little guy," she said. "I'm your mother."

Chapter Twenty-three

GUS WAS BACK at Victory Hill sitting at his desk when the phone rang. He grabbed it and barked, "Yes."

"Montgomery is dead," Kelly's voice reported.

Gus closed his eyes and slumped back in his chair. *"Dead?"*

"Yeah. Sorry it took so long. We searched the house from top to bottom. Then we spread out over the grounds, but the weather's turned bad. A regular blizzard. One of the gardeners finally found her in the family cemetery completely covered over with snow. All she had on was a nightgown. She was lying with her arms around the marker for the stillborn baby."

So that's whose baby was buried there. *Montgomery's.* But he couldn't think about that now. At some later time, maybe he would process the information. Right now he had to deal with the situation at hand.

"And the girl?" he asked.

"I sent two men out in a truck with snow chains. They managed to get all the way to Alma and didn't see a sign of her. The service station was closed but they asked at the truck stop. Lots of truckers and travelers are holed up there. No one had seen her."

"How bad are the roads? Could she have even gotten that far?"

"I suppose, but I don't see how she could have gotten any farther. The interstate and state roads are closed."

"Who says?"

"The highway patrol. They aren't allowing any traffic onto the interstate. Apparently there're dozens of jackknifed eighteen-wheelers. I'm thinkin' maybe she headed north, in which case she might have beat the weather. Hard to say."

"Send men out on horseback. And get hold of someone in that little town north of there."

"Monroe?"

"Yeah. Monroe. Call law enforcement in any town where she might be holed up, but tell them not to approach the girl. Tell them she's a psycho and may be armed. They're to keep her under surveillance and notify you."

Jamie cleaned the baby with warm water from the pot by the fire. Then she cleaned herself as best she could.

She had torn down there, and blood was flowing. More than when it was her period. A lot more. She tore a blanket into sections that she could fold into pads.

She winced as she wiped the blood off her buttocks and thighs, which were covered with bruises from her slips on the ice while unloading the car and gathering wood. Her shoulder also was badly bruised, and the lump on her forehead was excruciatingly tender.

She pulled on the same maternity jeans and top she'd been wearing, then let Ralph outside and closed the door.

In a few minutes, Ralph announced his return. She put out food and water for him and drank some water herself and ate a couple of crackers. Then she put more wood on the fire, curled up with her baby in her arms, and closed her eyes. Soon she would have to decide what came next, but right now she did not have the strength.

She slept off and on, waking to put more wood on the fire, change the makeshift pad between her legs, and make sure the baby was still breathing before surrendering once again to sleep.

Midday, the baby began to cry.

Probably he needed to be nursed. But how did one do that?

She wrapped him in a fresh towel, then bared a breast and propelled her nipple into his mouth, but he did not take hold. She changed positions and tried again, speaking words of encouragement. Still no luck. In desperation, she rubbed the nipple back and forth over his lips. He would suck a few times and then stop. She tried the same maneuver again and again, hoping he was getting something. Then she held him in her arms and surrendered herself once again to sleep.

It was dark when she nursed him again, this time with seemingly better results. While he nursed, she tried to plan.

She hoped that Kelly and Montgomery hadn't discovered that she was missing until morning and assumed she was already hundreds of miles away. She doubted if anyone would be looking for her this close to the ranch. Maybe she should just stay here for another day or two and give the roads a chance to clear.

Except she needed to find someone to stitch her up and either reassure her that the heavy flow of blood was normal or do something to stop it. And she needed baby clothes and diapers. Needed to buy a book on how to take care of a baby. Needed to find a place to stay. And a computer. A new name. And a cup of hot coffee would be really nice.

What choice did she have but to press on? Just the thought of loading her things back into the car made her exhausted, but she really should leave while it was dark. If she waited until tomorrow evening, she would have to find more firewood, and she had already scavenged most of the wood around the house. To find more, she would have to go farther out and leave the baby here alone. Besides, eventually someone was going to notice the smoke coming from the chimney.

Leaving the baby on the mattress, she ate a couple of granola bars and drank a bottle of water. Then she bundled up the bloodied towels and bedding and stuffed them into the trunk. After carrying her other possessions out to the car, she tidied up the house as best she could, collecting the trash in bags and putting them in the car to be discarded later.

By the time she was finished, she was exhausted and the baby was crying.

Once again she offered a breast to him. This time he grabbed hold like a little piglet. And Jamie laughed out loud.

"We learn fast," she told him. How beautiful he was, she thought as she looked down at him. How perfectly beautiful. *Her baby.* She was a mother now. Not a surrogate mother. An honest-to-gosh mother. She would die before she let anyone take him away from her.

When he seemed to have finished nursing, she put the baby in a nest she had made for him among the items piled on the backseat. Ralph jumped into the front seat.

She got in the car and took a last look at the house, thinking of the long-dead family that had once lived here. Their house had saved her life and that of her baby.

She drove with her headlights on low beam, crawling along at a snail's pace, almost sliding off the road several times. Once, she saw headlights up ahead and panicked, but the vehicle turned and headed toward a cluster of lights a half mile or so off the road.

At dawn she met a pickup truck. She could tell that the driver was an elderly person with frail, hunched shoulders.

The sun had cleared the horizon when she met a second pickup, this one driven by a man wearing a cowboy hat. He raised a finger from the steering wheel by way of a greeting. Jamie nodded then watched in the rearview mirror, half expecting him to turn around and chase after her.

She drove a bit faster now that it was daylight. The roadbed was covered with loose snow but not icy. After an hour or so, she reached the intersection with U.S. 54. Just a few more miles and she would be leaving Marshall County. *Forever.*

The lone service station in the tiny town of Monroe was closed, but it took less than an hour to reach Stratford, where she stopped at a convenience store. She filled the gas tank and purchased diapers, baby wipes, Kotex, and a cup of coffee and a doughnut. Back in the car, she diapered the baby and wrapped him in the last clean towel. Then she drove around to the back of the store and deposited her trash bags in a Dumpster.

From Stratford, she drove northeast on Highway 54. In less than an hour, she crossed the state line into Oklahoma. Will Rogers offered a smile and a wave from a billboard, welcoming her to the Sooner State. She took a deep breath and gave a prayer of thanks.

Just minutes later, she was driving into the town of Goodwell, population 1,192, according to a sign posted at the city limits. She pulled abreast of some children waiting for a school bus and asked for directions to the local cemetery.

It looked as though considerably more people had been buried in Goodwell's cemetery than now lived in the town. She drove up and down the lanes, hoping she could spot a suitable grave marker from the car. She could not. So she tucked the baby inside her jacket and, with Ralph following along behind, walked up and down the rows until at last she found what she was looking for.

Janet Marie Wisdom had been born the year after Jamie's birth and died at age three. Jamie took note of the girl's birthday then touched the tombstone, thinking of the grieving parents who had buried this child here. "I hope you don't mind if I borrow your name, little Janet," she said. "I'd rather your family name was Smith or Jones, but Wisdom is a fine name."

Then it was on to Guymon. The town was considerably larger than Goodwell, with a downtown clustered around a courthouse square. She stopped at a service station and looked in a phonebook for midwives. Only one was listed. Mae Vandegrift, certified nurse-midwife. She dialed Mae's number and explained that she had had a baby unattended yesterday morning and was bleeding pretty badly.

"What's your name, dear?"

Jamie hesitated. "Janet," she said. "I can't go to the hospital. I don't have any insurance. I can pay some, but not much."

"You on the run?"

"Yes," she said. "From my boyfriend."

Mae explained how to find her house.

It was a one-story brick dwelling set well back from the road. A pair of horses watched over the fence as Jamie turned into the driveway.

A middle-aged woman with graying hair answered the door. "You and that baby get yourselves in here out of the cold," she ordered.

Jamie stepped into a cozy living room warmed by a gas heater installed inside a flagstone fireplace. Family pictures smiled from the mantel. A large and well-worn Bible sat in the middle of the round coffee table.

"The boyfriend do that to you?" Mae asked, pointing at the lump on Jamie's forehead.

Jamie nodded.

Mae sighed and shook her head as she reached for the baby. "And no one was with you when you had this baby?"

Again Jamie nodded.

"You poor child. Where are your folks, honey?"

"Dead," Jamie said, blinking back tears. The kindness and concern in the woman's voice threatened to erode the force of will that had kept her going until now. She squared her shoulders. She was strong, she reminded herself. She would always be strong. She had to be for her baby's sake.

"So, what are you going to do?" the midwife asked, indicating that Jamie was to sit on the sofa.

Jamie sat down, putting the baby to her shoulder and laying her cheek against his head. "I don't know yet," she admitted.

"I can give you information about state assistance programs for single mothers," Mae said as she reached for the baby and placed him lengthwise on her lap. The baby's eyes were open, and he seemed to be looking up at the midwife. "Well, aren't you a handsome little fellow. I bet your old aunt Mae can find some clothes to dress you in."

Jamie reached over and stroked her baby's cheek. "I've never been around babies much. I need to buy a book and learn how to care for him."

"I'll give you some reading material, and your own instincts will kick in. He seems calm enough. Have you tried to nurse him?"

Jamie nodded. "But the stuff coming out of my breasts doesn't look much like milk. Maybe I should buy some formula."

"No call for that. He's getting exactly what he needs."

Mae asked Jamie how she was feeling, then, carrying the baby, she led the way to her clinic, which was housed in a room that been built onto the back of the house. "My mother built this room for a beauty parlor," Mae said as she struck a match and lit a gas heater. "I grew up shampooing hair and taking out curlers."

After washing her hands, the midwife thoroughly examined the baby, then listened to his heart and lungs, took his temperature, cleaned the cord stump, and weighed him. At five pounds nine ounces, he was a bit undersized but seemed quite healthy, Mae assured Jamie. She explained how to care for the cord stump and that the greenish stuff that was starting to come out of his bottom was normal.

Once she was finished with her examination, Mae diapered the baby, dressed him in a pair of fleecy pajamas, wrapped him in a pink blanket, and placed him in an infant carrier. "Sorry about the pink blanket," she said.

Jamie had the feeling that she wasn't the first woman who had showed up at Mae's door with a baby wrapped in a bath towel.

"Now it's your turn, Janet," Mae said, handing her a flowered gown and pointing to a curtained-off corner of the room.

With Jamie sitting on the end of the examining table, Mae took her blood pressure, checked her pulse, listened to her heart and lungs, took her temperature, then helped her lie back on the table. With her head resting on a clean, soft pillow, Jamie realized how exhausted she was.

Mae covered her with a sheet, guided her feet into the stirrups, and sat on a stool at the end of the table.

"Good grief, girl!" she exclaimed. "You're just one big bruise! That so-called 'boyfriend' should be arrested!"

Jamie said nothing, feeling almost guilty that she was allowing some nonexistent man to be maligned.

"Well, you tore some," Mae said, "but not too bad for a first baby. I'll clean you up and stitch you back together. You'll be just fine."

When Mae finished her examination, she explained that she was deadening the perineum as best she could but that Jamie was still going to experience some pain.

Jamie clenched her fists and tried not to cry out, which proved to be impossible. Still, it was nothing compared to what she had been through giving birth.

The stitches in place, Mae helped Jamie into a sitting position and rattled off a list of instructions for her and the baby. "I've got all this in writing, so it's okay if you don't remember everything."

"What about a birth certificate?" Jamie asked.

"We'll get to that," Mae said. "First, I want to watch you nurse this little guy."

Mae showed Jamie how to position the baby and discussed how long and how frequently she should nurse him. "It's best to nurse him on both sides each session," she instructed. "You may have to tickle his cheek or jiggle him a bit to keep him awake."

Once the baby had nursed on each breast and was sleeping contentedly, Mae put him back in the infant seat. Jamie got dressed and carried the baby into the kitchen. Mae gave her a cup of hot tea and a generous slice of homemade banana-nut bread, then sat across the table from her, holding an official-looking form.

"Since you obviously just had a baby, I can sign this form as 'certifier.' If I had delivered the baby, I would be 'attendee.' But either way, it's all legal and aboveboard."

"Do I have to list the father's name on the birth certificate?" Jamie asked.

Mae shook her head. "No. If you had a husband with you, I'd be required to report his name, but otherwise, I can just leave that line blank. Okay, now, what is your full name, dear?"

"Janet Marie Wisdom."

Mae looked up. "There're some Wisdoms over Goodwell way. You any relation to them?"

"Actually, I was born in Goodwell."

"That so," Mae said, studying Jamie's face.

Jamie's heart skipped a beat. She should have driven on to the next county before looking for a midwife. Or found a less common family name to borrow. Goodwell was too close to Guymon. Mae probably knew most of the families in this county.

"Okay," Mae said, returning her attention to the form. "Mother's birthplace—Texas County. Baby's birthplace—Texas County."

When she asked Jamie her date of birth, Jamie told her the date on the long-dead three-year-old's tombstone.

Mae paused again, regarding Jamie over the top of her reading glasses for several heartbeats before returning her attention to the form. "So, what are you going to name the baby?" she asked.

"William Charles Wisdom."

The midwife wrote down the name. "Okay, Janet, I'll send this in the morning. You can get a copy of the official birth certificate from the state health department."

Jamie asked to use the bathroom before leaving. When she returned, Mae had carried the baby into the living room and was copying down something from the Bible on the coffee table.

Loaded with booklets on infant care, useful addresses, foiled-wrapped slices of banana-nut bread, and a bottle of orange juice, Jamie asked the midwife how much she owed her. Mae shook her head. "I know what it's like to be in an abusive relationship. You can pay me by taking good care of yourself and little William."

"Billy," Jamie said. "I named him for my father, and everyone always called him Billy."

"Billy Wisdom. Now, that's a right nice name."

"I can never thank you enough," Jamie said, her eyes misting over.

Mae opened her arms and Jamie stepped into them gladly. "I know, honey, it's been rough," Mae said soothingly, patting Jamie's back. "But you have your health and a fine baby boy. And it would seem that you've taken the necessary precautions to keep the boyfriend from tracking you down."

Mae handed Jamie some tissues. She blew her nose then bent to lift the baby from the infant carrier.

"No, you take that along with you," Mae said. "I have a base for it that turns it into a car seat. I keep a lookout for used ones. And baby clothes. You'd be surprised how many mothers get caught unprepared."

"I'll send you money someday," Jamie said. "I promise I will."

"Never you mind," Mae said. "You just take good care of yourself and little Billy."

Mae put on her coat and carried the base out to the car. "Oh, your poor little dog," she said when she saw Ralph. "You should have brought him inside."

Ralph raced around the yard while Mae helped Jamie clear a place in the backseat and install the base for the infant seat. Once Billy Wisdom and his carrier were securely fastened in place, Jamie hugged Mae once again. "I'd all but forgotten that there were good people in the world," she admitted.

"Lots of good people," Mae said. Then she reached inside the pocket of her coat and pulled out a folded piece of paper. "My maiden name was Wisdom. I've written down the names, birth dates, and birthplaces of Janet Marie Wisdom's parents. You're going to need this information to get a copy of her birth certificate and apply for a Social Security number in her name."

"I am . . . I am so sorry," Jamie stammered. "I didn't know what else to do. The baby's father comes from a very rich family. I was afraid that . . ."

Mae held up her hand. "No need to explain, and you can rest assured that if anyone comes around here looking for you, they'll get a blank stare from me. The good Lord is looking out for you, honey. He took you to little Janet's grave then turned right around and directed your path to her great-aunt's house. She was a sweet child and much loved. Use her name well."

For a moment Jamie thought her knees were going to buckle. "I will," she said. "I promise that I will."

Chapter Twenty-four

GUS LOOKED OUT the window as the plane banked for a landing. The freshly cleared airstrip stood out starkly against the white landscape.

His kingdom was laid out below him, with Hartmann land as far as the eye could see—a sea of snow-covered land. He remembered Grandpa Buck saying that a man could never have too much land. The more land a man owned the more important he was.

He could see the little cemetery where his grandfather, father, and Sonny were buried. And Montgomery's stillborn baby.

He'd always known that Montgomery worshipped his grandfather, but somehow it had never occurred to Gus that they might have been lovers. Poor Montgomery. How sad she must have been when her baby didn't live. Had his grandfather also been sad? Or just relieved?

Kelly met the plane.

"More bad news," she announced as she pulled away from the airstrip. "Jamie Long had the baby."

Kelly drove him to what once had been the McGraf farm. Gus went in and looked around. At the blood-soaked mattress. The thick pile of ashes in the fireplace. Trash left by previous visitors. No fresh trash, though. Jamie had cleaned up after herself and taken it with her.

He pointed at the mutilated second mattress. "What's the story on that?"

"Probably she used the stuffing for kindling."

He noticed something shiny sticking out from beneath the bloody mattress and bent to pick it up. It was a small pair of scissors. Not nail scissors. Larger than that and of better quality. He carried them over to the window. They were engraved with vines and flowers.

"She probably used those to cut the cord," Kelly said.

Yes, she would have had to do that, Gus realized. It was hard to imagine a woman being alone at such a time—a young woman who'd never given birth before. And with all that blood. She must have been very frightened.

What had made Jamie Long leave the ranch, Gus pondered. What things had she deduced on her own, and what things had his mother told her? Surely the girl realized that Mary Millicent was as crazy as a loon. But not always. Sometimes she understood exactly what was going on. Sometimes she played them for fools. Gus knew that she could walk. When the Mexican gardener had carried her down the stairs to Sonny's room, he noticed that the bottoms of her house shoes were scuffed.

"I remembered one of my men saying that he'd pointed out the McGraf farm to her," Kelly said. "I drove up this morning to take a look."

Gus wanted to be angry. Wanted to yell at Kelly and tell her she should have looked here first. But this wasn't the only deserted farmhouse on the ranch. He'd paid the back taxes on at least a half dozen of these small spreads and had the occupants evicted. He didn't like the property of no-count dirt farmers backing up to Hartmann land. Didn't like their animals wandering onto Hartmann land. Didn't like them using the ranch store and service station and thinking they should be allowed to attend the Hartmann City church. Didn't like them tapping into the same aquifer with their wells. Didn't like them observing the comings and goings at the ranch.

The McGrafs. That was the family who'd frozen to death after the sheriff evicted them. But what did people expect? That they could stay on indefinitely without paying their taxes? It wasn't his fault that dumb-ass McGraf decided to leave in the middle of winter without first checking the weather report. Even if his generator was broken, everyone should have a battery-operated radio for emergencies. Or he could have listened to the radio in his truck—if it had a radio. Surely the man could have gotten the weather report somehow. He could have asked the sheriff for another day or two or taken shelter with a neighbor. There was no excuse for putting his family in danger like that.

Or maybe it had been like this most recent storm. Kelly said it hadn't been predicted to come this far north. Somehow Gus knew that Jamie Long had listened to the weather report before she left—for all the good it did her.

Gus walked through the house. Faded wallpaper was peeling from the walls, and tattered remnants of curtains hung from some of the windows. Mrs. McGraf had tried to make the place pretty.

He needed to stop thinking about the McGrafs, though, and focus on Jamie Long. Judging from the pile of ash in the fireplace, she had gathered a lot of wood and been here for a significant period of time. Right under Kelly's nose. Once again he was all but overcome by the urge to blame Kelly. To berate her.

But he didn't want Kelly going crazy like Montgomery. He needed Kelly to keep things going at the ranch now that Montgomery was gone.

He walked into the larger of the two bedrooms. Had Mr. and Mrs. McGraf been happy in this room, he wondered.

And he wondered how tall a man Mr. McGraf had been.

With all his riches and power, Gus had never experienced true love and joy with a woman. But he had experienced something just as precious when he was with Sonny. A pure, unselfish love that went all the way to bedrock.

He hadn't kidded himself into thinking that he was going to love Jamie Long's baby with anything close to what he had felt for Sonny. Every time he saw the baby, he would think of what he'd had to do to the kid's mother. But he wanted his sister to have Sonny's baby to love and raise and to pass off as her own if that was what she wanted. And human nature being what it was, Jamie Long would not have been able to resist blackmailing Amanda or selling her story to the highest bidder.

The closest thing to joy he was going to have for the rest of his days was making Amanda happy. If there was a hell, he already was going to burn in it. One more major sin wasn't going to make it any worse. What he had to do now was figure out how to find Jamie Long and Sonny's baby.

"We checked all the hospitals within a hundred-mile radius," Kelly told him. "And I swore out a warrant with the county sheriff accusing her of stealing money and jewelry."

"Call the sheriff and tell him that you were mistaken," Gus said. "I will handle the search—*privately*. As far as anyone on this ranch or in this county is concerned, she left and was never heard from again."

What he needed to do now was crawl inside the girl's head. What were her needs?

Gus took one more look around the pitiful little dwelling, then walked out onto the porch and pulled his cell phone from his pocket. The message on the tiny screen informed him that service was not available. Which irritated him. Even if the population density in Marshall County wasn't significantly higher than that of the moon, it was ridiculous not to have reliable cell-phone service.

He motioned to Kelly and headed for her vehicle.

After she dropped him off at the ranch house, he went straight to his bedroom, where the phone line was secure.

A man's voice answered.

"I'm at the ranch," Gus said. "I need you to come right away."

"Is this official or unofficial business?"

"Unofficial," Gus said.

Then he sat staring at nothing.

Montgomery. It was hard to believe that she was really dead. She had always been there for him. *Always.* He shouldn't have yelled at her. He'd been yelling a lot lately. The pompous, swaggering ignoramus they'd put in the White House thought that he should actually be in charge. If Gus hadn't been so aggravated with him, he wouldn't have lost his temper with Montgomery.

Gus did not allow himself to peer over the edge of the open casket as he lit the candles placed around it. With the flickering candlelight penetrating the shadows in the vaulted hall, he brought the stepping stool from the library. Without it, he would not be tall enough to kiss Montgomery's cold dead lips. And he needed to do that. Not for Montgomery, but for himself. Maybe such an act would make him feel better.

She looked ghastly.

He touched her cheek. It felt like cold rubber.

He sucked in his breath and bent forward to plant a kiss on her lips. "I am so sorry," he whispered.

Now the only person in the whole world who loved him was his sister.

He had waited until right before he left for the ranch to tell Amanda. She was still in bed, a coffee cup in her hands. Gus told Toby he needed to talk to his sister alone.

Amanda took one look at Gus's face and put the cup on the bedside table. "What is it?" she asked, patting a place on the bed beside her. The bed was low enough that he was able to seat himself next to her with some degree of dignity. He took her hand in his and kissed it.

He didn't believe in euphemisms. People did not "pass away" or "depart this earth." But he could not bring himself to say the *d* word. He took his beloved sister in his arms and whispered to her, "We've lost Montgomery."

Amanda gasped and pulled away, her eyes wide as she stared into his face. "She's not . . ."

Gus nodded.

Amanda screamed and began pulling at her hair and clawing her cheeks, leaving angry red marks. Toby came rushing back into the room. "Get the hell out of here," Gus yelled, grabbing his sister's hands. He couldn't stand to see her like this. "No, my darling, please don't do that to your beautiful face. We still have each other. We will always have each other."

Finally she calmed herself enough to ask how Montgomery had died. Gus considered lying to her but decided that she would discover the truth sooner or later and said, "She went out to the cemetery in the middle of a snowstorm wearing only her nightgown. They found her next to that little tombstone where a stillborn baby is buried. I think the baby must have been hers and Grandpa Buck's."

That had set her off again, with anger creeping into her tirade. How could Montgomery do such a thing at a time like this? "I need her to help me with the baby," she wailed.

Gus didn't have the heart to tell her that Jamie Long had disappeared. He would let her digest Montgomery's death first.

At first Amanda insisted that she was coming with him to the ranch so they could bury Montgomery together. But he reminded her that she supposedly was in the final weeks of her confinement for what had been billed as a difficult pregnancy and it would seem irresponsible if she did such a thing. "But it's *Montgomery*," she wailed.

Before he left Victory Hill, Gus had informed Toby that he was under no circumstances to allow Amanda to come to Texas and that he would find himself divorced, penniless, and minus some body parts if he did.

Gus took one final look at Montgomery's lifeless face, then climbed down from the stool, sat down on it, and buried his face in his hands.

"I am so sorry," he said again. "So very sorry."

The crying was less satisfying than he wanted it to be and it was chilly in here, so he blew out the candles then climbed the stairs and headed for the tower door.

He wanted his mother to put her arms around him even if he had to beg her.

After leaving the midwife's house, Jamie drove to the local Wal-Mart and, with Billy in the carrier and the carrier in a shopping cart, hurried her way through the store, trying to remember all the items on her mental shopping list. She selected assorted articles of baby clothing and a couple of packages of receiving blankets and wash cloths. Then she spotted a cloth sling designed to carry a baby across an adult's tummy and tossed it into the cart. She found a knitted cap for herself, selected a couple of nursing bras, then headed to pharmaceuticals for the bottle of rubbing alcohol and cotton balls she needed to clean the baby's cord stump. Next she located the hair dye and selected a shade called "burnished chestnut." Last she selected a pair of scissors suitable for cutting hair. Her long blond hair and height were the two most noticeable things about her appearance. She couldn't do anything about her height, but as soon as she had a chance, she would do something about her hair. In the meantime, the cap would have to do.

Once she had loaded the baby and her purchases into the car, she stuffed her hair inside the cap then drove into downtown Guymon and turned into the ATM lane at the Bank of the Panhandle. She inserted the ATM card that she had never used and was relieved when the machine accepted her PIN number. Her money was still in an account at the Austin bank. Almost $2,000 remained of the original $10,000 advance and, with no job and a baby to care for, she was going to need every penny of it.

The ATM machine allowed her to withdraw only $250. She then drove to City Bank, where she was allowed $500.

Next she drove around looking for the library.

Only a few cars were parked in the library lot. Jamie unfastened the infant carrier from its base, carried her sleeping baby inside, and headed straight for the computers.

First she looked for classic-car dealers. As much as she hated to part with it, she feared that Gus Hartmann already had people searching for her car. She surfed around a bit and found one site full of friendly advice for selling worthy older cars and a warning against randomly driving onto just any secondhand car lot. That said, the site recommended a number of reputable classic-car dealers.

The baby was waving his arms. Jamie calmed him by rocking the carrier with her foot.

Next she searched for Joseph Brammer's telephone number and found a listing in the Austin white pages. With a pounding heart, she used a pay phone in the foyer to place a call but got a recording informing her that the number was no longer in service.

Back at the computer she tried the business listings in Austin. Then she Googled his name but found too many matches to deal with. Next she tried to locate a listing for attorney Joseph Brammer in numerous Texas cities then finally gave up. There was no telling where he had opened his law practice, she realized.

She knew that his grandparents had moved to a retirement community in Georgia, but she couldn't remember the name of the town. Hopefully, though, she could find a listing for his parents in Houston. She had met his parents on several occasions but either had never known or had forgotten his father's first name.

There were dozens of Brammers in Houston, but one listing jumped out at her. "Arthur S. Brammer." Joe's middle name was Arthur, and she was certain that Joe's grandmother had referred to her son-in-law as Art.

Rocking the carrier was no longer working for Billy, and she carried him out to the car. He nursed vigorously for a time then obligingly fell back asleep.

Jamie tucked him back into the carrier and headed back to the pay phone. A woman's voice answered.

"Mrs. Brammer?"

"Yes?"

"My name is Jamie Long. I hope I have the right number. Do you have a son named Joe?"

"Yes, I do, Jamie. You used to live across the back fence from my parents in Mesquite. I remember you well and was so sorry to hear about your grandmother. We all thought a lot of Gladys. You know, dear, Joe tried to track you down last summer. I remember him saying that you seemed to have dropped off the planet."

Jamie's heart soared. *Joe had been looking for her.*

"I've been trying to get in touch with Joe, too. His Austin number is no longer in service."

"Joe took his last semester of law school abroad—at Oxford," Mrs. Brammer said. "Then he and some of the young men he'd met at Oxford decided to bike around the Continent. When winter came, Art and I thought for sure he'd head on home, but he and his companions headed south—for Greece."

Mrs. Brammer paused a second or two before continuing. Jamie had a sense that she was not going to like what followed. "Joe signed on as a crew member on a tramp steamer, Jamie. His last phone call was from some island off the coast of Turkey."

Jamie found herself having terribly conflicting reactions. God only knew when she would be able to talk to Joe. But trekking around Europe didn't sound like something a married man would be doing.

"So, Joe is not married?" she dared ask, trying to keep her voice a careful neutral.

"No, dear, he's not married. I always thought he was waiting around for you to grow up, but he got sidetracked with Marcia, who is a lovely girl, and they really seemed to care about each other, but I think she got tired of waiting around for him to get on with things."

Joe was not married. *Not married.*

Jamie realized that she had been holding her breath. She let it out before asking, "So, when do you think he's coming home?"

"Believe me, we ask him every time he calls. And his father lectures him about how it's time for him to settle down and how risky it is nowadays for Americans traveling abroad. Joe's all but promised that he'll be home in time for his father's birthday in June, but I'm hoping it will be sooner. We do miss him so."

"Is there any way I could get in touch with him?" Jamie asked.

"Not that I know of. He was e-mailing his grandparents every few weeks from places called cyber cafés, but they haven't heard from him since he's been on the ship. Is there anything Art and I can help you with, dear? You sound so forlorn."

"No, really I'm fine. The next time Joe calls, tell him that you talked to me," Jamie said, disappointment displacing joy.

"Where are you, Jamie? And where in the world have you been? Before he left for Europe he checked with UT, but you weren't enrolled for the spring semester. And while he was in England, he searched for you on the computer—which I don't understand at all. Finally he decided that you must have signed up for the Peace Corps or something exotic like that."

Jamie took a deep breath. Joe had been looking for her. *Really* looking for her. "It's too complicated to explain on the phone," she said.

"But you have to be living someplace. Where are you calling from?"

A man and woman were coming through the front door. They looked down at the baby in the carrier parked at Jamie's feet and smiled. "A pay phone in another state," Jamie said, lowering her voice. "I'll try to call you back in a day or two and tell you where I can be reached."

"You can't even tell me the name of the state! Are you in hiding or something? You sound so tired, dear. Are you all right?"

The sympathy and concern in the voice of Joe's mother was too much for Jamie to bear. She choked up, unable to speak for several seconds, unable to hold back sobs.

"Oh, my goodness. You poor child. How can I help you? Please tell me where you are. Art and I will come to get you. Or wire you money. Send you a plane ticket. Just tell me what you need."

"I'll be fine. Really I will. I'll talk to you soon. Okay?"

"No. I want you to promise me that you will call back *tomorrow* with a phone number where we can reach you."

"I'll try," Jamie said and hung up the phone. She wondered if the Brammers had caller ID. She should have warned Mrs. Brammer not to tell anyone except Joe that she had called. And her husband. That would be okay. But no one else. She rubbed her forehead and tried to tell herself once again that her fears could very well be baseless. But how could she know for sure?

Chapter Twenty-five

JAMIE SAGGED AGAINST the foyer wall by the pay phone. She wanted to carry her baby back into the nice warm library and sit in an easy chair for a time to ponder her conversation with Joe's mother—to replay Mrs. Brammer's words, turning them over and over in her mind and examining them from every angle as one would a handful of pleasing pebbles gathered from a creek bed. Jamie had no idea when she might see Joe again or hear his voice. But *he was not married.*

Even so, she must put thoughts of him aside and decide what she was going to do next. She would get back to them, though.

With no way of knowing when Joe would return home, maybe she should find another lawyer.

She imagined sitting across the desk from an attorney. Imagined the incredulous look on his or her face as she tried to explain the predicament she was in. And what if in the process of checking out her story, the attorney alerted the very people who were looking for her?

Joe wouldn't think she was crazy. He would realize the threat against her was real.

She had always been in love with Joe. She could admit that now. It had not been just an adolescent crush.

She had tried to cure herself of Joe, telling herself that he was nice to her because he felt sorry for her. Sorry that her parents were dead. Sorry she didn't have cute clothes and wasn't popular and lost her one shot at being special when she hurt her knee and couldn't run track anymore. But now Joe's own mother had indicated that his feelings for her were not based on pity.

Jamie knelt and touched her baby's unbelievably soft cheek with a fingertip. "Let's go, my little Billy boy," she whispered.

She stopped at a Conoco station on the way out of Guymon. She paid for gas, a cup of coffee, and a cheese sandwich, then—with an ever watchful eye on the car and its precious cargo—studied the map of Oklahoma taped to the wall. The Oklahoma-Kansas line was only thirty-five miles away.

She got back in the car and started the motor. Then, absently stroking her dog, she sat there for a time, trying to decide what to do. She was exhausted and desperately in need of sleep. The stitches in her bottom hurt like hell. The baby was whimpering, and soon she would need to nurse him again, longer this time. Maybe she should get a motel room here in Guymon.

But she had used her ATM card here. Twice. She could be traced to this town. Gus Hartmann's henchmen might already be on their way. Jamie recalled a movie in which an on-the-run Julia Roberts discovered that her bank account had mysteriously vanished, leaving her without funds. Even though Jamie realized that she would be leaving an electronic trail by using her ATM card, she hoped to remove all of the money from her account before anyone had a chance to make it disappear. By then she would be far away from the town in which she made her withdrawals.

She needed to keep going. Needed to put miles between herself and Guymon. Needed to find other banks and withdraw the rest of her money before it vanished like Julia Roberts's had done. Of course, she was probably being paranoid. Probably Gus Hartmann could not simply pick up a phone and make her money vanish. But just in case he could, she needed that money and whatever she got for selling her car to live on until she had a Social Security number and was able to find a job.

She closed her eyes, trying to will away the headache that was planting itself inside her weary brain.

The next thing she knew her head was jerking back. And she realized that she had dozed off while sitting in the car beside a gas pump.

She could see a road sign indicating that Liberal, Kansas, was straight ahead. She would go there, withdraw more money, and then decide where to go next. She drove behind the service station. She let Ralph run around a bit then fell asleep again while she was nursing Billy.

During the drive to Liberal, when she felt herself starting to nod off, she would pull over onto the shoulder of the two-lane highway, get out of the car, inhale the cold air, swing her arms around for a minute or two, then get back in and drive a few more miles.

Finally she crossed the state line. Liberal was just ahead.

A large stone monument announced that she had arrived in the town. She continued driving until she reached the downtown, where she pulled into the ATM lane of the Bank of America and withdrew $500.

Then, at the Community Bank, the words "Invalid PIN" appeared on the screen.

Very carefully she entered the number again. Then she punched "enter." And the same words appeared on the screen.

"Oh my God!" Jamie whispered as goose flesh rose on her arms. Her worst fear had been validated. Any notion she had harbored that she had misjudged the entire situation vanished. Some ominous and seemingly omnipotent power had closed her bank account, and the electronic word of that closure had reached all the way to Liberal, Kansas.

She looked around, half expecting men with carefully trimmed hair and wearing overcoats and mirrored sunglasses to appear suddenly and pull her from the car. They hadn't arrived yet, but they would.

She rested her forehead on the steering wheel. *What should she do?*

She couldn't just sit here like a sitting duck. She needed to hide. And get rid of her car. *ASAP!*

The driver of the car in line behind her gently tapped on his horn, reminding her it was time to move on. For an instant, Jamie couldn't remember how to drive.

Push in the clutch, she told herself. *Put the car in gear.*

She followed the curving drive to the street. Left or right? She turned right and drove hesitantly for a block then pulled into a parking space.

Ralph pushed his head under her idle hand, and she absently began to stroke him. She couldn't take a bus or a train with a dog. And she couldn't hitchhike in frigid weather with a two-day-old baby.

What would she do with her possessions if she abandoned her car? She hated to give them up. They were all she had left of her past.

But they were only *things,* she told herself. They weren't worth losing her baby. Or her life.

She toyed with the idea of renting a car. But she would have to show her driver's license. How long would it take for the transaction to be traced, for the men in mirrored sunglasses to be looking for a specific rental car with a specific tag number?

Then a hopeful thought crossed her mind. Maybe the computer at the last bank had malfunctioned. Maybe she should try another bank.

She pulled out of the parking space and made a U-turn on the wide street.

She pulled into the ATM lane of a third bank. Her hand was shaking as she inserted her card and punched in her PIN.

Once again she was informed that she had used an invalid number.

She had to get out of Liberal, Kansas. *Now.*

She left the bank and headed back toward the highway. When she reached the intersection, she hesitated. Anyone pursuing her probably would expect her to continue heading north, putting as much distance and as many states as possible between herself and the Hartmann Ranch.

She turned south. Once she had crossed back over the state line, she stopped at the first service station and bought an Oklahoma map. She wanted the anonymity provided by a large city, and Oklahoma City was the largest city in the state. She would use only the least traveled roads to get there.

But first, she had to find a place to sleep for a few hours. Her vision was starting to blur. She was weak with exhaustion, probably from all the blood she was losing. She needed to change the pad again. Needed something to eat.

She went through a tiny community whose only businesses seemed to be a convenience store and a tavern. Then she spotted a sign that said COTTAGES FOR RENT.

She pulled into what was left of an old-fashioned tourist court—four cottages and a row of empty foundations. A crooked sign with the word OFFICE was nailed on the side of a frame house. Jamie climbed up the steps and knocked on the door. An elderly man in filthy overalls opened the door. "Twenty dollars' cash in advance," he said. Jamie returned to the car for a twenty-dollar bill, which she exchanged for a key to cottage 2.

She parked the car behind the cottage so it would be out of sight from the road and carried the baby and a few things inside. She watched from the door of the cottage while Ralph raced around the bare foundations then called him inside. She fed him and filled a bowl with water. After changing her baby, she nursed him once again, not because he was crying but because she needed him to let her sleep.

She had promised herself a nice long shower but didn't have energy left even for that. She drank the bottle of orange juice and ate the banana-nut bread that Mae the midwife had given her, then crawled into bed with her baby and her dog, which probably wasn't recommended in Mae's booklets. But first she needed to survive and then she would worry about the rules for child rearing.

She kissed the baby's forehead and his ears and hands. "I love you, baby Billy." She felt as though her heart had grown to enormous proportions in order to accommodate all the love she felt for this tiny infant.

With her cheek against the top of his downy head, she used the few minutes she had before sleep claimed her to think about the phone call with Joe's mother. She replayed the conversation in her head, considering its implications.

It could be weeks—or longer—before the Brammers heard from Joe.

He wasn't married.

He had searched for her.

His mother thought he had been waiting around for her to grow up.

What did mothers know about such things, though?

Jamie knew, however, that she was going to cling to Mrs. Brammer's words like a lifeline. Maybe she was setting herself up for disappointment, but she was going to allow herself to hope. What she had to do now was survive until Joe returned from his travels.

The baby woke in the night. Jamie changed him then wrapped them both in a blanket and leaned against the headboard to nurse him. He was getting lustier about the nursing, and her breasts suddenly were much fuller. Painfully so. She worried that she had an infection or that the milk ducts were becoming clogged. She definitely needed to read those booklets, but they would have to wait. Right now the best she could do was fly by the seat of her pants.

She slept a few more hours. When she woke it was dawn. She put on her coat and took Ralph outside for a few minutes, then fed him and set out a bowl of water. Then she stood in front of the bathroom mirror, took a deep breath, and cut her hair, leaving about four inches all over her head.

She had also planned to dye it, but the directions revealed a far more lengthy and complicated process than she had anticipated.

The water in the shower was freezing cold, but she was desperate for a shower. She hurriedly soaped herself and rinsed. When she turned off the water, she could hear Billy crying. She dried quickly and pulled on some clothes. "There, there, there," she cooed as she picked him up.

Her breasts were as hard as rocks, but their swollen state did not seem to impede the flow. Billy was obviously getting something out of them.

When he finished nursing, she changed him and sponged the cord stump with rubbing alcohol as per Mae's instructions.

She loaded up her possessions, baby, and dog in the car then pulled up in front of the convenience store and, keeping the car in her line of vision, bought coffee and a packaged pastry.

Billy slept for three hours, which took her as far as the town of Shattuck. She pulled into an empty church parking lot to nurse him and let Ralph out. Then she bought gas along with snacks and water bottles for the road and once again took up her meandering route eastward.

It was evening before she reached the outskirts of Oklahoma City. She pulled over to consult the city map that was printed on the back of the state map. She wanted to be close to the downtown and the inter-city bus station it would offer. Eventually she found herself in a neighborhood near a large hospital complex where formerly large gracious homes had been divided into apartments. Within walking distance were a park and a small commercial area that offered a grocery, bakery, drugstore, and service station. It was almost dark by the time she parked in front of a brick dwelling with an APARTMENT FOR RENT sign in a window.

She pulled the knit cap over her much shorter but still blond hair, lifted her baby out of the infant seat, and went inside. The word "Office" was written in magic marker on the first door. Jamie knocked and a seriously overweight woman with graying hair opened the door and stepped out into the hall. She introduced herself as Ruby Duffy.

"You got a husband?" she asked Jamie.

"No, ma'am. It would be just me and the baby."

Jamie followed behind the woman as she laboriously climbed to the third floor and unlocked the door to an apartment on the backside of the building.

The apartment was bleak. Jamie took in the dingy windows, worn linoleum, stained sink, and mouse droppings in the corners. The double bed took up so much room in the tiny bedroom that the two bottom bureau drawers wouldn't open all the way. The minuscule kitchen was an alcove off the living room. The living room's only furnishings were a sofa and chair, both upholstered in cracked brown vinyl, and a battered coffee table. The bathroom was no bigger than a closet, and the only closet was so shallow it offered only a row of hooks on the back wall from which to hang clothes. But the apartment was cheap and the water that came out of the hot-water faucet was actually hot.

Mrs. Duffy announced that she required a month's rent in advance.

"I have a dog," Jamie said.

"No dogs," the landlady said and started for the door.

"He's a very good dog. Could I just bring him in and let you meet him? You'll see what a nice dog he is."

Mrs. Duffy frowned. "You want me to *meet* a dog?"

"Just to see how well behaved he is," Jamie said. "Please. I've come a long way, and I just don't have the energy to look further."

Mrs. Duffy cocked her head to one side and regarded Jamie and then the baby. "How old is the baby?" she asked.

"Three days," Jamie said.

"Where's the father?"

Jamie hung her head. "He's not in the picture," she said.

"He the one that put that bruise on your forehead? I don't want someone like that showing up here and causing trouble."

Jamie touched her forehead. "No," she said, revising the story she had been about to tell. "I tripped and fell. The baby's father doesn't know anything about the baby," she said, thinking of poor dead Sonny.

The landlady looked dubious. "You have a job?" she demanded.

"Not yet. But I have enough money to tide me over until I find work." Jamie leaned her cheek against her baby's head. "Please," she begged. "I am exhausted, and it's getting late."

"If you're planning to write a check, you won't be able to move in until Monday morning—after I call the bank and make sure it will clear."

"I can pay you in cash."

Ruby stepped a bit closer and touched the top of the baby's head. "Three days old," she said reverently.

Then she stepped back and folded her arms across her ample bosom.

"Okay. A two-hundred-dollar security deposit for the dog. Up front. There's parking behind the building. Don't leave anything inside of your car if you don't want it broken into."

She followed the woman back down the stairs to her apartment, which was more spacious than the one Jamie was renting. Even so, two oversized recliners, a big-screen television, and an enormous rolltop desk filled up the entire front room. Ruby Duffy had to turn her body sideways to get to the desk.

Jamie paid the rent and deposit and signed the lease as "Janet M. Wisdom." The name was only temporary, she told herself. Someday she hoped to reclaim her own name, but for now she was grateful for Janet's.

She put Billy in the baby sling and, with Ralph following at her heels, began carrying her possessions up the three flights of stairs and dumping them in the tiny living room, which turned out to be a seemingly endless job. She took several breaks, once to nurse Billy, and others to simply sit and catch her breath. Her stitches hurt and every muscle in her body protested that she simply could not take another step. When she had the interior of the car emptied, she decided that the things in the trunk would have to wait until tomorrow. At least there was nothing visible to tempt thieves.

Then she loaded the baby and Ralph back into the car and drove to the nearby grocery store to buy a few groceries, mouse traps, and some cleaning supplies.

She made up the bed, got the baby settled, and ate a peanut butter sandwich and a glass of milk before walking down the hall to the pay phone.

She stood there for a minute, coins in hand. But maybe this call wasn't such a good idea. What if the phone was tapped?

It couldn't be, she told herself. No one knew that she was here. But what if Mrs. Brammer had let something slip to a friend or neighbor? Or her husband had? Maybe their phone was the one that was tapped.

Jamie felt as though she was going to pass out if she took one more step. Maybe she should wait until tomorrow to call Mrs. Brammer.

Instead, she loaded up the baby and the dog in the car one last time and, keeping to residential streets, drove to far north Oklahoma City and placed her call from a drive-up pay phone near a service station.

"Mrs. Brammer, it's Jamie. I'm sorry to be calling so late."

"Jamie, thank goodness!" Mrs. Brammer said. "I've been waiting all day for you to call. Are you all right?"

"Yes."

"Do you have a phone number where you can be reached?"

Jamie hesitated. "No, and please, you must not tell *anyone* about me," she added. "Except your husband and Joe, of course."

"Are you in hiding?"

"Yes. I am in hiding. I haven't broken any law," she hastened to add, "but I am in trouble. Serious trouble. Do you have any idea when Joe might call again?"

"Not really. It could be tomorrow or several weeks from now."

Jamie ended the call by saying that she would try to call again the following Thursday evening.

She drove home by another route, getting lost on the way. Almost an hour had passed by the time she returned her car to the parking space in the alley behind the apartment house. She waited for Ralph to relieve himself before going inside. She wasn't sure she had the strength to climb the stairs. Just one step at a time, she told herself.

She drank another glass of milk, fed the baby, and then at last was able to take a shower. A long, hot shower. Even though the bathroom was dirty, it was the most wonderful shower she had ever taken in her life.

She put on one of the flannel nightgowns that Amanda had given her, picked up her baby, and crawled into bed with him. Ralph jumped up on the bed and curled up at the foot. "We're home," she told her baby and her dog. Then she began to weep. She wept because she was more exhausted than she had ever been in her life and every muscle in her body felt as though it were on fire. She wept because she was lonely and faced an uncertain future. But mostly she wept because she was afraid.

So very afraid.

The next morning, she finished unloading the car and dyed her hair. The results were discouraging. Her hair not only looked as though it had been trimmed by a lawn mower, it was now a flat shade of brown that made her skin seem sallow. She wanted to cry, but she had already done enough of that.

Her aching body begged her to leave the cleaning and settling in for later, but she had been raised by a woman who believed that rest was allowed only after the chores were done. And it was such a small apartment.

Her grandmother used to say that scrubbing was good for the soul, and it did prove to be good for her spirits as she scoured away years of grime and mouse habitation and polished the two windows until they gleamed. Cleanliness gave the shabbiness a genteel quality that reminded Jamie of the little house in Mesquite.

"You mean that you couldn't find a single person in Guymon, Oklahoma, or Liberal, Kansas, who remembered seeing Jamie Long?" Gus demanded.

"Yes, sir. That is correct."

"You're using that picture I provided?"

"Yes, we are, sir."

"Have you looked at the security tapes from the ATMs?"

"Yes, sir. The girl had her hair stuffed inside a cap. None of the tapes revealed the presence of a baby, but she had a lot of clothes and boxes piled in the car, and it was impossible to view the far side of the backseat. There was a dog in the passenger side of the front seat."

Yes, Gus thought. Kelly had said she took her dog with her. "Can you get a still of the dog?" he asked.

"We can try."

"What about the hospitals in those two towns?" Gus asked. "The nurse here says the girl probably would have needed some stitches."

"We thought of that. No one fitting her description and circumstances showed up at the emergency rooms in either city. We also checked with the family practitioners, obstetricians, and midwives in both towns, but the girl had not contacted any of them."

"What about other towns?" Gus demanded.

"There aren't any other towns in that area large enough to have a physician or a midwife."

Gus looked at the map he had spread out in front of him. "Go on up into Kansas—to Ulysses, Garden City, Dodge City. To any town that has any sort of medical practitioner. And check at service stations, convenience stores, roadside diners. She has to buy gas and she has to eat. And if the baby is alive, she'll need diapers and other baby stuff. And she would have had to stop and sleep by now. Check motels for any young woman who paid cash. This is the highest priority. You got that! *Highest priority!* I want that girl and her baby found."

Gus slammed down the phone. The girl was outsmarting them.

He got up and kicked a wastebasket across the room. He started to throw a crystal decanter against the wall but decided instead to pour himself a glass of sherry. He downed it and poured another.

It was time for him to talk to Amanda.

Chapter Twenty-six

AMANDA HAD JUST stepped out of the tub and wrapped herself in a warm towel when Toby tapped on the door. "Your brother is on the phone," he said. Then he stepped inside and, wearing a playful look, tried to pull the towel away.

She hit the side of his head with her fist and stormed out of the bathroom. He knew how upset she was about Montgomery. She was in *mourning,* for God's sake. All the man could think about was sex.

"Gus, darling, why haven't you returned my calls?" she asked, allowing her voice to sound a bit angry. It wasn't like Gus to ignore her. "Are you still at the ranch? I thought you would be back home by now."

"I am still at the ranch," Gus said, his voice weary.

"Freda said the service for Montgomery went well, but I wanted to hear it from *you,*" Amanda said. "And we need to discuss a grave marker. Something in pink granite, I think. I still can't believe that she's gone and that I'm never going to see her again." Amanda closed her eyes against the pain.

And the anger.

How could Montgomery have done this to her? Montgomery knew how much she and Gus depended on her. How much they cared for her. Who was going to look after Mother now? And the ranch?

"Are you sure she didn't leave a note?" Amanda asked. "She owed us some explanation of why she would do such a thing. Or do you think she had a nervous breakdown?"

"Something like that," Gus said. "She was very upset, Amanda. And she had reason to be. Jamie Long left the ranch."

"Left the ranch!" Amanda cried out. "But why? Did she come back?"

"No. I have people out looking for her, but it's been three days now since she left. We think she's someplace in Kansas."

"I don't understand. Why would she be in Kansas?" Amanda demanded, her brow tightening with apprehension. "The baby is due in a couple of weeks. Surely she'll return to the ranch to have the baby."

"Amanda, Jamie Long has already had the baby. She had it by herself in a deserted farmhouse during a snowstorm."

Amanda sank to the side of the bed and put her hand to her throat. "The baby is all right, isn't he?"

"I have no idea."

"How do you know she had a baby if you haven't seen it?" Amanda rubbed her forehead. Her brother wasn't making any sense. No sense at all. But he was frightening her. *Really* frightening her.

"There was graphic evidence of a recent birth at that house," Gus said. "I seriously doubt if some other woman had traveled to Marshall County to have a baby on her own in the middle of a blizzard."

"That terrible girl!" Amanda shrieked. "You have to find her! To find our baby!"

"I will," Gus promised, "but it may take a while. I have been making some phone calls. I plan to arrange for a soon-to-be-born baby to use as a stand-in until we find Sonny's baby."

"No," she screamed. "I don't want another baby!"

"Amanda, I want you to take a deep breath and listen to me. Listen very *carefully*. What if your supposed due date comes and goes and there is no baby? Your followers will be expecting an announcement of his birth and a picture of you with a baby. They are waiting with bated breath for that picture, and I'm not even sure that Jamie Long's baby is still alive. It was three weeks early, and the girl was alone when she had it. I saw that house, Amanda. There was a lot of blood, and it was bitterly cold."

Amanda drew in her breath. "No," she gasped. "I would know if the baby died. God would have told me."

"That may very well be," Gus said, "but until I find Sonny's baby, we may need another one to use in its place."

"No, Gus, no," Amanda said, tears rolling down her face. "Please, I have to have *Sonny's* baby. I *have* to. You know that. I don't want Toby anymore. I just want you and *our* baby."

"And you will have him," Gus said, his voice breaking. "You have my solemn promise."

* * *

Gus hung up the phone and drew in his breath, filling his lungs and heart and mind with resolve. He would keep his promise to his sister. He *must*. What good was all this power if he couldn't give his sister the one thing that she wanted more than anything else?

He should have removed Jamie Long from the ranch long ago and put her in a more secure place. He knew as soon as he realized what Amanda was up to and that her plan was fraught with problems. His sister lived in a fairy-tale world of her own making. Gus had realized from the very beginning—even before he learned that Sonny's semen had been used to impregnate the girl—that one of two things was probably going to happen. The girl would realize that she was a goose about to lay a golden egg and hold out for more money, or, for quite another set of reasons, the girl might decide that she wanted to keep the baby for herself. The minute he found out that she was carrying Sonny's baby, he should have locked her up in a place far from the ranch. A place that she would never leave.

It was all his fault.

He rose from his chair and began to pace across the imposing bed-chamber—with its high ceilings and massive fireplace—that had once been his larger-than-life grandfather's. Back in his Grandfather Buck's day, the room had contained massive furniture—a huge four-poster bed that stood four feet above the floor, oversized chairs, and tall chests whose top drawers Gus could not reach. Now the room held different furniture. Chairs he did not have to scramble into. A bed he didn't need a stepping stool to climb into. But the furniture never looked as though it belonged in a room of such grand proportions.

He paused by the fireplace for a minute to warm his backside.

What if he couldn't keep his promise to his sister? What if he never found the girl?

But that was ridiculous. She was clever, but it was only a matter of time until she made a mistake. There was a limit to how long she could elude the net he had thrown out there. Not without unlimited money. Not without help.

Help. Was there anything he was overlooking? An all-points had been sent out on her and her car. He had found the girl's address book in Montgomery's desk and knew the names of her friends. And her sister. Those people were already being watched. Their phones were being tapped. Their mail would be examined. People in the girl's hometown were already being interviewed—neighbors, teachers, classmates, members of her church. They were shown a badge and the cover story was kept vague but strongly implied that it would be in Jamie's best interest for her to be located and that something ominous could happen to her if she were not. Even if those being interviewed were at first reluctant, eventually they would agree to help. They would let the interviewer know if they saw or heard from her.

It was only a matter of time, Gus told himself as he pulled the covers back and crawled into bed.

For so many years, whenever he was at the ranch, he and Montgomery would play gin rummy and drink scotch in the evening. And she would tell him stories about his father and grandfather. Coming here was never going to be the same.

He should not have yelled at her. What happened was his doing, not hers. He should have seen it coming. "I'm so sorry, Montgomery," he whispered. *"So sorry."*

He didn't want to cry. Not again. He turned his thoughts to Amanda. She didn't want Toby anymore. "I just want you and our baby," she had said.

Maybe they could name the boy Montgomery and call him "Monty." Or "Buck" would be nice. Buck was a good name for a West Texas boy. And that's what Gus wanted him to be. A rancher. A man of the land. He wanted to preserve his innocence, as he had with Sonny. Gus had convinced Amanda not to take Sonny on the road as a boy, claiming that some would see that as exploitation. There would be plenty of time for that after Sonny had finished college. But Sonny wasn't much of a student and didn't adapt well to college. Sonny wanted to spend his life here on the ranch—not saving souls and raising money to elect political candidates. But the boy had never had the courage to tell his mother. He was happiest here at the ranch. Like his great-grandfather Buck, the boy had loved the land. If he wasn't riding across it on horseback, he was racing around in that damned all-terrain vehicle. Gus had wanted to blame the accident on the company that manufactured it, but maybe it was the land itself that had killed Sonny. All that space was seductive. It made a man feel one with the universe. Made him long to be a wild mustang. Or an eagle.

Gus desperately needed a full night's rest and had taken something to assure that sleep would come. He felt his body relaxing as the drug took hold. A nice feeling. He closed his eyes and imagined himself and little Buck in the pony cart. He could hear the boy's laughter and the bells jingling merrily as the pony trotted down the drive. But to turn that vision into reality, he had to track down Jamie Long.

The baby was still alive. He had decided to believe that was so until he knew otherwise. He *needed* to believe that.

Monday morning Jamie found her way to the vital statistics office at the state health department. Using the information the midwife had given her, she filled out a form for the baby's birth certificate and one for Janet Marie Wisdom. The clerk said she should receive them in a week to ten days.

That was easy, Jamie thought as she picked up the infant carrier and headed for the door. As soon as she had a birth certificate, she could apply for a Social Security number and obtain a driver's license.

That afternoon she called a classic-car dealer in Wichita, Kansas, and told him about her car. He sounded interested. And honest, if one could determine such a thing over the telephone. Then she ran a few errands while she still had the car. At a secondhand store, she bought a baby bed, a floor lamp, and a radio. Then she went to a discount store where she selected more clothing for Billy, bedding for his bed, a huge package of diapers, a large bag of dog food, a rawhide bone, and a Frisbee. Last she stocked up on staples at a supermarket.

The landlady's door opened as Jamie started up the stairs with the last of her purchases. "How's that baby doing," Mrs. Duffy asked as she stepped out into the hall.

"Just fine," Jamie said. "He and I are learning more about each other every day."

Mrs. Duffy reached out and stroked Billy's head. "Such a pretty little boy," she said. "You be sure and enjoy him while he's little. Children grow up so fast."

"Yes, ma'am," Jamie said and headed up the stairs.

After she put away the groceries, Jamie put the baby in the sling and the leash on Ralph, and they went out for an evening walk. It was almost balmy, and she realized that spring was in the air, that the trees and shrubs were starting to bud.

Her long cold winter was over.

Early the next morning, she gave Ralph the rawhide bone in hopes it would help him pass a long, lonely day shut up in the apartment and headed for Wichita.

She avoided I-35 and took Highway 74 north until it ended at the town of Deer Creek, then she crossed under the interstate and took Highway 77 and then Highway 15 into Wichita.

She arrived at the classic-car lot before the appointed hour. She watched while a tall, lanky young man named Underwood walked around the car then lifted the hood. Then she and Billy waited inside the cluttered office while Mr. Underwood drove the car.

When he returned he asked what she wanted for the car. When Jamie told him, he looked as though she were demented.

"You told me on the phone that you are an honest man and would do right by me," Jamie told him. "I'm a single mother with a new baby and need the money from this car just to get by."

"I could take it on consignment," he suggested.

Jamie shook her head. She needed to sever all ties with this car. *Today*. Its very uniqueness made her feel as though she were driving around in a vehicle with a target painted on its side.

Mr. Underwood made an offer considerably lower than her asking price. Jamie made him a counteroffer, and they shook hands.

"I'll need the money in cash," Jamie told him.

He lifted an eyebrow. "Domestic trouble?" he asked.

She nodded.

He looked down at the car title. "I see the original owner of the car was a Gladys Simpson."

"She's my grandmother. You'll see on the back of the title where she signed the car over to me before she died. I have her death certificate—and her driver's license if you want to verify her signature."

She watched while he looked at the certificate and the license and made copies of both. Then he picked up her Texas driver's license again and stared at the image. "You have any other identification?"

Jamie produced her Social Security card, her birth certificate, and her University of Texas student ID. She wondered how many months or years would have to go by before she once again could identify herself as "Jamie Amelia Long."

Mr. Underwood gave her a ride to the bus station in downtown Wichita. "Where are you headed?" he asked.

"Florida," she said firmly. "I am sick and tired of being cold. And I have an aunt there who is going to look after my baby while I finish college. That's what the money from the car is for. I'm going to use it for tuition and books."

Her story amazed her. Should she be worried that she was getting so proficient at lying?

She purchased a ticket to Oklahoma City.

As the bus rolled down I-35 toward Oklahoma City, she tried to think if there was anything else she should do. Any mistakes she might have made.

Every mile she put between herself and her car, she felt safer. Soon she would have a new birth certificate with a different name, which would also make her feel safer, but not safe.

Would Amanda Hartmann find another baby to pass off as her own? Would Amanda ever tell her brother that he didn't need to look for Sonny's baby anymore?

No, Jamie decided. Amanda would never give up.

It was dark before a taxi delivered Jamie and her baby to the apartment house. Poor Ralph was so overjoyed to see her that he went absolutely crazy, leaping so high in the air that he did a complete backward somersault. "Wow!" Jamie said, putting down the infant carrier and kneeling to hug her dog. "We're going to have to give that Frisbee a try."

After she had seen to her dog and her baby, she carried a sandwich and a glass of milk to the coffee table. She planned to finally read the material on infant care that Mae had given her. But she ate her sandwich and then just sat there, allowing herself for the first time to address the horror that she had gone through. The bone-grinding pain, the blood, her ignorance of what was happening, the fear that she and her baby would die alone on an old mattress in the middle of a blizzard. And even after Billy had been born, how much determination it had taken for her to pack up the car and start out again with her body weak and torn and exhausted and hurting and bleeding, bleeding, bleeding. She was still bleeding. She hoped Mae's little booklets would tell her that all that bleeding was normal. If not, she would have to find someone to make it stop.

But for now she just wanted to sit here. She would read about motherhood tomorrow.

She thought of how not long ago her most immediate goal had been to return to college. Maybe she would still do that someday, but right now she had to plan her life around two things—caring for her child and keeping her little family safe.

She wondered if she would ever feel completely safe again.

Chapter Twenty-seven

JAMIE STRETCHED IN her bed and took note of the sun streaming through the window. The weather report on the radio had promised a beautiful spring day. And she had the whole day ahead of her to do as she pleased. For the time being, her travels were over. Now she began a waiting game—waiting until she could establish her new identity, buy a car, look for a job, open a bank account, and begin her life anew as Janet Marie Wisdom.

And more immediately, Jamie was waiting for tomorrow evening, when she would once again talk to Joe's mother.

But today, she had no agenda. She stretched, luxuriating in the thought that she could simply enjoy her baby, her dog, their new home, and the gift of a beautiful day.

Ralph was looking at her from the foot of the bed. "Good morning," she told him and he wiggled his way to her side, pushing his head under her hand. "Let's see, what shall we do today?" she pondered as she scratched his ears. "I want to give Billy a by-the-book bath, and we need to do some laundry. And this afternoon we can walk over to that little park and see if you can catch a Frisbee."

She read about bathing babies. Only sponge baths were allowed until Billy's cord stem fell off.

She put him on a folded towel beside the kitchen sink and talked to him while she washed his little body, and he looked up at his mommy with a somewhat puzzled but quite intelligent expression on his face. Everything about him was perfect—his little nose, his mouth, his fingers and toes. The slope of his little shoulders made her weak with love. She'd realized that having a baby was a life-changing event but hadn't had a clue as to how complete that change would be.

"I will be the very best mother I can be," she promised her child and herself.

That afternoon, except for some elderly men playing dominoes on the concrete picnic tables, they had the park to themselves. She spread a blanket under a tree, placed Billy on it, and picked up the Frisbee.

Keeping her baby in view, she tossed the Frisbee over and over again, and Ralph would race after it and wait for it to land, then dutifully pick it up and come trotting back to Jamie. She hadn't a clue as to how to make him understand what she wanted him to do until one of the domino players yelled at her, "Roll it to him a few times so he can learn to catch it while it's still in motion."

Jamie did as the man suggested, and Ralph would chase after the rolling disk and grab it. After they had that routine down pat, she sailed the Frisbee along a horizontal plane just a few feet above the ground, and lo and behold he made a leaping jump and grabbed it. Jamie was thrilled. "Good boy," she called and watched with pride as he trotted back with the disk in his mouth and his crooked tail wagging. She knelt and gave him a hug. "You're the best!" she said enthusiastically.

Then they got serious. The domino players applauded time and again as Ralph leapt high in the air, his body twisting and turning as though he had been catching Frisbees all his life. Finally Jamie grew weary of the game. She picked up Billy and walked toward the picnic tables with Ralph leaping happily at her side.

"Thanks for the advice," she told the man who had yelled the instructions. He wasn't as old as the other domino players, she realized. In fact, he wasn't old at all.

"Glad to be of service," the man said. His suit jacket was folded on the bench beside him, his necktie on top of it. He had rolled up the sleeves of his white dress shirt. The other men were more casually dressed. He was the only one who looked as though he had just been to a barbershop.

"He caught on fast," the man said as he reached out and petted Ralph. "Cute little mutt. Have you had him long?"

Jamie shook her head. "He followed me home a few days ago," she lied.

"Smart dog," the man said, picking up a domino and fiddling with it.

His nails were carefully trimmed. His shoes were polished to a high gloss.

"You live around here?" the man asked.

"No, I'm visiting my aunt," Jamie said, trying to keep her voice calm and friendly. "Well, thanks again," she said, backing away.

The man stood. "Well, Grandpa," he said to the man across the table from him, "are you ready to go? Grandma probably has that cake baked by now."

The elderly man nodded and, using the table for leverage, struggled to his feet.

Jamie watched as the two men walked across the street and entered a two-story house that, like the others in the neighborhood, had seen better days. In the driveway, a shiny black SUV was parked behind an elderly tan sedan.

Jamie went weak in the knees. She drew in several breaths to calm herself then carried her baby back across the park with her dog at her side.

She put Billy in his sling and snapped Ralph's leash back on his collar then gathered up the blanket. "That man *could* have been one of them," Jamie told Ralph. "*They* know I have a dog. Montgomery would have told them what you look like. They are looking for a tall girl with a baby and a scruffy grayish-brown dog with long legs."

She left Ralph in the apartment, then with Billy still in the sling walked to the neighborhood drugstore, where she bought inexpensive electric hair clippers.

Back at the apartment, she put several sheets of newspaper on the floor and trimmed off most of Ralph's hair. He didn't much approve of the procedure but tolerated it. "It's your summer cut," Jamie told him. "You'll be much cooler."

Then she sat back on her haunches and regarded her handiwork. Ralph was now a nonscruffy grayish-brown dog with long legs.

Mrs. Duffy did a double take when she saw him. "Is that the same dog?" she asked.

Thursday afternoon, Jamie—with Billy in the sling—walked to the downtown bus terminal and caught a bus to Norman, which was two towns south of Oklahoma City. Once she had arrived at the Norman terminal, she went to a secluded corner and nursed Billy. At six o'clock, she placed her phone call and closed her eyes and silently implored, *Please let there be good news.*

Mrs. Brammer answered almost immediately.

"It's Jamie. Have you heard from Joe?" she asked, holding her breath, her eyes still closed.

"Not yet, dear. How are you? Are things any better for you?"

Jamie let out her breath. "Yes. I have a place to stay. I'm okay for now. You haven't said anything to anyone about me, have you?"

"Not a word. But I have thought about little else."

"I am so sorry. I don't want to complicate your life."

"I understand that, Jamie. You realize that it could be weeks before we hear from Joe? And we have no idea when he'll be coming home."

Jamie recalled how, during their first conversation, Mrs. Brammer had been so certain Joe would be home in time for his father's birthday.

She listened while the woman suggested that Jamie wait at least two weeks before calling again. Maybe by then she would have some news.

Two whole weeks of waiting, Jamie thought dejectedly as she hung up the receiver. Of course, there might not be a damned thing Joe could do to change her situation. And what if she was endangering him and his parents by involving them in her troubles?

With that frightening thought, she took a seat in the waiting room. The next bus to Oklahoma City wasn't due for almost an hour.

It was after nine before she finally unlocked the door to her apartment and was greeted by her dog. With the baby still in his sling, she grabbed the leash and took Ralph downstairs for a short outing before settling in for the night.

She fed Ralph and warmed a can of soup for her own dinner and thought about what lay ahead while she ate. At this point, she had little else to do but take care of her baby, walk the dog, read, and check the mailbox daily to see if her and the baby's birth certificates had arrived. She was in limbo until hers came. She couldn't obtain the all-important Social Security number that would allow her to obtain a driver's license and look for work.

The following Monday the birth certificates arrived. Jamie felt like a thief as she looked down at the official-looking documents. Or maybe "grave robber" would be a better term.

She looked up the address for the Social Security office and checked her map of bus routes then loaded Billy into the sling.

The waiting room was filled with people. Jamie filled out the necessary forms and waited for her name to be called.

When her turn came, the plump female clerk studied the form Jamie handed her. "Are you Janet Marie Wisdom?" she asked.

By way of an answer, Jamie handed the woman the newly arrived birth certificate.

The woman looked it over then asked, "Have you ever been married or used another name?" Her tone of voice suggested she had asked that same question many times before.

"No."

"Have you ever applied for a Social Security number before?" the woman asked in the same bored voice.

"My parents are deceased," Jamie said, with no idea at all if Janet Wisdom's parents were still alive. "I don't know if they ever obtained a Social Security number for me or not," she fabricated. "I was raised by my aunt and uncle in Canada and haven't needed one until now."

The woman attached a note to the application. "We'll have to research it and see if you've already been assigned a number," she said.

"How long will that take?" Jamie asked.

"Two to three weeks," the woman said. Then she looked over Jamie's shoulder and called the next number.

Mrs. Duffy was sitting on the front porch when she returned to the apartment house.

"Hey, Janet, I've got some fresh sandwich fixings," she said as she struggled to her feet. "You bring that baby inside and nurse him while I set out lunch."

"That's very nice of you," Jamie said, thinking how strange it was to be called by another name.

She followed the woman through her cluttered living room to the kitchen. On the refrigerator door was a large, colored picture of Amanda Tutt Hartmann.

Jamie gasped.

"Isn't that the most wonderful picture!" Ruby exclaimed. "I ordered it from Alliance headquarters in Virginia."

Chapter Twenty-eight

WHEN THE TIME finally arrived for Jamie to call Mrs. Brammer once again, she and Billy rode the bus east to Shawnee, a small town with huge grain elevators towering over it. If anyone was monitoring the Brammers' phone calls, they would have realized that Jamie was living in central Oklahoma, but she was determined that they would not be able to pinpoint her location any more closely than that. Next time, if there was a next time, she planned to go farther east, rather than always fanning out from Oklahoma City.

Like before, Mrs. Brammer answered on the fourth ring.

"Oh, Jamie," she said. "Joe called, but Art and I weren't home so he called our next-door neighbor just to make sure we were okay. He was calling from someplace in Turkey and said it would probably be a couple of weeks before he called again. With that in mind, Art and I decided we'd head over to Arkansas for a little fishing. I hope that's okay with you."

"Of course it is," Jamie said, trying to conceal her disappointment. "I hope you have a wonderful time."

"Is your . . . your *situation* still the same?" Mrs. Brammer asked.

"Yes, still the same. But I'm okay for now," Jamie said halfheartedly. "Enjoy your trip, and I'll call in two weeks. If you're not back, I'll try the following week."

"Jamie, it seems to me that whatever your trouble is, you probably need someone with an established law practice. Joe has a law degree but has yet to take the bar exam. And I know I said that Joe was coming home this summer, but I don't want you to count on that. We really have no idea what his plans are. He has an inheritance from his great-aunt and can do pretty much what he wants. He might even decide to take another course at Oxford, so I really think you need to find someone on this side of the ocean to help you."

"You may be right," Jamie allowed. "It's just so complicated. I'm afraid someone else might think I'm crazy or paranoid."

The bus was only half full for the ride back to Oklahoma City. Jamie sat in the rear and went over the conversation with Mrs. Brammer, who was probably getting weary of all the intrigue. Just as Jamie herself was. After all, she was not in jail. Other than the abrupt cancellation of her bank account, she had no evidence that anyone was looking for her or following her or plotting her demise.

Then she remembered how she had felt at that ATM machine in Liberal, Kansas—like a housefly that was about to be swatted. She could not begin to imagine the power and resources of someone who had the ability to manipulate other people's lives in such a manner.

Jamie felt almost angry with Joe. He was off having the time of his life while she was having the worst of hers. What was the point of all this waiting around for him anyway, she asked herself. He had earned a law degree but he wasn't a practicing attorney. He hadn't even taken the bar exam. What could he do? What could anyone do to change her "situation"? She was living in limbo, and maybe she would have to settle for such an existence for years and years to come. To settle for always being afraid. Always thinking that disaster was just around the next corner.

She looked down at Billy, who was the reason for it all. What a confusing, frightening, catastrophic mess her life was in, yet at its center was love.

Evelyn Washburn watched through the screen door as the two nice-looking young men in dark suits walked down the front walk toward their car. With a sigh, she closed the door and headed for the kitchen.

She sat at the bar and picked up the telephone, anxious to tell her daughter and son-in-law about the two visitors.

Evelyn started to dial their number in Houston, then remembered that Millie and Art were on a trip. Millie was good about checking in every few days when they were away from home, but Evelyn wished that they weren't so stubborn about getting a cell phone. It was ridiculous for them not to have one in this day and age. And a computer, for goodness sake! Some folks were so old-fashioned.

She opened the sliding-glass door and stepped out onto the patio, where she had been watering her potted plants and hanging baskets before the two men rang her doorbell and flashed their badges. She turned on the hose and went over the strange encounter in her mind while she finished up. The badges had certainly looked official and the men were very polite, but the entire encounter had made her uncomfortable.

She had answered their questions but volunteered nothing. Yes, she and her husband had been neighbors of Jamie Long and her grandmother, but they hadn't seen or heard from Jamie since her grandmother's funeral. And no, her grandson Joe had never dated the girl.

When Evelyn finished watering the plants, she paused to admire her yard. Everything was so green and lush in Georgia. In Mesquite, it had been a battle to keep a pretty yard throughout the long, hot summer.

She went inside to wash some salad greens and start dinner. Shortly, she heard the garage door opening and dried her hands. "Good haircut," she said as her husband came through the door.

She accepted his peck on her cheek. "The strangest thing happened," she told him as she took her usual perch at the bar and watched as Paul poured two glasses of wine.

In the middle of her story, the phone rang. Evelyn had a feeling that it might be Millie.

"Hi, Mother. How's it going?" her daughter's voice asked.

"Where are you?" Evelyn asked.

"In Texarkana. We're having car trouble and will be here overnight."

"Well, I'm glad you called," Evelyn said. "I have something rather disturbing to tell you."

Ruby Duffy continued to make overtures of friendship toward "Janet" and little Billy, but Jamie found herself making excuses when the landlady invited her for lunch or dinner. Or offered her a ride to the grocery store, even though it would have made her life easier. She was fearful of giving herself away, what with the web of lies she had created around herself, and was disturbed by Ruby's adoration of Amanda Hartmann, whose name she seemed to work into every conversation.

Jamie tried to pass the time reading and walking but was growing more restless with each passing day. Her spirits rose, however, when her Social

Security card arrived. She could get a driver's license now and buy a car and look for a job. She looked in the phone book for the nearest tag agency.

After lunch, with Billy in his sling, she hiked over to Classen Boulevard.

The agency was quite busy, and Jamie took a number and the required form and headed for the waiting area. She filled out the form then watched as those ahead of her had their picture taken and then a few minutes later received their driver's licenses. It took her a while to realize that these people were also being fingerprinted. Jamie tried to remember if she'd been fingerprinted when she obtained her Texas driver's license. Or perhaps at some other time in her life.

She really could not remember.

She left before her name was called. On the way home, she stopped at a pay phone and placed a phone call to the tag agency in Mesquite, Texas. She told the woman who answered the phone that she was a reporter doing a survey for a story. Did the state of Texas fingerprint those applying for a driver's license?

The answer was yes.

No matter what name she used, if she obtained a driver's license, she could be traced through her fingerprints. She slumped against the wall, discouragement washing over her like a tidal wave. What other obstacles were waiting for her?

She felt like a hunted animal in the middle of an ever-tightening circle of native beaters with a man on horseback waiting to take the perfect shot.

Late that afternoon, when Ruby climbed the two flights of steps to tell Jamie she had a pot of homemade vegetable soup on the stove and cornbread baking in the oven, Jamie didn't have the heart to decline her invitation to dinner, which even included Ralph.

Except for the picture of Amanda on the refrigerator door, Jamie liked Ruby's homey kitchen, with a rocking chair in the corner, a herb garden on the windowsill, and a television on its stand with Jamie's old friend CNN often flickering on the screen. It was on now with the sound muted.

She sat with her back to the refrigerator. The soup and cornbread were delicious, and she accepted seconds. She was explaining how she hoped to find work in a day-care center so she could keep Billy with her when she realized that Ruby was no longer listening. Something on the television screen had captured the landlady's attention.

Jamie glanced at the screen.

It was Amanda Hartmann. Holding a baby.

Jamie felt the blood rush from her head and for an instant felt as though she was going to faint. She grabbed hold of the edge of the table to steady herself and closed her eyes.

"Would you look at that!" Ruby exclaimed as she grabbed the remote and turned up the sound.

Jamie could hear Amanda's voice praising the Lord for the miracle that He had brought her. She opened her eyes. Amanda was standing in front of a door. A very handsome paneled door with a brass knocker. A beaming Toby Travis was at her side. There was a close-up of the baby's face. Then suddenly the picture changed to a female news anchor at her desk. She explained that these were the first pictures of the internationally revered evangelist Amanda Tutt Hartmann and her baby, Jason Tutt Hartmann. The baby had been born three days earlier. In an effort to protect the family's privacy, the birth was only now being announced from their home in northern Virginia. The news anchor went on to recall the death of Hartmann's son after an accident involving an all-terrain vehicle on the family ranch in the Texas Panhandle. Then the woman smiled and said that the sports news would be up next, following a commercial break.

Ruby pointed the remote at the screen and muted the sound. "Praise the Lord!" she said. "I've been so fearful for Amanda. She was too old to be having a baby, but the Lord helped her through, bless her heart. After what happened to her son, she deserves this baby. She surely does," Ruby said, nodding her head in agreement with her own words.

"I heard Amanda's mother preach back when I was still a young woman," Ruby continued. "In Dallas. My mother and I went down front to confess our sins and accept the Lord Jesus Christ as our personal savior, and Mary Millicent put her hands right on my forehead," she said, placing her own hands where Mary Millicent's had been. "And Lord, did I feel the power! It went all through me, and one of the ushers caught me when I fell right over backwards. I've never forgotten the feeling of all that power just taking me over and scrubbing me clean. And sometimes when I really need it, I can close my eyes and feel it again."

Ruby sighed and brushed tears from her eyes.

Jamie rose and busied herself with carrying dishes to the sink. "Don't bother with that, Janet," Ruby insisted. "Do you feel all right? You look a little peaked."

Jamie smiled as brightly as she could. "Just tired," she said, picking up Billy in his carrier. "Thanks for dinner. The soup was delicious."

Amanda with a baby. *What did it mean?*

Jamie kept asking herself that question while she waited for sleep. Was she safe now?

Something had not been right about that seemingly joyous televised picture in front of the beautiful doorway. Amanda's voice seemed half a register too high. And the way she held the baby seemed stiff. Was it really her baby or just a stand-in until her brother brought her Sonny's baby?

When Gus was informed that the official report had been filed, he went to his computer and used his agency password to access it. The suspect had been located. In Oklahoma City. From the calls she had been making to Houston, they had known for several weeks that she was someplace in central Oklahoma. Then one of their Oklahoma City–based agents recalled seeing a girl in a park that fit Jamie Long's description. She and the baby were living on the third floor of a rundown apartment house in central Oklahoma City.

That evening Gus met with Felipe and handed him a handwritten list of salient points, which he would memorize then destroy the list before leaving the room.

"My first priority is the baby's safety," Gus said, drumming the desk with his index finger to emphasize his words. "I want him out of that apartment before you kill the girl. She is to disappear without a trace along with the mutt. I want it to look as though she bolted in the night with the baby and the dog with absolutely no indication of what actually transpired."

Felipe nodded.

"You have someone lined up to bring the baby here?"

Felipe responded with another nod.

"I don't want anything left in that apartment that identifies the girl as Jamie Long or would link her to me or my sister," Gus said.

Once they had gone over the entire plan, Gus leaned back in his chair and looked past Felipe into the meditation garden. His bowels were starting to churn. He sometimes wondered if his conscience was located in his colon. In fact, he'd had loose bowels off and on ever since he realized what Jamie Long's eventual fate would be. If he didn't love his sister so damned much, he could hate her, but out of this whole fiasco had come Sonny's child.

Gus rose from his seat abruptly. "Check in when you get to Oklahoma City," he told Felipe as he hurried toward the john, tightening his sphincter with all his might, but already he could feel it starting.

Chapter Twenty-nine

ONCE AGAIN JAMIE found herself at the downtown bus station. She had planned to buy a ticket to Seminole, which was southeast of Shawnee, the town where she had made her last phone call to Mrs. Brammer, but discovered there would not be a return bus to Oklahoma City until morning.

How necessary was it for her to go someplace else to make these calls? She was trying not to pinpoint herself in Oklahoma City proper, but maybe that was already evident by the calls she had made from different points on the far edges of the metro. And maybe there was no one sitting at a huge console like some technology wizard in a James Bond movie tracking on an electronic map every call made to the Arthur Brammer residence in Houston, Texas. Her connection to the Brammer family was just too tenuous for anyone to have made the connection.

Or was it?

Any number of people in Mesquite knew about the long-standing friendship Gladys Simpson and her granddaughter had had with their back-fence neighbors, Evelyn and Paul Washburn, who were the parents of Millie Brammer and the grandparents of Joe Brammer. And it was no secret that Joe often visited his grandparents and had befriended both Jamie and Gladys. How careful Jamie needed to be about the phone calls depended on how thorough a search Gus Hartmann was conducting.

She had three choices. The wisest one would be to forget about Joe Brammer for the time being. Or she could call his mother from someplace closer to home and save herself a great deal of trouble. Or she could buy a ticket to someplace other than Seminole.

She bought a ticket. She would go a second time to the town of Shawnee. Maybe the wizard at the console would decide that she was living in Shawnee or one of the many even smaller towns scattered along the interstate highway that connected Oklahoma City to Fort Smith, Arkansas, and points beyond.

It was time to feed Billy. She sought out the back of the bus and draped a blanket over her shoulder. A weathered man in a denim shirt sitting across the aisle and one row up kept glancing in her direction, which made her very nervous. She couldn't decide if he was just being lecherous or if his interest in her was something else altogether.

Once she had arrived in Seminole, she went to a pay phone. The phone rang eight times before the answering machine came on. A male voice announced that she had reached the Brammer residence. She hung up, waited fifteen minutes, and tried again. Then she walked around the block and tried a third time. When the bus for Oklahoma City was announced, she tried one last time but to no avail. Of course Jamie had told Mrs. Brammer that she would try again the following week if they weren't yet home from their trip. Or perhaps she and her husband had something more entertaining to do tonight than sit around waiting for a phone call from a girl they barely knew who might be in trouble or might be off her rocker.

Perhaps, as Mrs. Brammer had strongly suggested, it was time for her to find another attorney to help her. Maybe she should go to the Oklahoma City legal aid office, where attorneys helped people of limited means.

During her ride back to Oklahoma City, Jamie tried to imagine explaining her situation to a total stranger.

My baby is the grandson of Amanda Tutt Hartmann. Yes, the famous televangelist who just had a baby. Except the baby she is holding in those pictures probably is not really hers. It's just one that she and her brother are using while they are trying to track me down and take my baby away from me. I signed a contract agreeing to be artificially inseminated with semen supplied by Amanda Hartmann's husband, though actually the semen came from her son, who was supposed to be dead but really was being kept alive until Amanda was sure that I was carrying a healthy baby. For the eight months and one week of my pregnancy, I was held prisoner on the Hartmann Ranch in the Texas Panhandle, where I met Amanda Hartmann's mother, Mary Millicent Tutt Hartmann, who was also being held prisoner except she had a passkey and sometimes roamed around the ranch house at night. Mary Millicent was the one who told me that her almost dead grandson was really the father of the baby I was carrying and that

Amanda planned to claim that she was the child's biological mother, which would make him the heir to her ministry when he grew up. And Mary Millicent warned me that Amanda's brother was going to have me killed after my baby was born so that I couldn't tell anyone that Amanda was not the baby's mother and that God had not performed a miracle so that her barren body could produce one more kid.

All of which was definitely too far-fetched to be believed, Jamie realized, even for a long-haired, antiestablishment legal aid attorney. Maybe if she ever had the chance to tell the story to Joe, he, too, would think she was crazy. Maybe she should start operating on the assumption that she would never be believed so there was no point in ever telling anyone the truth about her baby's birth.

She wondered how many years it would take for Amanda and her brother to give up looking for Sonny's child. How many years she would have to hide.

But if hiding was going to be a way of life for her, she needed to make some preparations. She would have to buy a car. Without a driver's license she would have to drive very, very carefully—never speeding, always coming to a complete stop at stop signs, never having a burned-out taillight, never doing anything to get pulled over. But she could do that. And she would always keep the tank full of gas and have basic supplies in the trunk—diapers, blankets, clothes, dog food, some nonperishable food for herself, water bottles—in case she had to make a hasty departure. And she would never leave the apartment without money.

It was depressing to think she would probably be on the run for years and years. But depressing or not, she would sleep better at night with a car parked behind the apartment house.

It was dark when she arrived back at the apartment. She was climbing up the first flight of stairs when Ruby stepped out into the hall. "Janet," she called up to her. "I was hoping that was you. I have something to tell you."

Jamie wearily retraced her steps. "I have a new tenant," Ruby said. "A young woman with a baby not much older than Billy. She's applied for a job over at the medical center and asked if I knew of anyone who could look after her baby while she was at work. It occurred to me that might be a perfect way for you to earn some money and still stay home with little Billy."

Jamie could hardly believe her ears. *Good* news for a change.

"You look tired, honey," Ruby said. "Why don't you see to your dog then let me fix you a plate of spaghetti."

Jamie was too tired to argue with her.

"If you like, you can just leave the baby here with me while you take the dog out," Ruby offered.

Jamie backed up the first step as a knot of panic rose in her throat. "I, ah . . . I really need to change him," she stammered. "Just give us a few minutes."

"Honey, I'm not going to steal your baby if that's what you're worried about," Ruby said. Then she cocked her head to one side and frowned as she regarded Jamie's face. "And that *is* what you are worried about, isn't it? That someone's going to take that baby?"

Jamie did not know how to respond so she didn't. She simply rushed up the stairs as fast as she could with a baby strapped to her chest.

She greeted her exuberant dog with less enthusiasm than usual. She simply did not have the energy or goodwill it took to frolic with him and make him feel loved. She changed Billy, used the bathroom, splashed water on her face, and brushed her ugly hair. Then, in accordance with her new resolve never to leave her apartment without money, she reached under the mattress and pulled out the manila envelope that contained her cash along with her personal papers and her grandmother's ring. She removed three hundred dollars, slid the envelope back under the mattress, and stuffed the money in her pocket.

With Billy in the infant seat, she took Ralph to the vacant lot for a few minutes then headed back to the house.

Ruby had left her door ajar, and Jamie called out to her, "Is it okay for Ralph to come, too?"

Ruby stuck her head around the corner. "All three of you come right on in here."

Jamie closed the door behind her and wound her way through the crowded living room to the brightly lit kitchen, which was filled with the aromas of garlic and warm bread.

The refrigerator had a new picture—one from the newspaper of Amanda Hartmann holding the mystery baby. Once again Jamie sat with her back to the refrigerator.

Ruby dished up a generous helping of spaghetti, covered it with a thick sauce, and set it in front of Jamie. Then she filled Jamie's glass with iced tea and put a generous slice of crusty bread on her plate.

The spaghetti was wonderful, and Jamie had to admit that it was nice having someone fuss over her, even if she didn't approve of that person's taste in refrigerator art.

Over coffee Ruby told Jamie that she had once been a beautician and reached across the table to lift a strand of Jamie's hair. "Why don't you let me give you a decent haircut tomorrow and adjust the color a bit? If you don't want to be a blond anymore, I think you at least need some highlights for a more natural look."

Jamie was speechless. And had to blink back tears. First there had been Mae the midwife, and now there was Ruby the landlady. She had almost forgotten what kindness felt like.

"I know you got private troubles that run real deep," Ruby said, "but having bad hair and not having a friend you can count on shouldn't be among them. And besides, it does a lonely old lady's heart good to feel useful to another human being once in a while."

After leaving Ruby's apartment, Jamie sat on the front step while Ralph raced around the yard for a few minutes. Then she called to him and smiled as he came racing up the steps, his tail wagging and tongue hanging. Such a dear little dog he was.

In spite of her weariness, she climbed the stairs with a lighter step. It was amazing what a good meal and human kindness could do to raise one's spirit.

Jamie, Billy, and Ralph spent the next morning downstairs with Ruby. First she shaped Jamie's hair then touched up the roots and carried out a complicated procedure involving aluminum foil and a paintbrush. The morning was almost gone before it was time for Jamie to shampoo her hair at the kitchen sink and watch in the bathroom mirror while Ruby showed her how to use a handheld drier to fluff her hair into a soft, becoming style. The highlights softened the dark color and actually made it look more natural.

"I look like a different person," Jamie said with relief, thinking that if she ever did get to see Joe again, she wouldn't be embarrassed about the way she looked.

Saturday morning, Ruby introduced her to the new tenant. Lynette was a petite, gregarious brunette whose boyfriend was working on an offshore oil platform in the Gulf of Mexico. Lynette's baby was two weeks older than Billy.

Jamie felt almost like a normal young mother sitting there among the boxes and clutter of Lynette's apartment as they discussed sleep patterns and feeding schedules and took turns holding each other's babies.

Lynette explained that she had completed her LPN training the month before Sally Ann was born. She hoped to get a regular shift at one of the medical center hospitals, but for now she was going to fill in as needed. "I'd like to be assigned the night shift so I can spend more waking hours with Sally Ann if that's all right with you," Lynette said.

Jamie assured her that the night shift would be fine. In fact, she would prefer it. A little voice in the back of her head wondered if she should warn Lynette that she might not be permanent in Oklahoma City. But she didn't know that for sure. She didn't know anything for sure. And it would be nice to have an income, no matter how modest.

That afternoon, she left Ralph in the apartment and, with Billy back in the infant carrier, walked south toward downtown Oklahoma City and the used-car lots strung along North Broadway. The infant carrier was cumbersome and bumped uncomfortably against her leg, but she would need it if she took a car for a test drive.

As she wandered up and down the rows of cars, she wondered how negotiable the prices painted on the windshields were. The only cars with a price she could even begin to afford looked as though they belonged in a salvage yard.

At each lot, a salesman would follow her around while she checked the tread on tires and looked under hoods for clues as to how well the motors had been maintained—the condition of belts, how clean the oil was, if the filter needed replacing, if the spark plugs were clean or dirty.

At the third lot, she selected what she considered the best of the bunch and, with the salesman in the front seat and Billy in the infant carrier fastened in the back, took a test drive. The motor ran a bit rough, and she decided to look further tomorrow, but she took the salesman's card and said she would keep the car in mind. Then she started the long walk home with the afternoon sun beating down unmercifully.

Back in her apartment, she opened both windows. She could see that she was definitely going to need to buy a couple of fans or they were going to swelter this summer. She grilled a cheese sandwich and made a salad for dinner and entertained herself for a couple of hours working crossword puzzles with the radio as background noise. Then, with Billy in her arms, she took Ralph out front. It was a beautiful night, and she sat on the front step while Ralph carefully sniffed every bush and tree trunk as he decided the very best locations for him to deposit his pee, a few drops here and a few there. Billy's gaze seemed to be focused on the very bright moon that was directly overhead, and she took his hands in hers and, waving them back and forth, softly sang,

> *Oh Mister Moon, moon, bright and shiny moon*
> *Please shine down on,*
> *Have a heart and shine on,*
> *Please shine down on me, Oh Mister Moon.*

The night sky brought to mind an evening when she and Joe had stretched out on the grass in the backyard and looked up at the moon through a pair of binoculars. Jamie had been aware that Joe was watching her as she studied the pockmarked lunar surface, amazed at the details she could make out with just binoculars. He told her that her hair looked silver in the moonlight. And he had touched a strand.

With her dark hair and a baby in her arms, Joe probably wouldn't recognize her as the girl he had once known.

When Billy began to try to eat his fists, Jamie called to Ralph, who was nosing around under a yucca plant by the front steps. When he didn't respond, she used a firmer tone, and he backed out from under the bush.

"Good boy," she told him, scratching his head. "Let's go upstairs and feed this baby."

She had just finished nursing Billy when there was a knock on the door. She went to the door and, leaving the security chain engaged, opened it just an inch.

When she saw that it was Lynette, she disengaged the chain and invited her inside.

The hospital had just called, Lynette explained. The eleven o'clock shift was short, and she had been asked to fill in. "Could you look after Sally Ann?" she asked.

Jamie agreed, of course. Lynette said she would bring Sally Ann up around ten-thirty.

Jamie had hoped to purchase a secondhand playpen, which could double as a bed for Sally Ann, but she could manage for one night. She put Billy in the infant seat, changed the sheet on his bed, then took a shower. She had on a nightshirt when Lynette arrived with her baby and pink polka-dotted diaper bag.

She watched Lynette place her sleeping child in Billy's bed, cover her with a lightweight blanket, and leave a second blanket at the foot of the bed.

"I just fed her," Lynette said. "If she wakes up in the night, offer her a pacifier. If that doesn't work, give her a bottle. I'll pick her up around seven-fifteen or so." Lynette put a hand on Jamie's arm. "I can't tell you how grateful I am to have you looking after her."

Jamie locked the door behind Lynette and carried Billy into the bedroom. Ralph was already curled up at the foot of the bed. She sat on the side of the bed with Billy on her knees and told him what a very handsome little boy he was and how very much she loved him.

And he smiled.

It wasn't just gas. It was a real smile. But just to make sure, she kept cooing and talking.

Billy smiled again, waving his arms and legs and looking quite proud of himself. And Jamie's heart absolutely melted.

She convinced him to do it yet again. "Look, Ralphie," she said. "Billy is smiling at us."

Today had been a good day, Jamie thought. And yesterday, too. Two good days in a row. Her baby had smiled for the first time. She had an income and a new hairdo and had begun her search for a car. And she actually had two friends—Lynette and Ruby.

Before turning out the bedroom light, Jamie padded across the living room to check on Lynette's baby. Moonlight streamed through the open window, illuminating the sleeping infant. Little Sally Ann. Such a pretty little girl. Jamie pulled the lightweight blanket up to her chin and put a hand on her tiny fragile chest, feeling it move up and down. Babies were so precious. Life was so precious.

Then she went into the bedroom where her own baby lay sleeping.

Even though Billy was months away from rolling over, she had stuffed a rolled-up blanket between the mattress and the wall and another one between the mattress and the headboard.

She sat on the side of the bed for a time just watching Billy sleep. The feeling that swelled in her breast went beyond love, beyond adoration. It encompassed something quite elemental and even ferocious. No one was ever going to take her baby away from her. *Ever.*

She reached down to pat Ralph's head and tell him good night. He didn't open his eyes, but his tail swished a bit. "You're all worn out, aren't you, boy? Me, too. It's been a busy day."

Then she stretched out beside her baby and stared out at the sky for a time. She couldn't see the moon from this window, but the stars were bright and mysterious. She wondered where Joe was at this moment and what he was thinking.

Just before she closed her eyes, she glanced through the open doorway of the bedroom and could just make out the form of Lynette's sleeping baby.

Chapter Thirty

IT WAS A FEW minutes after one when Jamie discovered that Lynette's baby was missing. Billy had been trying to wake up. Sometimes he would go back to sleep if she walked around the apartment jiggling him in her arms. That's what she had been doing when she realized Sally Ann was no longer in the baby bed.

Panic filled Jamie's chest and clouded her mind. *They* knew where she was. They thought they had taken *her* baby.

Even as she tried to deal with the horror of the missing baby, her mind was trying to push ahead.

How long would it take before they realized the baby they had was a girl?

And why hadn't the person who took Sally Ann killed Jamie first?

Jamie imagined a shadowy figure putting a gun with a silencer to her temple while she slept and pulling the trigger. Or putting a pillow over her face and suffocating her.

But there was something wrong with both scenarios. And with Jamie sleeping through Sally Ann's kidnapping. Ralph would have alerted her the instant an intruder set foot in the apartment.

Ralph would have barked.

Ralph!

She raced to the bedroom. Her scruffy little dog was still curled up on the foot of the bed. Jamie knew before she touched him that he was dead. But still her mind cried out in protest. *Not her Ralph*. Not her sweet little dog who had been at her side for all these many months. Who had saved her sanity and been her devoted little buddy. Who had loved her unconditionally and trusted her completely.

She wanted to scream. To cry out in her grief. And rage. But she didn't have time to rage or grieve. Not even for Ralph.

She had to get out of here.

She put Billy on the bed, grabbed her backpack, and raced around frantically stuffing things inside. Some clothes for Billy. A couple of baby blankets. Diapers. The baby sling. The Oklahoma map. Then she realized she still had on her nightshirt. She threw on some clothes and stuffed an extra shirt and underwear in the backpack.

She reached under the mattress and pulled out the manila envelope and slid it under the pad in the infant carrier. Then she put her baby in the carrier and bent to kiss her little dead dog good-bye, her chest heaving with the pain of her loss. "I am so sorry," she whispered. "Good-bye, my darling Ralph. I'll never forget you."

Blind with tears, she slung the backpack over her shoulder and picked up the infant carrier. And glanced at the clock on the bureau. Less than ten minutes had passed since she realized Sally Ann was gone.

Billy was chewing on his fists and only seconds away from crying. On the way to the door she picked up Sally Ann's pacifier from the baby bed. She didn't take the time to wash it or even wipe it on her sleeve. Billy had never used a pacifier, but he latched on instantly.

Ever so carefully, Jamie unlocked the door and, leaving the chain lock engaged, peeked out into the hall. Then she closed the door, disengaged the chain lock, and opened it again. She took one last look over her shoulder and saw a pair of feet appear in the open window.

The kidnapper was coming back to kill her.

She slipped into the hall and gently closed the door behind her. Then raced down the hall. Down three flights of stairs.

Once she had reached the first floor, she unlocked the front door and opened it a few inches, then turned around and tiptoed toward the back of the house to the basement door. In the inky darkness she crept down the basement stairs. The laundry room with two high cellar windows was less dark. She paused to let her eyes adjust. Pushing the wooden table would make too much noise. It took all her strength to lift it and place it under one of the windows. She put the infant carrier and backpack on the table, climbed on top of it, unlatched the window, and carefully lowered it. It was a tight squeeze to get her long body through the opening. Once through she reached back inside for the infant carrier and the backpack. Then she reached down and pulled the window closed.

She was hidden by the bushes and crouched there unmoving for a time. She heard the front door being pushed open. Footsteps on the porch. Billy was trying to push the pacifier from his mouth, but she held it there with one hand and frantically unbuttoned her shirt with the other and scooped her baby from the carrier.

She was sure the kidnapper was not alone. He had already given Sally Ann to an accomplice and returned to kill Jamie. Probably there were others besides those two. They would fan out to look for her.

She nursed Billy until she was sure that he wouldn't cry then put him back in the carrier and crept across the deep shadows between Ruby's apartment house and the one next door, quickly taking cover behind its overgrown shrubs. Pressed against the wall, she made her way toward the front of the building and climbed over the railing onto the covered porch. Keeping to the shadows, she tiptoed across the porch and climbed down into the shrubbery on the other side of the building, which was on a corner. The bus-stop corner. She waited for a few minutes, watching for any sort of movement. Then she sat in the moist dirt behind a huge, overgrown lilac bush to wait for morning and to cry for her little dead dog. She knew what had happened. Someone had been watching her and knew that she took Ralph out front last thing every night and had left a piece of poisoned meat by the front steps.

After they had killed her, they would have disposed of her and Ralph's bodies and made it look as though she had fled in the night with her baby and dog. Ruby would have remembered her bruised forehead and concluded that Jamie was once again running away from an abusive boyfriend.

Except the kidnapper had taken the wrong baby. Soon someone was going to realize that. Jamie closed her eyes and prayed. *Please don't let them kill Lynette's baby. Please.*

She imagined Lynette coming in the morning and getting Ruby to open the door when Jamie did not respond to her knock. The police would be called. Would the police think that the woman who called herself Janet Wisdom had fled with both babies?

By now the kidnapper and his accomplices would be driving up and down the streets looking for her. Maybe they had called in others to help with the search.

She tried to make herself as comfortable as possible, leaning against the side of the house. She could feel the moisture from the damp earth penetrating the seat of her jeans and scooped a layer of dead leaves between herself and the ground.

And so she stayed. For hours. Grieving for her dog. Holding her baby. Wondering what was going to happen to them.

"We have the baby," Felipe said when he had Hartmann on the line. He was in the back of a panel truck parked inside a garage at the end of the alley. "Carl and Luis have gone back to deal with the girl."

"Is the baby all right?"

"Seems to be. It is with the woman in the other vehicle."

"Good. You figured out how to get the girl's body out of the apartment?"

"Toss it out the window. The dog, too. Then we will pick them up and be on our way. The plane is waiting at a rural airstrip south of here. After we leave the baby in Virginia, we will fly over the ocean and dump the bodies."

"Call me before you take off."

Next Felipe called the woman. "The baby okay?" he asked.

"Yeah, but I thought you said it was a boy."

Felipe's blood ran cold. "What are you saying?"

"The kid crapped and I just changed its diaper. This baby is a *girl*."

Felipe paused for only a moment. He'd always known a time like this would come—a time when he himself would become the focus of Gus Hartmann's rage. He got out of the truck, opened the garage door, then got back in and drove away. The waiting plane would take him to an island off the coast of Honduras. From there he would take a boat to the place that only he knew about. It was a relief, really. He had enough money in Swiss accounts to last three lifetimes.

At midnight, Amanda—wearing a flowing blue bathrobe—had joined Gus in his office. She would pace for a time then lie on the sofa, all the time offering a running monologue about how they needed to get this thing over with, how wonderful it would feel to finally have the baby in her arms, how no baby could ever replace Sonny but this child was the next best thing. How it didn't feel right when she was holding that other baby.

Finally she ran out of steam and dozed off. Gus didn't wake her after he'd talked to Felipe. He would wait until the plane was ready to take off. Until he was absolutely sure nothing had gone wrong.

He sat at his desk staring at the minutes ticking by on the clock. The plane would take off in about an hour.

After two hours had gone by, he finally had to admit that something was amiss, but he waited another thirty minutes to shake Amanda's shoulder. "Something's gone wrong," he said.

"How do you know?" she asked.

"My man would have called by now. I've tried to reach him, but his phone is either turned off or he ditched it."

"Why would he do that?" she asked.

"Because he screwed up and is running for his life."

"What about the men he hired to help him?"

"The same," Gus said, his jaw clenching.

"But you'll still be able to get the baby, won't you?" Amanda asked, panic in her voice.

"Yes, of course," Gus said soothingly. "But it may take a few days. You might as well go on upstairs. Take something to help you sleep."

"I won't have my baby tonight?" she asked, her voice getting shrill.

"No, not tonight."

Gus went to the sofa and took her in his arms. He spoke to her in his most soothing voice, telling her that everything was going to be all right, that it was just going to take a little bit longer than he had at first thought. He smoothed her hair and told her that he loved her and that they were going to be so happy with Sonny's little boy to raise and to love. But right now, he needed for her to go to bed and let him think. And make a few phone calls.

It was noon before he had pieced together the story. Jamie Long had been caring for her neighbor's kid. Felipe's man had taken the wrong kid, and Jamie Long had gotten the hell out of there. The woman working with Felipe had left the baby girl in a hospital waiting room.

"What rotten luck," Gus said with a slam of his fist on the desk. "Damned rotten luck."

Then he calmed himself. A young woman with a small baby and no luggage and no one to turn to for help shouldn't be too hard to track down.

When Jamie saw the morning's first bus approaching, she crawled stiff and dirty and disheveled from the bushes. She was greeted by startled stares as she walked toward the cluster of waiting people, the infant carrier bumping against her leg. She got on the bus last, gave a crumpled bill to the driver, and sat in the seat immediately behind him.

When the bus reached Classen Boulevard, she got off and walked to the last of the three used-car lots she had visited. The same salesman was already there unlocking the door to the office. "You come back for the car?" he asked.

"If you'll give me a good deal," she said. "Otherwise, I'll have to take my business elsewhere."

The man took in her disheveled appearance with a knowing look and shook his head. "The price stands as is."

Jamie shook her head. "If I pay what you ask, I won't have enough money to buy gas."

He dropped the price one hundred dollars.

Jamie could almost feel her pursuers getting closer by the minute. She nodded.

When he asked what name she wanted on the bill of sale, she told him Mary Johnson.

With the infant carrier anchored in the back with a seat belt, she drove south for fifteen or twenty blocks and stopped by a drive-up pay phone at a service station. She might as well call the Brammers' number in Houston one last time. By the time her call was traced and someone arrived at this location, she would be miles away.

A man's voice answered the phone. A young man. Jamie clutched the receiver saying nothing. Was it one of Gus Hartmann's men just waiting for her to call? Waiting to threaten her? To lie to her and tell her that all they wanted was the baby and nothing would happen to her if she would give him up?

But then the voice said, "Jamie, is that you?"

She leaned forward and rested her head against the steering wheel. It had been a long time—another lifetime ago—since she had heard that voice. "Joe?" she whispered.

"Oh, my God, Jamie, what in the world is going on with you?"

"I can't explain. I just called to say I wouldn't be calling anymore. *They* know where I am now. I have to find someplace to hide. They even killed my dog," she said, her voice breaking. "And they are listening to us *now*."

"Jamie, listen to me very carefully," Joe said. "Remember that Sunday afternoon when we planned to take your grandmother to a very special place?"

She tried to think. "I don't know what you're talking about."

"It was someplace historical that Gladys had never been to before."

Jamie rubbed her forehead. "I can't think, Joe. I don't know what you're talking about," she repeated. "And *they* are tracing this call as we speak. *They'll* be here any minute now."

Joe kept talking, his voice calm and low. "It started to rain, and we decided not to go. Gladys put a pot roast in the oven, and we played dominoes while it was cooking. Gladys won."

Jamie racked her brain. She was so afraid. And tired. Hungry. She couldn't think. She *couldn't*. Granny was always cooking pot roasts. Always beating them at dominoes.

But then she remembered. It had been a terrible rainstorm with ferocious lightning and thunder.

"The lights went out," she whispered.

"Yes. Can you go to that place—the place that we never went to?"

"I don't remember the name," she said, "but I remember what it was near."

"Get yourself there as soon as you can. I'll be there at noon tomorrow and again at dusk. And the next day, too. I'll be there every day until you come."

"I don't know how long it will take me. My situation is . . . difficult."

"So I gathered. You just get there, and I'll be waiting."

"But you'll be followed."

"Just come, Jamie."

"Yes. I'll come. I'm going to hang up now. Good-bye."

* * *

She quickly hung up the receiver, disconnecting herself not only from Joe but also from the ominous someone she knew had been listening to their conversation.

She had actually spoken to Joe. And had a plan.

She pulled out into the traffic and drove west instead of south in case she was being followed. Could they have put a tracking device on this car? She spent several minutes convincing herself that was unlikely. *Okay, think,* she told herself.

Her pursuers would realize the location she and Joe had agreed upon would have to be within a day's drive of Houston. They would be alerting the highway patrol and local law-enforcement agencies. She forced herself to think of the maze of highways and roads in Texas. Of the hugeness of Texas. And allowed herself to believe that it just might be possible. But she had to be clever. And she was too exhausted for clever. Too exhausted and hungry.

They were expecting her to head south into Texas, which eventually she would have to do. But not right away.

She would take her time. Let the searchers get in front of her.

She drove north, avoiding the main thoroughfares. She wound her way through an area where there were stately old mansions as large as hotels, and even farther north, past gated communities with brand-new mansions. She drove carefully, ever mindful of speed limits and stop signs.

Not wanting to waste gas, rather than driving around aimlessly she made frequent stops, pulling into a parking space and just sitting there for a time. She stopped at a service station to use the restroom and buy a sandwich and a bottle of orange juice. Twice she stopped to feed Billy and give him some time out of the infant carrier. Finally, keeping to secondary roads, she began winding her way south, continually checking her rearview mirror.

When darkness finally came, she filled the almost empty gas tank, bought a couple of candy bars, filled the empty orange juice bottle with water, then headed south on a county road several miles east of Interstate 35. Soon it was late enough that she had the rural roads pretty much to herself. When the moon rose, she turned off her headlights for long stretches, not exactly sure why, except that it made her feel invisible. She knew from her drive across the western half of the state that its county roads were laid out in one-mile squares, and she would go south for a time, then east, then south again, until she had to maintain an eastern course around sprawling Lake Texoma. She bypassed the town of Durant, then began winding her way south again until finally she turned south onto Highway 78.

Given her meandering path, it was almost dawn before she crossed the Red River into Texas. She knew that she had to sleep for a while. When she stopped for gas in Ridings, she studied the Texas map on the wall, then asked the elderly attendant if she could pull behind the building to nurse her baby and rest for a time. When he didn't respond, she asked him again in a louder voice, and he nodded.

The clock in the car didn't work, and she had left her watch in the apartment, but when she woke, she estimated by the sun that it was mid-morning. Arriving at her destination by noon was out of the question. But hopefully she would be there by dusk.

Still keeping to country roads, she headed south once again, ever watchful even though she hadn't a clue as to the form her enemy would take. She wondered if she would ever feel safe again. The word itself sounded elusive, like something at the end of a rainbow, something she might wish for but never achieve.

Now that she was in the state of Texas, however, she did allow herself to wonder what it would be like to see Joe again. She hoped that she could at least clean up a bit before she made her way to their meeting place.

Then what?

She knew that he would help her. That was the kind of person he was. And perhaps it was best not to go beyond that. If she didn't allow herself to expect more, she would not be disappointed.

That was hard to do, though.

Texas was not laid out in precise squares like Oklahoma, and she had to be careful not to lose her way as she endeavored to keep to rural roads. Early afternoon, she crossed over Interstate 30, which she knew connected Dallas to southern Arkansas. A couple of hours later she crossed Interstate 20, which connected Dallas to Shreveport.

The motor began to overheat south of the town of Athens.

She stopped at a service station and sprayed water on the radiator then drove very slowly into Corsicana. She parked the car near the bus station and gathered up her baby and her few possessions.

The bus didn't leave until the morning. After she bought a ticket to

Brenham, she had just enough money to buy a banana and two candy bars. She filled the bottle with water in the restroom.

The bus station closed at five.

She walked around for a time then returned to the car. She sang to Billy and played with him for as long as he was willing then nursed him to sleep. Whenever a car drove by, she ducked out of sight. She waited until dark to eat the first of the candy bars. For the second time she had not been at the meeting place. And she wasn't going to be there tomorrow, either. But Joe had promised to keep returning until she arrived. She clung to that promise.

The night was endless. Every muscle in her body ached with fatigue and discomfort.

She ate the banana for breakfast.

The bus arrived in Brenham just before noon. She described the place she wanted to find to the ticket agent. "It's a very old cemetery where some of the area's first settlers are buried."

"That would be the Independence cemetery," the woman told her.

"How do I get there?" Jamie asked.

"Just head up the street here to Chapel Hill and take a left. Chapel Hill runs into 105 which will take you to 50. There's no town to speak of anymore. Just look for Old Baylor Park. The cemetery is near there."

"How far?"

"'Bout ten or twelve miles, I'd say, but there isn't a bus."

Jamie had planned to walk anyway. She didn't have the money for a ticket if there were a bus.

A block from the bus station, she left the cumbersome infant carrier in a Dumpster and put Billy in the sling.

She reminded herself that she used to think nothing of running ten or twelve miles. All she had to do now was walk. But it was already warm. And she was exhausted. And she had a baby slung across her middle.

Climbing even the gentlest of hills left her breathless and sweating. And Billy was restless. She stopped several times, seeking out a shady, private spot where she nursed him, with no sense at all of how long it had been since the last feeding.

She ate the second candy bar a bite at a time and rationed her water. There were no service stations, no buildings at all except for an occasional farmhouse at the end of a winding lane. The sole of her left shoe came loose and made walking difficult. She tore a strip from the baby blanket she was using to shade Billy from the sun and tied the shoe back together.

I can do this, she told herself repeatedly, the words becoming a mantra. Several times a vehicle would slow as the driver considered asking her if she wanted a ride, but she would square her shoulders, stare straight ahead, and turn her dragging step into a marching gait.

The road signs told her that she was nearing Independence. She stopped at a large gardening establishment to ask for directions to the cemetery. A woman watering rose bushes pointed the way and filled her water bottle. "You all right, honey?" she asked.

"Fine," Jamie said with all the brightness she could muster. "It was just farther than I thought." Then she asked the woman what time it was and was on her way.

The water helped.

She passed by four stately stone columns in a grove of trees with a sign that said OLD BAYLOR PARK. A half mile or so past that sign was another for McCrocklin Road. A mile or so beyond that McCrocklin ran into Coles Road, just like the woman watering the roses had said.

A woman in an SUV pulled up beside Jamie and asked if she was lost.

"No, ma'am. I'm just out walking."

The woman had beautiful snow-white hair. She stared at Jamie for a moment. "You look awfully hot and tired to me," she said. "I live just past the cemetery. You and the baby are welcome to rest there for a time. I think I'll make a pitcher of fresh lemonade as soon as I get home."

Jamie thanked her again and kept on walking.

Fresh lemonade. She felt light-headed just thinking about it.

The cemetery was on the right side of Coles Road, set among a grove of ancient live oak trees. Just beyond the entrance to the cemetery Jamie sank to the ground by the moss-covered tomb of Moses Crawford, who died in 1857. She leaned against the backside so she wouldn't be visible from the road and nursed her baby. Then she lay down and, cradling Billy in her arms, curled her body around his and closed her eyes.

Chapter Thirty-one

AFTER JAMIE HUNG UP, Joe stood there for a time with the receiver still to his ear. He felt the anxious eyes of his parents. Still in their bathrobes, they were standing by the sink, his father's arm protectively around his mother's shoulders.

It was just three days ago that he had finally talked to his parents. The ship had just docked in the Libyan port city of Tripoli. He could tell the minute he heard his mother's voice that something was wrong. She was too chipper. When he started asking questions, she insisted that nothing was amiss and that he should continue his trip for as long as he wanted. Then she had handed the phone to his father, who had rambled on about how he wished that he had traveled more as a young man and had seen the world just as Joe was now doing, and experienced the glory that was Greece and the grandeur that was Rome, and taken advantage of what only youth can offer, which was a definite about-face from the paternal lecture on responsibility that Joe had received when he'd told his father about his plan to stay on in Europe after he'd finished the course at Oxford.

Joe finally interrupted him. "Dad, what in the hell is going on? Did the house burn down? Is Mom sick?"

"No, no, no. Nothing's wrong," his father insisted. "Your mother and I were a little put off when you decided to stay over there, but we do want you to enjoy yourself before you have to settle down."

Maybe there really was nothing wrong back home, but the phone call had left him with a deep sense of unease, and after roaming through the old city center for a time, he returned to the ship to collect his possessions. He didn't bother to announce his departure, unsure if international maritime law permitted him to terminate his employment before the end of the voyage. He had flown standby to London's Heathrow Airport, where he was lucky enough—after running at full steam through three terminal buildings—to arrive at the gate just as the last passengers were boarding a direct flight to Houston. The gate attendant said there was just enough time for him to make a quick phone call before he boarded.

His father answered. Joe blurted out the flight number and the time it was scheduled to arrive in Houston.

When his parents picked him up at the airport, his mother insisted they stop for coffee at an airport restaurant. That was when they told him that they couldn't talk at home. Or in the car. Just in case the house and car were bugged. They were absolutely certain that their phone was tapped and that they were being followed everywhere they went and were being watched at this very minute.

Bugged? Tapped phones? Being followed? Joe wondered if his parents had gotten senile during his absence.

Then they explained that it had all started with a phone call from Jamie Long.

Their coffee grew cold as they told him about Jamie's strange calls and how she seemed desperate to get in touch with him. How she behaved as though someone was listening in and wouldn't say where she was or what sort of trouble she was in. And they told him about the mysterious "agents" who showed up at his grandparents' house in Georgia in search of information about Jamie, including her relationship with their grandson. His grandparents had called friends in Mesquite and learned that these mysterious agents had been there, too, questioning all sorts of people—wanting to know who Jamie's close friends had been and implying that she was in some sort of danger and that they were trying to find her so they could protect her. "But the only one who had seen or heard from Jamie since she packed up and drove away from Mesquite was the stonemason at that monument place out by the cemetery," his mother said. "She had come by sometime in July and ordered a tombstone for her grandmother's grave and paid him with cash. Everyone says it's like she dropped off the face of the earth, and since Jamie was adamant that we not tell anyone we'd heard from her, we can't tell them otherwise. I know you've always thought highly of her, Joe. And we are sorry for her, but now that we realize how serious her trouble must be, your father and I don't want you to get involved."

Joe quizzed his mother about the phone calls, wanting her to describe each one. She recalled that when she asked where Jamie was, all she would say was that she wasn't in Texas. And she said that she was in trouble but had done nothing wrong. His mother hadn't talked to her in more than two weeks.

His father explained that they hadn't been home at the appointed hour for Jamie's last phone call because they were delayed when they had to replace the alternator in their car. "Truth of the matter was we were both relieved that something beyond our control had prevented us being there. That way we didn't have to feel guilty."

They wanted him to get on the first available flight back to Europe. His mother had even put his name on standby for an Alitalia flight to Rome that left in two hours.

"Not until I've had some home cooking," Joe joked, picking up his duffel bag.

Despite her nervousness, his mother outdid herself with some of his favorites—garlic grits, smothered pork chops, coleslaw with bacon and vinegar dressing, and strawberry shortcake for dessert. He knew that his parents didn't eat like that anymore and that he shouldn't either, but once in a while it sure was good.

And it felt good to crawl into his own bed rather than a narrow berth with not even enough headroom to sit up, although he did miss the motion of the ship plowing through the waves. More and more of late his before-sleep musings turned to Jamie.

He had really screwed things up with her.

He'd all but decided it was time to expand the parameters of their relationship when Marcia took his hand and led him out onto a tiny crowded dance floor in a downtown Austin bar and plastered her body against his. At the end of the dance, she led him to the ladies' room, where she pushed him down on the toilet seat and straddled him. As they walked back to the dance floor, she reached over and shook his hand, then said, "I'm Marcia."

Joe had been screwing Marcia for almost a year when he stopped at the dry cleaner's to tell Jamie that he was getting married even though he wasn't yet officially engaged. But he knew it was coming. Marcia expected it, and Joe felt like she was entitled.

Jamie seemed so forlorn, standing there at the counter in that dreary, steamy dry-cleaning establishment with rows of plastic-covered clothing hanging behind her, her hair damp with perspiration, putting on a brave, smiling face as she wished him well. A few weeks later he learned from his grandmother that Jamie had dropped out of school and gone back to Mesquite to look after the ailing Gladys. Joe knew he should call her. Or drive up for a weekend. But he hadn't. Marcia would have expected to come with him to meet his grandparents. And he didn't think he could face Jamie with Marcia at his side. Of course, no words had ever been spoken between him and Jamie. And there had been almost no touching—only high fives and crashing into each other when they grabbed at rebounds. But there was a place in his heart that belonged exclusively to the long-legged little girl whom he'd watched grow up into a lovely young woman with the most beautiful smile imaginable and eyes that glowed when she looked at him. But he felt kind of stupid being hung up on a kid, especially one who considered him a big brother of sorts. And if his thoughts about her turned the least bit sexual, he felt like a pedophile. Then, after Jamie developed into a shapely young woman, sexual thoughts seemed incestuous. She was still in high school when he started law school. And Marcia was gorgeous and funny and outrageously inventive when it came to sex.

For the most part, he hadn't allowed himself to have anything but the most ethereal sort of daydreams about Jamie.

But not always.

Joe awakened early and went for a run. There was a FedEx truck parked at the end of the block. The dark tint of the windows prevented him from seeing who was inside. Since when was FedEx tinting its truck windows, he wondered.

He headed for the track at the high school, where he did laps for almost an hour. When he returned, the FedEx truck had been replaced by a black panel truck with tinted windows.

He smelled the coffee as soon as he opened the door. His parents were in the kitchen, his mother at the stove, his father setting the table. When the phone rang, Joe had gotten there first.

And now, he stood facing his wonderful parents who loved him completely and would do anything for him and said, "I have to go."

Tears began to roll down his mother's face. "Please, no," she said, her head moving back and forth. "When Jamie first called I wanted you to help her. But whatever trouble she's gotten herself into is too big, Joe. Too dangerous."

His father nodded his agreement. "Wait until they catch her. Then maybe you can help with the legal side of things."

Joe considered. He could do that, of course. But something in his gut told him that Jamie's problem was outside the normal boundaries of the law. She knew something that she was not supposed to know. At one time, he would have encouraged her to turn herself in no matter how frightened she was and let the law straighten things out, but the more he learned about the law, the more he realized that being innocent sometimes wasn't enough. The rule of law was like religion. At its heart it might be pure, but all too often it was bent by those in power to serve their purposes.

Strong voices within him warned him that getting involved in Jamie's problem could be his undoing and cause his parents great anguish. He should look the other way.

But what kind of person would he be if he did that?

Or was it just that he was in love with Jamie Long and had been most of his life? And she never even knew it.

"I have to try to help her," he told his parents.

The look on their faces was one of absolute fear with just a touch of pride. He was across the kitchen in an instant and put his arms around the two of them. "You're all we have," his mother cried, clinging to him.

Joe showered and ate breakfast. The black panel truck followed him to the bank, where he cashed out a CD.

He waited until dark—a long day, with the three of them trying to act normal as they watched a golf tournament on television and puttered about the kitchen fixing first lunch and then dinner. After the late news, he went upstairs to his bedroom. He waited until midnight, put on his backpack, and crawled out of his bedroom window onto one of the thick, spreading branches of the ancient post oak that had been the reason his parents had built their home on this particular lot.

Keeping well in the shadows cast by the six-foot fence, Joe made his way to the back of the yard, scrambled over the fence, and dropped into another backyard. He went along the side of the house toward the street.

Before he stepped out of the shadows, he watched a long time for any movement.

He took a circuitous route to the storage facility on Gessner Road. When he arrived he hid behind the small office building for twenty or so minutes. Finally convinced that he had not been followed, he entered the code on the punch pad to unlock the outer gate, then closed it behind him.

He got a bit of a thrill when he opened the overhead door to his storage unit and saw the vintage Harley parked there among the other possessions that he'd acquired during his Austin years.

Minutes later, he was on his way. Even though he was fairly certain that he was not being followed, he rode around the Memorial area for a time, then took a turn through downtown and headed south on Galveston Road. Only when he was absolutely certain that he was in the clear did he make a U-turn and head north, cutting over to Interstate 45. He then took I-610 to Highway 290, which took him into Brenham. He was there before dawn and checked into a generic motel where he slept for a few hours, then ate a huge breakfast at a pancake house and got directions to the Independence Cemetery from the waitress. He arrived well before noon, parked his bike in the back of the cemetery, and wandered around for a time. With its stately old trees and ancient tombstones, the cemetery was a poignantly beautiful place. Maybe someday he and Jamie could come back here and poke around.

He waited until after one o'clock, and since he hadn't passed any semblance of an eating establishment on the ride out from Brenham, he made his way back to the town. He ate lunch in a vintage hotel and wandered around the quaint downtown for a time.

Around five, he headed back up Highway 50 to the cemetery. He waited until dark before heading back to town.

He downed a few beers at a tavern to take the edge off his disappointment, then fell asleep watching TV in his motel room.

The next morning he killed time poking around the rolling countryside, arriving at the cemetery well before noon. He wandered up and down the rows of headstones, glancing up every time a car approached, which wasn't very often.

At two, he got on the Harley and headed back to town. At five-thirty he was back at the cemetery. Once again there were no people, no vehicles, no Jamie.

But it was not yet dusk.

To pass the time he began to make a more methodical inspection of the cemetery. He hadn't taken two steps when he saw a pair of tattered athletic shoes jutting out from behind a tombstone.

The wearer of the shoes was a sleeping female with a baby in her arms. Her face and arms were sunburned and smudged with dirt. Her brown hair was dusty and disheveled. Her clothing was filthy. She looked limp—more like she had passed out than fallen asleep. The baby was awake and seemed to be studying the gently moving leaves on the low-hanging branch of a live oak.

He felt as though he should look further. This person could not be Jamie. Jamie had long, beautiful blond hair. Jamie was a lovely young woman. This woman wasn't lovely. And Jamie wouldn't have a baby.

But this person had her long legs. And the sweet curve of her chin.

He knelt and put a hand on her shoulder. When she opened her eyes, she smiled.

"Jamie?"

"Hi," she said, struggling to a sitting position, the baby cradled in one arm. He grabbed her free arm and helped her to her feet. Once she was upright, she closed her eyes for a few seconds and took a deep breath.

"Are you okay?" he asked.

"Just hungry and thirsty," she said. "And I desperately need a bath."

Joe fished a water bottle and a small bag of peanuts out of one of the Harley's saddlebags and watched while she wolfed down the peanuts and drank the entire bottle of water.

He helped her put the baby in a cloth contrivance she wore across her stomach, then held her arm as she slung a leg over the Harley. When he climbed on, she grabbed hold of his belt. "Don't go fast," she said. "I'm feeling kind of dizzy."

He drove at a very sedate pace back into Brenham, enveloped in a cloud of disappointment. He had expected more from finally seeing Jamie once again. A great deal more.

He pulled into the same motel, wondering if he should find someplace nicer. But Jamie felt pretty limp behind him, and the baby was crying. He helped her off and took her into the room. "I'll go get you something to eat. What sounds good?"

"Anything. And I need diapers. And I'd really like to see a newspaper."

"What about some milk for him?" he asked, nodding toward the baby.

She shook her head. "I'm nursing him."

"So, he's *your* baby?"

She closed her eyes and nodded. "Oh, yes. He's *my* baby."

When he arrived back at the motel, Joe knocked on the door. There was no answer.

He unlocked the door and peeked inside. He could hear the water running in the bathroom. The baby was lying in the middle of one of the double beds. Joe put his purchases on the table, iced the beer, then stood looking down at the baby. He was quite small and had big eyes and was waving his arms about aimlessly. "I'm sure you are a nice enough baby," Joe said, "but I must admit that I'm not very happy about you."

Jamie came out of the bathroom with a towel wrapped around her body and another around her head.

"Do you have any extra clothes?" she asked, heading for the table. "And I need to borrow a comb," she added as she picked up one of the milkshakes, took off the lid and gulped some down. Then she ate a handful of fries and unwrapped a hamburger.

Joe produced a pair of gym shorts, a T-shirt, and a comb. Jamie went back into the bathroom. When she emerged again, her wet hair was combed, and she was wearing his clothes. She picked up the phone and called the office to ask if there were laundry facilities.

When she hung up she covered the now sleeping baby with a corner of the bedspread, picked up the newspaper, and glanced at the headlines on the front page. Apparently she found what she looking for on page two. She read the story and ate the rest of the hamburger. "You have any quarters?" she asked.

While she was in the laundry room, Joe read the article on page two. A baby girl kidnapped from an Oklahoma City apartment house had been left in a hospital waiting room apparently unharmed and was returned to her mother's arms. A woman named Janet Wisdom had been caring for the baby in her apartment. Wisdom was now missing, along with her own child. There were no signs of violence in the apartment, but there was a dead dog on the bed. Police were searching for Wisdom and her infant son.

When Jamie returned, she glanced at the baby, then sat across the table from Joe and reached for his hand. "Thank you," she said and burst into tears.

Joe knelt in front of her and took her in his arms. Then he helped her to the empty bed and stretched out beside her, cradling her, stroking her damp hair, her arms, her back. His shoulder grew wet with her tears. At one point he went to the bathroom for the box of tissues. She blew her nose and tried to regain control. But she couldn't. Not yet. She said something about a dog named Ralph. And being so afraid. So very afraid.

Finally, she was cried out. She blew her nose again then went to splash water on her face. When she returned the baby was starting to thrash about. Jamie picked him up, leaned against the headboard, propped a pillow under her left arm.

Joe carefully looked away as she placed the baby at her breast. He felt jealous of a very small baby.

He wanted to ask who the father was—and if she had loved the man. If she had been married to him. Or maybe he should turn on the television. He couldn't just sit here not watching her nurse a baby. He offered to get her clothes from the drier.

He took his time, jogging around the block several times before searching for the motel laundry room. When he returned, Jamie was curled on the bed. The baby was asleep in a dresser drawer with a folded blanket for a mattress. Jamie opened her eyes and offered a small smile. "I'm in terrible trouble," she said.

"Yeah," he said. "I figured out that much on my own." He covered her limp body with a blanket then sat beside her and stroked her shoulder.

"They killed my dog so he wouldn't bark while they stole my baby, but they took the wrong baby. Then they came back to kill me."

He could hear the utter exhaustion in her voice. "You go ahead and sleep," he said with more gallantry than he felt. "We'll talk tomorrow."

"This isn't how I thought it would be when we first saw each other again," she said, her eyes fluttering closed.

"Have you thought about that—about us seeing each other again?"

"Yeah. What about you?"

"Me, too," he said. He ran a finger along her jawline, then briefly touched her lower lip. She had a beautiful mouth. As a sixteen-year-old boy he had felt like a dirty old man because he thought that ten-year-old Jamie Long had the most beautiful mouth he had ever seen.

She kissed the tip of his finger, then gave herself over to sleep.

He understood that she was exhausted, but he felt cheated. And a little regretful that he was here at all. Maybe more than a little.

He drank two cans of beer then took a shower and crawled into the empty bed.

Chapter Thirty-two

THE SOUND OF HER baby crying pulled Jamie back to wakefulness. It took her a few seconds to remember where she was, but in the darkness she felt disoriented.

The only light in the room came through a tiny opening between the heavy draperies that covered the room's one window. Not daylight. She made the opening wider to admit more light and picked up her baby. She made soft shushing sounds as she pulled a diaper from the open package beside the drawer-turned-bed, then groped around for the package of baby wipes. The baby continued to vocalize his hunger as she changed his diaper.

"I'm sorry," she said into the darkness.

"It's okay," Joe said. "Obviously the kid is starving to death."

Jamie felt herself smiling. "Yes, he does have a good appetite."

She propped pillows up for an armrest and got the baby situated. Silence immediately descended over the room, the only sounds coming from an occasional vehicle driving by.

"Joe?"

"Yeah."

"You want to talk now?"

Even in the dim light, she could see him stretching under the covers. And noted the empty beer cans on the bedside table.

She sensed Joe's disappointment. He had expected something more dramatic and rewarding for his efforts. Deservedly so.

She had known all along that trying to involve him in her troubles had been a selfish act. If her need had been for herself alone, she would not have tried to contact him, and she was not without guilt. At some level, she had always wanted Joe to be the man in her life. But now she had lured him into her fight for survival. He could lose everything. His parents could lose their only child, his grandparents their only grandson. It was more than her not wanting to die. It was because she wanted to be the one who raised this baby. She had acted as a mother, not as a lovesick female.

Poor Joe.

"I'm sorry," she said again.

He said nothing.

She closed her eyes and began.

Her story sounded unbelievable even to her own ears as she explained how she was deeply in debt and had entered into a contract with a televangelist and her young husband and found herself a virtual prisoner at the Hartmann Ranch with the formidable Miss Montgomery as her jailer. How Miss Montgomery and everyone else at the ranch idolized Amanda Hartmann. How she herself had fallen under the woman's spell.

When she got to the part about the crazy old woman and Amanda's brain-dead son locked up in a tower, her story sounded even more farfetched. Joe interrupted her, saying she must be mistaken. He had read about Sonny Hartmann's death in a London newspaper months before Jamie would have arrived at the ranch.

"Well, he wasn't dead," she said. "I saw him. The poor boy had been raised to follow in his mother's footsteps, and his mother kept him alive so she could get herself another heir. Being raised by Amanda Hartmann wasn't the sort of life I would want for any kid. And I was afraid for myself. Mary Millicent said that I would be murdered after the baby was born. And you know what? I could understand why they would do that. I would be the living proof that Amanda's claim to some sort of miracle birth was not true."

Jamie paused in her story to put Billy back in his makeshift bed. Joe closed the draperies, turned on the lamp, and sat on the side of his bed.

"At first I thought all the things that Mary Millicent told me were just the ramblings of a crazy, paranoid old woman," Jamie continued, leaning against the headboard. "Then, over the months, I began to realize that there was truth in everything she said. I'm not sure how much Amanda had actually planned what was going to happen to me. Apparently she relied on her brother to take care of things for her, like having her first husband murdered."

Joe was leaning forward, his elbows on his knees, his hands folded. "But you don't know any of this for sure," he said, staring down at his hands. "Just because some senile old woman said these things doesn't mean they are so. Maybe these people did misrepresent themselves in the contractual arrangement they made with you, but that doesn't mean they planned to kill you."

Jamie heard the disbelief in his voice. She saw it in his body language. And it made her angry.

"Gus Hartmann's henchmen poisoned my dog so he wouldn't bark when they stole my baby and then came back to murder me. I was looking after my neighbor's baby that night and had put her in Billy's bed. They took the wrong baby! That's the only reason I still have Billy. And I'm still alive because I grabbed him and got the hell out of there."

Joe retrieved the newspaper from the trash can and opened it to the second page. "Is that what this article is about?"

Jamie nodded, remembering the horror of that night. She had been so relieved to learn that Lynette had her baby back.

Joe ran a hand through his hair. "Okay, I need for you to back up a bit. You said you were held prisoner. Why couldn't you just leave?"

Jamie was feeling very tired. A few hours of sleep had not been enough to revive her. And the telling of her story was making her stomach twist into knots. She asked if he would get her a Coke.

Joe gathered up some change and shortly returned with two cans.

Jamie took a long swig then attempted to describe the enormous ranch in the middle of vast, empty Marshall County. She told him about the ranch-house compound with its electric fences and security system. And how she was not allowed to leave the house without a guard following her, not allowed to make phone calls, not allowed to send or receive mail. How the servants avoided her like the plague.

"I would have gone crazy if it weren't for Ralph," she told him and had to cry for a time. Joe came to sit beside her and took her in his arms.

"I think this is enough for now," Joe said, stroking her back. "Why don't you sleep some and you can tell me the rest in the morning."

"No," Jamie said. She got up, blew her nose, and used the bathroom. When she returned, Joe had moved to a chair. She took another swallow of her drink then described how she had memorized the security code and threatened a hunger strike if her car wasn't brought over to the ranch-house garage. How she and Ralph had crept out in the night and how surprised she had been that her escape had actually worked.

She said very little about Billy's birth except that she was alone and it was difficult. Perhaps someday she would tell him more, but for now that was all she could manage.

"The weeks I was in Oklahoma City, I found myself wondering if it was overkill to go to all that trouble to make sure that every phone call with your mother was made from a different location, but at some level I *knew* that Gus Hartmann's people were trying to find me. Even when there were stories on television and in the newspaper about Amanda giving birth, I knew that wasn't the end of it. And I couldn't think of anyone else to turn to except you." Jamie paused before adding, "I knew that I could trust you. You were always so good to Granny and me, and I guess I was always a little in love with you."

"Just a little?" he teased.

"Well, maybe more than just a little," she allowed.

"The older you got, the more eager I was to spend part of my summer in Mesquite," Joe admitted. "No matter how old you got, though, it seemed like I was still too old for you."

At first, Joe had tried to play devil's advocate with Jamie's story. As farfetched as it seemed, however, there was no questioning the fact that someone had marshaled impressive forces to track her down. People with official-looking badges had come to his grandparents' home in Georgia to ask about her, and they interviewed people in Mesquite. And apparently there were taps on his parents' and grandparents' phones. He did not doubt that her fear was warranted.

"This Hartmann guy must be a very powerful man to be able to launch an illegal investigation like that," Joe acknowledged. "And close your bank account. The people who broke into your apartment were probably paid henchmen, but the others involved in the search must be some sort of government agents. It's just so hard to accept that it's possible for someone to abuse power like that."

Jamie didn't so much as finish telling her story as run out of steam. She would think of things she had not told him, and he would quiz her in search of more details. But what he needed to do now was get them some breakfast and let her sleep for a few hours. He had two last questions, however. Did she still have a copy of the contract she had signed? And what was the name of the attorney in Austin who had arranged for her to enter into a surrogate-mother contract with Amanda Hartmann and her husband?

Jamie explained that when she was packing up her possessions at the ranch, she realized that the contract was gone. "I'm sure that Miss Montgomery took it, but by that time, I knew I was leaving and wasn't about to raise any more issues with her."

While he was waiting at the pancake house for their carry-out breakfast, he placed a call to one of his former law professors at the University of Texas. Franklin Billingsley had served two terms as state attorney general and knew just about everything there was to know about the Texas legal system.

"I understand that you've applied for a job with the FBI," Professor Billingsley said.

"What makes you say that?" Joe asked.

"A woman from the agency showed up at the law school asking questions about you. She said you'd put in an application with them, and the agency was conducting a background check."

"That's very interesting," Joe said, "but I'm calling about something else. I wonder if you know an Austin attorney named Bentley Abernathy."

"Abernathy? I've met him. He's given a couple of guest lectures at the law school. He made quite a name for himself sorting out the mess left by old Buck Hartmann, who founded Palo Duro Oil and Gas and acquired a mountain of mineral rights through hook or crook. The bulk of Abernathy's practice continues to deal with Palo Duro and handling in-state affairs for the Hartmann family."

"What sort of person is he?"

"In what way?"

"Shady or not shady?"

"I think he's managed to keep things on the right side of the law. Old Buck's grandson runs Palo Duro now and maybe the whole damned country if you believe some of the rumors."

The professor paused a second then added, "But don't you go around asking questions about Gus Hartmann, Joe. I hear things from time to time. Hartmann is not someone with whom you want to get at cross-purposes. And reconsider this FBI business. You belong in a courtroom, son."

Chapter Thirty-three

THEY ATE AT THE table next to the window with the draperies still tightly closed. They could hear the footsteps and voices of people walking by the window and packing up their cars.

Joe told her about the phone call to his professor then added, "I think we should be moving on—before someone discovers that I own a motorcycle."

"Any ideas as to where?" Jamie asked.

Joe nodded. "As a matter of fact, yes."

They packed up their few possessions and loaded them in the Harley saddlebags. Jamie had no choice but to climb onboard, with her baby slung out of sight across her stomach. Carrying an infant on a motorcycle was not only unsafe, it was surely against the law. She wanted to tell Joe to drive carefully, but he must realize how disastrous even a minor accident could be to her unprotected baby.

He stopped at a Target on the way out of town and waited while she replaced her tattered shoes.

Staying on country roads and driving at a very sedate speed, he wove his way south. By midmorning they had crossed under Interstate 10. When Billy started to fuss, Joe headed down a country lane, and Jamie leaned against a tree trunk while she fed her hungry baby. Joe had stopped looking away, but he didn't stare either. When she was finished, she handed Billy to Joe and found a sheltered place to relieve herself.

They ate chicken sandwiches in the town of Wharton and rested for a time on a shady patch of grass at a small park with Billy lying between them and entertaining himself by kicking furiously and waving his arms. "We're heading for the gulf, aren't we?" Jamie asked.

Joe nodded. "Yeah, there're some cabins near a place called Neptune

262

Beach. At least I hope the cabins are still there. My grandparents and I stayed there for several days back when I was in grade school. As I recall, it's on the primitive side but very out of the way."

"What about money?"

"I got some before I left Houston. Don't worry, I won't be using any ATMs or credit cards along the way."

"I'm afraid that I've ruined your life."

Joe propped himself up on an elbow. "I walked into this with my eyes wide open," he said.

"Not really. You didn't bargain for a baby or for the scope of the mess I've gotten myself into."

He didn't say anything for a time then he stretched out again, his hands behind his head. "There's a way out of this, Jamie. We just have to figure out what it is."

"I hope so. I wouldn't have gotten you involved if it weren't for Billy," she confessed. And felt better for saying the words.

"You really love him a lot, don't you?"

"Yeah. I do."

She closed her eyes and dozed for a time. She woke when he put his hand on her shoulder. "Time to go," he said, handing her a bottle of water.

She touched his cheek. He moved his face so that his lips were touching her fingers. It was a sweet moment, one that filled her heart with hope.

By midafternoon, she could smell the ocean.

The cabin was one of a dozen or so scattered along a low bluff and overlooking a series of dunes and the cobalt-blue gulf beyond. They both stood for a minute to take in the view before Joe put the key in the lock.

Jamie noted the rough siding on the walls, faded linoleum on the floor, and iron bedstead covered with a lumpy comforter. The kitchen had an ancient refrigerator, a galvanized-steel sink, and was equipped with mismatched dishes and dented cooking utensils. The back porch overlooked the ocean. "It's perfect," she said.

"Will you be okay here by yourself while I go buy some groceries?"

She nodded.

She wasn't really okay, though. As nice as it would be to sit on the back porch while she fed Billy, she locked herself inside and got a butcher knife from the kitchen before curling up in the bed with him. Then she closed her eyes and prayed. "Please, let this turn out all right. *Please.*"

When Billy drifted off to sleep, she closed her eyes and slept for a time, awaking when she heard the motorcycle approach. Joe parked behind the cabin, where the bike would be hidden from the road. Judging by the sun, it was already late afternoon. He must have had a hard time finding a grocery store.

Billy was still sleeping soundly. She left him on the bed and hurried out back to help carry in the groceries.

The saddlebags were overflowing, and a cardboard box was tied to the back of the motorcycle. Apparently their stay here was to be more than a one-night stand. Jamie was glad.

Together they put the groceries away. He had done a good job. In addition to several days' worth of food, he had bought her two scooped-neck T-shirts, one a rosy pink and the other a black-and-white stripe, a couple of pairs of knit shorts, and a set of navy sweats. When she pulled a package of women's underpants and a nursing bra out of the sack, Joe blushed. "The saleswoman had me watch the women walking by and point out one who was about your size."

And there was more—baby shirts, pajamas, and receiving blankets, and a baby rattle. Another sack held a big bottle of sunscreen and some toilet articles for Jamie. "I asked for the essentials," Joe explained. "I told the saleswoman that my girlfriend's luggage had gotten lost."

Girlfriend. He had called her his girlfriend. "You've done a wonderful job," Jamie said. "Thank you."

They stood there awkwardly for a few seconds. Then she busied herself putting away her new possessions. Together they put away the groceries and filled the cardboard box with the things they would need for a picnic on the beach.

As darkness fell, with Jamie carrying Billy and Joe carrying the cardboard box, they headed down to the beach. They gathered driftwood and built a fire in a secluded place among the dunes and, with Joe wearing Billy in the sling, walked along the beach. The waves washed over their bare feet as the sun sank closer and closer to the horizon until it became a huge orange ball and gradually slid from view, leaving streaks of vivid color in its wake. When they turned and made their way back up the beach, Joe reached for Jamie's hand.

He added more driftwood to the fire, and she spread out a blanket, put Billy on it, and watched delightedly as he became mesmerized by the flames. She took a few small sips of Joe's beer, taking enormous pleasure in the intimacy of passing the can back and forth. It was a thrill to put her lips where his had been and wondered if he felt the same.

She fed Billy while Joe downed a second beer on his own. By unspoken agreement, they did not talk about the circumstances that had brought them to this place. She told him about her hope to attend medical school and maybe to specialize in the care of very ill children if she had the courage. Joe told her about Oxford and how exhilarating it was to study at such a venerable place. And how he had spent every weekend prowling about London—the ethnic neighborhoods, street markets, used book stalls, pubs, museums, Westminster Abbey, Trafalgar Square, dining on the Indian tacos he bought from street vendors. "I'd like to take you there someday," he said.

"I'd like that," she said. His words empowered her. She reached over and touched his hand. Then, after years of dreaming about such a moment, she was in his arms.

He kissed her neck first. Then her eyes. Her hair. And finally her mouth. She couldn't get enough of his mouth. Or his tongue. And the feel of his strong body against hers. She had always wondered if she would know what to do should she ever find herself in his arms. But there was no thought. No plan. Just craving. Lust. Need. Her body was on fire. She strained against him, wanting more. Wanting all.

They tugged at each other's clothing, making themselves naked in the firelight. "You're beautiful," he told her, his voice filled with awe.

Jamie was amazed by his words. Did he really think that? "Oh, but you're the one who is beautiful," she told him. And he was. His body was lean and brown and muscular. His erect penis was amazing. It was a magnet pulling her toward him, her desire so great she felt as though she would cease to exist if she did not take it inside of her. She had been waiting her entire life for this moment and had no fear. Only desire.

She gasped as he thrust himself into her. And then she thrust back, marveling at the feel of him. She felt herself melting around him as wave upon wave of sensation cascaded over her skin and through her belly and veins and mind until finally sensation was all that there was—white, hot, intense sensation that filled every pore of her body and lifted her higher and higher until finally it exploded inside of her.

And for a span of time—a hundred years or a few seconds—she lost herself. She could not have said who she was or where she was. All that existed in the entire universe was her body and his.

When finally she could speak, the only word she could say was his name. Over and over she said it. He held her tenderly and stroked her hair and covered her face and neck with kisses. Then he began to speak, telling her that he had always loved her. Even when she was a little girl, he had felt a kind of sweet, protective love for her. And he knew that this love was something that would linger and grow and one day become the center of his life. He had even told his mother that he would like to marry Jamie Long when she grew up. Then Marcia came along, and they didn't so much as love each other as use each other. They skirted the issue of commitment, but he had begun to feel as though it was inevitable, as though it was something he owed her. When he told her about his plan to go to Europe, Marcia suggested that they should go their separate ways for a time. He'd been gone for months before he called her. The conversation had been cool. He didn't call her again. While he was trying to decide if he should come home when his fellowship was over or trek around the Continent with some of the guys he'd met at Oxford, he'd called his grandparents to ask if they'd ever heard from Jamie. Then he called Austin information. And Mesquite information. And he'd gone to a cyber café to search for her, but there were countless Jamie Longs. And he didn't know her middle name or initial.

"What *is* your middle name?" he asked, rising up on his elbow and looking down at her face.

"Amelia," she said. "It was my mother's name."

"Amelia," he said softly, then he continued explaining how it seemed as though she had vanished off the face of the earth and he realized that he didn't want to decide about his future until he had seen her again. So he simply drifted along with the other guys. He had been drunk when he staggered onto the ship.

"I thought about you even more on shipboard than I had on dry land. The waves made me think of you. And the wind. And the night sky. Remember how wonderful we thought the night sky was in Mesquite? I knew I had to find you and take you out into the middle of the ocean to show you what a night sky really looks like."

"I love you," she told him, "and I will love you for the rest of my life."

* * *

By way of disguise, Joe shaved his head and let his beard grow. Jamie's cheeks turned red with whisker burn, but after several days of growth, the whiskers became less bristly.

They allowed themselves a week to put the future on hold and enjoy being in an isolated, beautiful place while they explored each other's bodies and hearts and minds. They had no radio or television to interrupt the process. The rest of the world could have vanished, and they wouldn't have known it. They walked for hours on the beach and took turns swimming in the ocean while the other watched over Billy. Joe became proficient at diapering and learned how easy it was to make Billy smile and gurgle and wave his arms and legs. They both knew this idyllic time was only temporary, but that made it all the more precious.

Only when they held a planning session did reality intrude. And only then did they argue. Jamie refused to be left alone. Joe insisted it was too dangerous for the three of them to go. It was bad enough to have had Billy onboard while they traversed little-used secondary roads, but there was no way he could avoid Houston traffic. And by now, Gus Hartmann's people would be looking for them on a Harley, which was the reason he had to go to Houston in the first place.

On the last day before Joe's departure, they hiked to a convenience store and stocked up on diapers and other provisions. Jamie bought some magazines and newspapers to help her fill the time of waiting that lay ahead. Joe had already paid another week's rent on the cabin in advance and given her a roll of bills that she'd put in her backpack along with diapers, a change of clothes for herself and the baby, a couple of water bottles, a bag of trail mix, and a road map—just in case she had to make another hasty departure. Joe knew that she was remembering Oklahoma City and how she could have been out the door minutes sooner if she had been better prepared and came within seconds of losing her life.

That evening, with Joe carrying the baby, they had taken an evening walk on the beach and sat cross-legged on the warm sand while they watched the sun set. "I should be back here by tomorrow evening or the day after," Joe told her. "But if I have to lie low for a time, it might be longer. If I'm not back by the end of the week, you probably should assume the worst."

He tried to engage her in a discussion of what she should do then, but she refused to go there. "You have to," he said, "for Billy's sake if not your own."

"Later," she said. "Let's just sit here for a while longer and listen to the sounds."

And they did. To the wind and waves. And the methodical clanging of a distant buoy bell. Joe reached for her hand.

When Billy began to fuss, they walked back to the cabin. Jamie changed him and nursed him to sleep. Then they talked. After considering all the difficulties involved with fleeing to a foreign country, they finally decided that if he did not return she should go through the same process as before—find the grave of a child who would have been close to Jamie's age had she lived and use her name to get yet another birth certificate and Social Security number. The money Joe had given her should be enough to last for several months. By then, hopefully she could find a job and start a new life.

"How can we sit here and talk sanely about how I should live my life without you?" she asked. "We only just found each other. And if you die, it will be my fault. I created this impossible mess. If anyone should die, it should be me. But if I die, my child will be raised by a religious fanatic who thinks she speaks for God and by her insidiously evil brother."

"I don't want to die, Jamie," Joe told her. "I want to live on and make little brothers and sisters for Billy. I want to live to a ripe old age with you at my side. But if I die tomorrow, I will be grateful for this time we have had together."

She nodded. "Me, too."

Then she reached for him, and they made love with tears and poignancy and frantic professions of eternal love.

Joe woke at dawn surprised that he had slept at all. Jamie was curled on her side beside him. He lay there for a time, reminding himself why it was necessary for him to get on with things, why he couldn't wait a few more days to make this trip no matter how gut-wrenching it was to think of her here alone and defenseless. Their time here had been glorious, but always a nagging voice in the back of his mind kept reminding him that the longer they stayed in one place the more likely they were to be discovered. Someone could make an innocent remark about seeing a young couple with a baby walking on the beach. Or helping this clueless guy who was trying to buy clothes for his girlfriend and her baby. Or renting a beach cabin to a young couple who arrived on a motorcycle with a baby and not much else.

He swung his feet to the floor.

After he'd pulled on his clothes and picked up his boots and knapsack, he looked toward the bed. Jamie was watching him. When she started to speak, he shook his head. Instead of words, he put a fist over his heart in a gesture of eternal fidelity.

Chapter Thirty-four

LENORA PICKED UP the phone. "Law office," she said.

"Lenora Richardson," a man's voice requested.

"This is she."

"I am a friend of Jamie Long's."

"Oh, my God!" Lenora said, clasping the receiver more tightly. "How is Jamie? And *where* is she? We lost track of her."

"I wonder if it would be possible to speak with you privately. I have Jamie's permission to make this request."

Suddenly wary, she asked, "Why? What's going on with her?"

"Jamie's life is in danger as a result of the surrogate-mother arrangement negotiated by Mr. Abernathy. She speaks highly of you and asked me to consult with you as to the best way to handle this situation."

Lenora took a few seconds to replay the man's words. "I'm not an attorney," she said. "You need to speak with Mr. Abernathy."

"Perhaps, but I would prefer to speak confidentially with you first."

Lenora tapped her pencil on the desk. "This is highly unusual," she said softly, glancing over her shoulder to make sure the door separating her office from Bentley's was closed.

"I'm aware of that," the man said.

He sounded earnest, Lenora decided. And worried. Maybe even frightened.

"I wouldn't ask this of you if it weren't very important," he added.

"I gather you don't want to come here to Mr. Abernathy's office."

"I'd like for you to meet me at the bar at the Holiday Inn on Mockingbird Lane. At six o'clock."

"Will Jamie be there?" Lenora asked.

"No."

"How will I know you?"

"I'll find you. Jamie said you look like a runway model."

Lenora had trouble concentrating on her work the rest of the afternoon.

Bentley left at five-fifteen. Lenora was locking the door minutes later. As expected, the traffic at that hour was impossible. She was ten minutes late when she walked into the hotel bar. It took a few seconds for her eyes to adjust to the dim light. Several men at the bar had turned on their stools to stare. One man was watching her more surreptitiously in the mirror over the bar. Then she saw the young white guy with a shaved head and whiskery face waving at her from a corner booth.

She headed for the corner, taking in his jeans, black T-shirt, heavy black boots, and great build.

She sat across the table from him. "What's your name?" she asked. "And what's your connection to Jamie?"

"I'm Joe. I've known her since she was in grade school. She said to tell you that someday she hopes you and she can lunch together again at the Driskill Grill."

They were silent as a waitress approached. They both ordered coffee.

"Okay, so you know Jamie," Lenora said. "But why all the cloak-and-dagger stuff? And what makes you think that her life is in danger?"

For more than an hour Lenora listened to Joe's tale, interrupting with frequent questions. And at one point she took out her cell phone to call her husband and tell him she would be later than she had at first thought.

What she was hearing was just too bizarre to be believed. But why would anyone make up such a story?

She switched from coffee to a gin and tonic. Joe stuck with coffee.

Lenora confessed that she'd been worried about Jamie. Even though they had agreed to stay in touch, Jamie had never responded to her phone messages or her letters. And when she showed up at the ranch, she was told that Jamie had packed up and left without leaving a forwarding address. A nagging voice had said that Jamie would have let her know that the surrogate-mother arrangement hadn't worked out and given some indication of her plans for the future. And it seemed strange that Amanda herself had not told Bentley that the arrangement with Jamie Long had been terminated—and perhaps asked him to find her another young woman to use as a surrogate mother. Lenora had been stunned when she heard that Amanda Hartmann had given birth to a baby boy. There hadn't been nearly enough time for that to happen, unless she got pregnant about the same time Jamie was inseminated, and Lenora was positive that Amanda had once indicated she was no longer able to have children. And besides, Lenora just couldn't see Amanda putting her carefully augmented and liposuctioned body through such an ordeal.

But using her brain-dead son's semen to impregnate Jamie?

The newspaper story about the return of a kidnapped baby in Oklahoma City that Joe had showed her was convincing, however. The missing woman was described as tall, slender, and in her early twenties. And she had a baby about the same age as Jamie's would have been.

Lenora rubbed her forehead in an attempt to ward off a threatening headache. *That baby in all those photographs wasn't really Amanda's? And Jamie's baby is Amanda's grandchild?* "Okay, Joe, I want you to tell me why you called this little meeting so I can get home to my husband."

"I need a copy of the contract that Jamie signed. And I need your boss to act as an intermediary between Jamie and the Hartmanns. And as soon as she and her baby have undergone DNA testing and we have irrefutable proof that she is indeed the mother of the baby, I want Abernathy to inform Gus Hartmann that this has been done. Then the burden will be on Amanda's husband to prove that he is the father of the child. Since that would be impossible, the contract that Jamie entered into with Amanda Hartmann and Toby Travis would be invalid. I plan to obtain a court decree saying just that. And I want Gus to know that if anything happens to Jamie or if her baby is kidnapped, the contract along with the DNA tests and the court decree will be made public along with Jamie's sworn testimony as to the circumstances surrounding the kidnapping of the baby girl in Oklahoma City."

Lenora shook her head. "The only thing Bentley did was locate a suitable candidate and draw up the contract. Bentley had no idea what Amanda had in mind."

"I realize that," Joe said, running a hand over his bald pate. "But Bentley Abernathy is the Hartmann family attorney. He has access to Gus, and I don't."

Lenora leaned forward and narrowed her eyes. "I know without asking that my boss would do just about anything not to get involved in this mess.

And after what you've told me, I'd be afraid to let him or anyone else know that I've been in contact with you."

"Then I have no recourse except to go the criminal route," Joe said, sitting up straighter and squaring his shoulders. "I will file a complaint against Amanda Hartmann and her brother for holding Jamie Long against her will and conspiring to steal her baby. Furthermore, I will see that the media receives copies of this complaint and is notified well in advance of the time and place of the filing."

"The place of the filing would be the Marshall County Courthouse," Lenora pointed out. "Don't think that you're going to get a fair hearing out there. In fact, I predict that any filing you make against the Hartmanns in that courthouse would be summarily dismissed. In Marshall County, Gus Hartmann is God."

Lenora reached across the table and put her hand on Joe's arm. "You are playing with fire, young man," she said softly. *Poor Joe,* she thought. He was not only earnest, he was in love.

"I know, but what else can I do?" Joe asked. "Jamie can't spend the rest of her life hiding from him."

"You have a life, too. Don't waste it on a lost cause."

Young Joe's eyes widened. "You think I should just let Gus Hartmann have Jamie murdered and hand her baby over to Amanda?"

"I'm saying that no matter what you do, this thing probably will not end well. Even if Jamie gave up the baby, I'm not sure that her troubles would be over. In fact," she said, tapping the newspaper clipping with her finger, "if this business in Oklahoma City truly was a failed attempt to kidnap Jamie's baby and murder her, your troubles aren't ever going to be over. Look, Joe, I see fear in Bentley's eyes when he talks to Gus Hartmann on the phone. All the work Bentley has done for Gus over the years has been within the letter of the law, but I think Bentley has figured out more about Gus Hartmann's business and life than is healthy and it scares him shitless. It scares *me* shitless. I wish I hadn't come here tonight. But I'm going to walk out of here and forget everything you told me."

She stood. "I wish you well, Joe. The only advice I have for you and Jamie is to change your names, leave the country, and watch your backsides. *And* hope that Gus Hartmann has a fatal heart attack sometime *real* soon."

He grabbed her hand. "What about the contract?"

"It's gone," she admitted, pulling her hand away. "I decided I'd look it over before I came here tonight. It's been erased from my computer, and there are no copies in the hard files. I don't know if Bentley did it or someone else, and I don't want to know. And I don't want to ever see or hear from you again."

Chapter Thirty-five

JOE WATCHED AS Lenora picked up her purse, scooted out of the booth, and stood. Once again men at the bar turned on their stools to stare as the stylish, shapely black woman walked by.

He sat there for a time, stunned by what Lenora had said. And by her fear. His hope of finding a sane way to deal with the threat against Jamie was evaporating.

It was his threat now, too. He had no doubt about that. At this very minute there were people looking for both of them. And that knowledge made him more afraid than he had ever been in his life. Even so, there was an inviolate corner of his being that believed that if he and Jamie could keep their wits intact, they would find a way to prevail, that right would win over wrong.

Maybe they should follow Lenora's advice and leave the country. But to pull that off they would need new identities and passports. That wasn't something he could make happen overnight. At some point he would have to get more money. He had invested most of the money that he'd inherited from his aunt Lacy, and he wasn't sure how quickly he could access those funds. But what if Gus Hartmann had made it all vanish the way he'd made Jamie's bank account vanish? What if the only money they had was the cash he'd left with Jamie and what was in his billfold?

He left enough money on the table to cover the bar tab and tip then headed for the door. The men who had stared at Lenora paid no attention to his departure. Except for one man. The guy seated at the end of the bar was watching him in the mirror. Joe could tell by the tilt of his chin. The man had the bulked-up muscles of a dedicated weight lifter and was wearing black jeans and a blue shirt.

Out front, Joe looked up and down the parking lot, taking note of the vehicles parked there, then got on his bike and drove around aimlessly for a while. When he spotted the black Ford pickup in his rearview mirror, Joe abruptly turned into a service station and lingered for a time, using the restroom, filling the Harley's half-full tank, sipping a cup of coffee that tasted as though it had been brewed this morning. When he left the service station, he drove a few miles then without using his turn signal, turned into a convenience-store parking lot and stopped by a drive-up pay phone. As the black truck turned into a McDonald's across the street, Joe took off down the side street.

The phone lines at Bentley Abernathy's law office had been tapped, Joe realized. Someone had listened to his phone conversation with Lenora. And the driver of the black truck had been waiting for him at the Holiday Inn.

Fortunately he had lived in Austin for the seven years it took for him to complete his undergraduate and law degrees and knew the city well. He spent a couple of hours randomly driving through a maze of back streets, waiting until he was absolutely certain that no one could possibly be following him. But just to make sure, he headed for I-35, traveling north for a time, then made a U-turn and headed back into central Austin, where he abandoned the interstate altogether and headed across town to Highway 71. He pulled in at the first truck stop.

He parked in the shadows behind the building and carefully wiped the dust off his Harley. Then, leaving the key in the ignition, he retrieved his backpack, gave the bike a good-bye pat, and headed into the sea of parked rigs.

It took him a while to find a ride. The driver was heading for Galveston with a load of wrecked vehicles that had been smashed and stacked on the flatbed like decks of cards. Leon was his name. An older guy with bad teeth. He'd been driving twelve hours straight and needed someone to keep him awake. That was Joe's job. "I prefer sports talk," Leon said. "No politics unless you're a Democrat."

Once they were on the highway, Leon said, "Start talking, kid."

In spite of a punch-drunk state brought about by his own sleep deprivation, Joe somehow managed to conduct a mumbling discourse that went from baseball to the historical development of the Democratic Party to the role that team sports played in character development.

* * *

After spending a long, lonely day and sleepless night without Joe, the walls were beginning to push in on Jamie. She gave Billy a bath and looked through the newspapers. When she reached the religion section, she read and reread an article printed there, then carefully tore it out of the newspaper and put it into the side pocket of her backpack along with the roll of bills Joe had put there.

Even antsier than before, she washed her hair and did some push-ups. Finally she put Billy in his sling, shouldered the backpack, and headed out the back door. She locked the door behind her and tucked the key in the backpack.

It was a beautiful day with only a soft breeze to ruffle her hair. The gulls circled overhead and the sandpipers raced along the beach. Far out at sea, she could see a large tanker. Closer in there were smaller craft—pleasure and fishing boats.

She walked for a couple of miles. The only people she saw were an older man and a young boy digging for clams. She waved and continued on her walk. On her way back, they were still there. A happy sight. She imagined bringing Billy back here someday to dig for clams and throw pieces of bread in the air for the gulls to catch.

Billy was beginning to protest his confinement, so she took him out of the sling and, holding him so that he faced outward, cut inland a couple of hundred yards for a change of scenery and wound through the dunes, occasionally spotting a hermit crab scampering about. At one point, she knelt in the sand to take a better look at one of the ugly little creatures that confiscate the shells of sea snails for their portable homes. "See there, Billy," she said. "He carries his house around with him. That's what we're going to do when Joe gets back."

While she was kneeling there, she saw something moving just beyond the stand of beach grass. Holding Billy like a sack of potatoes on her hip, she crept forward a bit and parted the grass just enough to see two men heading toward the cabin. The men were young, athletic-looking, and dressed alike in jeans, navy blue T-shirts, and matching baseball caps. She might have mistaken them for two regular guys out for a walk on the beach except that they were hunched over and keeping to the depressions between the dunes as they approached the cabin.

It was happening again. They had tracked her down.

Immediately she dropped lower and scooted in among the clumps of grass, where she lay on her side clutching Billy against her chest. His little body was tense. She could tell that he was about to cry. Hurriedly, she curled her body around him, pulled up her T-shirt, and unhooked the flap on her bra. Just as Billy was about to voice his displeasure, she got a nipple into his mouth.

She heard the screen door slam as other men came running toward the cabin. "Fan out," she heard a voice call. With her arms around Billy, she used her feet to scoot deeper into the stand of grass as men headed up and down the beach. Others were running toward the other cabins and pounding on doors. She worked hard to control the panic that filled her chest and pushed on her rib cage, making it hard to breathe. She dug in the sand with her free hand, making a trench to lie in. When it was finished, she rolled into it and bent the tall grass so that it arched over her and Billy.

Harvey Morgan was half watching a baseball game and making a second perusal through the morning papers when the doorbell rang. Since he wasn't expecting anyone, he assumed it was either a kid selling something to raise money for his or her school, scout troop, or church, or a pair of bike-riding Mormon missionaries fresh from the barbershop. Harvey always bought something from the kids. The missionaries got a less friendly response.

The unshaven man standing on his front porch wasn't a kid, and he certainly wasn't a Mormon.

"Mr. Morgan, it's Joe Brammer," the man said, removing his hat.

"*Joe?*" Harvey queried, looking over the top of his reading glasses. "Where's your hair? You look like hell."

"Yeah, sorry about that. I need to talk to you. It's very important."

Harvey pushed open the screen door and stepped to one side while the young man entered, then led the way to the room he and Betty had built onto the back of their house that most people would call a family room, but since he and Betty didn't have kids they referred to it as the back room. Marvin, the elderly beagle, looked up from the sofa when they entered the room and thumped his tail a few times.

"I remember you," Joe said, bending to scratch the dog's chin. "Glad to see that you're still around."

Harvey picked up the remote and switched off the television. "Sit down," he told Joe as he gestured toward the unoccupied end of the sofa. Then he settled himself back into his well-worn easy chair, where he now spent too damned much of his time. He and Marvin were going to turn to stone pretty soon if they didn't start moving around more.

Harvey watched while Joe continued to pet the dog as he glanced around the room, which—except for being dusty and cluttered with stacks of newspapers—was pretty much the same as it had been when Betty used to give the boy milk and cookies after he finished working in the yard. Or sometimes Joe had simply showed up at the door wanting to return a book or looking for a chess game. Harvey had taught the boy to play. Joe was a reasonably good player but not exceptional. Mostly, though, Joe had wanted to discuss whatever book he was returning, which was always from Harvey's collection of what Joe called spy books. These books included histories, theoretical treatises, exposés, biographies and auto-biographies, and novels detailing careers in and the business of intelligence gathering. And the boy would ask countless questions concerning Harvey's own years at the CIA. Harvey's area had been profiling. After years as a double agent, he had become one of the early practitioners in the field and had compiled profiles on world leaders, dictators, political figures, military leaders, and sometimes other spies. Only when he had a heart attack and was forced to retire at age fifty-two did what was left of his family learn the true nature of his government service. He moved back to Houston to be near his ailing mother, renew old friendships, and figure out if there was life after danger and cigarettes. The wife of a friend from his high school days convinced him to accompany them to a school reunion and made sure he met up with his former high school sweetheart, who had been widowed a number of years earlier. He and Betty had had twenty wonderful years together, especially after she retired from her teaching job and they began trekking about the country in their RV. Now he felt lost without her. He even thought about taking up smoking again.

"Mom saw Mrs. Morgan's obituary in the newspaper," Joe said. "I'm really sorry. She was a great lady and the best teacher I ever had."

Harvey nodded. "Your mother wrote a nice note. She mentioned that you had finished law school and were spending some time abroad."

Harvey recalled how Betty had commented on more than one occasion that if she'd ever had a son, she would have liked him to be just like Joe Brammer. Harvey had agreed with her. Joe was a good kid.

"Okay, son, you need to tell me why you showed up at my front door unannounced, on foot, and unshaven except for your head."

"I'm afraid that I'm involved in an extremely unusual situation," Joe explained. "I can assure you that I haven't done anything illegal or even unethical, but my girlfriend and I are being hunted down by some sort of government agents whom I believe answer to someone high up in the national government. I'm sure the agents involved think they are tracking some sort of international terrorists or a spy who stole national secrets, when what is really at issue is a gross misuse of power over something quite personal and has nothing to do with the law or international intrigue or any sort of threat to the United States government or its elected leaders."

Harvey nodded. "Wouldn't be the first time," he said. "So, tell me, just what is it that you want from me?"

Joe sat up straighter. "Transportation," he said. "Do you still have the camper?"

"It's a 'recreational vehicle,'" Harvey corrected. "And yes, I still have it. I've only used it once since Betty died, though. Traveling around the country isn't the same without her."

"I need the RV," Joe said. "It's a matter of life and death."

"That bad, huh?"

"Yes, sir. I would like to sign some sort of lease, but I'd rather not leave a paper trail. If I live through this, you'll get it back. If not, I'm sure my parents will reimburse you out of the money I inherited from my great-aunt, unless it has mysteriously disappeared, which is what happened to my girlfriend's bank account."

"So you want to just get in and drive away without me telling anyone that I've seen you or that I no longer have an RV in my garage?" Harvey asked.

"Yes, sir. Not even my parents, should you happen to run into them. I know they're worried about me, but their phone lines are tapped and their house is being watched. I don't dare call them or go over there, and I really need for you not to mention to them or anyone else that I've been here."

"I'll make you a deal, son," Harvey said. "You tell me about your troubles, and I'll let you take the RV."

Joe shook his head. "I can't let you get involved. You can always say that I stole the RV, but if these people thought that you knew what was going on . . ." He paused, apparently not wanting or unable to put into words the seriousness of the risk.

"Joe, there was a time in my life when I carried around a little pill to put under my tongue if my cover was blown. Now the love of my life is dead. I don't have any children. I'm bored as hell. And I just might be able to help you. It might be the last opportunity I have to be significantly useful to another human being, so I'll get you a beer and I want you to start talking."

Joe closed his eyes and slumped against the back of the sofa. Marvin actually roused himself enough to scoot closer and push his head under Joe's hand. Absently Joe began stroking him. Harvey could well imagine what was going on in the boy's head. Here he was in the presence of someone who would be a knowledgeable listener and just might have some insights as to how he might extract himself from the situation in which he found himself. But anyone who helped him might also face the same danger that he faced.

Finally Joe's eyes opened. "I didn't come here to get you involved."

"I know you didn't, son. You need my RV so you can better manage being on the run. But it would be absolute torture for you to leave this retired old spy sitting here in his easy chair not knowing what the hell you're running from."

Joe actually grinned.

Harvey grinned back. "Before we get to the serious stuff, though, let's have a bite of lunch." He installed Joe on the kitchen stool and put a bowl of chips and a can of beer in front of him. He actually felt happy or something closely akin to it as he bustled about the kitchen making tuna-salad sandwiches and iced tea. While he worked, Harvey asked Joe about law school and his travels abroad.

Harvey was touched when Joe turned the conversation to Betty, saying how all the kids at Memorial High School knew they could go to her with their problems whether they were enrolled in one of her math classes or not. He found himself telling Joe about Betty's final illness and how valiant she was and how much he missed her. "Don't get me wrong," Harvey said. "Betty and I had our disagreements and pouts like anyone else, but all in all it was twenty damned good years."

After they'd eaten, Harvey took Joe out to the garage and showed him the RV, which had traveled more than 200,000 miles over its two decades and was on its second motor but had been diligently maintained and ran like a top. The vehicle was almost too large for the garage but was considerably smaller than Joe had remembered. But with a double bed, minuscule bathroom, kitchen facilities, and small table, it was all they needed. Harvey explained how to fill the water tank, dump the holding tank, and turn on the pilot light for the hot-water tank. The vehicle was fully equipped with dishes, towels, and bedding.

Then they settled down in the back room. Joe did most of the talking, of course, but Harvey listened with great care and asked questions when appropriate. The look on Joe's face when he spoke of Jamie Long brought the ache of missing to Harvey's heart. When he learned of Jamie's involvement with the Hartmann family, his heart sank.

At the end of Joe's tale, Harvey went to the kitchen to fix a pot of coffee. Over coffee he told Joe what little he knew about the Hartmanns. From time to time, during his decades-long career as a profiler observing and drawing conclusions about the inner workings of the minds of world leaders, he had come across the Hartmann name. He knew that Buck Hartmann had had no qualms about doing business with tyrants, and that those same tyrants had looked forward to the day when Buck's son, Jason, would be president of the United States. But Jason had died, and old Buck had groomed his grandson to take over the family's business interests but not to enter the political arena. Gus Hartmann was too short for that. And probably too smart.

"Probably Gus wants an heir as much as his sister does," Harvey speculated. "He needs someone to take over the family business, and she probably wants a child who can carry on the family ministry. Your Jamie has gotten herself into one hell of a mess, that's for sure. And now you're right in there with her, Joe."

Joe looked exhausted, and Harvey wanted to mull things over before he said any more, so he suggested they call it a night and showed Joe to the guest room. "I'll get up early and take the RV in for servicing," Harvey said. "When I get back we'll continue our discussion."

Harvey was already organizing his thoughts for tomorrow's session. And spent several hours at the computer before finally going to bed. He was quite certain that Joe was never going to get to Gus Hartmann. But Amanda Hartmann was a very public person.

He wasn't even sleepy when he finally went to bed. He felt more alert and vital than he had in years.

Chapter Thirty-six

FOR HOURS, JAMIE lay on the sand, hidden by the sea grass, barely moving, moisture seeping into her clothing, relieved that in spite of his strange surroundings Billy had fallen asleep. When he seemed to be waking, she patted him and whispered to him in her soothing go-back-to-sleep voice.

She wondered about the men who were searching for her. And wondered just who they thought they were looking for. Some Mata Hari who was spying for enemies of the state with a baby on her hip? Unlike the men in Oklahoma City, who were surely hired killers, she realized that these men were simply doing what their superiors had told them to do, and their superiors apparently answered to Gus Hartmann or someone who answered to Gus Hartmann. Probably when these men went home to their families at night, they were just normal guys. But right now they were her enemies, and if they did their job well, her life was probably over. Not that these men would kill her. They would turn her over to others, but eventually death would be her fate. She would never see her son grow to manhood. He would grow up thinking that Amanda Hartmann was his mother and would be taught that he was God's chosen and didn't have to play by the same rules as everyone else.

From time to time, she heard people talking, and then she heard a vehicle and parted the grass long enough to see a van drive up to the cabin. The next time she looked two men had dumped her trash on the ground and were meticulously going through it, even opening up Billy's soiled diapers and peering inside.

She tried to plan. She didn't dare leave her hiding place until darkness fell. But then what?

If only there were some way to contact Joe and tell him what had happened. Some way to warn him not to come back here. And together they could decide where she should go, what she should do. The man Joe planned to see in Houston was named Morgan. *Mr.* Morgan. She didn't know his first name. All she knew about him was that he had an RV and his wife had been Joe's math teacher in high school. There would be long columns of Morgans in the Houston telephone directory. Here she had been hoping that Joe would return this evening. Now she prayed that he was *not* on his way back and that it would be days before he returned and these men would be long gone.

Even if it seemed as though the men had left, Jamie wouldn't dare go back to the cabin. Some of them might continue to keep the cabin under surveillance, waiting for her to do just that. With all the discussion about what to do next, she and Joe had not designated a meeting place should they become separated.

She waited throughout the rest of the afternoon, moving her legs and arms only enough to relieve the cramping in her muscles. Finally, when she couldn't keep Billy asleep any longer, she nursed him again. When he finished nursing, he filled his diaper and, keeping her head low, she changed him and buried the soiled diaper in the sand. Then she dug her trench deeper and, sitting cross-legged, she played with him for a time, keeping her head down, talking softly. From time to time, she peeked through the grass. Visible activity around the cabin had ceased, and the van had gone.

When darkness finally fell, no light came on in the cabin. But Jamie not only *knew* that there were people still inside waiting for her to return, she *felt* their invasive presence in what for the past week had become a home of sorts to her.

It was Oklahoma City all over again. Fleeing in the night. Leaving everything behind. At least this time there had been no beloved dog for them to kill.

Her chest began to heave with sobs. It was all too much. If she survived this night, was this to become the pattern of her life? Always hiding? Always running?

So what was the alternative? To give up? To die?

She cradled her baby in her arms and forced her mind away from hysteria. She had to be calm. To think. To plan.

She tried to remember what time the moon had risen last night. She probably should leave now, taking advantage of the moonless darkness. Yes, that was what she should do. But still she waited a few minutes more, taking deep breaths, willing whatever residual courage still resided within her to come forth and fortify her. Then, clinging to her baby with one arm, she crept out of her hiding place.

Keeping to the low spaces between the dunes, she headed away from the cabin. She walked for a long time, an hour or more she estimated, staying south of the beach road until the terrain changed, and the cover offered by the dunes and grasses diminished in favor of wide beaches. She waited out of sight by the road, watching for any sort of movement or sound, then took a deep breath and dashed to the other side, where the cover was better. Finally she took the time to put Billy in the sling and catch her breath. Then, keeping the road on her left, she kept out of sight as best she could, which was difficult in the darkness. Several times she stumbled; twice she fell, putting out her hands to protect Billy. Her hands and knees were cut and bruised, her arms and legs scratched and bleeding from brambles. If only she had pulled on sweats this morning instead of shorts. Her only spare clothing in the canvas bag was a T-shirt and a pair of underpants. She ate a handful of trail mix and drank some more water, but she was still hungry. And exhausted. Filled with self-doubt. What if she was doing the wrong thing? What if Joe was apprehended when he returned to the cabin? Maybe she would never see him again. But for lack of another plan, she kept walking. When she reached an intersection, she turned north and, still keeping well out of sight of passing motorists, followed the new road. Occasionally she would take a few more bites of trail mix and drink a little water.

The sun was almost ready to peek over the horizon when Billy began to protest his confinement. She pulled him out of the sling and carried him over her shoulder as she headed down a country lane. He was howling with hunger by the time she found a sheltered spot in a dry creek bed where they could spend a few hours. The creek bed's sandy bottom welcomed her exhausted body. When the sun rose, a nearby black willow would shade them. She drank some water while Billy nursed, then gratefully closed her eyes. Billy would just have to amuse himself for a while.

She wondered where Joe was at this moment. Were those men still waiting for him back at the cabin? What would they do to him if they caught him?

It was all so unreal. Things like this weren't supposed to happen to ordinary, law-abiding people. Not here. Not in the United States of America.

Joe muttered a curse when he saw the signs warning that there was roadwork ahead and all traffic was being funneled into the right lane. Getting stuck in traffic at this hour of the night was unanticipated, to say the least. Joe got more and more impatient as he drove at a snail's pace behind the impossibly long line of vehicles.

He felt like a middle-aged man driving a recreational vehicle down the highway. He would have to keep his speed under the posted limit at all times. Speed was the only thing that might attract attention to the vehicle. He was certain that the RV and its license number weren't on any law-enforcement watch list. He and Jamie and the baby would seem like an ordinary family on vacation. Mr. Morgan had given him a nationwide listing of campgrounds. Once he had Jamie and the baby onboard, they could move around the country effortlessly. Maybe if they could stay pretty much continuously on the move for a few months or even a year, the baby thing would become a moot issue. Amanda Hartmann would have learned to love the other baby and forgotten all about Jamie's kid.

Of course, Joe knew that such a scenario was just wishful thinking on his part. Fear was going to be their constant companion until the business with the Hartmanns was resolved. Already his stomach was in knots because he had been away from Jamie and the baby too long.

Joe and Mr. Morgan had spent much of the day tossing out ideas to each other and searching for information on the Internet. When the garage finally returned the RV, the two of them put away the provisions that Mr. Morgan kept carrying out from the house—canned goods, paper towels, toilet tissue, soap, beer. Then they had dinner, and Joe suggested a game of chess, not because he wanted to play but because he knew Mr. Morgan was itching to. And he had decided that he shouldn't leave until Mr. Morgan's neighbors had bedded down for the night and wouldn't be out in their yards or walking their dogs and observe an unfamiliar person driving away in Harvey Morgan's RV.

At ten o'clock, they walked out to the garage. Joe unscrewed the light-bulb mounted on the overhead garage-door opener so he could make his exit in darkness. Then he punched the button to open the door and embraced Mr. Morgan.

"I wish I could tell you to call me and keep me posted," Mr. Morgan said, "but don't even think about it. No postcards with cryptic messages. The next time I see you I want you to have hair on your head and Miss Jamie and little Billy at your side."

Joe had waved out the window as he drove away. And now, an hour later, he was less than fifteen miles from Mr. Morgan's home, but the roadwork was behind him.

Finally he reached the Freeport turnoff, and shortly he was driving through Neptune Beach, with its darkened stores and restaurants. He parked the RV near a picnic area, locked the vehicle, shoved the key deep in his pocket, and made his way across the beach. When he reached the hard, wet sand by the water's edge, he broke into a run. He ran with joy in his heart, each step taking him closer to Jamie.

A thin sliver of moonlight reflected on the water and provided sufficient illumination for him to avoid stranded jellyfish and pieces of driftwood. When he reached familiar terrain, he cut inland and wound his way through the dunes for the last couple of hundred yards—just to be on the safe side.

Finally the cabin, silhouetted against the night sky, came into view. He dropped low behind a clump of beach grass to survey the scene and make sure that all was well.

The cabin was dark, which didn't surprise him. Then he noticed that the trash container had been moved from its former position alongside the building to a place by the back porch. Which hardly would enhance the view. And besides, the thing smelled like shit.

Maybe the trash container had been pushed over by a stray dog or an armadillo in search of leftover food, Joe speculated, and Jamie had simply turned it back over and not bothered to drag it back to its original position.

He was still pondering the trash container when he noticed that the only vehicles in the entire enclave were two identical black vans, each parked by a different cabin.

As much as he wanted to go dashing up to the cabin and tap on the door, Joe decided to hunker down and watch things for a while. For fifteen minutes, he would do that, he decided, and looked down at the glowing dial of his watch.

He watched. Everything was peaceful. The only movement was the waves on the beach.

At the end of fifteen minutes, he decided to stay put for another fifteen. Just to be sure.

And then he saw something out of the corner of his right eye. Just a glint of reflected moonlight from up there on higher ground.

Or had he imagined it?

Joe waited, trying not to blink as he watched to see if he saw whatever it was again. His eyes began to water and finally blinked of their own accord.

Then he saw it again. Or thought that he had.

He backed out of his hiding place and crawled through the clumps of grass angling toward the road. When he was certain that he would be out of the line of vision of whomever might be up there watching the cabin, he dashed across the road. On the other side, the vegetation began to change. Within a few yards, kudzu vines were everywhere, impeding his progress as he climbed to a place that would put him directly behind the area from which the mysterious reflection had come. A reflection from the lens of binoculars, perhaps. Or night-vision goggles.

When Joe neared the top of the incline, he dropped to his belly and scooted over and through the vines, trying not to think about the possibility of snakes and scorpions. When he calculated that he was getting close, he stopped and simply listened for a time.

At first he thought it was just the rustling of leaves he was hearing. But there was no breeze. It was voices. Very soft voices.

When he lifted his head, he saw them. Two men dressed in dark clothes, surveying the quiet scene below, waiting for something to happen.

Joe considered the possibilities. They could already have apprehended Jamie and the baby and were waiting for him to return. If that were the case, Jamie could already be dead and the baby already delivered to the Hartmanns.

But since that particular scenario was unacceptable, he tried to imagine one in which Jamie would have gotten away.

She had seen them coming and went racing out the back door.

But they would have had the back door covered. He tried again.

She had gone for a walk on the beach.

He imagined her leaving by the back door, locking it behind her, and strolling up the beach for a couple of miles then heading back. She saw the men before they saw her. And she turned tail and ran. She would have her escape bag with her. That was what they had decided. Anytime she left the cabin.

He liked that version better. *Much* better.

Okay, if that was what had happened, Joe reasoned, those two men and probably others who were watching from different vantage points would have no way of knowing that he wasn't with Jamie and the baby. With their possessions still in the cabin, the men were probably waiting for the three of them to return.

Joe made his way back down the slope through the maze of vines, which were like living things from some horror movie. His feet became tangled in them, slowing his progress.

Where would Jamie have gone, he asked himself. With all that talking and planning they had done, deciding that he should go to Houston for the RV and where they should go when he returned, they had neglected to include a scenario like this one. He didn't have a clue as to where she would go.

Or did he?

Once he had made his way back to the beach, he took off his shoes and ran full out on the wet sand. As fast as he had ever run in his life.

Chapter Thirty-seven

JAMIE STOOD AT the perimeter of the tarmac and looked longingly at Flossie's Truck Stop and Diner. It was a frame building that hadn't seen a paintbrush in decades, but business was brisk. At least a dozen vehicles were parked in front, and several others were being fueled by their owners.

She could almost smell the coffee. But she hesitated to go inside. She was filthy and had cuts and scratches all over her arms and legs. She could imagine people turning to stare. What if there was a highway patrolman seated at the lunch counter? He might ask if she had been in an accident or take an interest in Billy's welfare. He might want to know where she was going and how.

She had Billy over her shoulder with a blanket over his head to protect him from sunburn and was trying to jiggle him to sleep while she tried to decide if she dared go inside the diner.

An elderly rig with the words "Phillips Hauling" painted on the side rolled past her and came to a stop by a diesel pump. She watched while an aging couple emerged from the cab. It took her a few seconds to realize that an opportunity might have just presented itself.

The man headed inside the station, while the woman lifted the nozzle from the pump. Jamie started toward the truck, mentally composing her story.

The woman watched her approach with a wary look on her round face. She was a formidable-looking woman with broad shoulders, wide hips, and her graying hair in a no-nonsense ponytail.

"I suppose you want a ride?" the woman said, her tone challenging.

Jamie nodded. "The baby's father pushed us out of the car last night down by Freeport," she said. "I've been walking ever since, putting as many miles as I can between him and me, except for a couple of hours early this morning when I just had to get off my feet."

"You heading home?" the woman asked.

"Yes, ma'am. I've been afraid to accept a ride in the middle of the night from just anyone who might pull over so I kept off the road. It's been tough going."

"How old is the baby?" the woman asked as she inserted the nozzle into the truck's gas tank.

"Almost two months. My boyfriend decided that he wasn't the father. But he is. I doubt if I'll ever see him again, though. I've got family up in Washington County. If you're heading that way, I'd be ever so grateful if you would give us a ride. I'm pretty much walked out."

The woman cocked her head to one side as she regarded Jamie. Then, with a nod she said, "I reckon. We'll be pulling out in about ten minutes."

Jamie thanked the woman then went inside. Her first stop was the restroom, where she cleaned herself up as best she could and put on the clean T-shirt from her backpack. In the diner, she bought an apple-cinnamon muffin and a cup of coffee to go.

The couple was waiting by their truck.

"My name is Beverly," Jamie said.

The woman nodded and got behind the wheel. Her husband crawled into the bed in the rear of the cab. Jamie climbed aboard.

"You ought to have that baby in a car seat," the woman said.

"It's in my boyfriend's car along with all our clothes," Jamie said.

Billy had drifted off to sleep after just a few minutes. Jamie ate the muffin and sipped the coffee. She was grateful that the woman didn't want to chat. Lying was so exhausting.

She wondered where Joe was at this moment. Would she and Joe ever lead a normal life?

Would she ever see him again?

Once he was back behind the wheel of the RV, Joe waited a few minutes for his heart to slow and his nerves to calm. Jamie was physically strong and had the will to do what needed to be done, he told himself. She had escaped before. He would go on the assumption that she had done it again.

He drove with great deliberation, keeping his speed well below the speed limit. He knew that Jamie would stay out of sight as much as possible, which meant that he probably wasn't going to spot her walking along the side of the road. But he looked anyway, hoping to catch a glimpse of her walking along one of the country roads that paralleled State Highway 36. And he carefully scanned fields and groves of trees. Maybe she had managed to catch a ride with someone. An old farm couple, perhaps. Every elderly vehicle he passed he looked to see if Jamie was inside or riding in the back.

In Brenham, he stopped for coffee. Then he drove slowly along the winding road, looking for Jamie.

He passed Old Baylor Park and paused to get his bearings.

He pulled into the Independence Cemetery and stood on the running board calling her name, but there was no response.

He drove to the back corner of the cemetery, fixed a sandwich and grabbed a bottle of water, then walked up and down the rows just to make sure that Jamie wasn't there. He sat in front of a monument marking the grave of a man named Abner Martin, who, according to the inscription, was a veteran of the Texas War for Independence. From this vantage point he could see anyone approaching the cemetery.

He ate the sandwich and drank half the water then settled in for a wait. With no sleep the night before, he kept nodding off, and would wake with a jerk then look around frantically to see if Jamie had arrived while he was asleep. To keep himself awake he would walk up and down the rows, ducking out of sight when an occasional vehicle went by, reading the inscriptions on the headstones then returning to Abner's grave until he started nodding off once again and would force himself to take another walk.

At dusk, while he was taking a walk, he realized that someone on foot was walking toward the cemetery. But in the fading light he could not tell if it was someone out for an evening stroll or a woman carrying a baby.

The person was hunched over and walking with a lagging step. He or she was either elderly or very tired. He watched as the walker stumbled and almost fell. When he started walking toward the road, the person stopped and stared in his direction. And lifted a hand.

It was *her*. It was Jamie!

Joe took off at a dead run. "Jamie," he called, waving his arms in the air. "Jamie."

When he reached her she handed him the baby at the same instant her legs collapsed beneath her. He knelt and with his free arm embraced her, saying her name over and over again. She put her face against his shoulder and wept. He kissed her forehead, her cheeks, her cracked lips. "My Jamie, my poor darling Jamie," he said.

"I was so afraid that I'd never see you again," she sobbed. "Some men came while I was taking a walk. I was afraid that they would be waiting for you when you got back."

"They were, but I saw them first," he said. "I got the RV. It's parked at the rear of the cemetery."

"I can't walk another step," she said.

He left her sitting on the ground leaning against a fence post. Holding Billy tightly in his arms he raced through the cemetery. Billy began to cry. His lusty cries seemed quite out of place in the silent burial ground.

Once he was in the RV, he put the still unhappy baby in the center of the bed and drove back up the dirt track.

Jamie was sitting where he had left her. He helped her to her feet and into the vehicle. Billy was still crying. She lay down beside him, fumbling with her T-shirt. Joe bent over her and kissed her forehead.

"We're together," she said in a hoarse voice. "I'll be all right now."

Joe reluctantly returned to the driver's seat. After a half hour or so, he pulled off onto a dirt road and went back to the bed.

Billy was asleep. Jamie looked like a rag doll. "Would you please take off my shoes?" she asked.

Joe did as she asked. Her feet were filthy, her heels and toes worn raw. He got a pan of water and a bar of soap and gently washed her feet. He prepared a simple meal for her, then helped her to a sitting position, propping pillows behind her. Billy was sleeping peacefully next to her.

She sipped tomato soup from a cup and ate several wedges of apple, then fell back against the pillow and closed her eyes. "We can't keep living like this."

Joe left her there.

He continued to head north, winding his way toward Bryan, where he caught 190 and headed northeast. It was dark when Jamie came to the front and stood beside the driver's seat, her hand on his shoulder. "I've ruined your life," she said.

"Well, you've certainly *changed* it," he said. "Are you feeling better?"

"I'll be all right as soon as I'm clean," she said, caressing his neck and hair. "Does the shower work?"

"Yeah. Billy okay?"

"He's asleep. Where are we headed?"

"We can talk about it after you have a shower."

"Joe?"

"Yeah?"

"You are my hero. And you are the only man that I've ever loved and ever plan to love."

"And you are the love of my life. We are going to get through this, Jamie. We have to."

She stood there caressing his neck. He didn't want her to stop.

"Are you going to drive all night?" she asked.

"No. I didn't sleep at all last night and am running out of steam. That little dining area turns into a second bed. I thought we could put Billy there. I'd like to have you to myself back in the big bed."

"That's what I have in mind, too. I have never been so exhausted in my life, but I need you, Joe. I need endless kisses and to feel you inside of me."

Joe reached for her hand and kissed it, then watched in the rearview mirror as she opened the narrow bathroom door.

In the town of Cottonwood, he stopped at a convenience store to buy diapers then parked the RV behind a boarded-up service station. He prepared Billy's bed while Jamie nursed him.

Once the baby was taken care of, they stood clinging to each other. Joe relished the feel of her wonderful body against his and the scent of her. He couldn't tell her enough times that he loved her. Could not kiss her deeply enough. He had thought they had reached some sort of pinnacle back at the cabin on the beach, but he realized that there were limitless pinnacles spread out in front of them, enough to last a lifetime. A *long* lifetime. Not one cut short by evil people who stopped at nothing to get their way.

He backed her toward the bed. Toward heaven. He wished that he were more clever with words, that he could say something more profound to express his feelings than simply "I love you" over and over again. But oh, how he did love her. And she loved him back with the same intensity.

Her body was wonderful. And she gave it so completely.

*   *   *

Billy slept until dawn. Jamie brought him back to the bed and nursed him.

Then the talking began. It continued while Joe drove, a coffee cup in his hand. Jamie read him the article she had clipped out of the newspaper. Joe nodded. Mr. Morgan had found the same information online. Amanda Hartmann would be holding a three-day crusade in Dallas.

For hours they tried to come up with a game plan, debating back and forth, sometimes arguing vehemently and having to take a break, during which they would sulk a bit and calm themselves, then begin anew, knowing full well that whatever scheme they decided upon would either save their lives or end them.

Chapter Thirty-eight

GUS CLIMBED THE freestanding staircase that curved its way gracefully to the second floor. He took the stairs slowly to accommodate the discomfort in his joints that had grown more pronounced with each passing year. For the last decade, his quarters had been located on the first floor. Gus seldom visited the second floor—until recently, when the babies came into his life.

Even though Victory Hill had been his primary residence since childhood, he had never loved it the way that he loved the ranch. But when he began his accession to power, it was necessary for him to be a limousine ride away from the nation's capital. Now he seldom went into the city; if he needed to see someone, that person came to him. Only when he was extremely displeased did he put himself through the drama of strolling unannounced into the White House.

At the top of the stairs, Gus paused and reached down to rub his aching knees, then made his way down the broad corridor with its many-paned, arched windows that looked out onto rolling green acres. Gus tapped gently on the door to Sonny's old room then opened it and stepped inside. The two sari-clad women smiled, and the younger one, Randi, called out in her precise English, "Good morning, Mister Gus."

The babies were lying side by side on a pallet wearing identical blue sailor suits. Randi's baby was brown-skinned with dark hair, and the other was fair-skinned with a bit of light fuzz on the top of his head.

Gus grabbed hold of a nearby chair and gingerly lowered himself to his knees. Then he held out his fingers for the babies to grasp. He found them equally beautiful and equally appealing. Amita and Buck. Both were boys—fine boys who were fat and happy.

Gus had fallen into the habit of stopping by to see the babies morning and evening. Sonny's old suite was now a nursery. His books were still on the shelves, but most of his possessions had been removed and packed away in the attic. Gus hadn't even bothered to ask Amanda if that was agreeable with her; he had simply ordered it done. Randi looked after the babies, and her mother, who was called Patty in lieu of her very long and unpronounceable name, came in the morning to help her and often spent the night so that Randi and her baby could be at home with her husband.

Gus produced two musical baby rattles from his pocket and began shaking them in front of the babies' faces. Then he placed tiny fingers around the rattles and watched the babies' delight as they waved them around.

"Has Amanda been by to see Buck lately?" Gus asked. He had taken to calling the baby Buck even though Amanda planned to name Sonny's baby Jason after their father. What would happen to Buck after baby Jason arrived was beginning to weigh heavily on Gus's mind. To acquire the child, he had given substantial amounts of money to the birth mother and her parents. And to obtain legal custody, he had filed for adoption. Of course, he had no intention of going through with the adoption. No intention at all. He would make sure that the boy went to a good home, however. And perhaps he would maintain some sort of relationship with him in the years to come.

In response to his question, Randi shook her head, her lovely face sad. "No, Mister Gus. Miss Amanda has not seen her baby since the magazine people came last week to photograph them together. I think that Miss Amanda has the sickness in the head that some women get after their babies are born."

"Postpartum depression?" Gus responded.

"Yes," Randi said with a nod. "Miss Amanda is not a happy lady. Not happy to have a beautiful son. Not happy with her handsome husband. She is here at Victory Hill so seldom now, and when she does come to this room, Mister Toby is not with her and she does not want to hold her own baby. She just looks at him and leaves. It makes me weep to see her that way, Mister Gus. Miss Amanda, she is our guardian angel. My mother and my husband and I love her so very much. With all of our unworthy hearts, we love her."

Patty nodded vigorously in support of her daughter's statement.

"You cannot imagine the kindness that Miss Amanda has shown us,"

Randi continued. "And now we are afraid for her and pray for her many times every day to the Christian God and to Uma, who is the Hindu goddess of motherhood."

Gus grabbed hold of the chair, pulled himself to his feet, and stood watching the babies for a time.

How perfectly beautiful they were.

He bid Randi and her mother good day and headed downstairs to his office, where he tried to reach Amanda on her cell phone for the fifth time in two hours. She still did not answer. Every day that went by she became angrier at him. He had promised that he would deliver Sonny's baby to her, and he had failed to do so, which shook him to the core. How could a young woman with a small baby and no resources outwit all the muscle that he had thrown against her? Gus had developed a begrudging admiration for Jamie Long and would actually feel sad when she met her eventual fate. And her boyfriend. Gus had been furious when he learned that Joe Brammer had slipped out of Houston on a motorcycle that no one knew about. And when they finally tracked them to that place on the beach, Brammer and the girl weren't there.

The whole thing seemed like a bad movie in which he was the supreme villain. Which maybe he truly was. Gus knew that eventually he would prevail. He had to. Every day that went by Amanda became more and more difficult, acting out like a petulant child who no longer got her way. It wouldn't be long before the press got wind of her behavior, and he would have a devil of a time keeping a lid on bad publicity. Fortunately, with the consolidation of the media, it was far easier to pull in chits with various CEOs than it had been in the old days, when he was forced to make good on threats to feisty managing editors who thought they had some God-given right to print "The Truth." Nevertheless, squelching bad publicity was time consuming and still not a fail-safe process.

Amanda had put him on notice. She would behave herself and come back home to Toby only when she had Sonny's baby in her arms—a baby who would be genetically tested just to make sure that Gus was not trying to pull a fast one on her. Only Sonny's actual child would do. She was even threatening to cancel her next national tour. Right now she was holed up in a hotel in Brunswick with some tattooed piece of shit who probably would infect her with a sexually transmitted disease. And her so-called husband was still living down the hall and spending his days tanning, swimming laps, pumping iron, eating nuts and sprouts, and praying to keep himself in shape for when Amanda came home. For the most part, Gus avoided Toby, but he had gone from being appalled that Amanda actually married a brainless bodybuilder to wishing she would honor her marital vows and cleave only unto him.

But Amanda was so much like their mother that it was frightening. Of course, Gus himself had a healthy sexual appetite, but he conducted his activities with great discretion. And he did not preach one thing and do another. His sister—like their mother before her—presented herself to the world as a virtuous woman who not only believed her own sermons but also lived them when nothing could have been further from the truth. But while Mary Millicent and her old reprobate of a father had been hard-core con artists, Amanda actually seemed to believe all the godly rhetoric that flowed from her lovely mouth. Her rationalization seemed to be that God held her to a different standard, that, after all, God had made her beautiful, appealing, clever, and persuasive so that she could bring Him souls, and was therefore perfectly willing to look the other way when those same attributes attracted adoring men. Except that beauty didn't last forever. In spite of Botox and peels and procedures, Amanda wasn't going to be able to keep her looks forever. And then, he feared, she would become pathetic like their mother had become. But he would always love her.

Gus called his sister's cell-phone number once again. This time he left a message. "I miss you terribly and am greatly worried about you, Amanda. I desperately need to see you. We need to make the final plans for your crusade or cancel it. And surely you realize that it's past time for you to conduct another one. Just popping in and out of a city here and there is not the same as a full-fledged crusade. We have worked too hard to make you one of the most beloved and powerful women in America to let it all fade away. And the president's reelection committee is counting on both the funding and the loyal voters that only the Alliance of Christian Voters can provide. No one else can fill your shoes, Amanda. You are the greatest evangelist of our times, maybe of all times. No one has ever saved more souls to glorify God or mobilized Christian voters like you do. But all that aside, I miss my darling sister. You know that I love and adore you above all others. You are my life, Amanda. Please come home to me. I swear that you will have Sonny's baby in your arms. Soon. It is my solemn promise."

Chapter Thirty-nine

THEY NEEDED TO go to Dallas. But not yet. Not for a week.

Jamie insisted that they spend that week outside the state of Texas. And as soon as they crossed the state line into Arkansas, she felt safer—for a time at least.

North of Murfreesboro they passed up a couple of RV parks for not being scenic enough. The one they finally selected was located in a wooded grove with mountains all around and a quaint village within walking distance. They bought groceries before settling in at their campsite, which overlooked a small creek and had a picnic table and a grill. While Joe busied himself hooking up the RV to water, electrical, and sewer lines, Jamie put foil-wrapped potatoes in the oven, then told Joe to keep an ear out for Billy while she walked to the camp store to buy charcoal and ice.

Joe grilled steaks while Jamie made iced tea and a salad. They ate at the picnic table, with Billy sitting at one end in his infant carrier studying the gently waving branches overhead. "This is wonderful," Jamie said, reaching for Joe's hand.

"Yeah," he agreed, kissing her fingertips. "A preview of things to come."

"I hope so," Jamie said, a surge of emotion filling her chest. "Oh, God, I hope so."

With Joe carrying Billy, they took an after-dinner walk following a path along the creek. The night was clear, the air crisp. With the absence of city lights, an amazing number of stars revealed themselves, which made Jamie think of the ranch. The sky had been spectacular there, too. And the high plain landscape with its lonely vastness had offered an unspoiled beauty of sorts. It was people who had made it an evil place.

Back at their campsite, they sat at the picnic table while Jamie fed Billy and Joe drank a beer. She helped herself to a few sips and wanted more.

She allowed herself to think of a time when she would no longer be nursing a baby and could enjoy a couple of cans of beer or a glass or two of wine in the evening and not have to wear unattractive nursing bras.

She had become unaccustomed to alcohol, and the sips of beer made her a bit light-headed, which was delightful, and her mind drifted forward to lovemaking. She had found a box of candles in the kitchen cupboard and had thought all day how lovely it was going to be to make love by candlelight. And now her imaginings were becoming more graphic and brought wonderful responses to her body. She closed her eyes to savor them.

"Hey," Joe said, "are you thinking about what I'm thinking about?"

"Oh, yes," Jamie said, her eyes still closed.

Taking turns with Billy in the sling, they spent hours each day on long hikes. Sometimes they lingered beside a small lake, watching turtles sun themselves on rocks and engaging in rock-skimming contests. Every morning they walked to the village to buy newspapers and whatever groceries were needed. In the afternoon they returned for double-decker ice-cream cones. In the evenings they made a production out of dinner, with the picnic table nicely set and a candle burning in a hurricane lamp. Fresh trout was readily available at the village grocery and tasted wonderful grilled. Sometimes they went for hours or even an entire day without talking about the threat that hung over their future, but it was their constant companion, making every moment they shared all the more intense.

Their last afternoon at the camp, Joe caught a ride into town and used the computer at the local library to check out the mass-transit schedule for Dallas and its environs. Then he went to a site featuring Texas RV parks. He wanted a large one where they would be hidden away among a sea of vehicles.

Early the following morning, Jamie battened down the hatches inside while Joe unhooked the RV and filled the water tank in preparation for their drive.

They stopped in Greenville to buy clothing to wear in Dallas.

It was dark when they drove into a huge RV park near the Six Flags Over Texas amusement park.

* * *

Marcia Kimball picked up the receiver and identified herself.

"There's a guy out here asking to see you," the receptionist's voice announced.

Holding the receiver to her ear with her shoulder, Marcia continued to type words into her computer. "Who is he?" she asked.

"Won't say. He said to ask you if you've ever ridden on a Harley."

Marcia frowned then took hold of the receiver and leaned back in her chair. "Is he tall, dark, and handsome?"

"Well, he's tall and he's handsome, but his head is shaved."

"Ask him where he took me on the Harley."

Marcia listened while the receptionist inquired. The man answered, "Padre Island."

Marcia drew in her breath then slowly exhaled. "Give me ten minutes then send him back," she told the receptionist, then headed for the prep room with its lighted mirror and assorted cosmetics.

She was back at her desk, pretending to be engrossed in her work, when Joe tapped on the partition that formed the wall of her cubicle. She spun her chair around. "Well, look at you! I wouldn't have recognized you if I'd bumped into you on the street. What's with the bald head and facial hair?"

Joe looked up and down the corridor, then stepped closer and said in a very soft voice, "Actually, it's meant to be a disguise."

Another quip was composing itself in her head when she realized that Joe was serious. *Dead serious.*

He was wearing khaki pants and a navy dress shirt. No tie. He was leaner than before. And very tan.

She stood and motioned for him to follow her. She made her way through the maze of cubicles to one of the station's two conference rooms. She closed the door behind her and motioned for him to sit down.

"We can talk here," she said.

Joe shook his head and pointedly looked around at the corners of the room and put a finger to his lips. "What I had in mind was lunch. I'm starving."

Marcia frowned. What in the hell was going on with him? Was he actually afraid that the room might be bugged?

Could it be? The thought had never occurred to her.

She glanced at her watch. "I'm on for the noon news and have lots of loose ends to take care of first. How about dinner?"

Joe glanced toward a credenza, then made a motion of writing something on his hand. Marcia realized that he wanted a piece of paper and something to write with. She opened a drawer in the credenza and produced a tablet and pencil.

"You're looking good," he said as he wrote, but there was no flirtation in his eyes or his voice. He showed her what he had written:

Where can we meet? Not your apartment.

"Why don't you just call me in a day or two," she said as she wrote:

I'm driving a blue Kia SUV. Be in front of the Crescent Hotel at six p.m.

He nodded and tore off the piece of paper and stuck it in his pocket. She showed him back to the waiting room, asking about his folks and saying that hers were doing well.

Back in her cubicle Marcia realized that she was shaking. Either Joe Brammer had gone crazy or something was terribly wrong. And she would have to wait almost seven hours to find out what the hell was going on with her old boyfriend, whom she had never quite gotten over—even though she had been the one who finally ended things between them. But only because she realized that she was beating a dead horse. She saw herself living in New York City, and Joe planned to practice law in Texas—as a public defender, of all things. They had argued endlessly about whether the Lone Star State should adopt a kinder, gentler criminal-justice system. But oh, when they finally stopped arguing, they had been damned good together. In bed, on sofas, in dark hallways, in public restrooms, and even once with her bent over the back of the Harley. The sex she had had with Joe had become her gold standard, and it had never quite measured up since, though Lord knows she had tried.

But it definitely wasn't sex that Joe wanted from her now. Although it was hard for her to comprehend what sort of major trouble someone as smart as Joe had gotten himself into, she knew that he had come to her for help.

She was accustomed to people coming to her with their problems. She had handled all the consumer-watchdog stuff before she got the noon anchor job. The station had a reputation for looking out for the little guy—helping people who had been swindled or had unfortunate run-ins with city hall. Nothing cloak-and-dagger, though. Now, with her promotion, she could concentrate more on hard news, which was more compatible with her immediate goal of becoming an evening anchorperson either here in Dallas or in some other major market, which she hoped would be a stepping-stone to a network position or a cable job that provided nationwide exposure. After all, some of the big-time broadcast divas were getting a little long in the tooth, and Marcia wanted to be experienced enough and have proven herself to be aggressive enough to be next in line. It was only a matter of time, and she wanted sooner instead of later.

But she also wanted a husband and kids. A normal side to her life. And Joe Brammer was the only man with whom she had ever imagined herself growing old.

Don't go there, she warned herself. Just see what he wants. And hope it leads to a good story.

Still, she found herself wondering if he was with someone now. What if he wasn't in trouble at all but some woman was? His lover, or his wife?

Whatever the story was, it had better be a good one. She didn't have time to waste on dead ends or small stuff.

She forced herself to return to the story she had been working on before Joe's visit.

Somehow, she got through the rest of the afternoon. At a quarter of five, she was heading for the parking lot. She stopped by her apartment to freshen up and change into her best-fitting jeans and race around picking up clothes and shoes and tidying up a bit—just in case. Then she headed down the North Dallas Toll Road. The traffic was heavy. She was going to be late.

When she pulled up in front of the elegant Crescent, Joe was waiting.

As Joe got into the car, he handed her a piece of paper with the word "Denton" written on it. Once again he put his finger to his lips.

Marcia wanted to erupt. *Was the man nuts?* Did he actually think that someone might have bugged her car? She rolled her eyes at him then pulled away from the curb.

Marcia headed back up the toll road and found a pop-music station on the radio to end the stifling silence that hung over the interior of the car. She took the George Bush to I-35, and twenty minutes later, following

Joe's unspoken directions, she took the second Denton exit. She pulled into the drive-through lane of a Mexican restaurant and ordered two meals and two large iced teas. Then she drove until she saw a school playground and pulled into the parking lot.

She grabbed one of the food sacks and an iced tea and headed for a bench near the swings. "Are you crazy?" she demanded as Joe approached.

"Maybe," he said with a shrug.

They sat on a bench. "You care if I eat something before we talk?" he asked.

"Suit yourself," she said.

She watched him practically inhale a burrito and decided that she was hungry herself. They ate in silence. Finally Joe said, "My grandparents lived in Mesquite while I was growing up. I spent a lot of time there . . ."

Marcia listened while Joe explained the special feelings he'd always had for an orphaned little girl named Jamie who lived with her grandmother in a house just over the back fence from his grandparents' house. As Jamie got older he could never quite decide how to classify his feelings for her.

At first Marcia listened through veils of anger. If she'd known that she had competition, maybe she wouldn't have let herself fall in love with the guy. But as his story got ever more intriguing, she felt her reporter's instincts kick in. It was like listening to the plot line of a far-fetched movie with shadowy government agents tracking down innocent people who knew too much. She came to understand his paranoia and wondered if indeed her phones and office and car might be bugged because she was Joe's former girlfriend.

But as she listened to Joe relate what he wanted her to do and explain what little hard information he had on Gus Hartmann, she wondered if she *really* wanted to know more. "I'm sorry that you and your lady are in someone's crosshairs," she told Joe, "but I don't want to join you there."

"All I want for you to do is cover the event just as you normally would," Joe said.

"A religious service is not a *news* event," she protested. "You need to talk to someone from the Christian channel."

"It is a *political* event, Marcia. Amanda Hartmann's organization raises many millions of dollars to assist candidates who supposedly support their worldview but also just happen to be pro big business, especially the energy business."

* * *

Gus couldn't sleep. He took a midnight walk then went upstairs to make an unprecedented middle-of-the-night visit to see Buck. Randi's mother was flustered at first but then realized that he wasn't checking up on her, he was just looking for solace. She disappeared into the sitting room, leaving him to gaze down at Buck's innocent sleeping face and gently touch his achingly beautiful and exquisitely soft cheeks.

More and more he wished that he could simply end the quest for Sonny's baby. He could be satisfied for the rest of his life with little Buck. But things had gone too far. There was no way to back out of the chase. Too many laws had been broken. Jamie Long and her boyfriend had to be silenced. And Amanda would have the baby she wanted.

Not that he expected his sister to be a great mother. She would swoop in and out of the boy's life as she had with Sonny, as Mary Millicent had with them. Gus closed his eyes, remembering how he had lived for those times with his mother. When they were together, she couldn't hug and kiss him enough and would question him about every facet of his life and listen attentively to his answers. When Mary Millicent was with her children, especially at the ranch, she belonged just to them, but those times were separated by long, lonely weeks and sometimes by months. She would call on the phone, of course, but she always seemed to be giving instructions to her secretary or some other subordinate while she talked to him.

And that was the way Amanda had been with Sonny, overwhelming him with love when she was with him but leaving him to be raised by his uncle Gus or Ann Montgomery or the staff of some boarding school the rest of the time.

Jamie Long was a wonderful mother who had given up all of her dreams and any semblance of a normal life to be with her baby. Gus admired her for that. Admired her and Joe Brammer for their cleverness and their dedication to each other. They were two worthy young people who might have had a wonderful future together, who would have made sound, normal, loving parents for Sonny's baby and provided him with sisters and brothers and a good home. But that was not to be.

The die had been cast.

It had been impossible to maintain surveillance of all of Joe Brammer's former classmates and friends, but they had all been investigated and certain associates of these individuals—such as secretaries, receptionists, doormen, neighbors—had been put on alert. They were led to believe that they would be doing their nation a great service if they reported seeing anyone who remotely resembled Joe Brammer. Such efforts had finally paid off.

At first Gus had been inclined to eliminate Brammer's former girlfriend from the list until he found out that she was a newscaster with a Dallas television station. The more he thought about it, the more he wondered if Marcia Kimball might be the key.

And now his instincts had paid off. The receptionist at the television station had reported that a nice-looking man with a shaved head had shown up at the television station asking to see Marcia Kimball. He would not give his name but mentioned a Harley as a means of identifying himself to Miss Kimball.

According to the receptionist, the young man had stayed less than ten minutes.

A bug had been planted in Marcia Kimball's vehicle, and from the time she left the building at 4:47 that afternoon, she had been under surveillance. She picked up Brammer in front of a hotel and they hadn't said a word as they drove to Denton, where they bought food at a drive-in and drove to a school playground. They stayed at the playground for several hours, sitting on a bench. Nothing was known about their conversation, but Gus had no trouble imagining what was discussed. On the return trip, Marcia Kimball wound her way through a parking lot surrounding a shopping mall. Apparently Brammer exited the vehicle during this maneuver. He was not in the car when she returned to her apartment building.

He wanted to call Amanda and tell her about what was going on, but he feared that she might give something away. It was best just to let things play themselves out. And he looked forward to seeing the surprised look on her face when he finally was able to put the baby in her arms. She would be overjoyed. After all, it was *Sonny's* baby.

Chapter Forty

SHE INTRODUCED HERSELF as Sister Lola. A tiny woman, she wore a floral, tentlike garment that fell from her narrow shoulders to a pair of childlike feet ensconced in blue rubber sandals. Her long gray hair was plaited into two thick braids.

"Larry Carter," Joe said, extending his hand. "I spoke with you yesterday on the phone." Hanging from his neck on a lanyard was what he considered to be an authentic-looking press pass that he had designed, printed, and laminated the night before at an all-night copy shop. He also had designed and printed business cards that identified him as a reporter for *The Religious Times,* a publication that—according to the card—was published in Gayleth, New York. Of course, neither the publication nor the town actually existed, but he thought their names sounded quite legitimate.

"Yes, Mr. Carter," Sister Lola said amicably. "You're here in Dallas covering the Amanda Hartmann Crusade."

Joe nodded. "I need to get some background on the Temple of Praise, and I'd like to take a tour of the facility."

Already Joe was impressed by the church's size, if indeed it was correct to refer to a structure that looked like a sports arena as a church. Perhaps "house of worship" might be more correct.

Sister Lola spoke to someone on the phone and shortly a young man appeared wearing a bright gold knit shirt bearing the church name and its three-cross logo over his heart. Sister Lola explained that Freddie was one of their summer interns and would be taking him around. She would be delighted to answer any questions Joe might have at the end of his tour— or if he would like—she could schedule an appointment for him with Dr. Lawrence Goodpasture, founder and senior pastor of the Temple of Praise.

As they headed toward the sanctuary, Freddie told Joe that he was a student at a Free Will Baptist college in Oklahoma and planned to dedicate his life to serving Jesus. "Dr. Goodpasture is such an inspiration to me," Freddie said. "Have you heard him preach?"

"Oh, yes, I've seen his Sunday morning show on television," Joe fibbed as they walked through a broad hallway whose walls were decorated with murals depicting scenes from the Bible. "But actually I'm in town to cover the Amanda Hartmann Crusade."

Freddie stopped in his tracks and clasped both hands to his heart. "She is the most inspiring woman of our times," he said. "Don't you agree?"

"Without a doubt," Joe said.

"Sister Lola told me that it was quite a coup that Amanda Hartmann decided to forgo one of the usual downtown venues and hold the Dallas segment of her crusade here at the temple," Freddie continued. "I'm sure it's because our acoustics and sound system are considered to be among the finest in the world."

Freddie stopped in front of a pair of massive wooden doors offering Bible scenes carved in bas-relief. "Are you ready?" he asked.

Joe nodded. He was ready.

Freddie pulled open one of the doors and stepped aside, allowing Joe to enter first. The sanctuary was even larger than he had expected—a vast cavern of a room with a deep balcony on three sides and main-floor seating that sloped down to a huge stage and was divided by two wide aisles with narrower ones along each wall. The stage curtain was open, revealing tiered seating on both sides for choir members and a huge gilded pulpit under an enormous wooden crucifix that seemed to float above the stage. Freddie explained that the choir lofts, pulpit, and crucifix could all be lifted into the rafters, leaving the stage free for lavish theatrical productions—the annual Passion Play and musical and dramatic productions celebrating Christian living—for which the temple had become internationally known. The pulpit also could be projected out over the audience, and a metallic scrim curtain—the largest such curtain in the world—could be lowered in front of the choir during the preaching. Retractable flooring in front of the stage covered an orchestra pit. Under the stage was a large baptismal pool that could be raised to stage level. State-of-the-art lighting and sound systems offered a variety of special effects including sunrise, sunset, night sky, the northern lights, thunderstorm, volcanic eruption, and even Armageddon.

As Freddie explained the wonders offered by the Temple of Praise, Joe carefully limited himself to nonblasphemous expletives such as "wow" and "gee whiz." He wanted to ask what the price tag was on a place like this and what sort of financial support was expected of church members but didn't go there. Nor did he ask what Armageddon sounded like.

He did ask a number of questions about the choir—how large a group would perform during the Amanda Hartmann revival, where the choir members would practice, what robes they would wear. Just as Joe suspected from the research he had done online, Freddie explained that at Miss Hartmann's request, the choir assembled for the three revival services would include choir members from evangelical Christian churches all over the metro. And yes, the visiting choir members would bring their own robes to wear. "Sister Hartmann prefers traditional Christian music," Freddie pointed out as he showed Joe the large practice hall where both the Temple of Praise and visiting choir members would assemble. The practice hall had its own outside door and restroom facilities.

At the end of the tour, Freddie returned Joe to the amicable Sister Lola, who told Joe more than he really wanted to know about Dr. Goodpasture. Joe made a show of taking notes while the woman talked, and he asked a number of questions. When the other people in the office began pulling out sack lunches and heading for what was apparently the break room, Joe thanked Sister Lola and told her how impressed he was by everything he had seen and heard. "Would it be possible for me to attend choir practice this evening?" he asked. "And I would like to spend a half hour or so of personal meditation time in the sanctuary."

Joe headed first for the restroom then wandered the halls for a time and revisited the choir room before making his way back to the sanctuary. He sat in the back row of the main floor and studied the room, getting things straight in his head. He even thought about saying a prayer but decided he would save his prayers for a more holy setting. Someplace where he was surrounded by nature with the sky overhead.

Marcia and her cameraman showed their ID badges to a uniformed security guard before being admitted into the suite on the top floor of the stately old hotel in downtown Dallas. The spacious suite looked as though it had been furnished with visiting royalty in mind with ornate rococo furniture,

luxurious Oriental rugs spread over hardwood floors, and huge arrangements of fresh flowers on the tables and sideboards. They were greeted by
a sleek gray-haired woman in a designer suit who introduced herself as the
public relations director for the Alliance of Christian Voters.

"I watched your noon broadcast," the woman told Marcia.

Marcia expected some comment to follow as to whether or not the PR
director enjoyed the program. Instead the woman asked, "Can you assure
me that Miss Hartmann's interview will be aired on this evening's news
broadcast as well as on your own show tomorrow?"

"Barring a major fast-breaking news event, that is correct," Marcia
said, adding that the station's reporters usually did not interview evangelists, but with Miss Hartmann's Texas roots, her tremendous name recognition here in the state, and her position with the Alliance of Christian
Voters, her visit to Dallas was considered newsworthy.

Marcia had anticipated resistance from the station's news director
when she pitched her idea to him, but he hadn't given her any flack at all.
"Stress the political angle," he said, "and if your story turns out well, we'll
send it along to the network."

Network was the magic word. Marcia had stayed late at the station
viewing archived footage of Amanda Tutt Hartmann and checking old files
for information about her parents and brother. She discovered that Mary
Millicent Tutt's father had been an evangelist before her and that Jason
Hartmann's father had founded the family oil company. She'd found
nothing on Gus Hartmann.

The PR director asked them to have a seat. "I'll let Miss Hartmann
know that you have arrived," she said.

Marcia sat. The cameraman prowled around the room deciding where
he wanted Marcia and Amanda to sit. Then he adjusted the brocade
draperies and existing lights and set up his camera and the portable lighting that he'd brought along. That done, he joined Marcia on the sofa, and
they waited. For almost an hour they waited.

When Amanda Hartmann finally entered the room, Marcia's first
thought was how lovely she was. And how gracefully she walked across
the room. Marcia's irritation at having been kept waiting dissipated somewhat, and her pulse began to race just a bit in anticipation. After all,
Amanda Hartmann was one of the most famous people she had ever interviewed.

Amanda was wearing a cream-colored pants suit and a matching silk blouse with a softly draped neckline. Her blond hair was in a soft upsweep, her complexion lustrous, and her makeup flawless. And beyond her looks, Amanda had a calm, regal presence about her as she extended her hand and offered a greeting. Marcia felt a bit tongue-tied as she thanked her for agreeing to the interview and showed her where to sit and attached a tiny microphone to her lapel.

Marcia took her own seat across from Amanda and explained that her lead-in would be done during the broadcast, at which time she would explain about Amanda's Texas roots and her illustrious parents. And she would announce that Amanda was holding a revival in Dallas that would begin tomorrow evening and would run for three nights.

Then Marcia nodded at the cameraman.

"When did you first know that you would follow in your mother's footsteps?" she asked Amanda.

"I always knew," Amanda said, her hands resting gracefully on the arms of the wing chair. "God has been in my life ever since I can remember, but I formally gave my life to Jesus when I was four years old. We had already moved to Washington, D.C., following my father's election to Congress, and my mother no longer conducted regular Sunday services in her Glory Temple over on Taylor Street right here in downtown Dallas. But once or twice a year, she would hold weeklong revivals there. The building was torn down to make way for the Central Expressway, but I remember how beautiful it was. My father had brought me to the services that day as a surprise for Mother. When she looked down and saw her own little daughter kneeling in front of her, she cried out and lifted me in her arms and asked if I felt the love of our Savior the Lord Jesus Christ filling my heart. And I did," Amanda said, touching her heart. "I still feel that love, and I have spent my life helping others to open their hearts to God's love and saving grace."

Marcia realized that this was a story Amanda had related countless times before, but she told it well. With that bit of background out of the way, Marcia moved on to her next question.

"Your mother is not only remembered as an evangelist but as the founder of a political action group, the Alliance of Christian Voters, which supports evangelical Christian candidates running for political office. And you apparently have no qualms about asking your followers to support these candidates and using the money donated to the Alliance to run political ads. How do you justify this practice in light of the constitutional dictum of separation of church and state?"

"The Alliance does not tell people whom they should vote for," Amanda said, her voice even but firm. "We ask only that voters consider what is in a candidate's heart before they support him or her with their prayers and their money and their votes. And if they choose to make a donation to the Alliance, we use that money to encourage voters to vote for evangelical Christians, but the Alliance does not support specific candidates."

"But what if the most qualified candidate in a race is *not* an evangelical Christian?" Marcia asked.

"We believe that the nation can be best served by those who consider God's wishes when they lead and legislate," Amanda said.

"Many observers believe that your organization was an important factor in the election of our current president. Has he lived up to your expectations?"

Amanda looked directly at the camera and said, "He has grown in understanding as to the special role he plays in bringing goodness and hope to all Americans, and I am sure that in God's eyes there is no one better qualified to lead our country."

"So will he have your vote for a second term?" Marcia asked.

"Yes, he will," Amanda said with a nod.

"I understand that you are expecting a full house at all three of your revivals here in the city, which begin tomorrow evening and will be held at the Temple of Praise."

"Yes," Amanda said. "The Temple of Praise is an inspiring house of worship."

"Will you have your baby with you?"

Amanda beamed. "Definitely. I keep him with me as much as possible."

"I understand that you consider your baby to be somewhat of a miracle."

"Oh, yes," Amanda said, offering a beatific smile that seemed quite genuine. "My baby is a miracle from God," she said, lifting her hands to her chin and clasping them together. "He is a wonderful little boy who looks so much like my darling Sonny that it takes my breath away."

"When your son, Sonny, was killed in a tragic accident more than a year and a half ago, I understand that many of your followers wondered if you would give up your ministry."

"My grief overwhelmed me for a time," Amanda acknowledged, "but God sent my husband, Toby, and then our beautiful baby to heal my broken heart. We have named our baby Jason, which was my father's name. The name means 'healer,' and this baby was sent by God to heal me and help me rededicate my life to His service."

"Obviously you are a very youthful woman, but weren't you surprised to find yourself pregnant at this point in your life?" Marcia asked.

"Surprised and overjoyed," Amanda answered, offering another radiant smile and placing her hands prayerlike under her chin.

"Did you have any problems during your pregnancy?" Marcia asked.

"It was a bit difficult at first, and my doctors insisted that I suspend my public activities during the last four months. But after a rocky beginning, I actually felt quite wonderful. And you cannot imagine the outpouring of love I experienced when Jason was born. I received cards and letters and telegrams from all over the world. And people traveled to the Alliance headquarters in Virginia to leave flowers at the gate and light hundreds of candles. Maybe thousands of candles. It was a spectacular sight. I cannot tell you how touched I was."

Marcia asked a few questions about the remainder of Amanda's tour then thanked her for her time and nodded at the cameraman, indicating that was a wrap. Then she chatted with Amanda for a few minutes, outlining their plan for tomorrow evening. "Since the local Christian station will be covering the event live, we would like to offer a different view—shots of backstage preparations and of you arriving at the facility with your husband and baby."

"My husband has pressing business in Virginia and probably won't be coming to Dallas," Amanda explained, glancing at her watch. "And the baby and I will be arriving separately. His nursemaid will carry him onstage during the service."

"I see," Marcia said. "Well, we'll take shots of you showing him off to . . ." She paused, uncertain about what to call people who attend revivals. *Audience* seemed too secular. "To the worshippers," she said. "And I especially want some shots of you delivering your message taken from offstage. In my research I came across an incredible picture of your mother on the cover of *Life* magazine that was taken from offstage, and I plan to include it in the segment and then show you from the same angle."

"Yes, I know the picture well," Amanda said. "That's very creative of you."

"Is your baby here with you?" Marcia asked. "Maybe we could get some close-ups of the two of you now."

Amanda's expression changed slightly. "He and his nursemaid won't be arriving until tomorrow."

"Well, then, we'll see you tomorrow evening," Marcia said.

Amanda rose and Marcia followed suit. Amanda reached for her hand and smiled warmly. "Thank you so much, Marcia, for your time and professionalism."

"You are very beautiful," Marcia said, surprising herself. But it was true. Amanda Hartmann was positively radiant.

"Why, thank you, my dear," Amanda said. "The years do seem to have been kind to me. I do hope that you enjoy the service tomorrow evening and feel God's blessing upon you."

"I look forward to it," Marcia said. And she did. In fact, she would have liked to stay here in this room with Amanda a while longer, listening to her speak, watching her expressions change, her hands move. Amanda Tutt Hartmann was mesmerizing.

Marcia started for the door then paused. "Does your brother attend your revivals?" she asked.

"Not usually," Amanda responded.

Jamie showered first and nursed Billy while Joe took his turn in the bathroom.

At first she hoped that he wouldn't want to make love. She was too tense. Too preoccupied about tomorrow.

But what if this was the last time?

When Joe crawled into the bed beside her, she reached for him. Afterward, they held each other and cried for a time. Then they once again went over their plan for tomorrow.

During the night, they had their first quarrel. Jamie wanted Joe to unhook the RV and drive them to Oklahoma City, where she would turn herself into the police. She would explain to them what had happened to her that night at Ruby Duffy's apartment house. Why Lynette's baby was taken. Why Jamie had fled with her own baby.

"With Amanda having a baby to which she claims to have given birth with her here in Dallas, the Hartmanns can't say that Billy belongs to them," Jamie pointed out. "And Billy couldn't be her baby anyway. There are people in Oklahoma City who can testify that I was in Oklahoma City with Billy while Amanda was in Virginia supposedly having a baby."

"There's a warrant out for your arrest in Oklahoma City," Joe pointed out. "On that basis alone, they would take Billy away from you and put you in a cell at least until you are arraigned."

Joe held his thumb and forefinger less than an inch apart. "Gus Hartmann's people have come *this* close to killing you twice now," he said. "Once in Oklahoma City and again down at Neptune Beach. What makes you think they wouldn't find a way to finish the job? Gus Hartmann has already shown that he has the power to operate outside of the law. He has the power to have your throat slit while you're in some jail cell and then lay claim to Billy."

Jamie broke down and wept. "We don't have a chance against him," she said.

"Our plan is going to work," Joe insisted, holding her close. "When we confront Amanda Hartmann, millions of people will be watching. They will be our jury, and we have right on our side. That has to count for something."

Her whole world was here with her on this bed, Jamie thought. She found herself wondering if this world would end tomorrow. If tomorrow would be the last day of her life. If after all this running and hiding and planning and gut-wrenching fear, Amanda would end up raising Billy after all and he would never know that there had been this other woman who had given birth to him and loved him completely. "If it looks hopeless, I don't want you to do anything idiotic," she told Joe. "If they kill me, just get the hell out of there. And out of the country."

"It's all going to be on live television," he reminded her.

She tried to take comfort in that fact. Usually people weren't murdered in front of television cameras. But it wasn't unheard of. It had happened once before in this very city, when Jack Ruby shot Lee Harvey Oswald.

Chapter Forty-one

FOR THE FIRST HOUR of the flight, Gus sat in the front of the jet with Randi and the babies. When Buck grew tired of being confined in the baby carrier, Gus unfastened him and walked up and down jiggling him. When he sat back down, he held the baby on his knees and talked to him, telling him what a fine boy he was.

"When I signed those papers in Dallas, I didn't realize that I was going to be keeping you forever and ever," Gus told baby Buck, "but that is exactly what I am going to do. You are going to be *my* son, and I will raise you. We'll still live in Virginia but spend lots of time at the ranch. You'll have the best education that money can buy—you and your cousin Jason and your little friend Amita—and the Mexican children, too. I'll build Amita's family a house there. And you three boys will raise chickens and have a vegetable garden and climb trees and learn to swim and ride on your very own ponies. Your aunt Amanda will come visit us from time to time, and probably she'll take your cousin Jason on trips with her, but most of the time he'll be with us. Such a happy life we will have."

Gus had tears in his eyes just from imagining it. If only Montgomery were still alive to enjoy this new life with him. But he would have Randi and her family to help him with the boys. And having young children around would be good for his mother.

This new life had become what he thought about in the night and during his morning walks. He had trouble concentrating during the day because he was thinking about it. Only yesterday, he had been on a conference call discussing what to do about a holdout senator who refused to vote for an upcoming administration-sponsored bill when Gus realized that he had completely lost his train of thought and was focused instead on the playground he planned to build at the ranch.

Gus felt profoundly happy—except for the times he was thinking about Jamie Long and her boyfriend, whom, ironically, he held in high regard. He knew that they could not be bought or tempted in any way to back down. Not that he would barter with them. Things had gone too far for that.

Amanda may not have birthed that baby, but it never would have been born if it weren't for her. And he had been born of Sonny's seed. He was a Hartmann, and his rightful place was with the Hartmann family. Gus would fulfill his promise to his sister.

But Jamie Long and Joe Brammer would be the last, he promised himself. The very last.

He nuzzled Buck's neck and inhaled the baby sweetness of his flesh. An intoxicating scent. It was almost enough to make him believe in God.

"Daddy loves his little Buckie," he told the baby. "Daddy loves you very, very much."

When Buck drifted off to sleep, Gus put him back in his carrier, feeling quite proud at how adept he had become at handling babies. He kissed the top of Buck's head then leaned over the carrier that held Randi's sleeping child and kissed his head, too. "They are so beautiful," he told Randi.

"Yes, Mister Gus, they are so beautiful," she said with a lovely smile.

He liked the way Randi said "beautiful," enunciating every syllable. He liked Randi. She was both intelligent and pragmatic. "Have you ever been to Texas before?" he asked.

Randi shook her head. "No, sir. I understand that Dallas is a very large city."

"Yes, it is. Lots of people in cars driving around on a maze of highways, just like lots of other cities in lots of other states. Before we head back to Virginia, we'll fly out to the ranch for a few days. It's very peaceful there and quite beautiful in its own way."

"I would very much like to visit this place that you and Miss Amanda love so much," she said.

Gus patted her shoulder then walked to the back of the plane and sat at the conference table next to Zubov, his new head of security—a former KGB agent with piercing black eyes. After the fiasco in Oklahoma City, Gus had decided to take charge of the planning and be on hand for its implementation. Facing them across the table were three members of Zubov's team: a lean Russian woman he called Bella, a large young man known as Johnny who looked to be either a Pacific Islander or a Native American, and a hard-bodied black man with a British accent called Frank.

Zubov and his three associates were wearing navy-blue uniforms complete with nightsticks and holsters hanging from their belts and shiny badges on their chests. Four additional men, also in uniform, would join Zubov's team in Dallas.

By tomorrow night it would all be over, Gus thought. *Finally.*

He wasn't quite sure of the explanation he would give Randi when another baby turned up, but she was pragmatic and would not ask questions. Randi understood that her continued association with Gus meant good things for her family. And she realized that Gus sincerely cared about her son and would someday send him to a fine university along with any other children that she and her husband might produce.

Zubov produced a file folder filled with photographs of Jamie Long and Joe Brammer that obviously had come from high school and college yearbooks. There were the usual head-and-shoulders—Jamie with her high school track team, Brammer in a basketball uniform, Brammer with some other guys in front of a fraternity house. And there was the picture taken by Bentley Abernathy's secretary—Jamie with her long blond hair, looking scrubbed and young and wholesome. "The girl does not look this way now," Zubov said. "Her hair is short and brown. Look for tall young woman with blue eyes and body of athletic person. And for young man with brown eyes and athletic body. His head is shaved and maybe he have beard. The baby is same size as those two," he said with a gesture toward the front of the plane.

"I have two goals," Gus told them. "The first is to gain possession of the child without harming him in any way, and the second is to eliminate the man and the girl even if others are harmed in the process."

"Do you think they will be together?" Bella wanted to know.

"The man and the girl may or may not arrive together," Gus said, "but yes, I am sure they plan to be together when they attempt to confront my sister on live television."

Gus had no trouble at all crawling inside the heads of Jamie Long and Joe Brammer. They envisioned a scenario in which, after Amanda shows the stand-in baby to her adoring followers in Dallas and around the world and claims to be his biological mother, they confront her with Jamie's baby. When Amanda insists that Jamie's baby belongs to her, people will realize that she has been lying to them. Jamie will get a fair hearing. The correct questions will be asked. The entire situation will be dealt with in an aboveboard way, and Jamie will be allowed to tell her story. Amanda and Gus Hartmann's criminal acts will be exposed. The truth will solve everything. Except that Jamie Long and Joe Brammer were not going to live long enough to tell it. Ideally the two of them will have been dealt with before Amanda appears onstage, and the baby she shows off to her flock will be Sonny's.

As usual, the Alliance had hired a force of fifty uniformed security guards from local security companies who would be posted throughout the parking lot, at every entrance to the facility, and throughout the building. They would have pictures of Jamie Long and Joe Brammer and be told that the couple had made threats against Amanda. One of the two would be carrying a baby. If the guards spotted them, they were to keep them under surveillance and immediately notify Zubov. Under no circumstances were they to approach the couple or do anything that might jeopardize the safety of the infant.

Gus hoped that Jamie and her boyfriend would be apprehended before entering the sanctuary, but he was certain that they would both be disguised in some way and, with the flood of people that would be pouring through those doors, they might slip through unnoticed. In which case, everything was to be put on hold until the end of the service, when Amanda invited worshippers wanting to confess their sins and dedicate their lives to Jesus to come forward. After giving the invitation, Amanda would make her way down the steps to greet the penitent. Gus had no doubt that Jamie and Brammer would join the stream of people coming forward.

Zubov unrolled a floor plan of the Temple of Praise. Five doors opened into the sanctuary from the large lobby area. There also was access to the sanctuary from both the office and education wings. And there were fire exits on both sides of the stage area. In addition, there were two outside doors into the stage area and two more into the practice hall.

Just before the service began, Bella, Johnny, and two of the Dallas contingent were to take positions in front of the stage. The rest of the floor crew would remain in their positions throughout the sanctuary until Amanda made the invitation, at which time the floor crew would make their way forward. As soon as Brammer and the girl were sighted, Zubov's people would surround them. Brammer was to be killed immediately. Those closest to Jamie were to grab her and assist Bella in removing the baby from her possession. "If the girl won't relinquish the baby, threaten to put a bullet through his head," Gus told Bella.

To the three men, he said, "The instant the baby is out of harm's way, shoot the girl."

Then the men were to surround Bella and the baby and get them to the fire exit on the east side of the stage. Three vans with flashing lights and sirens would be waiting. Zubov and Bella with the baby were to board the first van and be taken away separately.

Gus knew that by the time local law enforcement arrived, they would be greeted with pandemonium and conflicting stories. It could be hours before he could extract himself from the investigation and escort his sister, Randi, and the two babies to the hotel. It might be morning before he could travel to a motel in Lewisville, where he could finally claim Sonny's child.

Gus leaned back in his chair, his hands folded on the table. He looked at each of the faces around the table in turn. "Pull this thing off," he said, "and I will double what Zubov has promised you. Just make sure no harm comes to that baby. The instant he is safely out of the girl's arms, shoot her."

Suddenly exhausted, Gus slumped back in his chair. After today, no more killing, he told himself. *No more killing.*

He rose, nodded at Zubov, and made his way back to the front of the plane, where he sat down next to Buck asleep in his carrier. Just sitting there watching the sleeping infant calmed Gus. So innocent he was. So perfect. Gus touched the baby's cheek with a fingertip. Buck opened his eyes and rewarded him with a toothless smile.

Gus's heart turned over in his chest.

He would step down as chairman of the Committee of Five. Maybe he would even resign from the committee. Resign as president of Hartmann Oil. From now on he was just going to be a rancher. And a father to Buck and an uncle to Jason and a godfather to Amita. The three boys would grow up as best friends.

Tomorrow, after everything was over and he and the babies and Randi and his sister were all at the ranch, he would go to the little chapel and pray for forgiveness. Yes, he would do that. Pray with all of his heart that

God in heaven will wash away his sins and make him worthy of three innocent little boys.

Jamie and Joe spent the day intentionally keeping Billy awake. They covered the drain in the shower and filled it with a couple of inches of water then took turns holding Billy so he wouldn't topple over while he slapped the water and kicked with his feet, squealing with delight. And when he lost interest in splashing, they took turns carrying him up and down the lanes between the campsites, jiggling him, talking to him, constantly moving him from one position to another. They put a blanket under a tree and tickled him and shook a baby rattle in his face. They sang songs and fed him spoonfuls of applesauce—his very first solid food. When he got absolutely frantic with hunger, Jamie would nurse him for a short time then play with him some more. Jamie and Billy both cried during the drive to the Temple of Praise. "He must think I'm the worst mother in the whole world," she sobbed over his wailing. "The poor little guy is starving to death."

"Not much longer," Joe kept telling her.

But the traffic was terrible. The trip was taking longer than they had planned. Jamie felt as though her breasts were about to explode. And with every cry that came from Billy's mouth, she would feel spurts of milk erupt from them.

Joe parked the RV behind the building in an area reserved for such vehicles. Jamie sobbed as she forced her furious baby into the sling then finally slipped a leaking nipple into his mouth and felt his little body go limp with relief. Joe pulled on his choir robe then put another one over Jamie's head. She looked like a woman soon to give birth to a very large baby.

"Billy's going to suffocate," she said.

"It's just until you get inside," Joe told her. "Then you can hide out in the restroom until it's time to go onstage."

"What if someone figures out I have a baby with me?"

"Just go, Jamie. *Now,* while Billy is quiet."

"I've never been so scared in my life," she told him. "Not even when I was alone in that old house giving birth."

"I'm scared, too," Joe said. "We're doing this so we won't have to be scared anymore."

A guard was posted outside the entrance to the choir room. He smiled pleasantly as they pushed open the door.

Marcia and her two cameramen—actually a cameraman and a camera-woman—surveyed the huge sanctuary that was already beginning to fill with people. Marcia explained that once the service began, she wanted them to shoot from the stage, the balcony, and the back of the sanctuary to show the vastness of the space and the sea of people. Then they were to go backstage. Marcia showed them a copy of the *Life* magazine cover. "I want dramatic footage that is reminiscent of this historic photograph," Marcia explained. "And I want up-close-and-personal shots of Amanda onstage with her baby. And of her preaching, of course. Wait until she really gets into it and be sure to get the part where she invites people to come to the front. Apparently she goes down those center stairs to meet them. There's one family I'm particularly interested in—I'll let you know when I spot them."

"You mean we have to stay for the whole thing?" Jill the camerawoman protested.

"We'll stay until I have my story," Marcia said.

Marcia was nervous and jumpy, in part, she supposed, because she hadn't slept well the night before. She didn't like buying into conspiracy theories. Didn't want to believe that there were powerful people who operated outside of the law. Part of her hoped that nothing was going to happen today. But part of her wanted *The Big Story*.

Chapter Forty-two

GUS AND RANDI, with assistance from Zubov and Bella, carried the babies and their accompanying paraphernalia to a backstage dressing room.

Gus was perspiring profusely. He could smell the odor of his own body and worried that Randi might notice.

And his bowels were beginning to churn.

He used the restroom down the hall rather than the one in the dressing room. When he came out of the stall, he unbuttoned his shirt and sponged his underarms with wet paper towels. His face in the mirror looked pale and drawn. Today was the most important day of his life, he realized. Failure was unacceptable.

He walked back to the dressing room, squared his shoulders, composed a smile on his face, and opened the door.

"Are you all right, Mister Gus?" Randi asked, her forehead creased with worry.

"My stomach is a bit upset," he told her.

Gus checked his watch. Were Jamie Long and Joe Brammer already on their way to the Temple of Praise or would they wait until the last possible minute to arrive? He hoped they came early and were dealt with without causing any disruption. Zubov and his people would take them away, and it would be as though Jamie Long and her boyfriend had never existed. Then he could relax and enjoy the evening. He hadn't seen his sister preach in person in years.

After sipping a Seven-Up that Randi had brought him, his innards seemed to settle down a bit. He left the room to search out a private corner so he could call Zubov.

No sign of them yet, he learned. But it was early still. The service wouldn't start for two hours.

Already, though, there was a beehive of activity backstage. Electricians were running one last check on the lighting and sound systems. A tiny woman in a long Hawaiian-looking garment was bustling about inspecting the floral arrangements on the stage and repositioning them.

People were trying not to stare at Gus, taking furtive glances or waiting until they thought he was looking elsewhere to study him. An item of curiosity. A man who wasn't short enough to be a midget but definitely not normal-looking. It had been years since Gus had been around this many strangers. He had spent his entire life avoiding strangers. But today was a unique day. A day that marked a new beginning. He felt almost feverish in his excitement and wished that Amanda were here so he could embrace her and feel her cool hand on his forehead. Not that he could tell her why he was in this state of disquiet. Amanda had no idea what a special day this was.

His sister claimed that dressing rooms gave her claustrophobia. She did her own makeup and arrived minutes before it was time for her to walk onstage. Sometimes she arrived late, but no one ever got mad at Amanda. They probably just assumed that she was having a last few minutes with God in preparation for her words of praise and redemption.

Gus walked over to the curtain and peeked out into the sanctuary. Musicians were setting up their electronic equipment in the orchestra pit. Four seats in the middle of the front row were roped off. He hoped that there would be no need to use them, that Zubov and his team would have already apprehended Jamie and her boyfriend and be long gone before the service began. By the time Amanda walked onstage Jamie Long and Joe Brammer would be dead.

Early comers already occupied the rest of the seats in the first row. In fact, the lower half of the main floor was practically full, as were the front-row seats in the balcony.

God, he was nervous. He would like something alcoholic to drink but in lieu of that would settle for another Seven-Up. The vending machines were just around the corner, but he never carried money.

He called Zubov again.

Still no sign of Jamie, Joe, and the baby.

He went back to the dressing room and played with Buck for a while then fed him a bottle and jiggled him to sleep. Then he stepped outside the room to call Zubov again. The Russian reported that Marcia Kimball and her camera crew were roaming around the sanctuary talking to worshippers. But there was still no sign of Jamie Long and her baby and boyfriend.

Doubt was beginning to nag at Gus. Had he read Jamie and Joe's actions all wrong? Maybe they had some other reason for being in Dallas.

Except that Joe's former girlfriend Marcia Kimball was out there waiting to capture the meeting of Amanda and Jamie on camera.

A meeting that was never going to happen.

The orchestra began playing. Gus pulled the curtain aside and looked out front once again, scanning the faces in the crowd.

Zubov called to tell him that Amanda had arrived.

Gus watched as the choir members filed in and took their seats in the tiered choir stalls on either side of the stage and a robed minister with hair that looked as though it were made of plastic stepped into the golden pulpit under the heroic-sized and agonizingly graphic floating crucifix.

The curtain began to open as the voices of the choir boomed forth:

Love divine, all loves excelling,
joy of heaven, to earth come down,
fix in us thy humble dwelling,
all thy faithful mercies crown.

A spotlight illuminated the pulpit as it rose and floated over the stage until it was hovering over the orchestra pit. People in the first rows tilted their heads back and were looking up at the minister. His voice boomed forth, "This is a day the Lord hath made."

Gus kept scanning the faces in the audience while the minister welcomed everyone to the Temple of Praise and said what an honor it was for the temple to welcome one of God's most eloquent and beloved messengers, Sister Amanda Tutt Hartmann. The man gave a brief overview of Amanda's incredible lineage and ministry. Then he offered a prayer in which he asked the Lord to open the hearts of all assembled and help them accept the message they would hear today and leave the temple praising His holy name.

Gus was beginning to feel ill. *Where were they, damn it!*

The choir sang another hymn.

Come, Thou almighty King,
Help us Thy Name to sing,

Help us to praise!
Father all glorious,
O'er all victorious,
Come and reign over us, Ancient of Days!

Then suddenly Amanda was walking out onstage. And the audience rose as one. The ovation was thunderous and reverberated all around Gus. The floor trembled under his feet.

As was her way, Amanda was dressed in a flowing white gown. She wore no jewelry. Her hair was down and brushed smooth and shining. Gus glanced up at the close-up of her face on one of the huge overhead screens. So beautiful she looked. Like an angel. His heart swelled painfully with pride and love.

Amanda smiled for a few minutes, seeming to enjoy the audience's response. Then she lifted her arms, and in just a few seconds a hush came over the vast sanctuary. It was as though everyone was holding their breath, waiting to hear the first words that came out of her mouth.

Amanda put her hands over her heart. "I love you," she said.

And the applause began again. Wave after wave of it. The audience was overjoyed that Amanda loved them.

Once again she lifted a hand and quiet fell. "I have a baby," she said with a broad smile, her voice girlishly breathless. "Everyone said that I was too old to have a baby. My physician told me I was too old to have a baby. My body told me that I was too old. But God granted me a miracle after my beloved son died. I thank God a hundred times a day for the gift of this child, and I want to share him with you today."

Once again applause began to erupt, but Amanda lifted her hand to stop it. "Applause might frighten him," she explained, her voice barely above a whisper. "We named him Jason, which means 'healer.' We named him that because this beautiful child healed my broken heart and has taught me to live again, just as God intended." Then Amanda gestured offstage to Randi, her arms outstretched, ready to receive her child. Gus was standing just behind Randi. Amanda's eyebrows shot up in recognition and surprise.

Randi carried Buck to center stage amid a soft chorus of "ahhs" from the audience, placed the baby in Amanda's arms, and backed away.

Gus watched as Amanda's body seemed to stiffen just a bit. There was awkwardness in the way she held the child. She kissed the baby and offered a smile to the audience that was a bit too broad, a bit too dazzling. Gus held his breath as little Buck's body tensed at the feel of unfamiliar arms—arms that were not as loving and tender as those to which he was accustomed.

Amanda held on to her forced smile as Buck began to wail, but her shoulders became rigid. The muscles in her neck grew taut as she lifted him to her shoulder and began to pat his back. But Buck's back arched as his cry turned into a scream of protest.

Gus could see that his sister was beginning to panic. She was doing all the wrong things. Her disquiet was transferring itself to the baby. He wanted to rush out there and take Buck from her, or at least tell her to relax and talk soothingly to the child. And to jiggle him, for God's sake. If Gus had learned one thing about babies in the last two months, it was the value of jiggling. And pacifiers helped. Amita didn't respond to a pacifier, but Buck did. Buck could soothe himself if he had a pacifier. There was one dangling from a ribbon clipped to his shirt.

"Use the pacifier," Gus called to her, but Amanda didn't hear. Didn't respond.

He was about to repeat his instructions in a louder voice when suddenly the voice of a lone, unaccompanied male singer filled the stage. Gus glanced toward the choir loft on the left side of the stage. The singer was standing—a bald man wearing a gray choir robe. The man grabbed the hands of the choir members on either side of him and pulled them along with him as he walked down the steps. The words he sang were familiar ones.

> *Jesus loves the little children*
> *All the children of the world*

As he sang, another voice joined in. A female voice. A heavy woman who had been sitting behind him stood and grabbed the hand of the woman on her left and followed the bald man and his companions, who were now singing along.

> *Red and yellow, black and white*
> *They are precious in his sight*
> *Jesus loves the little children of the world*

When the young man reached Amanda's side, he turned and gestured expansively to the other choir members, indicating that they, too, were to come forward and raise their voices with him. The choir members glanced at one another as though unsure of what they should do, then slowly began to come forward. Orderly, row by row, they came, drifting to the center of the stage, singing. Once the exodus was in progress, the bald man reached for the crying baby. It all seemed so rehearsed that Gus assumed it was an intended part of the proceedings.

Amanda hesitated then relinquished Buck to the man, who immediately began to jiggle him. Gus sighed with relief when the man put the pacifier in Buck's mouth.

Dozens of the choir members were now gathered around Amanda, singing the familiar song remembered from their Sunday school days. With smiles they were singing. And the audience joined in. Each round of the song grew stronger and more triumphant.

The heavy woman had stepped behind the others, but from his vantage point, Gus had a clear view of her. With her back to him, he watched as she unzipped her choir robe and let it drop to the floor. She wasn't heavy at all. Her body was slim and straight and young. She seemed to be unfastening some sort of harness.

It took Gus several heartbeats to understand who she was and what she was doing.

And suddenly there he was. *Sonny's baby.* The child for which Gus had been searching. The child his sister wanted more than anything.

Jamie Long bent to kiss the baby and whisper to him. Gus could well imagine what she was saying. She was telling Sonny's baby that she loved him, that everything was going to be all right. And Gus could tell by the language of her body and the look on her face that this young woman did indeed love her baby. Her love was bountiful.

Over and over audience and choir sang the familiar refrain. With faces radiating love and hope, they sang. Jesus did indeed love little children. And here was one of those children for them to love right along with Jesus—the child of their beloved Amanda, who promised them hope and glory, who told them of a God who loved them and cared about them and knew what was in their hearts. A God who was here with them now.

With her own baby reassured, Jamie Long tucked him close to her body and made her way through the cluster of singers until she was standing beside Amanda. And the singing grew louder. Here was another little child for them to love. An anonymous child.

Gus watched Amanda's face as she looked first at Jamie and then at the baby in her arms.

Suddenly Amanda was trying to grab the baby away from Jamie, who was backing away and shaking her head.

"That's my baby!" Amanda screamed, looking around frantically for someone to help her.

One by one, the choir members stopped singing. A wave of silence swept through the audience until every voice was stilled and the vast sanctuary became eerily silent as puzzled worshippers tried to discern the meaning of the drama they were witnessing onstage.

Amanda screamed again. "She has my baby."

Gus took a step forward.

"Gus," Amanda shrieked. "It's her. It's Jamie Long. She has Sonny's baby."

Gus took a tentative step forward as Amanda abruptly turned to Jamie. "Just let me hold him for a minute. Please let me hold him. I promise that I'll give him back. In front of all these people, I promise. In front of God, I promise. I just want to hold my son's baby. *Please.*"

Amanda's arms were extended. "Just let me touch him and hold him," she implored, her voice being carried electronically throughout the vast hall to the absolutely silent audience. So silent they were. Six thousand people and not a whisper. Not a cough. No shuffling of feet. Just immense and total silence.

"I won't try to take him away from you," Amanda pleaded. "I understand why you left. Really I do. But I need to be part of the child's life. Please. In God's name, *please.*" She looked in Gus's direction. "Tell her, Gus," she called to him. "Tell her that we won't take the baby away from her. But we have a right to know him and to love him." Then she turned back to Jamie. "Please, in God's name, just let me hold him."

The bald young man, still cradling Buck in his arms, was now standing beside Jamie. He shifted Buck to the crook of his left arm so that he could put his right one protectively around Jamie's shoulders. She was looking questioningly into his face. Into Joe Brammer's face.

Joe Brammer leaned forward and the two of them touched foreheads. Such an incredibly sweet gesture. One of complete trust. Complete love.

Gus felt his heart give a painful lurch. What he wouldn't have given to have had such love and trust in his own empty life.

Then Jamie looked at Amanda and nodded her head.

Suddenly Gus took off running toward the center of the stage. He reached the cluster of people standing there just as Jamie was placing her baby in Amanda's arms.

Gus turned toward the front row and screamed, "No." At the top of his voice, he screamed.

"No," he screamed again as he threw his arms around the mother of Sonny's child.

But the shot rang out anyway as per his own instructions to shoot the girl the instant that the baby was no longer in her arms.

Houston

A PLEASANT-LOOKING middle-aged woman answered the door balancing a sturdy baby boy on her hip. *The* baby, Bentley assumed. He would be about eight months old by now.

Wearing a very serious expression, the child regarded him with large blue eyes.

"You must be the lawyer from Austin," the woman said.

"Yes, ma'am. Bentley Abernathy."

"I'm Joe's mother, Millie. And this is Billy, of course," she said, kissing the baby on his cheek. "Joe and Jamie are out back. They're expecting you," she said over her shoulder as she led the way through the house. A nice comfortable house, he thought, as he walked through the family room with its reclining chairs, oversized leather sofa, and big-screen television set. No such amenities would be found in the restored Victorian mansion that eventually would be his home now that Brenda had almost returned the house to its former glory. He was thinking about adding a retreat for himself over the garage except that, while he wanted to separate himself as much as possible from Victorian furniture and its accompanying bric-a-brac, he did not want to retreat from his wife.

Millie Brammer slid the patio door open for Bentley but didn't follow him outside. The large deck was covered by a lattice roof that had been completely engulfed by a very aggressive wisteria vine—a vine that Joe Brammer and a man Bentley assumed was Brammer's father were attempting to tame, with Jamie gathering up the cut branches and piling them on a tarp. The three of them stopped midaction, guarded expressions on their faces—expressions that Bentley understood. He was, after all, here representing Amanda Hartmann, and he had gotten Jamie into a situation that had almost ended her life.

Joe Brammer's father stepped forward to introduce himself and offer a perfunctory handshake. Then he announced that he was going inside to help Millie with the baby. Joe didn't bother with a handshake. He simply nodded.

As did Jamie. She was wearing jeans and a black, sleeveless shirt, with no jewelry, no discernible makeup. Her hair was back to its natural blond but shorter than before.

"You're looking well, Jamie," Bentley said. Which was true. She was lovely to look at—like before. But he realized that he was looking at quite a different person than the hopeful young woman who had come to his office almost a year and half ago. This new Jamie would be forever wary, the innocence with which she had once met the world gone forever.

Bentley felt perspiration collecting in his armpits and under his collar. He was a bit nervous, and the air was muggy and still. He would have liked to remove his jacket and loosen his tie but decided it was best to maintain a professional appearance.

He did, however, accept Jamie's offer of iced tea. He watched while she poured three glasses and seated herself at a glass-topped table. Joe sat by her and Bentley sat across from them.

He took a swallow of the tea, then set down the glass and picked up his briefcase. He pulled out the yellow legal pad on which his notes were written, placed it in front of him, and cleared his throat.

But Jamie spoke first. "I want to thank you for intervening that night. If you hadn't contacted that judge and convinced her that I was Billy's mother and his sole legal parent, she would have taken him away from me and put him in foster care until a custody hearing could be held. I would have lost my mind if they had taken him away from me." She spoke calmly, but Bentley realized that her statement was meant to be taken literally.

He thought of the frantic middle-of-the-night phone call from Lenora. It had taken Bentley a while to comprehend what she was telling him. That someone named Joe Brammer had called her. That Brammer and Jamie Long had been on the run with her baby. That Gus Hartmann was dead. And some judge in Dallas was about to put Jamie's baby in foster care. What had gotten Bentley's attention was the statement about Gus. *Dead?* If that was true, then his own life had just been irrevocably changed. It was hard for him to concentrate enough to piece together Lenora's tale of her meeting with Brammer and the young man's insistence that Gus

Hartmann was trying to have Jamie murdered. With all the publicity about Amanda having a baby, Bentley had assumed that Jamie must have returned to the ranch and that the baby in the newspaper pictures was the one that had been contracted for. "You've got to do something," Lenora kept saying. "You can't let them take Jamie's baby away from her."

The judge he contacted in Dallas had been a law-school classmate of his. "But I thought you worked for the Hartmanns," she said, puzzlement in her voice.

Bentley had explained that Jamie Long was the birth mother and that no matter what Amanda Hartmann was claiming, Miss Long had never relinquished legal custody of the child. The judge had given temporary custody to Jamie until a hearing could be held. In the meantime, with the help of Toby Travis, Bentley had been able to convince Amanda that all sorts of ugly things would come out if there were any sort of legal proceedings.

"It was the least I could do," he told Jamie then glanced down at his list. "I assume you've been in touch with the district attorney's office in Dallas," he said by way of inquiry, glancing from one to the other. They made a handsome couple. Both were tan, young, and athletic-looking. Joe's head was no longer shaved; his dark hair was longish and curled around his ears. Joe had scooted his chair closer to Jamie's and moved his arm so that it touched hers.

"Yeah," Joe said. "We were informed that the shooter agreed to a plea bargain but that the information he gave didn't amount to much. As we understand it, he and the other three men who joined Hartmann's people in Dallas were Honduran nationals and apparently had been hired through a third party in Tegucigalpa. The four hired guns who arrived in Dallas on the Hartmann jet have not been apprehended."

Bentley nodded. "The man known as Zubov apparently worked for Gus Hartmann, but he was off the books. No one knows his real name or those of the woman and two men he brought with him."

"We were amazed at how little media coverage the shooting garnered," Jamie said.

"Yes," Bentley agreed, "even in death, Gus Hartmann has remained a very private person. There are those in high places with a vested interest in keeping anyone from probing too deeply into his life. And his death."

"But all those people saw him die," Joe protested. "Thousands of people. And two television stations were there filming the event, yet it barely got a mention on the morning news—just something about a crazed shooter killing the brother of evangelist Amanda Hartmann. The Dallas television reporter covering the assignment resigned the next day, and we later learned that she had accepted a position as a network correspondent in London. The newspapers weren't any more forthcoming than the television broadcasts. The AP story said that a Honduran man in the country illegally went berserk and tried to kill Amanda Hartmann and that her brother died trying to protect her. Which wasn't what happened at all. And Amanda isn't being held accountable for anything. Or her dead brother. Gus Hartmann had Jamie's money stolen from her bank account. He had God knows how many people's telephones tapped. He used government agents to track us down, and he brought in illegal aliens to *kill* us. A baby in Oklahoma City was mistakenly kidnapped because of him. And the men he hired killed Jamie's dog. She has been through absolute hell because of the Hartmanns, and no one knows it."

"Perhaps it's just as well," Jamie said, reaching for Joe's hand. "I certainly don't want the notoriety. This way Billy can maybe grow up as just a normal kid."

"That would be nice, but he is not just a normal kid," Bentley pointed out. "He will be forever linked to Amanda Hartmann."

"Not unless Amanda goes public with the unusual circumstances of his conception," Joe said.

"What about the baby she adopted?" Jamie asked.

"Amanda Hartmann and her husband plan to raise him and see that his future is assured. But understandably she desperately wants a relationship with her grandson. And I must point out that by shutting the boy off from her, you could be denying him a vast inheritance. However, if you grant her partial custody of the child, she is willing to pay you . . ."

"Stop," Jamie said, holding up her hands. "All I want from Amanda Hartmann is for her to leave us alone."

"And if she doesn't," Joe said, "we will file charges against her for knowingly entering into an invalid contract, unlawful imprisonment, conspiring to murder Jamie and kidnap her child, and anything else I can think of."

Bentley sighed. He really had no taste for this at all. "You realize," he said to Jamie, "that when your son reaches maturity, Amanda will legally be able to contact him."

"We'll deal with that when the time comes," Joe said hotly. "You tell that woman that if she attempts to call us or to contact us by mail or have us followed or interfere with our lives in any way whatsoever, I will file those charges."

"I don't think you understand what a sheltered life Amanda has lived," Bentley said. "Gus kept anything distasteful from her. She really had no idea . . ."

Jamie slapped her hands down on the table and leaned forward, glaring at him. "Don't you try to tell me that Amanda didn't realize what was going on. She would caress me and kiss me and tell me how much she and God loved me, all the while knowing that I was to be killed after the baby was born. Her mother isn't playing with a full deck, and Mary Millicent certainly understood what was going on. And by the way, we contacted the sheriff's office in Marshall County about Mary Millicent, and they ignored us. So we have contacted the state department of health and the victim services office in the state department of public safety to report the conditions under which Amanda Hartmann's mother is being kept. So you better tell Amanda that she's going to have to get that old woman down from the tower and start treating her like a human being. I'm just sorry that Ann Montgomery is dead so that we can't include her name on the complaint we have filed on Mary Millicent's behalf."

"Have you no pity at all for Amanda?" Bentley said, forcing himself to make eye contact with the impassioned young woman. "After all, there never would have been a Billy if Amanda hadn't hired you to have a baby for her."

"You expect me to have *pity* for Amanda Hartmann?" Jamie asked, her tone incredulous. "How can you even ask such a thing? She wanted me *dead,* Mr. Abernathy, so she could turn my baby into what she wanted him to be. She would have paraded him around while people screamed Hallelujah and wept when they touched the hem of his robe. Sometimes I wonder if Sonny didn't end his life intentionally so he wouldn't have to live the life his mother had laid out for him."

Bentley had wondered the same thing himself.

He sighed and slumped back in his chair, signifying defeat. He hadn't wanted to come here, but Amanda had insisted. And he was, after all, her attorney. He had become a wealthy man representing the Hartmann family. But those days were drawing to a close. Amanda's husband was in the process of engaging another law firm, and he pretty much ran the show now, which was somewhat amazing except that Amanda had never had a head for or interest in business, and she was no longer the same woman as before. She was totally passive and did whatever Toby Travis said. Travis claimed that he wanted Amanda to continue with her ministry. But at least for the time being, she had retired to the ranch and backed away from saving souls and raising money for the Alliance of Christian Voters, which had already brought a new spiritual leader onboard—a woman named Aurora. No last name. Just "Aurora." She was a longtime friend of the vice president, who would probably run for the presidency in four years if he and the president were reelected in November. And it certainly looked as though that was going to happen.

"I never liked Gus Hartmann," Bentley admitted, "or people like him—people who think this country should be run to benefit the few on the backs of the many. But, then, in many ways I am as guilty as Gus. I never broke the law for him, but I certainly bent it. But in the last few seconds of Gus's life, he did the right thing. The shot that was meant for Jamie's heart blew his brains out. I suppose that if there is such a thing as redemption, Gus Hartmann earned it."

"Yes, and it leaves me in a terrible quandary," Jamie admitted. "I can't begin to add up all the grief and pain and fear that he caused Joe and me, but in the end, he apparently had a change of heart. It's hard for me to know if I should curse his evil life or be grateful for his few seconds of atonement."

Silence fell over the table. The only sounds were the chirping of birds and the distant sound of traffic. Then Jamie stood.

Bentley and Joe followed her lead.

Bentley felt their watching eyes while he put his yellow legal pad back in his briefcase.

"I'm sorry for all the grief I've caused you," he told them.

"But out of all that grief came Billy," Jamie said. "There's no point in looking back or even in casting blame, I suppose. The only place we can go is forward."

She extended her hand across the table, and Bentley hastily grabbed it. "You are a remarkable young woman, Jamie Long. I knew that the first minute I laid eyes on you. A remarkable woman."

"It's Jamie Brammer now," she corrected, withdrawing her hand and taking a step toward the patio door.

"Yes, of course," Bentley said. "I believe that I knew that. I wish you both the very best. Will you make your home here in Houston?"

"Maybe someday," Joe said.

"We're proud to be Americans," Jamie said, "but until I know that sort of abuse of power can no longer happen in this country again, I think we'll feel safer raising our family someplace else."

Joe put an arm around his wife's waist. "We're expecting Billy's little sister in March, and we both like the idea of raising our children as citizens of the world. I have an inheritance that will allow us to float for a time. I may take another course or two in international law at Oxford. Or we're thinking about studying Italian and attending the university in Bologna. Jamie wants to study medicine, and medical education was invented there."

Such a remarkable couple, Bentley thought. He wanted to tell Jamie and Joe to appreciate their youth and beauty and lives full of promise, but after what they had gone through, he suspected that they already did.

"I wish you well," he said and took his leave.

As he slid the door closed behind him, he caught a glimpse of Jamie putting her head on her husband's shoulder and him kissing the top of her head. The expression on Joe Brammer's face was so tender it brought tears to Bentley's eyes.

The Surrogate

1. Gus Hartmann is described as being an atheist who is more interested in political power than the religion he uses as a tool to achieve his family's goals. But when his beloved nephew, Sonny, is left in a persistent vegetative state from a horrible accident, he prays fervently to God. What does this tell you about Gus's character? So many people who are otherwise nonreligious find themselves praying in dire circumstances. Do you think their prayers are hypocritical or somehow less sincere? If you believe in God, do you think he listens even to the prayers of nonbelievers?

2. Jamie has to weigh "mortgaging her future" to pay off her debt and finish her education versus mortgaging her body and a year of her life to the Hartmanns. What would you do in her situation? What is a year of your life worth to you? Can a price be put on an unborn child or any human being for that matter?

3. On the one hand, Jamie's decision to become a surrogate is altruistic: she wants to help a couple who cannot successfully conceive on their own. How do you feel about the other hand: the idea of pregnancy as a business arrangement?

4. Does Jamie's virginity make you more or less sympathetic to her decision to become a surrogate? Do you think she has less of an understanding of what she's about to do because of her inexperience with sex and love? How does a healthy sex life affect the relationship a woman has with her own body?

5. Amanda Hartmann and her followers are often described in terms reminiscent of dictators and cult leaders. How much do you think her apparently sincere belief in God or her "saintly" actions differentiate her from other charismatic leaders of more overtly insidious persuasions? Can you pinpoint the moment when Amanda crosses the line from following the word of God to using religion as an excuse to satisfy her own desires? Do you think she is ever truly aware of the depravity of what she is doing?

6. The novel carries some heavy political implications. Do you relate any of the people or situations in the book to current conditions in the United States?

7. How do you feel about the statement that "it's easy to be 'good' when you have someone do your dirty work for you"? How guilty is Amanda with regard to the crimes her brother commits to further their joint agendas?

8. Bentley Abernathy remarks that "if there is such a thing as redemption, Gus Hartmann earned it" when he sacrificed his life to save Jamie's. Do you agree with this statement? How much wrong can be righted with one truly sacrificial act? What is it, ultimately, that transforms Gus?

9. Jamie and Joe say they want to raise their family outside of the United States until they "know that sort of abuse of power can no longer happen in this country again." Do you think such abuses are happening now? Do you agree that leaving the country is the best course of action, or do you think people should stay and fight such egregious constitutional violations?

Enhance Your Book Club Experience

1. In the biography on her Web site, the author shares that she meets once a month with friends to discuss books. Spend some time browsing Judith Henry Wall's Web site (www.judithhenrywall.com).
2. As a supplement to your discussion about Amanda Hartmann and religions versus cults, try doing a little research to find out how others are debating the issue. These sites will get you started:

   http://www.spiritwatch.org/cultdef.htm
   http://www.ex-cult.org/General/identifying-a-cult

A Conversation with Judith Henry Wall

Q. *What sparked the idea for this intriguing, controversial novel?*

A. My increasing discomfort in recent years with the blending of politics and religion that is taking place in the United States.

Q. *Authors often remark that they put a little bit of themselves into their characters. Which characters in* The Surrogate *do you identify with, and why?*

A. Creating characters is like method acting. An author must, in a sense, become each of his or her characters and see through their eyes, hear through their ears, think their thoughts, feel their pain, etc., which means that all characters—good or evil—come out of an author's imagination and his or her particular set of experiences, observations, education, relationships, etc. And I believe most authors keep in mind as they create their characters that even very evil people love their children or have some other redeeming quality and that even the most saintly are not perfect.

This is the first book in which I have created true villains and was rather proud of them. Gus, Amanda, Miss Montgomery, and Mary Millicent were united in their genuine love for Sonny. I didn't like them, but I understood them.

Jamie, as the story's protagonist, is the character who most closely shares my own sensibilities. I liked her a lot and suffered along with her, but she is not me. I have never birthed a baby in a blizzard or been on the run.

Q. *Did you have any particular religious leaders or televangelists in mind when you created Amanda Hartmann?*

A. As a child, I sometimes watched a very famous televangelist "healing" people during his weekly telecast from Oklahoma City. As a college student, I lived one summer near a small church, where—with its windows and doors open to the night air—people "talked in tongues" in very loud voices until the wee hours of the morning. And over the years I have watched televangelists conduct their crusades and have always been amazed by the power these people have over their flock and how readily people give over their own free will to others.

Q. *On a similar note, did you have particular businessmen or politicians in mind when you created Gus Hartmann?*

A. Yes.

Q. *Your story seems to carry some heavy political implications. Are there current conditions in this country that prompted you to craft this layer into the novel?*

A. Yes.

Q. *The kind of power that Gus Hartmann wields and manipulates to find Jamie Long and baby Billy seems frighteningly possible. What kind of research did you do to prepare that aspect of the story?*

A. I interviewed a former CIA agent and closely follow current events.

Q. *Are you a mother? What kind of relationship do you have with your family?*

A. I am very close to my three children and five grandchildren and all the other members of my large, quite wonderful family. We like and love each other and have great family gatherings.

Q. *Have you ever known a surrogate mother? Do you think your portrayal of the dilemma a potential surrogate faces is accurate, one that women who have served as surrogates would identify with?*

A. I have never known a surrogate mother but can understand why a woman might want to enter into such an arrangement. In writing the book, I tried very hard to in no way criticize surrogate motherhood per se.

Q. *Physical beauty plays a subtle but large role in this book. Amanda is described repeatedly as angelic and beautiful, as is Sonny, while Gus is short and somewhat deformed. It is critically important to Amanda that her surrogate be attractive and athletic. What was your intention with this line of detail?*

A. It seemed only natural to me that Amanda, whose own beauty had been such an important part of her appeal and power, would do everything possible to create a perfectly formed, beautiful child to replace her handsome son and to follow in her footsteps.